UNTIL WE ARE LOST

Until We Are Lost

A Novel
by

LAO-TZU ALLAN-BLITZ

Adelaide Books
New York / Lisbon
2020

UNTIL WE ARE LOST
A Novel
By Lao-Tzu Allan-Blitz

Published by Adelaide Books, New York / Lisbon
adelaidebooks.org
Editor-in-Chief
Stevan V. Nikolic

For any information, please address Adelaide Books
at info@adelaidebooks.org
or write to:
Adelaide Books
244 Fifth Ave. Suite D27
New York, NY, 10001

ISBN13: 978-0-9996451-8-5
ISBN10: 0-9996451-8-8

Printed in the United States of America

"*Every man has to learn the points of the compass again as often as he awakes, whether from sleep or any abstraction. Not until we are lost, in other words not till we have lost the world, do we begin to find ourselves, and realize where we are and the infinite extent of our relations.*"

–Henry David Thoreau

To the love of my life

The light of my eyes

The wind in my sails

The stars in my skies

BOOK ONE

Chapter One

The sky is getting lighter. We should go back. It looks almost gray now. It'll be brown soon. And the gray light makes the wasteland look pale and flat. It's hard walking through this garbage, especially after the rains. After the rains it gets soft, and slippery. There are still puddles in the creases of the trash bags. They're almost frozen. She's off in front of me, far enough away for her coat to blend in with the waste, and she bends and rummages through a bag. I hear it rattling. I watch the horizons. It's quiet. Except the wind, it's quiet. And still. Nothing moves. There're no birds. Or squirrels. Or anything. Maybe some roaches down there under the trash. And as far as I can see, more trash. Only trash, in bags and out. A sea. Old buildings, crumbling, sinking, sacked and glass-shattered, empty and stark buildings sticking up. I see the tops of a couple sticking over the trees further down, built into the cliff, the brown bricks looking pale and dim. Sinking into the sea of garbage. Below them an open parking lot, the cars broken into and drained and buried. Far off to the left and across a wide empty expanse of trash on the other side of more decaying woods, the mountain. I can barely see it. Disappearing into the graying sky.

I catch up to her. Her boots are worn, and slimy. Covered in something fresh. I can't smell it anymore. Any of it. Except when it gets really bad. I can't smell her either. I miss her smell. She looks at me. Her hair is in her face. It's still golden, but it's a darker gold. She smiles. She looks tired. And she walks away. I walk behind her. Quietly. Over the soggy trash that clacks and rattles under us.

The sky is getting lighter. We should go back. It's been long enough. The bag over my shoulder is still empty. Not even anything. I catch up to her again. We turn back without looking at each other and walk back over the mounds of trash, careful to avoid the sharper pieces of metal and broken glass.

"It's still empty." She whispers.

"I know."

Her hands are in gloves in her pockets. Her head hanging a little. The gray light makes it hard to see the wrinkles in the sides of her cheeks and around her eyes. She looks younger. I can see her breath.

Something cracks in the distance behind us. We stop. She crouches down and I turn. We wait. Staring, and scanning the far edges of the trash. Listening. I can hear her breathing. We don't move. Not for a while. It's quiet, and after a while she stands up again and we keep walking. We walk until we see the edge of the old forest. The trees are black and smoky and bare. They barely look like trees anymore. There's less trash the closer we get to them, and we walk along the edge where the walking is easier. The twigs are still a little wet from the rains so they don't make too much noise when they crunch under out boots. She'll probably need new boots soon.

The sky is already a little brown in the distance. The sun will be up soon. We walk along the edge of the tree line until we get to the path that cuts through the wood and we follow that over the frozen plastic, unsteady and loosely-packed old roadway of trash bags. On the far edge of the wood is the wide empty expanse of large, almost-browning sky above the stretch of trash between us and the mountain.

We walk quicker the lighter it gets. She looks worried. We should have left earlier. Before it got this light. We shouldn't have gone out this far. We're okay. It's not morning yet. The empty canvas bag over my shoulder sways as I walk. I hold the end of it with one hand, but my fingers are getting cold even through my gloves. Maybe I need new gloves. These have too many holes. She looks up at the sky. I know what she's thinking. But we're okay. We walk quickly. Always listening to the forest, to the wasteland. Only silence.

"We're okay." I whisper.

She nods.

We follow the curves of the mountain up until it peals away from the mounds of trash along the cliff and we stand in the stiff black dirt waiting. It's easier to stand here. We watch the edges of where we can see and listen and watch and wait. There's a road under us somewhere. Wide, all the way to the edge of the cliff where the metal guard rail is, barely poking up through the trash. And the metal looks bright and rusted-brown in the brown light directly over us. The sun is up and so are they. But they can't see us against the mountain. We wait. It's quiet except the wind. But we still wait. Until we are sure they are not near. Then we move. Across the wide road of trash as quickly as we can without making a sound. Always listening. Up the road the brown light makes the black trash pale. Nothing. Down the road, off the cliff to the horizon. I think I can see the skyline of the City. But I can't, of course.

She almost falls, and I reach out, but she's already caught her balance and is walking ahead. We reach the hill of trash we built around the house and look back just to make sure. It used to be a nice view from the edge of this cliff. It doesn't look like much now. Just the vast expanse of the waste.

We crawl over the mound. We built it pretty high, but maybe we should add more. We wipe the slime off our boots in the rim of dirt around the door. Inside is still cold, and dark. She lights the candle before she takes off her coat. The candle is short, and almost burnt down to the base. Wax drippings stick to the wrinkled and creased wood of the table. The small orange light makes her skin look tan. Her cheeks are flushed from cold. She smiles. And the wrinkles around her eyes look dark. I take off my coat and hang it next to hers. It's cold. And we're tired. And hungry. She hasn't eaten all day. She didn't eat breakfast either.

We don't have much. There might be some peanut butter left. She's already wrapped herself in the sheets. I look through the cabinets. No more peanut butter. There's a can of beans. She doesn't like those much.

I take my boots off. My socks are slippery on the scrapped and dry wood floor. I lay down next to her and put my arm over her shoulder. Her hair is across my face and my nose is at the base of her neck, but I can't smell her. I miss that smell. I breathe deep and imagine I can smell it again. Like that flower back home. The one with small white pedals that are pink before they bloom. Growing in the cracks of the bright, sandstone rocks along the driveway under the oak tree. The one with the bee hive in the trunk. I don't like bees much.

"We only have beans." I whisper.

"I'm not hungry." She says. Her voice is soft. And small. It used to be a loud voice. A big voice. But now we whisper. All we ever do is whisper. And I miss her voice, too.

"You didn't eat breakfast either, love."

"I'm all right."

"To drink?"

"Tomorrow."

I kiss the side of her cheek. Cold. The glow from the candle makes her hair shine, and the shine moves up and down as the small flame flickers. I stand up and walk back to the kitchen.

"Come sleep." She says.

I undress and blow out the candle. I can still see her in the little bit of light that comes through the cracks in the wood. The air is very cold and I shiver crawling under the sheets. But she's warm and her skin is soft and she rolls over to face me and I can see her eyes even in the dim light.

"We'll go somewhere else, tomorrow." I say.

"All right."

"Maybe the other side of the mountain."

"We've found a lot there before, haven't we, darling?"

"Your boots."

"Maybe we'll find more."

"And maybe we can go to the City the day after."

"We don't have enough."

"We have a little."

Her breath is warm on my cheek.

"It's a long ways." She says.

My stomach rumbles. I hold her close. She's very thin. She kiss my neck. I wish she didn't have to go through this. I wish it harder than anything I've every wished for. She deserves so much better. So much more. Than trash. There's so much we never did. And so much we lost. We lost to this trash. And slime. And now she's so thin.

She puts her face against my chest. Her eyelashes tickle when she blinks. My hand against her ribs rises and falls with her breath. Her ribs stick out distinctly from her soft skin, and I can feel the grooves between them.

"It's a long ways." She says.

"We're okay."

"Do you think we have enough?"

"We'll find more tomorrow. Then we'll have enough."

"You're not worried?" She asks.

"A little."

"Me too."

"But we're okay, love."

It's quiet. And the air is still. But outside I can hear the wind.

"We should see if we can find another candle when we go." She says.

"That would be good."

"This one's almost done."

"We'll look."

"They remind me of the fireflies. Do you remember the fireflies, darling?"

"Yes."

"In the trees. I didn't know we had them out here."

"I never had them back home." I say.

"I did."

"Did you ever catch them in jars like in the books?"

"No. We never did that. I just liked looking at them."

"Me too."

"Isn't it strange we never saw them before?"

"Yes."

"I think she brought them with her."

"Maybe."

"I think she did."

"It's nice to think so."

"I miss her. I miss her so much, darling."

"Me too."

My throat feels tight and my eyes burn a little, but it's quiet again. The little bit of light poking through the crack in the wall streaks across my arm that's wrapped around her. It makes my hairs look white. My arm is cold. But the morning outside is just starting, and the sun will warm things a little. Her breathing is slow and shallow. I'm tired. And a little hungry. We'll eat tomorrow. And maybe we'll find something on the other side of the mountain this time. If we're lucky.

Chapter Two

Dark crimson. It splashes into the bowl of the old and cracked sink and the cracks are brown and rusting, and the crimson turns brown and the color fades mixing with the water. I wash my hands with the pot of water she was boiling over a very small fire of twigs. The fire is warm and makes my cheeks feel hot. The blood-water swirls and spins down the drain. I put the pot back over the fire. It rustles and the dry leaves cough smoke and sparks. She smells sweet. And a little bitter. It's soured by the ending. When everything lets go. That always sours it. And the trash. That sours it, too. And the smoke from the small fire smells chalky and makes the sweet smell and the sour smell fade. But the sweetness is still there. It smells familiar. I breathe deep, and feel good and blissful.

Her skin prickles and I can see the little bumps in the orange light from the fire. Small bumps on her smooth skin. Very soft. Her blood isn't pooling anymore. There's no more left. And the puddle around her is as wide as it will get and very still. It looks black in the orange light and makes her skin look pale in comparison. The surface of the puddle looks shiny and filmy and smooth. Her red hair glows a little too, and the tips dip into the puddle. They're almost the same color. Clipped short to her ears, and very straight, it covers one of her eyes. She looks more angry than anything else. It's not how I wanted her to look. But she looks angry. And her eyes are clouding. They look gray now, and the gray makes her look more angry. They were very blue. Crystal blue. And sharp. She was very pretty. The prettiest I've had. And confident. Even now she is confident. I liked watching her. And she was so careful and confident and pretended to be so haggard so nobody would know how pretty she was, or how confident. And she didn't look as angry when her eyes were blue. I don't like that she looks angry. It's not right. But I breathe deep and still feel good and blissful and her smell is still there and the smoky smell is nice, too.

She doesn't have much in this small room. But it's impressive she kept this much. And this much a secrete. They'd kill her for it. But now they won't. They'd kill me for mine. But they'll never find it. She has some books. I've heard of that one. And she has that pot and enough to make a fire to boil the water and sterilize it and she has a mattress, but it looks pathetic and stained and droops in the middle. And she has a painting on the wall. A painting. The walls used to be red. Like her hair. But they're stained and brown now. Ugly brown. And she still looks angry. Still pretty, and her features are still good, but angry. I don't like that. It makes me feel angry. And it's ruining the good feeling.

"Stop that." But she doesn't stop.

I wash my hands again because they still look filthy, and shake them dry. A small droplet of water falls into the blood and floats peacefully. The surface ripples and doesn't look filmy anymore. The spot is dark against the black crimson puddle. A blemish. And her eyes are almost completely gray now. There's only a little of that crystal left at the edges and behind the gray. I breathe deep, but don't feel as good or as blissful. Damn it. It disappears so quickly now. It used to last a long time. I take her shirt from the ground at my feet and drop it over her face. It ripples the puddle against her pail arms, leaving a wet wine stain on her perfect skin. That's better. But she has such a pretty face. Her skin is still prickling and still looks alive, but it's very pale. I take the knife from the counter. I cleaned it well. It almost shines. I step around her and avoid the puddle. I breathe deep again, but the feeling doesn't come, and I feel low and sick and I don't feel good. I smell the mattress, and it smells like her. Sweet. And familiar. But the smell doesn't help. I like it, but I don't feel good now. She's ruined it. Ruined it with her stubbornness. She had to be angry. They're never angry. But she had to be angry. I'll have to look for another.

From this angle I can't see her face. All I can see is her twisted figure, mostly on her back, twisted and naked in the puddle glistening around her. And her skin soaking in it. Trying to get it back. The water in the pot goes back to boiling and it fizzes and hisses and the steam rises up to the small painted ceiling that doesn't look white anymore.

I leave through the small door. I have to push hard to move it and the trash bags she used to hide it. The narrow hall with the wall paper torn and tearing off. The floor lined in newspapers that scratch under my boots. No lights, but I don't mind the darkness. I prefer the darkness. I toy with the small bellybutton ring in my pocket that I tore off her, and I feel a little better. I didn't expect there to be a piercing. And my hand found it. And it was exciting. She didn't seem the type. She was always so careful. A very careful person. Not the kind to have a piercing. As long as I watched her I never would have guessed that she had it. But she didn't seem like the type to dye her hair either. I liked watching her. And she was so pretty. I feel angry again. And hate her for being so pretty. But I've already had her. And I should feel good. But I don't feel good. I feel angry. And hot. Even though it's cold and the wind blows hard and I close the outside door and crouch and listen in the darkness. But there's nothing out there, and I walk the two blocks two the subway station. The trash isn't too thick on this block. And the streets are wider up here, and the graying sky is big through the buildings that look ghostly in the dim and pale light. Stones and bricks and glass, all pale. The streets are covered in the black trash bags and I can't even tell where the sidewalk would end. The lampposts are dark spikes sticking out of the dark trash bags, and one of them is down on its side in front of me and I climb it and down the steps into the dark subway back towards the markets.

A few candles on the rocks walls. They flicker and glow. Orange semi-circles of light around the tracks and pebbles and glass bottles and plastic bottles on the ground under them, but I walk in the darkness. I like the darkness better. It's very black down here when there aren't any candles. Very black. It wasn't this dark before. It was bright and noisy and annoying. It's hard not to trip on the old wood planks or the metal rails or the bottles or rocks or heaps of old papers between the tracks. But I like the dark better. And so I walk between the tracks in the dark.

I can hear the market up ahead. It's loud and I can see the light and the light looks hazy on the grainy black rock. There are more candles on the walls now and the rock looks black in the orange light. The metal support beams and the old track lights and the railings of the tracks and they all look a very dark brown. Almost black. But not like the rock. The rock looks very black.

And I pass the first few people sleeping in huddles of muddied clothing and soggy cardboard and old rotting newspapers on the sides. Worthless people, pathetic and dumb, piss-smelling, stained, shells-of-humans. The cold air makes the smell tolerable. More. Hunched over, swaying back and forth mumbling to themselves. All of them hunched. And all of them ugly.

I walk for a long time back down to the middle markets. There are more people the closer I get. Pathetic people. Ugly pathetic people. It's so hard now to find a pretty one. They're all old and wrinkled and piss-stained and covered in rock dust and dirt and trash and they sleep there on the side without any shame, huddled on top of one another. Rows of them on one side and cardboard shacks on the other with the rusted fences and more old and wrinkled people shouting and rattling things they'll trade. A big strong-looking man watches the crowd with a pistol in his belt and a scar on his cheek and a sloppy, sewing-needle-done tattoo on his forehead. Further down another just like him. I fiddle with the bellybutton ring in my pocket. They make me nervous. But they're only here in the middle. They don't bother us on the edges. Nothing's worth anything on the edges.

The smoke from the candles is thick and the smoky-rock-dust smell makes me cough. I watch the faces of the crowd in the orange candle light, but they're all ugly. No one's pretty anymore. It's so hard to find a pretty one. And she was so pretty. The prettiest. And her skin was smooth. And the small prickling bumps in the cold air and the orange light. And the red all around her. And her eyes. And her smell. Familiar, but I don't know from where. The crowd gets thicker and it's slower walking and I'm getting frustrated, and they waddle in front of me, blank faces glowing, and in the light the stains on their coats and pants and faces stand out. Disgusting. And they smell. They all smell. Like rot and piss. And I try not to breathe.

The market is louder, and brighter, and even smellier. And the track opens up into a large, higher-roofed, multi-leveled marketplace along the platforms, and the crowd moves along the walls and along the tracks and along the platforms. The old tiles are cracked and the floors are covered in dust and soot from all the candles. The shacks are built into holes in the walls and into where old metal newspaper stands used to be. And here there are more strong men with pistols or rifles and they stand and watch us. I push hard through the crowd and they grunt, but they don't mind. I walk on the edge of the raised platform and up the stairs to the next level of dirty-tiled walkways and dirty-peopled platforms, and from the edge of the walkway I can see down to the lower levels. And now I'm looking down on the balding heads with sunspots and soot stains. Disgusting. The gray smoke coming up from the candles makes me cough.

Walking is hard against the crowd, and slow, and I walk for a long time until I'm out of the market. It's a long walk to my apartment, and I walk as quickly as I can, but my legs are tired, and I haven't slept in a while and it takes a long time until I pass through the lower markets. And the lower markets smell worse because I can smell the ocean when I get close to the surface. The people are younger here. And maybe a little less ugly. But all the almost-pretty ones have scars, and if they don't have scars they have wrinkles, and they all smell like rotten fish and the ocean and it makes me sick and gives me a head ache. I walk faster through the lower market because I know the back way down the tracks.

I climb off the tracks and onto the platform and pass through the turnstiles that click when I pass through them. The steps are filthy, and the wind is cold, and I wait at the edge of the steps and listen in case they're nearby. But they're not and I walk quickly over the trash to the stone steps of my apartment - only the last step is showing over the trash bags - and I push through the revolving door and unlock the door to the stairwell and I climb over the boxes and filth. I'm very tired by time I get to my floor and climb over more boxes. But my apartment is nice and big, and I feel good inside and relaxed and I can breathe, and I don't smell the ocean from this high up. And it's colder this high up. I shiver. It's good to be home.

The wood floors aren't so sleek any more, and the marble kitchen with the nice wood cabinets is old and the marble looks pale and dirty and the wood cabinets look faded. The table is scratched and the mattress droops in the middle, like hers. But it's still comfortable. I put the knife in the draw of the bed-side-table next to the pistol and I kick off my shoes. They're hard to kick off, and I put them together at the foot of my bed. The sky is getting grayer and the gray light comes through the corners of the blinds and I can see my hands almost clearly in the light. I don't like the wrinkles. But they're good hands.

Strong hands. And they work hard for me. I pull the corner of the blinds back. The buildings are taller down here, and most of them are brick and stone, and then there's the occasional glass and metal one that's always taller and pokes up at the sky and disappears into the gray smog and the glass windows all look black and empty, or broken. And I can see into the building across the street through the large shattered windows, and the wind makes a mess of things in there. On the street I can see the trash bags more clearly in the morning light, and it looks black. All the way down every street and up every avenue, black trash bags, like an ocean. Like a sea of trash. Almost-frozen plastic..., and the grime and sludge and it all smells sour, but I can't smell it this high up. It's getting bright outside, and I should go to work, but I'm very sleepy, and I don't feel good. I feel low, and sick and don't want to work. I want to sleep. I never get enough sleep. But I have to. I have to go.

I lie down on the drooping mattress and breathe deep breaths and feel sick and angry. Because she made me angry. Her pretty face. And her soft skin. And the curves of her hips under my hand, and it prickled under my fingers and the bellybutton ring and she whimpered and tried to fight. She was stronger than she looked. And she was angry. I twist the bellybutton ring in my fingers. She was so pretty. The prettiest yet. And I hated her more than the others. I liked watching her, though. I felt angry and excited watching her. I didn't watch her as long as the others. I couldn't help myself. And I'm supposed to feel good and blissful now, but I don't. I still feel angry. And it's so hard to find a pretty one these days. I should go.

Chapter Three

It's very dark tonight. And we don't know this side of the mountain as well. We have to walk slower. Quieter. The moon is out there somewhere, but we haven't seen it in a long time. She watched for it again tonight. And the sky looked especially red at sunset. And the red light looked good on her. But she didn't eat again. She said she wasn't hungry. She'll eat tonight, though. Otherwise she'll get weak. And she's already so thin.

I can barely see her silhouette in front of me. She's bent over something and I hear her carefully moving things about and inspecting them. I listen to the distance. Quiet. We're okay. They're still asleep. As long as we're quiet. But we don't know this side that well. I listen harder.

She comes over to me with something in her hand.

"It's good." She whispers.

I can't see what it is. It's too dark. I let her put it in the canvas bag. It feels good to have some weight in there. Whatever it is bounces against the base of my back as we walk. It's cold tonight, too. And I have to switch hands holding the bag often to give my fingers a rest.

A trash bag partially opened at my feet. I crouch down and feel around it. Mostly solid objects. The plastic rustles as I tear at it quietly with one hand. Some empty glass bottles. They clink lightly against each other. Some paper. Maybe a newspaper. It feels soggy and partially decomposed. A thermos. With a top and everything. It looks intact. This'll be good. I put it in the canvas bag. Some more bottles. Nothing else interesting. My back aches as I stand up. It feels stiff.

Alex comes over to me. I can tell she's smiling even in the dark. She puts something else in the bag and walks away again. We keep walking. But we shouldn't go too far.

I look up at the sky. No stars. Or moon. Or anything. I can't tell if it looks dark red or dark blue or just black. I can see the clouds and smog, though. I think. They look low. The wind blows cold against my neck. I shiver. And walk. Some more bottles clink and crack under my feet. We stop. And listen. It's too dark to see anything far away, but we try anyways. I don't know what to look at, though. I don't know this side of the mountain. When it gets lighter it'll be easier. Except for the wind it's quiet. After a while we go on walking. Slowly. We should turn back soon. Double back and stay close to the mountain. There's a group of buildings close by, I remember. We should be careful not to go too close.

I step in a puddle still left from the rains. The water is icy, and my boots aren't thick enough anymore to stop the water from seeping through. I cringe. I try to breathe slowly and not make noise, but my foot is so cold it hurts. In front of me I can see the silhouette of a lamp post. It's still standing. Not many are. She is leaning against it looking through a bag at its base. Her coat makes her figure look larger than it is in the dark. When she stands up again I can see her hair blowing in the breeze. She ties it back.

She shouldn't have to do this. Any of it.

We walk for a long time. Slowly. And in the cold. The wind is getting worse. The large mountain to our right looks black and massive even against the dark sky. To our left, some ways away through the dark, trash-laden stretch, more street lamps stick up, barely traced against the blackness. And houses beyond them, I can hardly see; and through the wood I can see the old general-store, large, white-bricked, two-leveled, square. The parking lot in front still mostly filled with cars. We circle around the town along the slope of the mountain. The wood isn't thick out here, and neither is the trash, and at some places I can see the concrete of the road. I stand on it, and it feels solid and strong. She doesn't find much, and after a while I catch up to her and we turn back.

The sky is a little lighter, and it's easier to see. And in the graying light I can see the cracking, pale-red shingles of the pointed roofs of the small square houses, and the faded brown brick apartment buildings standing higher and starker over the bare trees. I didn't realize they were so close. We walk closer to the mountain, but there are fewer bags over here. The ground is hard. Stiff with cold. So are my cheeks. She's stopping for almost every bag now, but we can't find much. I wish there were a better way. So, she wouldn't have to do this. I wish she'd carry the bag and let me dig through the trash, so she wouldn't have to. *But it's gotten worse*, she said. When we were in bed and I asked if I could dig instead of her. And she said no. *We have to take care of your back, darling.* It's not that bad.

She is getting farther ahead of me, and it's still too dark to see very far. The wind hisses against the loose edges of the plastic bags. It starts small. But it gets louder and louder. So much plastic everywhere hissing like a thousand snakes. I hurry to catch up with her. I trip on something sharp and something cracks under my boot. Loud. I hold my breath, still lying on top of several trash bags. I look at Alex. She's frozen. Crouching. The hissing is loud still. We can't hear anything over it. Maybe they can't either. But I don't breathe. That was loud. I try to swallow, but I can't. The slime form one of the trash bags is oozing out around my glove. The wind slows a little as I push myself off of it. More bottles rattle under me. Something growls from inside one of the buildings. From one of the dark holes where glass windows used to be. The wind hurts my eyes, open wide and straining to see. My chest is pounding hard. So hard I can hear it. And feel it in my fingers. The canvas bag is on the ground and I pick it up slowly and move slowly to Alex. Together we crouch. She's shivering. I put my arm around her. It's still very dark. They probably can't see us. I can hardly see the faces of the buildings. The growl doesn't come again. But we don't move.

I can hear her breathing. And I see her breath, gray against the darker gray. We wait for a long time. My legs are starting to cramp, and my back is aching from slouching for so long. She looks at me and then back towards the buildings. She's holding my arm tightly. Her jacket rustling in the wind. Her hair coming loose from the hair tie. The wind is hard. I try to breathe slowly. The air is cold, but it's thick. And we stand. It's quiet. I can feel her hands shaking. We walk slowly, and don't look through the bags for a while. I hold her gloved hand as we walk. My chest is still pounding hard. We'd hear them if they were awake. We would. We're okay. But her hand is still shaking in mine. And we still don't look through anymore bags. Not till we're back closer to the road. Where it used to be. Then she starts off ahead again. The mountain is large and black and I can almost see the domed top. We used to hike up there. It was a nice hike. And at the top we had a nice view of things.

I catch up to her, so I can be closer to her. So I can imagine I smell her. She notices but doesn't look back. The bags around her feet are dark and different piles of metal and plastic jut out at awkward angles making shapes in the darkness. The bag under my boot slips. Mostly the pulp of decomposing food. I can feel more bottles under it. Maybe metal. I wonder how many layers there are. At some points it has to be really deep. She comes back to me with something small and puts it in the sack. We're making our way home. We'll be there soon. At least we have something. Maybe enough to trade.

The sky isn't even bright when we make it back to the pile of trash around the house. We crawl over it on all fours and wipe our boots in the dirt around the door. I wipe my gloves too because there's still sludge on them. The sky is looking gray, and in the gray light I can see her pale skin. Her lips. They look dark. Her eyes. She smiles, but she looks tired. We don't go inside. We sit in the dirt and I put my arm around her. The ground under us is solid and firm. It's cold, but the cold is nice. I watch the sky get brighter. Little by little the gray starts to look a little brown and the trash in front of us doesn't look so flat. I can see the shadows and layers. Maybe we should make it higher. It's high enough to block the wind. But maybe it should be a little higher. I listen. There're no birds chirping. No crickets. No squirrels rustling the bushes. It's quiet. Perfectly quiet. Even her breathing is quiet. And small. She kisses my neck and her breath is warm on my skin. And she puts her head on my shoulder. We listen and watch the sky get brighter. And we watch our breaths disappear.

After a while we stand up and go inside. She lights the candle and I open the can of beans. I give her the spoon with the handle not broken. She doesn't complain about the beans. We eat the can. They're very dry. But they look brown and good in the small orange light. And afterwards we drink the liquid left in the can. But I don't feel full.

"I don't like the smell of these." She whispers.

"We'll get something better tomorrow." I say.

"We're going? Do we have enough?"

"We have a little."

"It's a long way."

"We're okay."

Her hair makes a shadow over her face. She looks very pretty. I hold her gloved hand. She's shivering. I bring her hand over the candle to warm it. There's not much left to that candle.

"Do we have another candle?" I ask.

"No."

"Let's see if we can find one tomorrow."

I stand up and pour a little water into the can from our jug. She drinks and then I drink. I pour more, but she doesn't want any.

"It tastes like beans." She says.

I use my glove to wipe out whatever residue is left in the can and pour more water into it. She drinks it, and smiles at me.

"Let's go to bed." She says and blows out the candle.

I follow her, and undress her. She's cold, but she lets me look at her skin in the pale light that comes through the cracks in the wood. She's soft. And delicate. And I hold her close and tight under the blankets. I can feel her chest beating. She's so very thin. She runs her finger along my back.

"I'm worried about tomorrow." She whispers. "It's a long way."

"We'll be okay."

"But it's a long way. And there are more of them now."

"I know. But we'll be okay."

"All right."

I kiss her cheek. And then her lips. And she smiles. And I imagine I can smell her. She smelled like that flower back home. The white one. By the driveway. That feels so far away now. The sun. And the flowers by the brown gravel. And the trees in front of the wood house. And all the bushes. So green in the bright orange sun. And the dark wood door. When the sun hit it right it glowed and almost looked red. Alex never saw it. I wish she saw it. I wish a lot of things. There's so much we never did. And so much we lost. I hate it. I hate this trash. She could have been so happy. She deserves to be so happy.

The blankets are thick and she's warm and makes me warm and the light from outside makes the small room look pale. The large, now-empty, birch-wood dresser in the corner. The table between the bed and the kitchen. The small candle on the table. There's still a thin string of smoke coming from the candle. The bathroom to the side of the kitchen. It hasn't worked in years. I don't know the last time I was in there.

Alex nestles her face into my chest. Her breath on my skin. Her hair in my face. I run my thumb along the edge of her chin. And close my eyes. Tomorrow will be a long day.

Chapter Four

I don't feel good. I feel sick and angry. The beans might have been bad. But they didn't taste bad. They always taste bad, but not worse than usual. Just dry and smelly. I didn't sleep. That might be it. And they smell, all of them, like piss and dust and rot, and their smell makes me feel worse, but they don't seem to notice how bad they all smell. They're thick coats with holes and stains and covered in trash, that's all they care about. Just that they have their coats. And they walk around the markets like they have something to trade with, but they don't have something to trade with, and then they lie down, and they sleep. They sleep more than I do. Until they don't get up. One day they just don't get up. And they never notice how awful they smell.

The rotting wood on the tracks is hard with cold. It sounds especially windy out there, but the breeze isn't too bad down here. I push through the crowd. I climb into the dusty platform at the start of the middle market. The tiles on the wall are cracked and the candles line the passageways like the tomb of a king. I take the stairs to the top and can see the gray light coming through from outside. It makes the metal turnstiles look ghostly and gray and cloudy like her eyes became.

The clicks of my steps echo down the long underground walkway filled with candle smoke. The old advertisements are peeling off their frames and drooping low like dying plants. The faded bottom halves of women for the new adult Broadway show. The wind comes down from the outside and ripples the thick smoke overhead and I smell the ocean worse and walk faster.

My hands are deep in my pockets and I toy with the bellybutton ring and press the point into my finger until it hurts a little. I try to breathe deeply, but the smell of ash and dirt and smoke and sour ocean, and not-her make me angry. And I don't feel good. I feel low. And a little sick. And tired. I need more sleep.

The long walkway ends, and I hurry down the steps bellow the sign that says Path with the rest broken off. There are more people down here waiting. And a big man with a pistol lets us through in small groups. And I wait. It's a long wait. And it's colder here and I can see my breath in the candle light. And I can smell the ocean coming through the walls, and it's sickening.

He lets me through and I climb down onto the tracks with the others. They cough, and mumble and we walk. It's a cold walk, and we walk fast. At the far end the ocean doesn't smell as bad and we climb off the tracks following the candles and through a smaller tunnel with a lower ceiling and rough walls. Hammers and oxygen tanks and fires and men shouting and coughing and thick smoke and rock dust. The clinks of hammers and the hiss of torches and the coughs of men.

We walk in single-file. They point where to go. The big men. With pistols and rifles and knives. The same tattoos. The same scars. Only mine is thinner. Because the bullet was fast, and the knives use are dull and tear more than they cut. They give me a pickaxe and I walk further down the tunnel. It's a long tunnel and I can smell the rotting wood planks holding up the rock and men with black soot and rock dust smeared on their faces push past me in the narrow space and low ceiling. It's hard to breathe because of all the rock dust and smoke from the candles and it's loud down here because the passage ways are so narrow, and the hammers are hard and crack the stiff rock. But they don't have the strength to hit very hard at all. And their bulky coats make it difficult to hit hard also. And it's hot, so it's harder to hit very hard. And no one cares how hard we hit, just that we keep hitting.

It's hot. I'm already feeling the sweat. One of them stops and puts his hands on his knees and drops his pick, panting. He pulls his coat down past his shoulders but doesn't dare take it off. He looks at me suspiciously as I push past him. At the end I find a piece of wall that no one else is at and I start swinging the pickaxe.

The pick rattles and stings my hand, and my hand is still sore from a couple days ago, and cold, but it warms up quickly. I hit weakly because no one cares. Some chips of rock fall into the dust at my feet and I kick them away and keep hitting until the man with a pistol and a tattoo and a scar goes back up the tunnel to check on something else. We all stop and sit against the rough and jagged rock wall. When we hear him coming back, we start up again. People shout from up the tunnel, but down here only mumbles. And even though we're not hitting so hard, the clacks are loud, and the walls are narrow, and the sound makes my ears ring. I cough. And spit. And more men cough and spit. A lot of coughing and spitting. And I taste the dust from the rock and it's grainy against my tongue, and the back of my throat is scratchy.

All day I work on the same wall and only chips fall off. And it's hard to breathe and I cough more and spit more and hit the rock more. And sweat, but I can't take off my coat. They're thieves. We all are. Dirty filthy thieves. Can't take it off. Just keep going. And my hands ache and my arms are sore, and my back is sore even though I don't hit very hard. But I don't stop until I can't hit anymore. Until my fingers are stuck and cramping around the handle of the pick and my shoulders are so sore I can't move them anymore. Enough? Almost enough. A little more. I keep hitting. And I sit when he's gone back up the tunnel, until he comes back. A slab of rock falls off the low ceiling and almost hits the man next to me. I cough hard on the soot and dust it kicks up. They bring some wood down to support the ceiling, but it's not a very good job. It's a nice break, though. I hit again and wince because it hurts. I wipe the sweat and rock dust off my face and cough and spit. Enough. I can't open my hand from around the pick.

I follow the big man back up the tunnel. He nods to the man with the beans. They give me one fresh can and one bowl to eat there. It's more than I thought I would get today. I sit in the dust, my back against the rock, and eat next to another man who only got a spoonful. He's not wearing a coat and I can see his ribs pocking out through the holes in his shirt. Shouldn't have taken it off.

I walk back along the tracks through the stench of the ocean. Back to the market. I lean against the tiles and feel very sleepy and sore and my hands ache and still don't open all the way. I watch the people going around and around. The wrinkled and scared and scarred and drooping faces. Their big coats make them look puffy, but they're all just skin and bones. You can see it in their faces. Bones with wrinkly and stained skin hanging off.

She could be a pretty one. I follow her at a distance. She stops at a stand and talks to a man with a fishhook hanging out of his nostril. When she turns I see her face. She already looks dead. I walk away and lean against another wall feeling lonely. And sick. And angry. She ruined the good feeling so quickly.

I watch for a while, but I'm sleepy and I walk home.

I walk past one of the big men with a pistol in his hands and a tattoo on his forehead and a scar on his cheek. He nods at me. Do I know him? Or just the scar. He thinks he knows me. Just my scar.

It's a long walk back. And there are more people on the tracks leading out of the markets. The can of beans clacks against the bellybutton ring in my pocket, but nobody can hear it. She would be pretty too, if she didn't have so many scars. Her hair is long and black and matted but could be combed out to look nice. It doesn't matter because of the scars. Too many scars. Home will be good. I'll sleep okay now. I'm tired enough.

Chapter Five

The tunnel is dark. And we don't have a flashlight. I brush against the wall and my shoulder hits one of the candle holders nailed to it. I trip against the hard tracks. Pebbles clack out in front of us and echo against plastic bottles and the rock wall. The canvas bag is draped over my shoulder. The pistol is tucked into my pants and digs into the small of my back. Alex's hand is in mine so that we don't lose each other. She's not shaking anymore. We made it this far. We're safer here. And it's warmer down here. The wasteland was cold. Especially in the open where the winds are the hardest. And they can see us the easiest in the open. But we made it this far.

I can hear sounds from the market place up ahead in the distance. She's walking faster. She wants to get this over with. She doesn't like the market. And it took us all night to get here. We might have to spend the day here. Until it gets dark again. And she's already so tired. She didn't sleep last night. The screams kept us up. And snarls and screams and shouting; it all echoes in the silence and the waste. That's probably why she couldn't sleep. I couldn't either. We should probably spend the day here.

It's so dark that I can't see her even next to me. And I can't see the large rock walls. And we have to stay on the tracks or else we'll get lost. The sound gets louder. Soon we can see the small orange glow pushed against the blackness from a candle that hasn't burned out yet. Then another candle. The louder it gets the more light there is. The black and dusty stone walls, and the thick wax-smoke collecting on the low rock ceilings. The cold, stiff, metal rails of the tracks, and the wood planks between the rails and the large screws. The old track lights off to the side. We come to a platform with candles on the tiled walls and light coming down from the stairwell behind the black iron gate and the cloud-gray metal turnstiles. The platform is long, and the edge is painted yellow, but the paint is chipping, and I see the tiles under the paint. At the end of the platform is a door to a service room that's been pried open and inside a group of people are sleeping. Snoring. We pass the platform and it gets darker again, but there are more candles after a while and the orange glow is enough light to see where we step and we avoid the people sleeping on the tracks and the dips between the wood planks that have almost frozen water that looks black and still and the old papers in the water are nearly disintegrated.

We reach the outer edge of the market. It's very loud. And bright. A roar of voices, and clinking of metal on metal and glass bottles, and grumbling people off to the sides. In the center, between the thick support beams, cardboard shacks with candles and traders, and on the tiled platforms on both sides of the tracks, in the metal newspaper stands, people have set up shop and put what their trading on the shelves and counters. They all have thick beards and their faces are covered in dust from the rocks. On the edges are people sleeping. Or just lying down. Waiting. Covered in dirt and more dust. More cardboard covering them. Bundled in thick coats. It's very loud. And the candles are bright. So bright they sting my eyes, but my eyes adjust quickly. We walk further, and Alex holds my hand tightly. The further we go, the thicker the crowd gets, and the tighter she squeezes.

We walk close to the traders to keep an eye on what they have, but we won't find anything worth trading for out here.

There are so many people. Men and women. They all look tired. And move slowly. And grumble and mutter, but so many grumbling people make for a roar in the tunnels. We push through them. The wrinkles in their faces are deep and dark in the orange light. An old woman. Moaning and pleading. Begging for something to eat. Anything at all. She doesn't have any teeth left. She hobbles, slouched over herself. Alex pulls herself close to me as we push past her. More traders yelling to us to come to them. Holding out bottles and cans. Shaking them in front of us. Canned beans and canned fruit and empty cans. Yelling. We climb onto the platform and up the stairs to the higher level. Closer to the surface is colder and the smoke is thicker because it collects from the level below and I cough, and we walk quickly, but there's nothing here for us and I climb down onto the tracks and help her down and we walk into the dark tunnel with lower ceilings. She stares at the candles with wide eyes.

The crowd thickens again, and she squeezes my hand hard. She's breathing hard, too. Deep breathes. And there's a lot of smoke in the air from all the candles. And the crowed keeps getting thicker, and the walking gets slower. It's hard to breathe. And she's starting to shake again. I pull her off to the side where people sleep. We almost step on a man wrapped in an old, decomposing newspaper. She crinkles her nose. I can't smell it. It's very loud, and I don't try to yell over everyone. But I hold her until her breathing slows down. And I kiss her head. She holds her arms around me.

When she's ready we push back into the crowd. There's vomit on the tracks. On the metal rails. The wood blocks look old and rotting and the large metal screws are covered in the vomit that looks dry. We walk slowly with the thick, shuffling crowd through the narrow tunnel and climb onto the next platform where the ceilings are higher and the smoke hangs in thick clouds above us, gray against the black rock in the orange light, and we can breathe a little easier. The shacks are crammed together. A small man with one leg and a tortuous wood cane hobbles back and forth between two. Rusted metal fences cover the good stuff. The rust looks blood-red in the candle light. A man with a big hat with holes in the brim rattles a walking stick and points to a collection of dull knives. The blades are gray and rusty towards the handles. A few shacks down from him an old woman who doesn't have teeth and who has very red gums smiles at us. I like the look of the cans of beans behind her. They look in good condition. But she asks too much for them. Everything is too expensive, now. And we don't have enough. We keep walking, but it only gets more expensive, and we push our way back through the slow-moving crowd. We could try the lower markets. They have more. But she looks tired. I hold her hand tightly. She leads the way back.

Another rack of beans, but they look old, and the cans are broken, and cracked, and one's still leaking, brown liquid soaking through the cardboard shelf. Alex points to the peanut butter behind the cans. We trade for it, but it's expensive. She likes peanut butter, though, and she looks happy, so I'm happy. And we walk back towards the end of the markets. She finds a candle and we trade for that too, but it's very small - but better than the ones along the walls. She looks happy with it in her hands and doesn't let me carry it for her and we walk back. We don't have anything left to trade with. I can't believe that's all we got. There's not much of anything out there anymore. And it was more expensive. Too expensive now. But we're okay. We have the nut butter. That'll be good for a while. We're okay.

She looks tired. We lean against one of the support pillars between tracks. Her face is in shadows and she stares at the candle in her hands. I'm tired too. We should find a place to sleep for a little.

"Soon." I say. I have to talk loudly and talking loudly hurts my throat. She nods.

We walk along the side by the rock wall, next to the old train lights where it's flat and easier to walk. We walk along the rock wall until we get to the next market and find our way to the upper level platforms and down onto the tracks again. She holds my hand tightly in the thick crowd. On the far side of the market we have to walk along the tracks because of all the people sleeping on the sides, piled on top of one another, and I almost fall into the gaps between wooden planks a couple times. A large man with an eyepatch and around it a large area of redness and drips of ooze running down his cheek, and he watches us, leaning against the divider between the tracks.

We find an empty spot a good ways outside of the market against the black rock and Alex stares at the people sleeping across from us. It's quieter out here, but we can still hear the hum from the market. There aren't so many candles this far out. The dim light flickers, as if quivering under the immense pressure of the darkness. I clear away the trash on the ground and we lie on the rock and dirt behind someone else covered in a down coat that has holes in it, the feathers from the coat blowing everywhere in the small breeze. She puts her head on my chest. Her hair tickles my cheek. I hold her hand in mine. I keep the canvas bag tucked tightly under my arm and tied to my belt. The pistol digs into by back, but I don't want to move. She looks comfortable.

"It's good it's over." She says.

"We'll be home soon."

"I'm glad we found a candle."

"Me too, love."

I like the sound of her voice. I miss that sound. She's quiet for a long time, but she's not sleeping.

"We didn't have enough." She says.

"No. We didn't." I say.

"And we'll have to come back soon, won't we?"

"Yes."

"I don't like it here."

"Me neither."

"I wish we didn't have to come."

"I know, love."

"Was the candle worth it?"

"Yes."

"He didn't ask too much?"

"No. It was okay."

"All right."

She takes off her gloves and puts them under her head on my chest as a pillow.

"I'm glad we found a candle." She says.

"Me too."

We listen to the market. And to the breeze. And watch the dark shadows and the small orange lights and she breathes calmly.

"Are you hungry?" I ask.

"No."

"We have peanut butter, now."

"I'm okay."

I'm not hungry either. I'm just tired. And she's tired. And we'll have a long night tomorrow. It's a long way back home. I breathe deeply through my nose to smell her hair. But I can't. I wish I could. I close my eyes. Someone grumbles and hobbles past us. I don't move. But I watch him. He's small, and he drags his feet and kicks up dirt and rock dust. I can hear him for a while after he's out of sight. Mumbling. I watch the small orange lights flicker on the black rock walls and the metal beams and the metal of the tracks and the old rotting wood blocks on the tracks too and the large, rusty, metal screws in the wood blocks, and I listen to the hum from the market in the distance. My back is stiff, but I think she's sleeping, so I don't move.

I put my hand in my pocket to feel the small, smooth stone. It's only a little larger than a quarter. And very smooth. From so long ago. I'm surprised we still have these. We lost so many things. But we're okay now. We're okay.

Chapter Six

We should be closer than we are. The sky is getting brighter. And it's easier to make our way over the trash now that we can see, but we're still too far away for it to be this light. We even left before sunset. I look back, but the City is long out of sight. The sun will be up soon. We follow the old freeway adjacent to the elevated platform of the tracks, and from here the tracks stand out starkly against the pale sky. The town is close, and we do our best to avoid it, but it's too hard to walk further out. The trash is too thick and loosely packed, and our boots slip through as if it was fresh snow. It's bright. And we haven't passed the town. They're awake now. Or they will be soon.

We hurry. Along the rail of the old highway, down through the woods where the road slopes further into a shallow valley and then back up through more woods and then out into an open expanse of waste with the sky very large and very low over us, and very gray. The mountain is far off, but I can see it. I look behind us, at the tracks, but we've come away from them now, and they're out of site on the other side of the wood and the other side of the town.

The wind is bad and very cold. And the walking is slow because of the wind. Especially in the open. Alex is ahead of me. She stoops to look through a bag, but I get her attention and shake my head. Her hair keeps coming loose in the wind. And she keeps tying it back. And when she does, she holds her arms out over her head and her head up to the sky and the gray light makes her look pale and her hair look white. And for some reason that pose reminds me of the old crumbling buildings in the City. In the setting light they still looked beautiful. Grey, silent, mournful. She's off again. The forest is just there and the mountain behind it. We'll be back soon.

I pull the collar of my jacket up higher over my face, but it doesn't help very much. The wind is strong. And my skin feels stiff. And cold. And my hands are freezing even in my pockets. The canvas bag with the plastic jar of peanut butter bounces against the pistol tucked into my pants, digging into my back. The wind is loud, and it whistles through the trash bags and hisses against my jacket. We walk in the open space with the wind coming down on us from all angles. We hurry. I almost slip when I see them running through the woods just ahead.

I hear them before I see them. Snarling. She sees them too. We both drop as if shot dead. She's well hidden behind the top of a car. Pale figures, mostly naked, gray blurs, running through the black trunks of the trees. Shrieking and snarling and shouting. I crawl over the trash to get to her. She's gone white in the face and her eyes are wide, face blank, lips shaking. She's holding a metal rail sticking out of the trash. I pull at her hands, but she's holding so tightly. I whisper to her, but she doesn't let go until the last of them are out of sight and we can't hear them anymore. Then she lets go and holds my hand. But we don't move. Not for a long time. Crouching in the trash, boots soaking in the slime and sludge that looks black in the gray light. The wind biting at us. I hold her gloved hands and we stare at the tree line. Breathing hard. And fast. We crouch for a long time. Even when my back starts hurting I don't move. And my legs cramp. And the sky gets brighter. Brown now. We don't move. Not for a long time. And when we do, we stay crouched, and move slowly. Over the wasteland and the trash and the slime. The rotting newspapers flick in the wind, but they're heavy with the rains and rotting and don't blow like they used to.

We stay low. Down the bank of a shallow dried-up creek where we can walk quicker, and the bank hides us from the woods. And from them. We walk faster against the stiff, pebbled ground, and follow the bank until it meets the road and we climb up. We watch the still horizon. We move slowly over the loose trash, and I can tell by the look on her face that something smells rotten. But we stay low and close to whatever it is until we get to the dark tree line. And then we run.

The sun must be almost completely up now, and they're all out. All of them. Running. Snarling. Biting at the air. And when the wind is quieter I can hear them in the distance. We're still a long way from home, and now they can see us. We hurry through the trees. Like them. But quietly. Listening. The twigs aren't crackling under our steps. They must still be a little wet.

We stop at the far edge of the wood, leaning my hand on the black trunk and breathing hard. The soot rubs off on my glove. We wait, looking out at the waste land. The mountain is close. The wind is loud. The chorused hissing of a thousand trash bags. But empty. We step out into the bright and open wasteland without a single shadow between us and the mountain. It's bright. And gray-brown. And the light hurts my eyes. Nothing moves on the horizon. We listen, and I hear her breathing and see her breath, quick and shallow breaths. She's shaking. We move quickly across the stretch of space to the foot of the mountain and here we're safer and we follow it, walking in the dirt on the edge until the hill of trash, and then across the gap between the mountain and the hill of trash that used to be the wide road. We crawl over the mound of black bags and sit outside, breathing hard and fast and the cold air stings my lungs.

My back is stiff, and my chest is pounding. She's still holding my arm tightly, but we're okay. We're okay. I breathe and calm down a little and listen. Nothing's moving out there. It's quiet except for the wind. And the wind isn't so bad now. I haven't seen the sky this brown in a long time. The clouds and smog are low and the sun must be high behind them. It's bright, and I can see the colors of the trash and newspapers and slime. And I can see the colors in the dirt. And in the wood. And in her face. Her cheeks are flushed with cold, her skin white with fear. And her cheeks and nose look especially red against her white, very pale skin. Very pale. Her lips are big and red, and her eyes are crystal blue and sharp and she looks at me. We're okay. And the color of her cheeks looks good on her.

She looks cold. And her hands are shaking. I take off her gloves and take off mine and hold them and breathe onto them. Her hands are small, and soft and the small gold ring on her finger is cold and isn't well polished, and looks cloudy, but it's bright and shimmers in the late morning light. From so long ago. And so many promises. I turn it with my thumb and breathe onto her hands again. She's stopped shaking, and she looks at me. She's so pretty. A strand of her hair blows loosely across her face in the small breeze. I kiss her finger with the ring on it. And she curls her fingers around mine.

"Come inside, darling." She whispers. She stands up and pulls my hand. I stand up and my back feels stiff and we wipe the slime off our boots in the dirt and go inside. It's dark, and she lights the last of the candle and I unload the peanut butter. I pour water from the jug into the empty can of beans from a couple days ago. The jug is almost empty. We should fill this from the river soon. Maybe tomorrow. But we have enough for now. She drinks small sips and I drink the rest. She sits at the table and watches me, the small flame making her skin glow and I can't tell how red her cheeks are anymore.

"I haven't seen it that bright in a long time." She says. "It was pretty, don't you think? In its own way."

"It was very bright."

"And pretty, don't you think? Not like it used to be."

"No. Not like it used to be."

"Don't you miss it?"

"Yes, love. I miss it."

"I miss it, too. I miss it a lot."

"It was good back then."

"I miss the trees most, I think."

"I miss them, too, love."

"Do you miss the City?"

"Yes. I miss it sometimes."

"I never liked it so much. But I miss it sometimes, darling."

"I miss what it looked like."

"It was pretty." She turns the ring on her finger and stares at the small candle. It's almost completely burned down now.

It'll go out soon. It's a nice little glow. And outside is bright enough to make it look even smaller, and bright enough that I can see the house more clearly. The grooves and creases in the wood that she picks at. The pale color of the wax globules. The tan wood of the big and empty dresser. The kitchen and the old stove and all of it brighter than I've seen it in a long time.

"And the birds." She says. "I miss waking up to the birds."

"That was nice."

"And the fireflies."

"I miss them, too."

"And the trees. And when there wasn't so much trash everywhere. I hate this trash."

"I know."

"And I hate the markets, too." She says.

"I don't like them either."

"I wish we didn't have to go. Oh, darling, I wish we didn't have to."

"I know, love."

"It's very hard." She says. "So very hard."

"I know. But we're okay."

Her face is in shadows under her hair. And the candle makes her hair shimmer.

She's still turning the ring on her finger. She opens her mouth slightly but stops. Her eyes are wet. Outside the wind is picking up again. I can hear it whistling through all the plastic and the space and the trees around the mountain.

"Are you hungry?" I ask.

"No."

"It's been a long day. We should eat."

I open the peanut butter and imagine I can smell it. It's the kind with bits of nuts still in it. She eats a spoonful. And she eats slowly. I like the crunch. She leans her head against my shoulder.

"Remember the fireflies?" She asks.

"Yes."

"They were lovely, weren't they? Like Christmas lights in the trees. Especially when it was hot out. Weren't they lovely?"

"Remember the squirrel that thought it could catch them?"

"And the time the squirrel stole my sandwich." She says. "Out of my hand."

"And you screamed." And she threw it and the sandwich into the bushes. And stood up and ran around in circles.

"I didn't scream."

"You screamed."

"It jumped on my hand."

"It must have really liked peanut butter. At least we don't have to worry about them now."

The wind hisses through the cracks in the wood. She puts her spoon back on the table. I put mine with hers. The candle flickers and goes out and a thin string of smoke rises up. The tip of the tiny wick that's left still glows red.

"I miss the fireflies." She says.

"Me too."

It's cold without the flame. It would be nice to have a fire again. The bricks around the fireplace are pale in the gray-brown light, and the bed of ashes behind the thin metal screen is gray and looks soft and fluffy. Except in the places where the rains leaked through the chimney.

I undress and undress her and we climb into bed. I put the pistol back under the mattress. My eyes are heavy, and she feels good against my skin under the blankets. Her hand is on the back of my neck and her fingers are cold and gentle. I like the way she looks at me. I miss when she didn't look worried. Or tired. Or sad. The wrinkles in her cheeks and around her mouth and around her eyes look dark in the dim light. Her hands. Her small hands. And her thin arms. And bony shoulders. She's so very thin now. She smiles her small smile. Squinting smile. Her eyes wrinkle and her nose wrinkles and her eyes are bright and sharp. Even in the dim light. Her hair falls into her face. I brush it back behind her ear.

"We're okay, aren't we, darling?"

"We're okay."

She kisses me and nestles her face into my chest. Her breath is soft and warm on my skin. We're okay.

Chapter Seven

The rock is sharp and pokes into my back and the smell of the
ocean and the shouting and grumbling down here give me a
head ache. I need a new one. I feel so alone and angry and I
should feel good. But there aren't any pretty ones left. And the
last one smelled so nice and was so pretty. And they all smell
so gross, now. They walk slowly and watch their feet and kick
up dust and cough and piss themselves. And the orange light
makes their wrinkles look deep. And the ones without wrinkles have scars. Or they have both. And the light makes the
scars look thick, and ugly. Criss-crossing their faces. They're
so ugly. They should find a better way to mark their property
that doesn't ruin them.

I watch the crowds on the upper level for a long time.
Until my back hurts from leaning against the rock. And I go
to the lower level and I walk along the tracks because there's
nothing else to do and my hands ache, but I'm not tired enough
to sleep yet. The smoke is thick and it's hard to breathe and the
smoke burns my eyes a little.

I follow the lower tracks towards home. They're less
crowded and I can walk a little faster but they're also darker

and it's harder to see the tracks and I trip and almost fall, but I don't fall. And I walk fast.

I pass through one of the lower markets and I can smell the ocean. The sour and salty ocean and it makes the piss smell worse. But the people aren't all so wrinkled down here. They're younger, and she's a little pretty. From behind. But not from the front. But maybe. And I follow her for a little bit because she's walking the way I'm walking. But she's walking with other people. They turn off and climb onto the platform. I don't follow them. She wasn't that pretty. From behind one of the cardboard shacks someone shakes a fistful of string in front of me.

"For you. For you." He shouts.

I shake my head and push his hand away.

"Ha'bout this? They good. Very good." He's pointing to knives behind him. But mine is better and I walk away.

The can of beans they gave me today is heavy in my pocket. I could trade it. But there's nothing to trade it for. But I have plenty of beans to trade. If I wanted something. I haven't traded for anything in a long time. Maybe a new knife, but mine is good and strong and I've kept it from rusting too badly. Maybe I could go back to a rope. But I can't see them when I use it. And I like watching them. It doesn't matter, now, anyways. I can't find anyone worth it.

Ahead a crowd stands huddled together. Not moving. And they're blocking the tracks. They stand and sway back and forth, staring at something on the ground. I push hard through them. Their black and stained and puffy coats rustle as I push past, and they grunt and mumble and I keep pushing. Hard. And almost step on someone lying on the ground. They're all staring at him. He's not that old, and his wrinkles aren't that deep. He has a large scar across his cheek. He's dead. And they stare. Blank faced. Swaying. I stare for a little, but it's not so interesting and I keep walking, pushing through them. I look back and they're still staring. Swaying. Back and forth. He wasn't bloody. Or hurt. Or anything. He was just dead. And they stare. I keep walking.

The soot on my gloves and coat is thick and I try and brush it off, but it doesn't come off. I wipe my forehead with a bare hand and my palm looks black after. I climb off the tracks and onto the platform and breathe deeply. The air is sour with trash and it smells and tastes bad, but it's not smoky or dusty and I breathe deeply again. It feels good on my lungs. And the cold is nice. I cough. And I walk up the stairs and wait by the top. The sky isn't so red yet. But it's getting there. I guess I didn't work so long today. But they still fed me and gave me an extra can. The sky is more brown than red, and the brown light makes the shadows of the trash look wide and the tall brick buildings start to blend in with the sky; and it's hard to tell, at the places where the tops disappear, where the smog ends and the buildings begins.

I sit at the corner for a while. The breeze is nice after the tunnel. And the open space is good, too. I don't like cramped spaces. The wind rushes hard through the tall buildings. The plastic of the trash rustles but nothing blows in the wind since the rains. That smell. So much worse. The acid burning through the plastic and letting it all out. I shudder remembering. But it's getting better since they stopped.

I stare at the highest points on the buildings I can see. The one with good stone work and the crumbling side stands out.

The stones are pale on that one, almost white, and I can see it clearly in the brown light. A crash of bottles and trash. I step back down a step. Snarling. And tearing through the trash. I move back quietly to the bottom landing. I hear them close by. And they shout and snarl and throw whatever they can find, and it echoes. I can see the shadow of one on the steps and it waits, and can see his pale foot with very long, brown toe nails. And then it shouts and runs back, and I wait. I wait until they pass. And I wait more. I walk slowly back up. They're gone, and the wind is the only thing tearing through the trash. I hurry through the revolving doors. The marble and exposed metal pillars in the lobby are all dark, and the only light comes from the reddening sky. I climb the steps.

That was a big pack of them. Bigger than normal. There are more, now. Every day more. And it was going to come down. Thinking about it. It wouldn't. Like that one through the broken grate. Was that the only time I saw one down there? I think so. Screaming in the darkness. Tearing at its skin. Biting at its arms. Its bright eyes. How could I not watch? But they all ran away shouting - cowards. How could I not watch? Screaming and tearing and then dead. I don't know why they can't stand it down there. But they must be getting desperate. And hungry. It was thinking about it. And no one is on the surface anymore. They must be getting hungry.

I slip on the newspapers on the floor of the hallway and the can of beans presses hard into my stomach. I unlock the door and lock it and feel better when it's locked and stand for a little in the shadows. But it's not very dark because the light is coming through the blinds and I stand in the black marble kitchen. The marble is hard and my boots clack when I step.

The wind whistles past the window and I watch the light at the edges of the blinds for a long time. Fading. From red-brown to red to dark, crimson red until it's gone. And no more light comes through. And I feel tired. And I take off my coat and pants and boots and fold them and put them by the foot of my bed and lie under the big blankets, but I don't feel warm. I never thought I'd miss the heat. The soggy, dusty, black, piss-soaked heat.

I can breathe easier up here. And there's no smoke or sour trash or ash. But I still cough sometimes if I breathe too deeply. I'm tired and breathing easier makes me feel better. But I can't sleep. I never get enough sleep. I should sleep at day and work at night. It'd be easier to get work in the tunnels. And better, too. With less of them stinking up the cramped space down there. But I never get enough sleep. And I need it. I'm always tired. But never enough. And even when I want to I can't.

I cough and roll over and try to feel warm. I don't feel warm. But I'm tired enough. I'll sleep eventually.

Chapter Eight

"What do you think, cowboy?" He asks. He yells so I can hear him over the clack of the hammer on rocks.

I hit the edge and a good-sized chunk falls at my feet and kicks up dust and we cough and spit.

"Did you want to?" He asks.

"No."

"Come on, cowboy. It'll be good. He said he has good stuff. When was the last time you had good stuff? Or any stuff, cowboy?"

"I'm okay." His matted hair falls over his eyes and his bristling beard has soot in it that falls when he coughs. He coughs loudly and spits on the rock and hits hard at the wall next to me. The sound rings in my ears. He's not too old. Maybe a little younger than me. His hands have spots on them from the sun. And his hair has gray in it, but it's hard to see through the black soot. And no scars. That I can see at least.

"It'll be like the old days." He says. "The old days were good, weren't they, cowboy? But maybe even better, because it'll taste sweeter. You know, things get sweeter when you haven't had them in a long time."

The rock dust gets in my eyes and stings a little and I wipe it out with the back of my hand. My glove almost falls out of my pocket and I shove it back in. And hit the rock hard. My hands are hurting pretty bad now. And I lean against the rock when the man with the pistol goes back up the tunnel. He looks at me and stops hitting for a little bit, wiping the sweat from his forehead and smearing the dust across it.

"*Sweet, sweet whisky.*" He sings. His voice is loud. People turn to look at him. "*I miss you sweet whisky.*" He leans back against the rock. "He says it's good stuff, you know? My friend. He says it's really good. Like the old days."

"I'm okay."

"Okay, cowboy. Your loss." He hits again at the wall. He's the only one hitting now. And it's loud and I wince when he hits. We all start again when the man comes back, and I chip at the rock. He's still singing to himself.

"Cut that out." The big man says.

He stops singing but keeps humming to himself. He hits hard. Harder than he needs to. And large chunks fall off and he kicks them away and spits on them.

"You don't have to hit so hard." I tell him.

"I know."

"You shouldn't hit so hard."

"The way I see it, we have to get to the other side eventually. I'd rather it be sooner than later. I want to still be here when we get there."

"We're never going to get there."

"Sure, we will. We just have to dig far enough."

"It's not there."

"Sure, it is, cowboy. Sure, it is."

He keeps hitting hard, and I keep chipping small pieces off. The shorter men that collect the chippings come down and run back up with their large oil drums filled with rock, hauling the bits out of the tunnel. My back is hurting, and my hands are very sore and I lean against the wall and wait a while but the man with the gun waves the pistol at me and I go back to chipping away. I cough into my sleeve. My throat feels scratchy and dry and I cough for a long time.

"You alright there, cowboy?"

"Fine." I cough again and hit the wall a few more times, but I'm done and I walk back up the tunnel and turn in the pick, my hands still cramping and it's hard to let go of it, and the callouses look very red and dry and I sit down to eat and they pour a soup of something into a small bowl and hand me a can of beans. The soup tastes rotten, but it's warm and the warmth is nice going down and makes my throat feel a little better. It could be better with salt. I eat quickly, but I don't want to stand up and I pretend to be eating for a little while longer. I leave and walk in the cold with the beans in one pocket and the bellybutton ring in another. Alone, I take it out. It's a pretty stone. I like looking at it. I lean against the dirty tile of the stairwell and look at it in the brown light. It's pretty. But not a gem. An actual pebble or something. But pretty. And green. And not perfectly smooth either.

I smell it, but it just smells cold. The light is reddening already. It must be getting late. I put the ring away and walk back down the tunnel. It's cold and the wind hisses down it and the candles flicker and the ocean smells rotten. One or two of the candles go out. Along the walkway the paper advertisements droop even lower and I can't see much of the naked women anymore. Another one has been torn and a piece taken off of it.

If there's something worth trading for, I'll trade today. But there's nothing worth trading for. And I walk slowly with the crowd and the loud mumbles and sometimes I can hear people actually talking with each other. But mostly it's just the people behind the cardboard shacks talking to the people in front of them. The rusty parts of fences they've locked around the more valuable stuff look dark in the flickering light. The clippers look good and strong, but I don't need them for anything. And they'd probably want more than a can of beans. But I have plenty back home. I walk around the market with the crowd, shuffling my feet, and staring at their faces. Ugly faces. And the black ceiling of rock that's higher up on this level and the way the rock looks grainy in the orange light. And the smoke looks thick up there, but it's probably not windy outside because it's not so thick as it can be if it is windy.

I cross the platform and up the stairs to get to another level where the tracks are just as crowded, and the smoke is thicker. But there's nothing I want. I walk up to the surface through the turnstiles and look out at the wasted City. It used to be impressive. I listen to the wind and walk out when I'm confident there aren't any of them out there. It's dark and even though the buildings are tall up here, the streets are wide, and I can see large swaths of the low black sky. I walk up the avenue and imagine it's still lit up like it used to be. And the avenue crosses another avenue running at an angle, but I can't remember their names, and the street signs have fallen off the posts and are buried under the trash somewhere. I turn down Fifth Avenue, the sign dangling from the lamp post, and follow the rows of broken windows, the dark and ominous storefronts. I look in through one of the windows. The long wooden table in the middle of the room is cracked in half, and the wooden chairs and smaller wooden tables stacked along the sides have been toppled. There's a kitchen in back, but I'm not going back there. There's probably still plenty to find up here, if we weren't too scared to look. I keep walking. It's very dark. Down the street are more gray bricks above black trash, silent. Dark. The wind comes hard down the avenue and I walk faster. The trees in the park are still standing but look stark and black and the bushes are thin. Twigs really. There's not much trash along the dirt pathway, and dirt pathway, and I follow it through the small park. The grass is good to walk on, and feels soft under my boots, and I walk slowly, but I shouldn't stay out here too much longer. I'm too far from a subway entrance.

I grit my teeth. I hate it. They've run us underground. Like rabbits. Like dogs chasing rabbits. The cowards down there. Too hard up here for them. Pathetic. Little rabbits.

I follow the grass to the small gate around the park and leave. The street narrows, or the buildings get taller – I can't tell. The black sky looks narrower. I walk quickly to the corner.

I climb back down the stairs and hop through the turn-stiles. The cold metal is good on my sore hands. My keens hurt when I land. I put my gloves back on and climb onto the tracks, waking quickly back home.

Chapter Nine

We should have gone out tonight, but we didn't. We shouldn't have, but we stayed in bed. We always do this after we get back from the City. We feel like we have a lot. And don't go out. But we don't have a lot. And we shouldn't have stayed in. But she looked so tired. And she was so warm in bed. And her skin was so soft on mine. She looks at me with her sharp, bright eyes. Her neck is thin and the shadows under her clavicles are dark. I feel her ribs under my hand.

After a while we dress and sit at the table. I bring over the peanut butter and the two spoons and we eat slowly, and she leans her head on my shoulder and we stare at the shadows in the darkness. There's no light coming through, and it's very dark, but I can still see her outline and the outline of the table. It's cold. I bet if there was light, we'd see our breath clearly. And a lot of it. But there's no light. And we shouldn't light the candle. Not till the sun comes up. But I can see her toying with it. I lick the spoon clean and leave it on the table by the wax.

"It's so dark." She says.

"I know."

"The sun will come out soon, though, won't it? It'll come out soon."

"Soon, love. I know."

"And then we'll light it. We'll light it when it comes out, won't we darling?"

"Yes, love. When the sun comes out."

"Soon."

"Yes, love."

"I dreamt about the fireflies, again." She says looking at the candle in her hands. "They were in the tree, and the sky was orange and the tree was very green and very dark." She's quiet. "Didn't you dream, darling?" She asks.

"I don't remember."

"I always remember my dreams."

"I wish I could."

"I used to dream about her." She's quiet again. For a while. And I hear her running her fingernail over the rough surface of the wood table. I stare into the shadows until I can see the outline of the large dresser by the bed. "I don't anymore. I only dream about the fireflies, now."

She puts her spoon over mine and puts her head back on my shoulder.

"The fireflies are pretty." She says. "Aren't they, darling? Aren't they pretty?"

I feel tired. And my eyes feel heavy. But we slept long.

"Let's sit outside. Just for a minute, darling. Let's sit outside."

We zip up our coats and close the door and lean against it in the dirt outside. It's a little easier to see, but it's still very dark. The small breeze is nice, though. And she closes her eyes and smiles a little. There used to be a road right there. Instead

UNTIL WE ARE LOST

of the hill of trash bags. I stare at where it should be. Winding down the cliff. And how it was before. You could see over the whole valley and the trees, oh the green trees. And the small brown buildings of the town far out. If it was clear. I look up at the big mountain. I can see the impressive outline against the sky, just ever so slightly a different shade. It used to be so green. And the big bright boulders on the face we can't see from here – I guess those are still there. But so green, and alive. And now dirt and gray and dead trees and no birds or anything. I liked those hikes to the top. And the view was broad and endless.

We can hear the wind rustling through the plastic in the distance. It stops, and nothing moves. It's quiet. Perfectly quiet. We watch the sky, but it's not getting brighter. And there are no patches of light like they're used to be. It's all the same dark blurry overcast. And it'll all be the same gray and then the same brown when the sun starts to come up and is up.

"Don't you think it looks pretty, sometimes?" She asks. "The emptiness. All the space. Don't you think so?"

"Sometimes."

"I don't like all the trash. But I like the space. And how quiet it can get. But I miss the birds."

"I would like to see birds again."

"And I miss the fireflies. I miss them most, I think."

"Not the trees?"

"I miss the fireflies more."

"I liked the fireflies."

"Don't you miss the sky, too? I miss the sky. Especially at night. And during the day. I miss it."

"I miss it, too. And how blue it could get. Remember, love, how blue it could get?"

"But it looks pretty out there, sometimes. When you think about it."

"I guess so."

"Not pretty like the old days."

"No. Not like the old days."

"But pretty in a new way."

"I guess so."

"I would like to see it in the afternoon time. When it's the brightest. Wouldn't you?"

"I don't know it would look much different."

"I would like to see it. I think it would be pretty. Not like it used to, but in a deferent way."

We're whispering too loud. I take off my glove and I run my finger through the cold dirt, stiff with cold, and coarse. I drop the small pebbles and put my glove back on. I look back at the cliff. I can't see anything beyond it, it's too dark. The big oak with the thick trunk was right there. I look at the mound of trash. Maybe we should make it higher. It's high enough to block the wind, but maybe it should be higher.

"I don't like the trash, though." She says. "I hate the trash."

"I know. I hate it too."

"I hate it." She's whispering loud still.

"I know."

"Awful. Poisonous."

"We shouldn't think about it. Not now."

"I hate it. I do." She's shaking.

"I know."

"Darling, I hate it."

We're quiet for a long time. My throat feels knotted. The wind rises and falls, and we sit, leaning against the wood of the small house in the dirt. The trash in front of us looks dark and it's hard to see where one bag ends and another begins. I push my boot out and straighten my leg when my back gets stiff. It rakes through the dirt. Grinding. The wind is loud around us. The hissing rustle of plastic and paper, no leaves or bushes.

She watches the sky.

"Are you thirsty, love?"

"No, I'm all right."

"Okay."

She nestles into me and after a minute her shaking gets softer.

"It's sad, isn't it? To think that they're all gone." She says quieter. "It's awfully sad to think about."

"I know."

"But they might not be."

"Maybe."

"I never got to meet your parents." She says.

"They would have loved you."

"Mary was always very sweet on the phone."

"I wish you could have met her."

"Isn't it sad to think that they're gone?"

My back is stiff and aches a little and I sit up straight.

"Maybe they're not." She says.

"Maybe." I say.

"I miss them all."

"I miss them, too."

She's quiet. And the wind is quieter, too. She takes a deep breath. "It would have been so good." She says. "I hate this trash. I really, really do."

"I know. I do too."

"We would have been so good at it, too. Don't you think so?"

"You especially."

"But we shouldn't think about it, isn't that right? It hurts to think about. And I miss her so much, so we shouldn't think about it."

"We shouldn't."

"But we're okay." She says. "Aren't we okay?"

"We are, my love. We're okay. And we shouldn't think like this now. It's been a long couple of days."

"It's just so hard."

"I know."

My lips are cold, and my teeth chatter a little. But I feel hot. And my eyes burn a little and feel wet and the wind chills them. We watch the sky. It's a little brighter. And it'll get bright quickly now. But it's still dark. Too dark for me to see the red in her cheeks from the cold. Too dark to see the wrinkles around her eyes. But it's light enough for me to see her pale skin. And her bright eyes. She looks so sad. And tired. She deserves so much better. Than this. This trash. I hate this trash. But she won't break. It won't break her. She was always strong. And stubborn. Very stubborn. My arm is around her, and her hair is tied back, and the bun rests against my arm. She curls into me. And I feel her pressing her hands into my chest.

She looks so white in the dark. And ghostly. But not before. Not before. By the church, leaning against the tree, her in my arms, the sun coming through the bare branches and making her arms look tan and her hair shine, and her eyes were so blue and sharp, and she looked at me. She was always a little pale, I guess, but not like this. I hold her tight to my chest and I feel her breathing and I breathe and it's nice and quiet and only a little cold.

"You never met my father, did you darling?" She says.

"No."

"It's probably for the better."

"I would have liked to."

"And we never traveled, like we said we would."

"I wanted to."

"Me too."

"I wanted to go to New Mexico with you." I say.

"That would have been lovely."

"And you could have come home with me."

"I would have liked that."

"And for the holidays. Mom always had big dinners on the holidays."

"That would be good."

"With lots of food. And wine. And we'd be drunk a little and it would be warm and good and we'd be with all of them."

"That would be lovely." She says.

"And you and my mom could read by the fire on the big couches." She leans into me and I can feel her breathing and her hair is coming loose and flicking in the breeze coming over the hill of trash. "The holidays are always good." I say.

"And everyone would fawn over her and they'd all want to hold her."

Around the top of the mountain the sky is looking a little brighter. And the mountain looks flat, and dark, like it was cut out of the sky. It'll get bright quickly now, and the sun will go up soon. I can hear the wind out there. It's loud, but down here it's not so bad. And she doesn't look so cold. She's not even shivering. I take off my glove and run my fingers through her hair. Her hair is dry and mated, but soft like it always is. My fingers get cold quickly and I put my glove back on and we go inside and sit at the table again and eat another spoonful of peanut butter each. She picks at the wax with the end of her spoon.

I pour a little water into the bean can. I offer it to her. She smells it. It's okay to use, she says. We drink a little each and I pour the rest of the water from the jug. She shakes her head.

"We'll get more tomorrow." I say.

"The river is a long way away."

"We have to go soon anyways."

She drinks a little. And I drink a little. There's only a little left but she won't drink it. I leave it in the can on the counter and hold her. The sky is getting brighter and the light comes in a little and I can see the table and the wax a little more clearly. They'll be awake soon. If they aren't already.

She's toying with the candle. It's almost bright enough to light it. She picks at the wick with her gloved fingers. It's a small candle. And it won't last very long. It looks gray and small and smooth in the pale light.

"I like the candles." She says. "Don't they remind you of the fireflies?"

"Yes. And I'm glad we found a good one."

"It's so small, though. But it's lovely. We'll need more matches soon." She shows me the small match box. "There's only a couple left."

"We'll find more in the market when we go again."

"You should light it tonight."

"Okay."

She hands me the matches.

"Not yet."

"All right."

I turn the small match over. The little bulb on the end pokes through the hole in my glove.

"I don't like the markets." She says.

"I don't either."

"I wish we didn't have to go."

"I know."

"I wish we could just stay out here. Like we used to."

"Even then we had to go."

"*You* had to."

The light from outside is pale and white. She's let her hair down and now I can't see her face.

"It was good, though. Wasn't it, love?"

"It was so good, then." She says. "It was so very good, then. Oh, wasn't it good then, darling?"

"Yes, love."

"And she was so little. And you would come home. And the fireflies came. She brought them. I think she brought them."

"It's nice to think so."

"I wish we didn't have to go. To the market. I wish we could just stay in. And the fireflies would be here."

I roll the rough bulb of the match along my thumb where the hole is.

"And I wish there wasn't so much trash everywhere. There's so much trash, you know? I hate it. And that something was alive out there. I wish that, too. Other than them."

"I know."

"It's so damn hard." She says. "It's just so damn hard."

"I know."

"Don't say that. Don't just say that. That's not enough."

She's whispering very loudly. And she stops. "But I'm sorry, darling. Don't mind me. I'm sorry, darling."

The sky is brighter now. I strike the match and it flares up in my fingers with a small hiss and I imagine the sulfur smell. And it nearly goes out, but it doesn't go out, and she holds the candle towards me and I light the wick. She puts the candle in the holder on the table and I stare at the match and the candle until the match gets too hot to hold and I shake it out. It was warm. And felt good on my cold fingers.

"Sorry." She says.

"Don't be sorry."

"I'm just so tired. So very tired."

"I know."

She doesn't say anything. We watch the candle for a little while and then blow it out and climb into bed.

"She'd be happy you lit it tonight."

She curls into me and we try and sleep. But it's hard to sleep. And I stare at the outline of the wood planks of ceiling and listen to the wind. Snarls and shouts. But they're far away. After a while I feel tired, and it's easier to close my eyes. She's warm against me, and her breathing is slow and relaxing.

Chapter Ten

One can was enough. I don't feel hungry anymore. But my stomach doesn't feel right. I cough in the cold breeze and the sour smell of the ocean and stand in line and wait for them to hand me the pick. They always give me the pick. I've never done anything else except pick. My hands are still sore and stiff. Hmm. The callouses look better. Not red anymore. I move my fingers and they don't hurt so much. They give me the pick and I walk down the dusty tunnel with the low ceiling and narrow walls. Men are holding a wood post against one side of the wall and others are nailing it to another post against the ceiling. It won't do much. The wood looks rotten all the way through. They talk loudly to each other over the clack of hammers and picks on rocks and I can hear an oxygen tank welding something down one of the offshoots and smoke billows out. I cough. The candles along the walls add more smoke. Black smoke.

There's an open slab of wall at the far end of the tunnel and I start hitting it with the pick. I hit it harder than I mean to and my hands hurt and the pick rattles. But they'll warm up quickly, and I hit hard until my hands are warm and I can't feel it anymore and then I don't hit so hard. I won't feel it for a while. I just have to think about other things. About her. And her lips. Her big lips. And bright, dyed-red hair and prickling skin and how it was harder to pull out the bellybutton ring than I thought it would be. And how her hands were small, but strong. And she was shanking, but not crying. She was angry. I wish she wasn't angry. I hit the wall hard and a large chunk falls at my feet. Slow down. It's gonna be a long day. But I don't feel tired and I keep chipping away, and I cough when the dust gets too thick and I spit. It's not as loud as usual. I look around. There aren't so many people. Maybe it's early still?

"Hey there, cowboy." He says and takes a big swing at the wall next to me. It hits with a loud clack and I wince and cough. The same man with the dusty beard. He's smiling, and he spits onto the wall and his spit sticks and looks a little green. His teeth are broken and brown. And his nose has been broken and re-healed crooked.

"You sure missed out." He says. "Man, it was sweet. And it burned good. Just like the old days. Expect better."

I hit the wall again with my pick and he hits with his hammer against the flat head of the chisel. His hammer is very loud, and he hits many times and gives me a head ache. I close my eyes and take off my gloves because my hands are getting hot and I wipe my forehead and put the gloves in my pockets. The big man with the pistol and the tattoo and the scar grunts behind me and I go back to hitting with the pick at the hard, stiff, black rock. Small pieces fall off and dust plumes up, and from where they fell the rock looks jagged and sharp.

"*Sweet, sweet whisky.*" He sings.

We keep hitting the wall without talking for a long time and more people find spaces on the wall around us and soon it's too loud to talk without shouting and he turns to me. "My friend says he'll let me know when he gets more. Said it shouldn't be too long. Said he's always getting some in."

I hit hard to drown him out.

"You should come this next time. Man, oh man, it was sweet stuff."

"I'm fine."

"What's your name, cowboy?"

I hit at the wall and my hands are starting to feel it.

"Name's Josh. Josh White." He puts out his big, dusty, calloused hand and I take it and then hit at the wall some more. His voice is annoying and loud. And his beard is dirty. And he spits often.

"Okay. *Cowboy's* fine with me. You must live close by, don't you?" He shouts.

More of the shorter people come with their empty drums to collect the scraps and chunks of rock in the dust. There are big chunks by his boots and small ones by mine.

"I see you here all the time." He says. "You must live close, right? I'm not too far, myself. I have a good place too, not too big or nothing. But good and close enough."

"You shouldn't talk like that." I say.

"It ain't nothing to talk about, cowboy. Just something, is all."

"You shouldn't talk about it."

He hits a couple more times in succession, and we take a break when the man with the pistol walks back up the tunnel. I'm sweating hard now, and I breathe heavily, but I cough when I breathe too deep.

"You from here? The City I mean."

"No."

"Me neither. I'm from back west a ways. Came out here a long time ago for something or another, but I can't remember what, now." He spits on the wall when I don't say anything. "Where you from, cowboy?"

"Out west a ways."

"Where? That's where I'm from. Not originally. But that's where I'm from mostly. Ohio. That's where I'm from."

"Same."

"No kidding? Cleveland?"

"Yeah."

"I knew it. I knew I had a good feeling about you. You drink, don't you? I can tell by the look of you, you're a drinker."

"Sure."

"I knew it. Could tell by the look of you. You got that drinker look about you."

I lean hard into the rock and it pokes at my back, but it doesn't hurt too bad because of the coat.

"You gotta try this stuff my friend's got." He says. "He says he's always getting more in. Says it'll be soon. And man, it's good stuff. And burns so good."

"I'm fine."

"He doesn't live too far away, neither. So, it won't be nothing for you."

"I'm fine."

"And it has that color, you know? And it's sweet as anything."

I can hear the man coming back down the tunnel and the others along the wall start hitting again and it's gets very loud and we start hitting again and my hands hurt and I cough on dust. It's not the same man as before. He leans back against the wall behind us and chews on an old cigar. An eyepatch over one eye. He's very big and doesn't fit in the tunnel under the low rock-ceiling. I watch him out of the corner of my eye when I cough, but he doesn't seem to mind us very much and so I go back to hitting weakly. Small chips fall at my feet and large ones fall at John's. Josh? Whatever his name is. The cracks in the rock look very black in the orange light and the candles nearest us go out when a strong breeze comes down that smells like ocean and I can barely see the wall and I can barely see John. I hit, but I hit a bad spot and the pick rattles hard in my hand and my hands hurt and I drop it into the dust. I feel around and find it and wait for the candles to be lit again, and that takes a while. The big man isn't behind us anymore.

"Kind of spooky, right, cowboy?"

"No."

We're leaning against the wall and waiting, and I twirl the pick in my hand. I can see the orange light from a few other candles on other walls down other off shoots. And the light makes the walls around us look flat and black and him look flat and black. I hear other people coughing, and him scratching his beard and spitting into the dust and tapping the hammer at the wall impatiently.

They light the candles and we go back to hitting when the big man comes back. The short people with their drums look up at John angrily when they see the large chunks at his feet. He doesn't seem to notice. Other people near us look at him angrily, too. But they don't say anything. And he keeps hitting very hard and large chunks fall at his feet and kick up rock-dust and soot and we cough and spit.

The big man doesn't leave often, and we have to hit for long periods at a time and my hands start to hurt bad and I wince every time I hit, and I try to shake them out but they're already cramping. And my back is hurting bad now too. I open and close my hand, and then switch hands again, but nothing is helping. I don't think I've been here long enough though. So, I stay. We hit in silence for a little while longer. Until the callouses start to crack. They'll bleed soon. I stop and walk back and John follows me. He sits with me while we eat. Cold stew. I eat quickly, but he doesn't. And he says we've made good progress today, and that he'll see me tomorrow and I get up and he gets up, slurping the last of it quickly and the dripple runs down the sides of his mouth into his thick beard. The can they gave me looks good. I hold it above my head as they pat us down. John follows me down the long tracks and a strong breeze hits us that smells sour like the ocean and the smell makes me feel sick. Or maybe it's the stew. Or the beans from this morning. They didn't taste right. But I like the cold air on my forehead.

"What were you before?" He asks when we're a good ways away from the tunnels.

"Nothing."

"I was a taxi driver. It was awful work, but I was good at it. And it wasn't for one of those damn yellow cabs or nothing. It was for a nice, good taxi service with good customers and all, you know? It was awful work, though."

A lot of the candles along the walk way are out, and look cold, like they've been out for a while. And it's hard to see much, but I can see the brighter light at the end where there are more candles along the tracks and we climb off the platform and walk back towards the markets. He's still talking loudly, even though it's quiet on the tracks, and his voice echoes. He kicks at bottles and they clack and crack. He tells me I shouldn't be so quiet. Everyone now is quiet, he says, and that that's why they're all dying off. Because they're too quiet.

"Is that so?"

"That's so." He says. "First, they're like us, and talking normal, you know? Then it becomes mumbling, and it's hard to hear them, then they just start mumbling to themselves and then they just stop talking all together. I've seen it. And then they stop walking around and just sleep all day and then, one day, they don't get up. I've seen it."

"I like it better when it's quiet."

"Don't say that, cowboy. It's a dangerous thing to say. Don't say that."

The market is loud and crowded. He follows me through them. I wish he wouldn't. My hands are very sore and I'm tired. I walk further north, away from my apartment. I look back hoping he's gone. But he's not. So I keep going.

"See them." He says when we've passed the market, and points to the side of the tracks. "That's what I'm talking about. They just lie there. And one day they just won't get up."

"Or they go up top." I say.

"Or they go up top. But that's different, cowboy. I've seen that too. But I don't know what causes that." He shutters and is quiet for a second. Then he continues, "I saw one once. Have you seen 'em? I mean when they're just about to change?" I walk faster and he rushes to keep up. "I've seem 'em when they first start shouting. This one fella just started going off the rocker. Had big fistfuls of hair." He holds up his hands. "That's what I tell 'em. Most folks don't know that. But I warn 'em, if you see a fella starts pullin' out his own hair..." He trails off.

"It's the small spaces they can't stand, I think. Drives 'em crazy. Small spaces and quiet."

"You've seen them up there?"

"Once. And it was bad, cowboy. Real awful. A terrible thing to become. Pray you go the other way."

We've walked a long way past the middle market and the platforms up here have different markings over them, and the people we pass have different scars on their cheeks. Not like the middle and lower markets. These are worse. Instead of horizontal along the cheek bone, they're up and down across the front.

"This is me." He says and points to the platform across the tracks. "I'll let you know when my friend gets more stuff in. He says it shouldn't be too long, now. Says he's always getting stuff in." He crosses the tracks, humming to himself. I watch him until he's out of sight. And I watch a little longer just to be sure. Then I turn and walk back south.

I walk quickly, trying to hide the scar across my cheek. I hear a crack from behind me and I look quickly, ready to run. Nothing. I don't like being this far up.

Past the lower markets I walk slower because I'm tired. And I follow the tracks and pass the different platforms that all look the same except with a different configuration of candles and sometimes the stairs leading up to the street are on one side, and sometimes they're on another. I cross the tracks at my stop and climb up on the platform, but it's hard because my arms are sore, and it takes me a couple tries to get up. I'm getting too old for this. The sign for Broad St. is swinging in the wind. I pass through the turnstiles and wait at the corner of the steps listening in the darkness. Nothing but the wind. I stumble quickly over the street of trash to my apartment building. I stand outside the revolving doors and look out. It's a nice night. Cold, but the cold is good, and I tuck my hands into my pockets and walk around the corner.

I don't walk too far, but it's good to walk. And I pass the old stores, sacked now, with the metal, locked gates cracked and pulled away, and the windows broken, and the shelves turned upside down. And I walk under the old scaffolding. I have to hunch over very far because the trash is so high that it makes the roof of the scaffolding low with the string of little lights that knock my head. They used to be white and bright but now I can hardly see them in the darkness. I walk around the block and look at the old buildings and how empty they all look and how pale and gray. There are many churches down here, and I pass one with short, sharp spires, and one tall one with chubby stones and broken stained-glass windows that look sharp, and the top of the cross is broken at the middle and looks like a "T." The doors are small and broken and I can see a short way in the entrance. The marble floor and the pillars and benches. I walk along the short gate out front and listen to the sounds along the windy avenue and look up as far as I can, but I can't see far. I stub my foot on the top of a fire-hydrant poking up and I curse under my breath and walk more in the middle of the avenue. It's a quiet night. Except for the wind. I listen, but there's nothing except the wind. And the wind is hard and cold on my face and my hands ache very much, especially when they're cold and I walk with my head low over the loose trash and back down the smaller, narrower streets and around the corner and up the one stone step and push through the revolving doors of my apparent building and climb the stairs.

I undress and fold my clothes and put them at the edge of my bed. But I've worn these clothes every day for a while, so I replace them with another set of very dirty and raggedy looking clothes from the large walk-in closet and fold those and put them at the foot of my bed right above my boots. The air is chilly up here, and I pull the thick blanket over me, but I still don't feel warm, and I sleep.

Screams. I sit up quickly, the sleep gone. Again, the screams. But they're from the street. Howling and screaming and biting. I stand at the window and look down but can't see them. And the screaming doesn't last long. The snarling goes on for a while, though, and they yell and howl and I hear tearing and the cracking of bone and it echoes through the narrow streets. I try but can't see them. I crawl back into bed and fall back asleep quickly.

Chapter Eleven

"Do you believe in God, cowboy?"

"No."

"Me neither."

I'm sweating and panting and leaning heavily on my knees because my arms are very sore, and my back is too.

"I don't know if anyone does anymore."

"They never should have."

"But what do you think happens after?"

"Nothing."

"Yeah, that's probably what it is. But it could be something."

"It's not. It's nothing."

"How do you know?"

"Because it's nothing."

"Maybe."

The big man comes back. He was only gone for a second. We go back to hitting and John shouts over the hammers and picks and coughs.

"My friend says he's got more stuff now."

I don't say anything.

"It's such sweet stuff, you wouldn't even believe. *Sweet, sweet Whisky.*"

He hits harder when he sings, and the loud, sharp clacks give me a headache. And I feel sick. Constantly sick. I feel like I haven't stopped feeling sick since her. When she ruined it so quickly. I need someone else. To make it feel better. But there isn't anyone left. They're all so ugly and so wrinkled and scared and smell so rotten. And she was so pretty. I don't know how I found her. Maybe I didn't. Maybe it was a dream. If it was a dream, it was a good dream. One hand in my pocket I feel along the stone of the bellybutton ring and hit the pick against the rock feebly with the other. It wasn't a dream. I remember her. I remember her smell. And for a second I don't feel sick. But it comes rushing back quickly. And now the more I think about her the worse it gets. I hit harder at the wall, and the callouses on my hands hurt bad, and I look at them. They're very red and almost cracking. But they're not cracking yet. When they crack they'll bleed, and if they bleed I won't be able to work for a while. Maybe I should take a break. I have plenty of beans to eat. Maybe I will. It will be good to take a break.

"I'll say this." He says. "If there is a god, he's a bastard."

"There isn't."

"But if there is."

He hits very hard and an impressively large slab falls off the wall and almost hits his toes and he jumps back.

"Look at that one! That's a nice one, cowboy." He says. "The biggest one yet." He hits again, but nothing larger falls off and he looks disappointed.

"We'll be through in no time." He says. "The rock is comin' down easier now."

"You're gonna bring the whole damn thing down if you keep hitting so damn hard." Someone else says from the other side of him.

"Buzz off, you lazy bum."

"It's coming down. I'm telling you. And we'll all be trapped under it." The man looks at the ceiling. He's very thin, and his beard is long and there is a thick scar on the side of his cheek that I can see clearly in the candle light.

A short man with the drum comes down our way and sees the large chunk at John's feet and frowns and curses under his breath. He picks it up and puts it in with the rest of the rocks, but he can barely carry the drum after, and he stops and curses more under his breath. The big man with the eyepatch kicks him and the short man falls face-first into the dust and coughs. He coughs for a long time and the big man yells at him to hurry up. The short man drags the drum with all the rocks in it, coughing and sputtering and the big man follows him up and we stop hitting at the wall.

The man on the other side of John leaves, muttering under his breath something about being trapped under the damn rocks. I look up at the low ceiling. Half an arm's length over my head. Not even.

"Lazy bastards." He says. "If it wasn't for them, we'd be through by now."

"There's nothing there."

"Sure, there is, cowboy. Just you wait. We'll be through soon, you saw that piece."

"There's nothing there."

"If there ain't nothing there, then why is it we still diggin'?"

"Because we're all idiots." I say.

"I ain't gonna argue with that, cowboy." He smiles, and I can see his broken teeth and how brown they are, and he spits. "But it's there. I know it is. They wouldn't feed us so good if there wasn't nothin' there."

The smoke is thick, and my throat is very scratchy, and I feel sick. Sick to my stomach. I lean forward to vomit, but nothing comes up. I feel like it's going to. But it doesn't. I stand, but the feeling doesn't pass. I feel rotten. Rotten all the way through.

"You alright there, cowboy?"

"I'm fine."

"You look a little green."

"I'm fine."

"I know what you need. You need some of that *sweet, sweet Whisky. So sweet, my Whisky.*"

"I'm fine."

"My friend says he's got more, now. And if it's anything like last time, man, oh man, oh man." He trails off and hums to himself.

I wipe the sweat off my forehead. The back of my hand looks black with soot and dust when it comes away. A loud crack from down a different branch of the tunnel and people run out yelling. We follow them out to the top quickly, coughing in the thick rock-dust and soot that fills the air. All the shouts stop at once as if sucked out and it's dead quiet. But only for a second. Nothing happens and the men with guns poke and prod us back down into the depths. The candles have gone out from the gust of wind and we have to light them as we go. A wooden beam broke and a bit of the rock-ceiling fell off. I see it through the cloud and haze of dust and soot when we pass back through.

"It's comin' down easier now. See." He says. "I told you, cowboy. We'll be through in no time."

"If it doesn't cave in on us first."

"It won't. We've dug a long tunnel. You see how long it is. We can't have done this for no reason."

I chew on my lower lip and hit the wall when the big man comes back. His hair is graying, but it looks dark in the orange candlelight. He waves us on with his large pistol. An Eagle. I remember those.

I hit as weakly as I can, but my hands still hurt and the callouses still crack and I walk back up earlier than I wanted to. John doesn't follow me this time. He says he's going to break through the wall and get us to the other side. He's right. It's a long tunnel. I turn in the pick and they give me a can of beans but nothing else and pat me down on my way out and I leave.

Chapter Twelve

When the sun is going down and the sky is red, and she's already woken up, I feel her running her fingers through my hair. She's not usually up before me. She looks at me and she looks happier, and younger, and she smiles and kisses me. The red light coming in through the cracks in the wood looks good on her, and her eyes shine. We stay here for a little longer until it gets too dark for me to see her clearly, and then we dress and leave. We climb over the hill of trash and walk down the steep slope of the cliff, carefully because the dirt and trash bags are loose. Pebbles fall ahead of us and the dead and blackened sticks of the bushes crunch lightly under our boots. It's easy to fall and to make a lot of noise. Like last time. That was too close. I've never seen one that close before. And it was so close. He was so close. I could see his scars and pale skin with crusted blood splatter and dirt and sludge, and fresh cuts and some of the fresher ones looked infected. And thin. Bones bulging through skin, wide-eyed, teeth-bared. Brown and broken bared teeth. Snarling, I saw him through the spaces between the trash bags. Heavier than I thought they'd be. After that we were more careful. And after that I couldn't smell anything anymore. The sludge and grime. I wince remembering. It ruined our jackets. I was so worried when we threw them out we wouldn't find more.

It's hard to walk with the empty water jug. I have to carry it in my hands, and it makes it hard to balance. We finally reach the bottom. The dirt we kicked up, a dry cloud around us. The back of my throat feels grainy. We muffle coughs. I help her over the black tree trunks that rolled down from up top. The ground is hard. And the twigs are dry, and they snap and crackle under our boots. There are only a few bags this close to the cliff. She stoops over one. She shows me a small book. It's mostly together. We keep it. There's not much to find down here. The tree line up ahead looks dense and black.

The small town is just there. Through the trees. But far enough. We're okay. They won't hear.

She leads me towards the tree line, towards the river. I should know better by now how to get there. But she knows for us. Within the trees is pitch black. We walk with our hands outstretched. On the other side there's more trash and it's harder to walk. I keep my eyes on the buildings. We come over a small hill and then back into more woods, but these are thinner and the trees are shorter. We climb over a fallen pine. I can tell even through my glove how thick the dust and soot are over it.

After a while I think hear it. Even through the wind, I hear the trickle of the water on the big round rocks in its bed. The woods slop gently down a long way and the sound gets louder. Then we see the mound of the bank. The water is wide and black except where it strikes the larger rocks, where it glows white in streaks. The large boulder is just down the bank. We fill the jug with the icy water using my dirty and tattered shirt as a filter and we drink a little from the jug and refill it, but it's hard to drink because it's cold. The full jug is heavy. The little splashes of water on the handle freeze and the freeze chills through my gloves. I have to switch hands often as we walk down to the boulder. We sit where we always sat, her in my arms, my legs around her, her hair tickling my cheek. We listen to the steady and quiet trickle of the water and imagine there's still moss growing on the wet stones and that there're still tadpoles on the surface. And that we could catch them if we wanted to, and keep them like we used to until they turned into frogs and then put them back in the river.

We walk back over the trash, and she looks through the bags on the ground. The sky is dark still. But is it already close to morning? The trees are close and maybe we can hurry through them. But we can't. It's still too dark to see clearly, and the jug hits a tree and makes a lot of noise and the water sloshes. I hope the plastic didn't break. It didn't. We crouch in the darkness against the black trunk of a large tree. She looks back at me after a while and we keep walking. We walk slowly and listen carefully, but it's still very quiet except for the wind. I can see the town through the trees. Not well because it's too dark, but I can see the outline of the buildings and of the swing-set just outside the tree line. I can hear it creaking. Back and forth. And the chains rattling in the wind. We're too close to it.

It's cold, and I'm shivering and my hand holding the icy handle of the jug is stiff and aching with cold. She doesn't look it, but she's cold too. I know it. And we didn't eat today. We need more than peanut butter. We need the beans. But we can't get them. Not yet. At least we have the water. That's good, for now. But we'll need the beans soon.

At the edge of the trees she walks away from me and towards the town. I try and wave to her, but she doesn't look back. I catch up to her and take her arm and she looks at me. I can't see her face very well, but I can feel her breath and she's shaking. I hold her close. And feel her sobs against my shoulder. And her shuttering. Silently. She holds me tight and I put the canvas bag and the water jug on the ground at our feet and we stand in the wind and she cries quietly. She stops crying and she's shivering now only because of the wind. We walk back into the trees and sit for a short while and I hold her and rub her shoulders and kiss her cheek. The tracks of the tears are frozen, and I wipe them away. We stand back up and I drape the bag over my shoulder and carry the jug in one hand and keep my other arm around her. We walk back towards the cliff.

Chapter Thirteen

I stand around the lower markets for a long time. For as long as I can take the smell of the ocean, and then walk up to the middle markets. I feel sick to my stomach, and stop often to vomit, but I don't. Not once. I just feel sick. And I cough constantly and spit onto the tracks. My hands hurt too much to go in today. And the beans I ate were dry and the syrup was bitter and tangy and probably rotten. Maybe that's why I feel sick. But it's not. I know it's not. I twist the bellybutton ring in my pocket and lean against one of the old hand railings on the platform in the middle market watching the crowd. They shuffle slowly along the walkways and down and up the stairs and kick up dust and soot and the smoke is thick on the ceiling and the whole place smells like smoke. Smoke and piss.

I feel sick, and angry, and I walk around the market quickly, pushing through the slow-shuffling crowd. And they grumble, and grunt and I feel more angry and hot, even though it's cold and I can see my breath. I scratch at the scruff on my chin and at my hair, and I lean against the tiled wall on the lower level closer to the tracks and watch. My hair is getting longer. I should cut it again soon. But I don't care much, and I scratch at it some more and the little pain feels good and calms me down. A man in a thick overcoat trips and stumbles and almost knocks into a cardboard shack, and the wrinkle-faced man with fidgety hands shouts at him. A woman walks past. But they're all ugly and disgusting and it makes me feel sicker to look at them.

I feel hot after standing for a while and walk down a tiled ramp and lean against an iron gate looking down onto the lower level and at the people shuffling past the shacks on and off the platforms. Along the walkway stone pillars hoist the low ceiling with metal pipes running in parallel. The stones of several pillars are cracked and have crumbled exposing the iron post in the center. A cold breeze comes in through the stairway around the corner. The orange flames flicker back and forth and make the people pushing past look blurry in the wavering light. There are no shacks on this narrow stretch of walkway, so it's not so busy with disgusting, pathetic, piss-smelling, shells-of-people. I keep walking and lean against a tiled wall next to an old newspaper stand that's become a shack for cigarettes and plastic bottles with different colored liquids. I can feel the cold coming off the tiles.

She could be pretty. She's walking faster than most of them, and her hair is shorter and matted, and from behind I like the way she moves. I follow her along the walkway above the tracks, and climb down them when she does, and follow her to a shack just before the tunnel narrows and the market ends, but she's ugly, too. I make my way back up through the market. Someone hunched over pushes past me, and I can see under the black hood that she's younger than she pretends to be. And she could be pretty. Like how I found the last one.

And I follow her. The limp is obviously fake. I'm getting excited. She pushes through the crowed and out of the mass of shuffling people. After a while in the darkness she straightens up and stops limping and lets her hood down. I can't get a good look though. I speed up to get closer. I see the vertical scars on her cheek. Just like the upper markets. That explains the hood. I try to see past the scars, but even still. She's disgusting. I go back.

The smoke is thick and gray. And I can see it moving slowly over us, back and forth, swirling. It's so thick I can't even see the rock-ceiling through it. The merchants in their shacks are yelling, but nobody is buying today. Mostly people just like to walk around. And the old lady in the shack next to me is yelling so much that she loses her voice and it sounds scratchy and she pulls a limp-looking cigarette out from her pocket and lights it in one of the candles. She smokes quickly. Her gloves don't cover her finger tips and her fingernails are long and brown in the candle light and the red glow from the tip of the cigarette pokes out between her brown fingernails and shriveled fingertips. The cigarette smoke makes me feel worse and I walk back towards the lower markets.

I can hear the wind picking up outside when I pass the *Twenty-Third Street* station and the ocean smell is thick and sour and I stop to vomit, but I don't. I wish I would. I would feel better. But I don't. I pass a group of people whispering to themselves walking back up towards the middle markets. They walk quickly and with their hands in their pockets and I hear them whispering about the smell. The upper parts of the metal posts between tracks are lit by the gray light coming through the vent. And it looks very crusty and sharp and it's rusted bad.

I wonder what moved the trash off the vent. The smell is worse, but the smoke is thinner. And it's easier to breathe. And the light looks good coming through the stairs. I climb up onto the platform and walk up the stairs and look out.

A big red awning with yellow lettering that's turning brown and has holes in it flaps in the wind next to me, and inside it looks like it was a fast food place. The counter still looks clean and the old registers and the grill and oil vat, but it's all been sacked and torn through and there are papers on the floor and the chairs and stools are broken. Across the way a construction site fenced off with blue wooden planks, but the blue paint is coming off - probably because of the rains - and the wood looks rotted through and bubbles out in the middle. I listen, but all I hear is the wind and I walk out and smell the ocean and the trash and try to vomit again. But nothing comes up and I walk around the corner. It feels better to be up here. The lampposts stick up over the trash. The sky is brown and the buildings look almost as if they're melting into the sky. And at the entrance to the building next to me, a big revolving door with a podium for the doorman, and the light makes it look almost normal. Like it used to look. But there's no doorman, and the glass is filthy. I'm a block away from the subway station when I hear a loud crunch around a corner.

I crouch. It's too bright. It'll see me. The wind is loud, but I hear more rustling in the trash and more crunching of bottles. My chest is beating hard. I should run. Back to the subway. I should run. From around the corner a small man stumbles over trash bags, panicked, tripping over everything, and behind him another man. Their faces are very pale, and their beards are big and scruffy, and their hair is long. They fall into the trash and climb over each other and start to yell and then the howls. From not far up the avenue. I run. Climbing over the trash. My foot misses and I fall. The icy plastic against my face. That smell. Oh, that smell. I try to vomit it out, but I can't. I push myself up. I trip on something hard, but don't fall.

Screams. Loud and horrible screams. And their howls and snarls and it all echoes through the emptiness. I want to see. I stand in the wind and the screams, stuck to the spot. I want to see what it's like. Then a crash from close by. Around the side of the building maybe. I run in a white panic and stop, panting at the top of the stairs leading down into the subway. The screaming fades. I feel an ache and a disappointment. The howling and shrieking continue. I'm twisting the bellybutton ring in my pocket. I push the sharp bit hard into my finger until it hurts. I push harder. I take it out and look at the tiny green stone in the brown light. It's a pretty stone. But it doesn't help the feeling. Chewing sounds, and crackling sounds. It's not the same. I walk back down onto the tracks.

The sky is already turning a little red by time I reach my station and I climb off the tracks and look at the brown-red sky. I need a drink. A drink would be good right now. I take off my gloves and look at my hands in the light. They're good hands. Older now, and wrinkled, but they're good hands and strong still. And they don't look so old in the red light. The callouses are sore and look thick, but they don't hurt so bad now. They needed a break. I put my gloves back on and walk to the revolving doors. It's still very cold inside the metal and marble lobby, but there's no wind, so it's not that bad. My apartment is very cold too. I hang my jacket up and open the freezer as if I would find more whisky. A drink would be good right now.

I pull the corner of the blinds open and look down and in the reddening light the shadows look dark. The glass in the buildings across the way reflects the red, too. I feel sick looking at all the red; the red glass, the red stones, the red street lamps that stick out above the red and black sea of trash bags, and I let the blind close and undress and fold my close and lie on the bed. I feel very sick and I wish I would vomit. Or I wish I could find someone else to make this feeling go away. But there is no one else. So, I wish I would vomit. She was the prettiest, and the last. There are no more. No more to compare to her. And her smell. So sweet and familiar and her skin and her lips and her hair. It was probably blond before she dyed it red. And she kept it so straight. She kept herself so pretty. My stomach turns, and I roll over and heave, but nothing comes up. There's no one left. Not like her. And she ruined it. She ruined it so quickly with her stubbornness.

I try to sleep, but I can't sleep. My skin itches all over and I'm cold and feel very nauseated. There's no more red trim around the edge of the blinds and when I close my eyes it's very dark and I can almost smell the dust and the piss and the candle smoke from down below. And my eyes feel heavy, but my stomach keeps turning on itself and I roll over. I cough, and my throat feels scratchy and dry and I cough up phlegm and almost spit it out, but I'm not in the tunnel so I swallow it and feel worse. I cough more and cough for a long time. And finally settle down and my stomach doesn't feel so bad because my throat hurts now, and I sleep.

And I dream. I know that I'm dreaming. With her. And her short, straight, red hair and it glows in the red light at sunset and she's looking right at me. I want to touch her. So I touch her. And her skin is very soft and warm, and her eyes are very blue and we're standing on a hill of trash under a mountain. There's a cliff behind me. And a mountain behind her. And she looks at me and I want so badly to hold her and so I hold her. And I squeeze, and she starts fighting and I squeeze more and her struggling gets weaker. But I want her. I don't want her gone. And so, I stop squeezing and she comes away and her hair is blond and long, now, and she looks at me and walks away in front of me and I follow her and the sky is black now and I can hardly see the silhouette of the mountain anymore. And I follow her. And I want to squeeze her again, but I can't catch up to her. I try to run, but she's too far ahead of me. And I can't reach her. And now she's gone. Into the black. Gone. And I'm alone under this mountain standing on trash and I hear them out there. Howling. Snarling. And they're coming for me. They're coming. And I can't move. And I try to call out to her. But I can't make sound. And I can't breathe. There's screaming in the distance. Maybe they got her. Loud screaming. And snarling. And howling.

I wake up to more screaming on the street. I'm sweating. And I kick off the big blanket and my damp skin quickly chills, and I feel cold. I go to the window to look down towards the screaming, but the screaming stops, and I can't see them anyway. I go back to bed, but I can't sleep.

Chapter Fourteen

We stayed too long on that rock. And walked too slowly back. Damnit. We should have known better. The sky is bright already. We walk quickly along the foot of the cliff. I'm breathing fast and the cold air is sharp. I look up at the high cliff above. I look out, but I can't even see the town yet. To get to the road on the other side would take too long. Unless we go through the town. But we can't. We can't do that. I look at her. She looks fiercely at the sky, her hair in strands around her cheeks. She stoops to look through a bag. I take her arm and gesture up the cliff.

I pull her with me, the water jug sloshing, the canvas bag bouncing against the pistol tucked into the small of my back. We claw at the loose dirt, digging our boots in, trying to push up a little further. But it's too loose. Dust and pebbles and twigs sift back down and carry us with them. We try again. I feel panicked. I slide quickly down. She's a little further ahead. I hope for a second that she can find footing and keep going up. But she can't and she comes sliding down in a rattling dust cloud.

I stand on a rock to get a better view. My nose and cheeks are numb with cold. She stands next to me and holds my hand tightly. We have to keep going. But around it? It will be too long. Too bright. But through it is so close to them. And they're almost awake now. The wind is getting stronger and louder and colder. The jug is heavy. My arms are tired from carrying it. The line of trees just before the town pokes sharply and blackly against the graying sky. She squeezes my hand. She's shivering.

We step off the rock and walk towards town. Through the trees the buildings become clear and the light shines on them making them almost glow. We crouch and move slowly. Quietly. Crackling of twigs under us. It was nice when they were still wet. I breathe as slowly and quietly as I can. My chest feels tight. My hands are sweating despite the freezing wind. The hill slopes into the town and we follow it. Half of a house stands splintered. Brick crumbling like stale cookies. Windows black. Every sound could be them. Another short white building with a pointed roof. Past it, I can see the road. Or maybe that's not it. There aren't any shadows, and everything looks flat. We claw, more than walk through the trash, moving as little as possible. We stop at the corner of the short white house. I hear a sound from one of the windows directly above us.

I don't breathe. I look at her. She's staring at the window where the sound came from, the whites of her eyes stark even against her pale face. I can see her clearly in this light. I've missed her face. I didn't realize how much I missed it. Her hair is matted, the color of straw. Her cheeks and nose are flushed. The blue of her irises is piercing and crystalline. Her jacket brown with dirt from the cliff. I pull a twig out of her hair.

A growl and the creak of old wood. I pull her close to me and lie as flat as I can. The trash rustles under us. I drag a bag over our feet. Bottles rattle. I cover our middle with another bag. And another over my chest. I hold her close, covering her face with my jacket. My eyes burn. By chest is aching and pounding. The plastic is freezing against my skin and I try to cover all the parts of her that I can to protect them from the trash. Heavy slime leeches out and rolls over me. But not her. Not her. I try to cover her some more, but the more I move the more the bottles at our feet rattle. Another growl. And another. I pull at one last bag. It tears and the sound echoes in my ears. I pull almost frantic. It covers my face and I freeze. Something snarls from above us. The crackling of footsteps on frozen plastic from around the house.

And then more of them from across the way in other buildings. The sky is bright and almost brown, and we lie under trash in the freezing wind with the sludge soaking into my jacket and gloves, breathing very shakily and I can feel her chest pounding hard. Her shivering gets worse. I squeeze her tightly. Please don't let her smell it. Please. The sludge rolls over my shoulder and onto my cheek. I can smell this one. Just like last time. I can smell the slime. And I almost gag, but I don't gag. It's not as bad as last time.

I can hear them. Moving. Snarling. It's too cold, but at least the bags block us from the wind. A little. But she's still shaking, and harder now. I wipe off the sludge as best I can from my gloves and run my gloved-fingers through her hair. Her hands are pressing into my chest. Her breath is shaky and warm on my neck. The sky is bright. And browning. And the smell. The smell.

The edges of the trash bags, where it's only plastic, they look brighter and almost glow in the gray-brown light. And the wood of the building looks brown and black and the bricks look brown. And the metal frames are exposed and bent and gray and they shimmer on the edges. I see them through the spaces in the bags. The shards of glass still in the sills of some of the windows look dirty and brown and opaque. And pale figures move behind them quickly. Running back and forth. Like a blur.

The pistol digs into my back, but I can't move. The jug of water and the canvas bag are beside us under the trash. She holds me, and I hold her, and for a long time we shiver, but eventually we stop shivering. I can see my breath in the air and try not to breathe through the spaces in the bags. I think they left, but they're never far away. And we wait. Freezing. The bag over my face is sour and it's leaking, and I can feel the icy sludge soaking into my hair. We can't afford to lose these jackets like last time. I hope the other bags don't leak too bad. We can't afford that.

The sky is completely brown now and it doesn't look pretty. She thought it would look pretty, but it doesn't. It's ugly as ever. And I'm glad she can't see it.

She's shaking again. I try and reach my pocket, but I can't. I wiggle but the bag shifts, and something rattles and something else snarls and we lie still. But I can reach my pocket now. It's coming closer and stomping over the bags and throwing them and growling and the bags rustle, and glass is cracking. Running around the house and throwing more and laughing. I can see it when it runs around this side. Him, I can see him. Running naked. Mostly on all fours like an animal. And then he's gone around the next house. It's quiet for a second. He thunders back over the trash. Tearing at the ground. Snarling. Growling. Coughing and grunting. His skin is ash white and leathery. The veins in his thin arms and thin neck are engorged. He runs.

More of them follow him around the houses. They all look so white. And pale. And balding. And they throw trash and snarl. They stop, but not for long. And keep moving and I can hear them running off in the distance. And then it's quiet for a while until I hear them again. And they've caught someone. I can hear the screams. She cringes and holds me, and I hold her tight. And the snarls and tearing and coughing and screaming and then there isn't any more screaming, but there's still snarling and tearing and cracking. And then they move off and their snarls get quieter and fade into the wind. It's quiet again and the light is still the same color. Have we been here long? It feels like it. Or it could be seconds. It feels like that too.

My pocket is a little warmer, and I take out the small smooth stone. It's cold even through my gloves. I put it in her hand and I can feel her fingers tracing the edge. She holds it and I hold her.

They're gone for a long time. And we lie here for a long time. And the wind is loud and hard and even under the trash it's too cold. And the slime smells so sour and it's hard to breathe because of it, but I hold her close to me, so she doesn't smell it. And several times I think it's too much. That I'm going to vomit. But I don't. We're okay. And she'll be okay. She won't smell it. But she shouldn't have to do this. She deserves so much better. I've never been resourceful. I wish I was more resourceful. So, she didn't have to go through this. She's gone through so much. We wait for hours and the light stays the same color as it's been. Brown. And flat. Bright and brown and flat, and the brightness stings my eyes and my head pulses, and I feel nauseated again. I hear her breathing when the wind stops for a while and everything is quiet. Small breaths. Quiet, small breaths.

I miss her voice. I don't get to hear it anymore. Not very often. And her smile. It's not like it used to be. Coming back from the City. After she stopped coming with me. She was in the chair, and the sun was low, and the sky was orange and the wood of the chair looked very red and the purple bundle of blankets in her arms and the tree out front looked black against the orange sky and she pointed, and I saw the fireflies and we watched them for a long time. All of us. And her voice was so calm and sweet and small, and she smiled so big with her eyes crinkled and her nose crinkled up and her lips pulled back. But it was already getting bad. And there was already trash everywhere. And the fireflies didn't stay long. The trash killed them. The trash killed everything. I hate this trash. She shouldn't have to have gone through that. And she shouldn't have to go through this. She deserves so much better.

I'm tired. Very tired. And she's almost asleep. She's breathing calmly now, but still shaking from the cold. And my back is stiff and aching, but I can't move. I can't move. Don't move. I wish I could sleep. But I can't sleep. I might move in my sleep. I can't sleep.

They're back. I hear them tearing through the trash. And snarling and growling and biting at each other. They pass through the open space between houses where I can see them. Covered in slime. And dried blood that looks black in the brown light. But the light is darker now. And getting red. They snarl and keep running and disappear again and come back. We would have been waking up soon. Up the cliff. And the red light would look good on her and she'd smile. She's always happier in the mornings when she first wakes up. In bed, just covered in the sheet, a little darker blue than her eyes, and the light from the early morning through the blinds barely coming in and the City was quiet, and she would look so happy and she was so warm and I never wanted to get out of bed. I just wanted to stay there with her. In my apartment. Forever. And we were so happy. And never hungry. And never cold. And never sad. Not like this.

My stomach rumbles, but they can't hear it over the wind. And she moves a little, the stone still in her gloved hand. And I keep running my fingers through her hair. The sky is very red now, but the sun isn't down yet and it's still bright enough for me to see the buildings across the way clearly. And the bricks and metal and rotting wood clearly, and they all look red. I feel sick from this smell, and my head spins a little, but I won't throw up. I won't. We're okay. It'll be dark soon enough and then we'll have time to make it up the road and we'll be okay. And we can eat a little and we have water to drink. And we'll be okay. We're okay. We'll be back in bed soon. And her skin will be smooth and warm and soft on mine and the light will make her look happy and young and not so worried. And she'll smile the one with her eyes crinkled up and her lips pulled back. Like when it started to rain, and she couldn't stop smiling that smile and we got dressed and went to the roof and sat there in the rain until our shoes were soaked through and then we held each other because it was a little cold and her breathe was warm on my lips. Staring at the City from the roof and the rain was all we could hear, and it would roll down her face from her hair that looked darker when it was wet and everything was mostly clouds and the buildings looked ghost-like through the clouds. She liked the glass buildings, but I liked the older looking ones.

When the sun is completely down, and the sky is only a little red and mostly black I move the trash bag from over our faces and can breathe easier. I can still smell it a little, but it's not so bad and she looks up at me and her face glows in what's left of the red light. We stay here until it's completely dark and then we get up slowly and make our way to where the road was and follow it up the cliff. The road curves with the mountain. The wind slaps hard when we come around the bend. It's very dark, and we can't see more than a few feet ahead. And the trash all looks like one black blur at our feet. Slow. Easy. Just get there when you get there. It never took us so long before. From the train station didn't even take this long. But slow. We curve again with the road and the wind dies down.

We crawl over the hill and wipe the slime off our boots and jackets and out of my hair in the dirt around the door. Inside is dark and I feel good to be back and she sits down, and I can tell she's not okay, but I can't say anything. She wants to light the candle, but we can't. It's too dark. We eat more peanut butter and drink more water, but we're still hungry even after two spoonfuls and two cans of water. But at least we have it. And maybe we can find enough to trade tomorrow. If we're lucky. We undress, but I can't feel the air anymore. I just feel cold. And even under the blankets and wrapped around her, I'm still cold. And tired. And I still have the taste of the slime in my mouth. It takes a long time to feel warm. But we're okay. We're okay. And maybe we can find enough to trade tomorrow. Maybe. If we're lucky.

Chapter Fifteen

I hit the wall weakly, but it still hurts. Not the stinging hurt from hitting too much, when the callouses are about to crack and when blisters form and when they burn and look red, but the dull throbbing hurt when my hands are sore from yesterday, when they're not yet awake, and when they're cold; the aching, throbbing hurt. I hit more until they're warm. It's darker down here, on the offshoot, than it is down the main tunnel. And it's harder to breathe because the walls are narrower and the ceiling lower and so the smoke and dust are thicker in the air. My hair touches the rock above me. But the men with pistols and tattoos and scars don't really stay down this way too long and so I don't work very hard or very often and I can go for longer.

I hit the wall again and small shavings fall to my feet. I cough and spit and repeat. I cough hard to get it out. But I keep coughing and I cough for a long time. And it starts to hurt. I hit all day until my hands are sore like they would be if I were on the main wall and actually hitting, and my callouses sting and burn and I stop and wait for a while, but it's hard to breathe and I keep coughing, so I walk back up. John is sitting at the feeding bench. He waves me over. I sit down with the cold broth they pour into a metal bowl and eat quickly. It's sour and cold and there are chunks of something that aren't very soft.

"I didn't know you were here today, cowboy. Where were you? But hell, don't tell me you was down one them shoots."

I nod.

"Why would you go and do that? There ain't no benefit comes from working down the shoots, cowboy. We got to stick together and work on the front. That's where we'll break through. And you should have seen it today, cowboy. It's comin' away easier now. So much easier. Like butter. We'll be through in no time."

"There's nothing there."

"Sure, there is. You'll see. And you'll feel real silly when we get there."

"It's not there."

"It'll be good, and things will get back to something like they were, and we'll all be eating like kings for getting us through. And drinking like kings."

"Sure."

"And man, oh man, I sure can't wait to be drinking like a king. I might go ahead and drown myself in whisky. I would, too. That would be a good way to go."

"I can think of better ways."

"*Sweet, sweet whisky.*"

We're done eating, but we don't get up right away. And he keeps singing to himself. I cough a little more and shake out my cramping hands and stand up and he stands up and we leave. They give me two cans today for how long I worked, and they pat us down before we get out of the tunnel. He sings the entire way through.

"I'm off to get that *sweet, sweet whisky.*" He sings. "*And then my troubles will be drowned. In that sweet, sweet whisky.*" We're walking north again. Towards the middle markets. I can't tell if I'm following him or he's following me. I could turn around. But then he'd know. He's singing cheerily the entire way to his stop.

He climbs up onto the platform and holds out his hand. "You coming, cowboy?"

"No."

"Get on up here. We're gonna drink that *sweet whisky tonight.*"

"I'm fine."

"You aint never had anything this good. And it'll only take a minute. He says this is even better than last time. And man, oh man, oh man. Last time was something else."

"I'm fine."

"No, you ain't. You're too quiet. Get on up here before you lie down and never get up."

A drink? With him? No. I look back down the tunnel. And up the tunnel. He's just watching me with that nasty grin and those rotten teeth. A drink sounds good. Better than I want it to sound. I'm tired. I should sleep.

"Well?" He gestures to me.

It does sound good. Even just one sounds good. It's been so long. I climb onto the platform."

"You ain't gonna be sorry, cowboy. You'll be thanking me soon."

We wait at the edge of the stairs to make sure there's nothing out there. All I hear is the wind and his humming and I follow him onto the trash. I feel sick still, but it's not as bad as it was earlier, and the cold wind is good on my sweaty face. I wipe away some of the sweat and my glove comes away with a damp layer of soot and dust on it. We walk as quickly as we can over the trash and along a street that cuts across the avenues at at an angle. This used to be a small square with benches and tables with umbrellas and you could sit and watch the traffic go by and look at the very tall buildings and all the lights. And on a sunny day the potted plants and people and cars, they all looked very bright because there was no shade anywhere except under the umbrellas, and the glass of the very tall buildings made the sun even brighter. We continue down the street a short ways before turning. We're above one of the upper markets now and I can hear the hum of people below us and even over the trash I can smell the smoke from all the candles. We pass several more blocks. The station entrance is far away now. What if they hear us? We wouldn't make it back. Part of that scares me. Part of that excites me. I remember the screams from yesterday. The ocean smell is getting worse.

We come to an old parking garage that looks very small compared to the tall buildings around it. Across the street is an old laundry mat and a bank with broken windows and a pizza place with a long red awning that's coming down and a liquor store with a big yellow sign over it, but the "L" is missing. We walk down the cement ramp of the parking garage and around the retractable arm that used to block traffic. There are still more than a dozen cars down here. They look pretty good, too. The windows are broken and I'm sure all the insides are gone. But maybe some gas? Or probably not. It's probably been drained. We walk past them in a rush. The clacking of our boots on the cement echoes through the low-ceilinged space. There's a door at the far end that he knocks on and we wait until we hear someone coming and it opens a little.

"Who's this?" Says a voice behind the door.

"This is a friend of mine. He's good. He's from Cleveland, like me." Then to me. "This is Joe."

"What's his name?"

"What's your name, cowboy?"

"My name's also Joe." I lie.

"You hear that, Joe? You're both named Joe."

The man behind the door spits and opens it. He's short and bald except around the ears and his beard is gray and he's not wearing a shirt, even though it's freezing, and the gray hairs on this chest ruffle in the breeze.

He leads us up a dark cement staircase and into a small lobby that has mirrors on every wall, and each mirror is cracked, and the cracks are deep and look dark against the silver of the mirrors. We follow him up more stairs with reddish light coming through the windows on every other landing, and out into a narrow hallway that looks similar to mine, with boxes and newspapers everywhere, and he opens a door for us and lets us in and then walks back down the hallway and back down the stairs. Inside is warm and I can hear a fire going, and I unzip my jacket and smell the wood smoke and the orange light looks nice on the brown bricks. Another man comes around the corner with a pistol on his hip and a cigar in his mouth, dark skinned, yellow eyes with deep wrinkles around them and a scar along his cheek and straight, brown hair cut short. He breathes out a big breath of smoke.

"Josh, good you're here. You're gonna love this new batch."

"Earl, meet Joe. Joe works with me in the tunnels."

"Pleasure." We shake hands. His hands are big and calloused, and he grips hard. We sit around the fire and I look out the window and can see a good way down. It's a nice view. It must have been especially nice when the City was lit up.

The man with the cigar leaves - I can't remember his name - and comes back with a big metal bottle and three glasses. He pours out amber liquor into each glass, but only a little, and hands them around. The amber color glows when I hold it up in front of the flames.

"To the good old days." He says and takes his in one sip.

"Here, here." Josh says.

I drink. It's good whisky, and strong. And it burns and my eyes water a little, but it's very sweet and I lean back and feel alright. I haven't felt good in a long time. But I feel pretty close to good. And the fire is nice and warm.

"Man, oh man, oh man." Josh says. "That's even better than last time."

"Didn't I tell you? It doesn't get better than this."

He fills our glasses again, and we drink, and Josh gives him over a silver necklace he's kept in his pocket. The man looks it over and smiles and puts it away and fills our glasses full and we drink. We drink for a while, until we're all good and drunk and my hands are buzzing, and my head is spinning. I give him my two cans of beans because that's all I have with me, and Josh says that his necklace will cover me and that I'll pay him back later. I feel good, and don't feel sick, and we talk for a long time until it gets dark.

"And we'll be through in no time." Josh says. He slurs his words a little when he's drunk. "You should see these chunks that are coming off. The size of my fist." He holds up his hand and makes a fist. "Bigger. One after the other."

The man with the whisky laughs and takes a big sip and then a long drag on his cigar. "What do you think, Joe? Are they there? At the other end."

"No."

He laughs again. "Good man. A realist."

"They're there, alright. They're there. And they'll have whisky for us when we get there."

"Not better than this." The man takes another sip and refills his glass.

"No, nothing's better than this, cowboy." He takes another big sip. "*Sweet, sweet whisky. I love you. I miss you. My sweet, sweet whisky.*"

They both laugh and finish off their glasses. They're teeth look especially brown in the firelight. Gross. I drink, and our glasses are filled again.

"This is the last one, though. Honestly, this time. I can't afford it when you come around, Josh."

Josh laughs and coughs and drinks a big sip. I lean back and watch the fire. He finishes his cigar and throws the butt into the flames. We're sitting on the floor, leaning against old cushions. The wall paper has been torn off, and the brick exposed, and the brick looks good, especially in the firelight. Out the window I can see a balcony.

"It's a good view." He says to me. "You should go take a look."

"Alright." I stand up unsteadily and the room spins a little and then stops and I make my way outside. The cold wind is good and strong up this high, higher than most of the other tall buildings around us, and I look straight down and can't see the trash because it's too dark. Out in the distance I can see the tops of buildings barely traced out against the dark sky, and the tops disappearing into it. I can see far into the distance. I bet I could see all the way to my apartment if it was good and clear. I listen hard to the wind, but that's all I can hear, and I breathe deep and feel good, and there's no smell of trash or ocean up here. I go back inside.

Josh is talking very loudly, and very drunkenly about the tunnels again. And holding up his fists. And saying that he's cut away a piece as big as both of them put together, and he puts his fists together. And he says that I was there, and I say I didn't see one that big, and he says I wasn't there, then. And the man with the whisky is laughing, and asks what Josh expects to find, and Josh says that we'll reach the bunkers and that there will be thousands of people living in them and they'll have plenty of food, because that's what they said, you know? That they'd have enough food for everyone to live over a hundred years, and we'd all have good food and good liquor and good women and we'd all be able to live normally, mostly. And the man with the whisky says that that's a nice dream, but that he doubts it very much.

"How come, cowboy?"

"Because even if they're there - and I don't think they are, mind you - but even if they are, they wouldn't let us in. They wouldn't want us, because then we'd eat all their food and drink all their liquor."

"That ain't true. They'd want us. They'd want all the people they could find, so that when we can come back up, we can get things going again."

"They have enough people to do that already. And they have the good people to do that. The rich people."

"That ain't true. That just ain't true. They want us. Just you wait. We'll get there, and we'll be welcomed like kings for all the work we put in to get us all there. Heroes. And then you'll feel real silly. The both of you." He points at us and the man with the whisky laughs and drinks the last of the amber liquor from his glass. It shines in the firelight as it goes down, and he coughs and smiles, and Josh finishes his.

"We'd best be going." He says. I drink off my glass quickly and feel dizzy and light headed. "It's always a pleasure, Earl." Josh says.

"You're a good man, Josh. One of the last damn good ones left." He turns to me. "Nice to meet you, Joe. Till next time. Any friend of Josh's is a friend of mine."

We shake hands and leave the way we came.

On the street the wind is cold, and the trash smells sour and we stumble because we're both drunk and it's difficult as it is to walk on the trash, but especially so when you're drunk. And I haven't been drunk in ages. And it feels very fine. And I don't feel sick. There's an entrance a block or two down for the west side subway line and we find it after searching for a long time in the dark and arguing in whispers about which way to go and falling over the trash and Josh laughs every time I fall, and we climb onto the tracks. But the ocean smells awful on this line, and we have to walk along it for a long time until it meets up with the other line that leads to the middle markets. Josh leaves at the middle markets and I wait around, feeling drunk and good for a while, and looking for anyone pretty. Or close to pretty. I'd settle with close to pretty. But they're all ugly and smell rotten. So I walk home, still feeling fine and drunk.

Chapter Sixteen

"We don't have enough." She says.

"No." I say.

"But we're okay?"

"We're okay."

She stares at the small orange flame. The candle already looks smaller and there's already wax from this one on the table. It's a gray wax and it's paler than the other ones.

"Do you want more?" I ask.

"No."

"To drink?"

"No."

"Okay." I put the peanut butter and jug of water back. She's still staring at the candle. My jacket still smells like the sludge, she says. But I can't smell it. She says hers smells too, but not so bad. And we can't afford to get rid of them.

She looks tired, and her eyes droop. I'm tired too. We slept a long time, but we're still so tired. She holds her fingers over the flame to warm them.

"Do you want to go to bed?" I ask.

"Not yet." She says. She's still staring at the flame.

She cried for a long time tonight. I could tell by her shoulders shuttering in the darkness. And an occasional sob quickly quieted. She hid it well. Her eyes still look a little puffy and red, but she doesn't look up at me. I wish she'd have let me hold her. And not say it was the cold. That hurt the most, I think. That she pretended. I just wanted to hold her, to make it better. It hurts so bad in my chest when I see her suffer. And I wish we had more to trade with. I wish we found anything at all tonight. There's nothing left out there to find. But we're okay. We just need to keep looking. She shivers and looks down at the table and picks at the wax and looks back at the candle and the small flame that gets taller in the breeze that pokes through the cracks in the walls and makes her shiver more. Her gloves are in her lap. Her fingers look smooth and thin in the small light. She puts them closer to the candle, and the flame is almost touching the gold ring. She winces and pulls them back.

"Maybe we'll find more tomorrow." I say. "We'll go back to the other side of the mountain. There's still plenty to find out there."

"All right."

"Then we'll have enough for more matches."

"That will be good."

She's still looking at the candle. She breathes small breaths, and the flame flickers when she breathes on it.

"Don't you remember the summers?" She says. "You do, don't you? The heat was too much, and we would always say how we liked the cold best."

"We did like the cold best."

"Well I miss the heat now. I like the heat the best, now. Isn't that funny?"

"Heat would be good, now."

"I'm just so cold. And I can't get warm."

"Let's go to bed. It's warmer in bed."

"But I'm always cold. It's never warm enough."

I take her hands and breathe on them. She's still looking at the flame.

"I like the heat better now. Isn't that funny?" She says. "Even when the sky would be blurry because it was so hot, and we couldn't cool down at all. And the smell was so much worse when it was muggy out, remember, darling? I'd rather that. I'd rather the muggy heat, now."

"Let's go to sleep."

"I never thought that would change. I never thought about it much at all, but never about it changing." She says. "Isn't that funny?"

The light from outside is looking gray on the old wood. The sun must be up now, or close to it. We should sleep soon. She picks more at the wax.

"And the rain." She says. "I don't like that much either, now."

"It's different now."

"It's funny, isn't it? It's funny how things change. And so quickly. Without any warning. It's funny, I think."

"I guess it is."

"And you've changed, too."

"Let's go to bed, love. Let's not talk about this now."

"You don't laugh anymore. You used to laugh. And you used to only ever get out of bed when you had to. When you absolutely had to. And you used to hate this smell. You couldn't stand it. You'd throw up if we were outside too long." She's still staring at the candle. "And I'd take care of you, and stroke your hair, wouldn't I?" She says. "It was shorter then."

"You used to be able to make me feel better, too." She says. "But you can't anymore. You used to, but not now. No one can. It's not your fault, darling. It's not your fault at all. Things just change, and we can't do anything about it. It's funny, though. Isn't it?"

"Let's go to bed." I take her hands, but she pulls them back and holds them over the flame again until she winces from the heat, but she keeps them there. Until she can't anymore. And her eyes look red and wet and she finally pulls them back.

"It's funny, isn't it?"

Her lips are pulled back into a smile, but her eyes aren't crinkled up and her nose isn't crinkled up and her eyes are sharp.

"We're okay." I say. "We're okay."

"There's so much I never even thought about that's changed now. I think it's funny." She's whispering too loud. The wind is still whistling, but not as hard, and she's too loud. I can almost hear her voice. I miss her voice. And I want to not stop her just so I can hear it.

She looks more at the candle and her eyes still look red and wet and she looks tired. The creases around her eyes look deep in the orange light and around her mouth. She blows out the candle. The thin string of smoke looks pale in the gray light. And the whites of her eyes shine, and she looks at me. She's not smiling anymore, or frowning, or anything. Her face is blank. Like it was then. When she wouldn't talk or eat or move. Just blank. And far away. And then she comes back. Without warning, and her eyes don't look so distant.

"I'm sorry." She says. "I didn't mean that. Don't mind me. I didn't mean any of it, darling. I'm sorry."

"I know."

"I'm just so tired."

"I know."

"And cold."

"Let's go to bed, love."

"It's so cold. And I can never sleep very long at one time. And the smell. This trash. It's all I can smell anymore."

"We'll feel better when we wake up."

"I'm always nauseous. And when I'm not, I'm hungry. And you don't know what it's like. How bad it can get. It's so much worse than it was."

I hold her to me and she shutters but she doesn't cry. She breathes fast and I breathe slowly, and she slows down her breathing and holds me.

"I'm sorry." She says.

"Don't be sorry."

"It's just so hard."

"It's very hard."

"And I miss so much. So many things."

"We're okay." I say. "We're okay."

I run my fingers through her hair. It's colder without the candle, but it's not so bad. Her hair is dry and knotting. She picks at a thread hanging off the cuff of my sleeve. The wind is quieter now.

Her head is heavy against my chest. She's still shuttering, but not crying. But she's still shuttering. Maybe she's right. Maybe I can't make her feel better anymore. Maybe it's too hard. She hurts too much. She's suffered too much. And she deserved so much better. So much better. She's always deserved better. Better than her small dorm room with the small window and the stained tile floor and the dirty green couch. Better than our apartment with the narrow walkway between the table and the bed and no space for anything we had and so everything was in boxes. She deserved that small bundle of purple and pink blankets and the orange light on her face and the warm summer breeze and the dark grass and the birds chirping and fireflies glowing off and on. And I miss that little bundle so much. My eyes burn and feel wet and my throat knots. She would have been great. So great. And she wanted it so badly. And she was so happy when she found out and she glowed. I heard that before. That women glow. I didn't think it was true. But she did. She glowed. Her pale skin was glowing, and her red cheeks were glowing, and her bright eyes were glowing and her smile was so big and her eyes were crinkled and so was her nose. Her lips were big, and she would kiss me and smile and kiss me again.

I feel her reach into her pocket. She hands me the small, smooth, black stone. Identical to mine. It's cold in my hand. And perfectly smooth.

"I didn't mean it." She says.

"I know."

"I'm sorry."

"Don't be sorry."

The stone is so smooth it's soft and it warms quickly in my palm. I put it back in her hand and she kiss my palm and puts my hand against her cheek. Her cheek is cold.

Chapter Seventeen

I wake up sweating and lean over the side of my bed to vomit. Finally, I vomit. But I don't feel any better after, and it smells. I lay back and cough. There's a little light coming through, but it's still dark out there, and I don't want to get up yet. I haven't slept very long at all. And still feel a little light headed from the whisky. It was good whisky. But the vomit smells, and makes me feel worse, and so I get up and wipe it up with some of the newspapers from outside the door and throw them back in the hallway. The air is cold, and I feel sick and hungry, but I don't want to eat anything. And it stills smells like vomit. I walk into the kitchen. The marble is cold on my bare feet. I look at a can of black beans. I don't want them. I need to vomit again. I rush to the hallway. I feel a little better I think. I go back in and dress. I look out the window at the graying sky around the tops of the buildings. Down on the street I see the trash rustling in the wind.

I leave and walk across the trash into the subway. The ocean makes me feel sicker, but I don't vomit again. There's not much left in there to come up. The lower markets seem emptier now. Everyone's asleep, and only a few of the shacks still

UNTIL WE ARE LOST

have people behind them, and even they look asleep on their feet. It's quieter in the market when there are less people, and I like the quiet. But I feel hot and itch even though it's cold. I walk slowly because I'm tired and feel sick, and it takes a while to make it to the middle markets, and then down the walkway to the tunnel. There aren't many people here either, and I get chosen quickly and given the pick quickly and walk to the far end of the tunnel where I know Josh will be later and I start.

No one's here making sure we hit. I look around. The other two are leaning with their backs against the rock. Probably not worth it to watch three men. I hit the wall a few times. It warms my hands up. And makes it easier not to think about the sick feeling in my stomach. And this itching. I scratch again at my head and my under arms. I hit a few more times.

The rock smells wet and the smoke isn't so bad. There are only a few candles lit. They'll light more soon. I don't hit hard, but I keep chipping away until the dull soreness in my shoulders is gone and they're warm, and the stiffness in my hands from the cold and the morning is gone, and the sleepiness is gone. Then I stop and wait for the tunnel to fill up with more people and for the men to come down and keep an eye on us. But that takes a while, because it's still early, and it's quiet in the tunnel, except for the faint clacking from somewhere back up closer to the top. The top is far away and the clacking echoes off the walls and is small by time it reaches me. I wait in the darkness with only a little orange glow and stare at the bulges in the low rock-ceiling above me. It looks especially close in the dark.

I kick around at the dust and feel the ring in my pocket. She was so pretty. Perfect. And to find her when everyone else was so ugly and sour. And to have her. All of her. To myself. It was too good to be true. Then she ruined it. And now there's no one else. Her breath on my face. Her skin on mine. Her hands. Her lips quivering. The tips of her hair in her blood. She had good shoulders. The shadows under her clavicles were deep. She was perfect. But now there's no one else. And she ruined it.

I feel sick and bend over to throw up, but I don't. I stay bent over for a while because it's easier to breathe and my stomach doesn't feel so bad like this, but I straighten when my back starts to ache. I feel hot and I unzip my jacket and stuff my gloves into the pockets, but I still feel hot, and itchy. And I scratch. All over my chest. And the hair on my chin itches and I scratch at that. And on my head itches. And I scratch at that and pull at the hair and come away with a fistful of it. I must be sick with something. I look at my hand. Short hairs sticking to it and sticking out of it. Mostly brown, but a little gray, and I try and wipe it off onto my pants, but it doesn't come off because my hands are moist with sweat. And I still itch all over. I hit the wall hard so that I don't have to think about it, and I hit hard until my hands hurt and the itching dies down a little. But it comes back when I stop so I keep hitting.

"That's how you do it, cowboy." Josh says, coming down the tunnel with heavy steps that kick up the dust and soot from the ground. "We'll get through. You and I. We'll get through."

I still itch, but I try not to scratch in front of him. He takes a big swing and his hammer strikes the chisel hard and the sound stings my ears and makes them ring, and nothing falls away.

"The first one always hurts the worst." He says, shaking out his hands. Then he hits at it again, just as hard, and a chunk falls, and he smiles. "Like butter." He says. "Like butter."

I hit, but not nearly as hard as he does, and only a small flake comes off.

"Come on, cowboy. You can do better."

"You hit hard enough for the both of us."

"Good food, and good liquor, and good wine, and women. Lots of women." He hits harder and faster. "And we'll be heroes, so they'll all want us and we'll live like kings." We hit for a while without talking, large chunks falling at our feet, and I feel a little better, but still sick and I cough often and spit up dark looking phlegm.

"Good food. And good liquor. And good wine." He says, hitting each time. "But not as good as Earl's. Never as good as that. What did I tell you, cowboy? Didn't I tell you?"

"Damn good." I say.

"And Earl's a decent guy. A really decent guy. And very fair."

"He's fine."

"And man, oh man, that was good stuff. Wasn't that good stuff, cowboy?" Only a small piece comes off after a particularly hard swing, and he looks disappointed.

"It was damn good." I say.

"It sure was. Even better than the last time. And he says more's coming in soon."

"Where does he get it from?"

"Don't know. Don't care to. So long as he keeps getting it. And he keeps being fair. I don't care to know."

I cough, and my throat feels dry and scratchy and the itching comes back all over and I scratch at my chest and my beard and my hair and my hand comes away again with more short strands of hair stuck to the fingers. And I swing without thinking and hit hard and a good size piece of rock comes off and hits my feet and the dust makes me cough more and I cough hard and for a long time.

"You okay there, cowboy?"

"Fine."

"You don't look fine."

"Just a little sick."

"You shouldn't be working down here with all this dust if you're sick. It ain't good for the lungs."

"I'm fine."

"It ain't good, is all. It'll make things worse."

"I'm fine."

I hit hard against the wall to prove it, and he goes back to hitting and humming to himself. After a while my hands are hurting, and I take a break because there's no one down here to check on us, and he stops with me. There are more candles lit now, and more hammers and picks hitting at the rocks up the tunnel and the clacking is loud. The air is still cold, but I'm very hot and it's hard to breathe because of all the dust and soot, and I can see it in the candle light, grainy and black, hanging in the air. And it makes his face look a little hazy.

"You know what I kept thinking about last night?" He says, walking around and shaking out his hands.

"What?"

"The lake."

"What lake?"

"*The* lake. The great and eerie lake. And the Italian district. The bred was never any good, but we never really did have any good places to eat, did we, cowboy?"

"No." Italy? I can't remember Italy from last night. Maybe he means the river.

He spits and his spit lands on the rock wall to the side of us and looks a little green. "I miss the lake most, I think. Don't you ever miss it, cowboy?"

"Sure."

"But I can't remember it in the sunlight. I can only ever picture it cloudy. And overcast. And gray. And cold. I can't seem to remember it in the sunlight."

"Me neither."

"It wasn't always gray, was it? The lake looks black when it's gray overhead. And spooky. But it's probably all rotten and poisoned now."

He looks upset. And he scratches at his beard and I can see dust falling off of it when he scratches. He taps his hammer against the wall lightly, and then takes a big swing and curses because he hit it wrong and his hands hurt now.

"But that's why we gotta get through this here wall, cowboy. So we can get back to that lake with everyone else. When they say it's safe, of course. But that's why, cowboy."

"We're not getting anywhere."

"Don't loose faith, cowboy. You see these chunks?" He kicks at a particularly large slab at his feet that hasn't been collected yet.

"There's nowhere to get to."

"Don't be down, cowboy."

"Don't be an idiot." I say.

"Just remember the food. The hot and salty food. And the liquor and the women. Especially the women."

"It won't do to keep talking like that."

"That's the only thing that will do, cowboy."

"You're dumber than I thought."

Even though it's loud because of the hammering it feels quiet for a second. And then he goes back to hitting on the wall. Hard. There's no one here to make us hit, but he keeps going. And I cough on the dust that comes up when a large chunk falls into the dust on the ground. I spit, and it looks a little red, but that could just be the orange light playing tricks. The big man with the eyepatch comes down the tunnel, hunched over, and he leans against the wall behind us. I go back to hitting.

I hit all day and Josh doesn't say much else. And he doesn't take a break either. Not even when the big man goes back up for a long period of time, and I sit down and almost throw up. He looks over to make sure I'm okay, but he doesn't say anything. And just keeps hitting at the wall. And more people fill the tunnel as the day goes on, and it gets very loud down here, and fills with smoke from the candles, and rock-dust from the walls and from the ground, and at one point some men come down our way to put up a support beam that smells rotten, and we take a break until they're finished.

After a while Josh starts humming to himself again, and I can tell he's worked himself back into good spirits. My beard is itching really bad now, and I scratch, and pull away more hair. He doesn't notice. We cough and spit and hit at the wall until our shoulders are sore and our hands are cracking, and he takes breaks again when the big man goes back up.

I lean over my knees and sweat drips into my eyes and takes the dust from my forehead with it and it stings and I wipe it away. I'm sweating, and the more I sweat the more I itch, and my arms are too sore now to scratch.

"Then why do you come down here every day?" He asks. He's panting. And when he breathes too deep he coughs and spits and his spit lands close to my foot.

"They feed me."

"There are easier ways to get fed." He breathes. "With that scar, there are easier ways."

"I don't mind it."

"I don't believe you. You're digging just like me. You just won't admit it."

"They're not there."

"Sure, they are, Joe. They're there. And you think so too."

"They're not."

"Why else would you always dig at the front. There are other places to dig."

"It doesn't matter where I dig. They're not there. Don't be an idiot."

"You talk sure, alight. But you don't fool me, cowboy. Not for one second."

He's talking loudly, and his voice is grainy and annoying and gives me a headache. I stand up but feel sick when I do and lean back down. I don't vomit. But I scratch at my head. The itching goes away but comes back and I keep scratching. Josh is watching me. I push myself back up with the pick and the nauseated feeling comes again. I ignore it.

"You'll feel real silly when we get through one of these days, and they all come running up to us with bottles of whiskey and wine and we'll get you so drunk you'll forget this entire thing ever happened. And there will be women there. Good women. Without scars all over them."

"It's not good to talk like that."

"And there will be food, lots of it, and we won't have to dig no more, and we'll be drunk and full and sleep like babies."

"Sure."

"And you'll feel real silly. But I won't rub it in, I promise."

We go back to hitting at the wall when the big man comes back, but my hands are hurting bad now, and I can hardly hit at all. And when I leave Josh follows me, singing to himself, and we turn in our tools and sit down to eat whatever they give us, but they don't give us much, and it tastes bitter and dry and we eat quickly so as not to taste it. And it looks like it has beans in it, and they give us a can of beans each. The bellybutton ring clicks against the can of beans in my pocket.

"*Sweet, sweet whisky.*" He sings. We stand in line to leave. "We'll be through in no time at all, cowboy. You'll see. That'll be a good day."

"Sure."

I pull the can of beans from my pocket and hold it over my head for them to pat me down. Josh bends down and mutters something to me. And the guard patting me down with big shoulders and crystal blue eyes and a big pistol yells at him, and his eyes get big and white, and asks him where he found that and waves the pistol at Josh and Josh mutters and cowers away from the pistol and the guard with the big blue eyes and big pistol shoots him through the head. The red mist hangs in the air and glows in the candle light and falls quietly and slowly down onto him. And everyone stops and looks at him on the ground and it's very quiet after the shot and my ears are ringing a little. Everyone's staring. The guard bends down and picks up the bellybutton ring and wipes it off on his jacket. I walk away. I hear him say he had it coming. My sister's, he says. Annoying with all that singing, anyways, he says. I duck my head low and walk back along the tunnel that smells intensely like the ocean.

Chapter Eighteen

More trash. As far as I can see in the graying light. We've walked far this time. Maybe too far. We're okay, though. We'll turn around now. But she doesn't want to. We haven't found enough, and she wants to keep going, but we shouldn't keep going. The wind howls loudly and stings my face and blows her hair out behind her and I can see it lashing out. It looks pale. So, does she. And thin. Her face when she turns back looks very thin and pale and her eyes shine. The trash is thick here, and it's hard to walk, and bottles rattle when I slide and almost fall. But I don't fall. And we keep walking. We'll turn back soon. We'll be okay. She's huddled over a pile of bags that stick up in a mound over the rest. She stays there for a long time and I catch up to her. She hands me what she's found, an old wristwatch with the glass face cracked and the cracks are white, and she keeps looking but she can't find anymore, and we turn back and walk together for a while, at least until the wind dies down and then she goes back to looking through the bags. It's good to feel some weight in the canvas bag. But it's not enough. We need more. We always need more.

The clouds and smog in the sky look soft and gray and thinner than usual. But that could just be the way the light is. And the wind stings my neck when I look up so I don't look up too long and we keep walking. The lines of the mountain are sharp against the pale sky and black and massive and impressive. In the dark I can't tell that there's nothing left on it. I can't tell there aren't any trees or bushes or brambles or deer or rabbits or squirrels or birds. It looks like it always looked at night. Big and impressive. But bare. It's hard to believe still. All the bushes and brambles wiped clean off. I can see the grave yard of the big red and white spruces trees and pine trees, the trunks rolled against each other at the base of the bald mountain. Just dirt and boulders. Bare.

There's something hard there, that I just stepped on. I crouch I pick through the bag. The slime is cold and soaks through my gloves and I wipe it off on the plastic and pull out the layers of decomposing cardboard. And something soft, like a hand-full of pulp. It falls apart in my hand. I can smell this one. I feel sick and I throw it off to the side. There's nothing in this bag. Under it maybe. I pull at it but it's stuck and I pull harder and it tears, and I put it off to the side. A chunk of concrete. And a metal post poking through it. I wipe my gloves again and keep walking.

She's walking slowly, but we walk faster when I catch up to her. It's bright by time we get to the hill of trash and wipe our boots and gloves clean in the dirt. She stands and looks at the trash for a little longer in the light, and in the light, we can see it clearly. The brown and yellow sludge and the black plastic that's fading and looks almost frozen and the corners of metal or sharp plastic that poke through, or just make the plastic bulge and stretch and look even more faded.

It's dark inside and she doesn't light the candle right away. She stares at the gray wax and the small wick in the pale light for a long time. I bring the peanut butter and the spoons and the jug of water and the empty can of beans. She smells the can and cringes but decides it's okay and we eat the peanut butter and drink the water from the can. The peanut butter is crunchy. I like the crunch. And the water is cold and helps to get the peanut butter off the roof of my mouth where it's stuck.

"Maybe we shouldn't light it." She says.

"Why not?"

"We only have so few left. Maybe we should save them." She holds up the match box. Maybe two left, I can't see very well in the dim light.

"We'll find more."

"We don't have enough."

"We're okay."

She lights the candle and stares at it. The flare of the match is small over the rush of the wind, and the smoke coming from it hovers in the air for a bit before it thins and fades and disappears.

I imagine the sulfur smell. And that smoky wood smell like from the fireplace. I can see the outline of the bricks next to the wood dresser across the table. The flames would be big, and crackle and the logs would roll off each other and a spout of sparks coughed up with the smoke and smoke would fill the house when it was windy and we would have to open the door and the windows. The blankets on the hard floor, wrapped in the blankets and her head on my chest and the smoke above us and the fire very warm and very bright. And her toes were cold on my legs under the big blankets. Her feet are always cold. And outside we would hear the foxes in the bush and the birds flying in for the night and we could sometimes hear the sounds from the town down the cliff if it was a quiet night.

And the sound of rain against the roof. And sitting up there with her in my arms when it would rain and our shoes would be soaked and coming down soaking wet and dripping and sitting by the fire. Steam would come off her soft skin. And she'd sleep in my arms and I'd sleep with her in my arms in that smoky wood smell and the soft crackling of the fire.

Or when the fire would just be small or barely any embers glowing under the ashes because we left it going all night and in the morning we'd poke it and it would flare up, but only for a second and we'd lie in bed and watch until the embers were completely dark and she would lean into me and her eyes were bright and her hair would smell like the smoke, but still sweet - like that flower.

"I wish we could light the fire." I say.

She looks at me and the light from the candle makes her eyes glow.

"Wouldn't that be nice, darling?" She says. "I'd like that very much."

"Me too."

"Don't you miss it?" She asks. "It was so good for a while. Back then. It was so good for a while."

"It was."

"It was so very good. Perfect."

But it wasn't perfect. It was never perfect. But it looks so perfect now. The orange light on her face. On both of their faces. And the warmth from the flames and the smoky wood smell.

"Don't you think it could ever get back to the way it was?" She asks.

"I don't think so. I don't think it can." I say. "I wish it could, but I don't think it ever can."

"I wish it could, too."

"But it was very good for a while."

"Nothing that good can last." She says. "And it got so awful. So awful."

"I know. But let's not think about that part."

"It was all the worse for how good it had been."

"I know."

"I wish it was never that good so it wouldn't ever have been this bad."

"Hush, darling. Please don't say that."

Her eyes look red. And wet. And her hair curls down over her cheek and shines in the line. She looks at me fiercely. Now softly. Now her face is small.

"I'm sorry." She says. "I'm sorry for yesterday. I didn't mean it. I said awful things, and I didn't mean any of them."

"I know. You don't have to be sorry."

"But I am. I didn't mean them. Any of them. It's this trash. It poisons everything."

She's quiet and I'm quiet and we both watch the small flame, and I stare at it, at the brightest part nearest the wick, until my eyes sting.

"And for before." She says. "I'm sorry for that, too. I'm more sorry for that than anything, darling."

"Don't be sorry. We're okay now."

"I wish it could have been different. I really wish that. Oh, darling, oh darling. I wish I could have been different. And I'm sorry darling."

"It's okay. We're okay, love." I put my arms around her and quiet her and she turns the gold ring on her finger around and around.

"I'm just so sorry."

"Me too."

Her face looks blank again. Like yesterday. Like before. Like when she wouldn't talk. And wouldn't eat. And she wouldn't look at me. Just blank. And far away. But she's turning the ring still and she shutters, and I hold her close and rub her arms to keep her warm.

"We're okay now."

But she's still shaking. And her head is on my chest and I feel her cheek pressing into me and it feels wet and a little warm through my thin shirt, but the wetness quickly chills. A strong breeze shakes the wood and howls through the waste with all the anguish of a thousand mothers. The candle flickers and goes out. The smoke looks gray in the pale light.

"We should light it again." I say.

But she doesn't say anything. And we stare at where the flame had been until the wick stops smoking and we keep staring until it's cold to the touch. But that doesn't take long because it's very cold. And we undress and climb under the blankets, but even under the blankets it's cold. With no fire. And no light except the gray light poking through and making the hairs on my arm glow white. It's cold. And my stomach grumbles and I hold her close, so I don't feel it so much because she feels very warm and soft and I think about her instead. And not about the cold or the hunger or the sadness. She holds me, too. And her fingers trace my spine and shoulders and she kisses my chest and buries her head in my arms.

Chapter Nineteen

I finish off the bag of stale potato chips. Worth the one can. They're not very good, but it's a good change from beans. I drop the bag and brush the crumbs off my fingers onto my pants and finish the water from the plastic bottle and toss it. I'm still hungry. But there wasn't anything else. I sit on the old, greasy hand-rail in the middle market, watching the black rock walls and the smoke and the candle light and the people going around. I feel a little better after eating something different, but I still feel sick and I still itch. And it smells like smoke and cigarettes and it gives me a headache.

So quiet without him today. Just hammering and picking and soldering. It all sounded far away, like it was stuffed up by the top and had a hard time reaching me at the bottom. It is pretty far. Maybe we are getting somewhere. A stupid thought. I wonder how long they'll keep digging for. Maybe until they run out of food to pay people with. But even then, they'd still find people to dig. I wonder if they'll just go until there's no one left. Probably. My hands ache, but not bad, and my shoulders don't feel so sore anymore.

I scratch at my head until it burns from scratching too hard and I feel around it tenderly. There are spots without hair now. I don't know what's happening. I must be actually sick. I climb off the rail and cough and spit and the phlegm looks a little red again, but that's probably just the light. I cough more, and for a while, but nothing else comes up. My throat feels sore and scratchy after. The wind comes through from one of the stairs and through the black metal gate and the silver turnstiles and it hisses as it comes through. The dust on tile floor blows around my feet in the breeze, and the breeze ruffles what's left of my hair. I see little strands of it sifting away silently.

I walk north until get to the upper markets. I feel uneasy this high up. Like they're all looking at me. I walk with my head low and the collar of my coat pulled over the scar on my cheek. But I need someone. Soon. I feel my stomach rumbling. There's no one left down there. Maybe up here. Maybe at least one.

I walk through the crowd slowly, my eyes flick from face to face. Down the stairs in the dull shuffle. It smells the same up here. That piss and candle-smoke smell. I turn down an offshoot when I see a big man with a pistol wading through the crowd. There's no one. No one at all. They're all just as wrinkled and old and broken and sour and I feel sick. They shuffle the same. They smell the same. They kick up dust the same, they have the same damn tattered, soot-covered jackets, the same hunch in their empty spines. It's like I haven't even come up here. Except the scars. There's no one left.

I walk down the platform and lean against a post when my legs get tired. For a second, it's like I'm waiting for the train. Like it's all a long time before and it'll be here in a minute and I'll sit and get home and not have to walk. And I'll have a drink when I get back. And look at the skyline and the river through the tall buildings. And here it comes. I can hear it now. And the light against the subway walls. And it'll run over all the slow-moving people down there. Ugly people. She was the last. I reach my hand in my pocket for the bellybutton ring, but my pocket is empty. And I have nothing left. I feel sick and I walk fast down the platform. Scratching hard against my chest and my head and my beard. I pass another old newspaper stand, but it's empty and the metal shelves are bare, and someone is starting to unload new supplies onto them, and a man with a pistol and a scar along the front of his face and a tattoo on his forehead stands at the side of the shop watching us and I duck my head.

The platform is long, and I walk back and forth between the metal poles and along the very edge and almost fall off once, and then climb onto the tracks and cross them and climb up the platform across the way. Old and wrinkled and smelly. And she might have been pretty if she didn't have that rash on her hands and face. And she talks lively to a man next to her, and I hate that she talks lively, but she's ugly and scarred in multiple directions.

I walk further up, but there aren't any more markets for a while and my legs are getting tired, and I feel very hot and sick and I scratch. And there's nothing up here either. The market isn't as big, but the rock ceiling is a little higher, and the smoke isn't so bad. There are more people, crammed together, waddling and shuffling and grumbling, and on the side, they sleep piled on top of each other, and someone smells dead. I can smell the rot. A pale hand sticks out, palm up, from under a pile of sleeping bodies and coats and cardboard. The palm is ghostly white. All the blood has settled to the bottom.

Someone steps on it. It smells rotten. I walk back the way I came. It gets quieter and I feel worse. And I feel it come up. I lean over and vomit. But not much. I wipe my mouth with the back of my hand. In the darkness it looks pale.

It feels very quiet. It was quiet without him today too. I scratch. And feel hot. Very hot. And walk quickly. I scratch. Sick. No one else. I chew on my bottom lip and the little pains calm me. I scratch. Heavy quiet. And no one else to make it better. No one at all. I feel angry and hot and itchy. I scratch hard until it hurts. And even then, it still itches. This itching blackness. This itching quiet. I bite at my lip until it almost bleeds. It gets louder. That's a little better. Better than the quiet. And the candles. But it didn't used to be like this. Am I sick? I breathe a little easier. My sore palms are sweating. My lip is throbbing.

Chapter Twenty

The big tree. The trunk is thick. And very wide. The branches look like they're falling over the trunk and the leaves look like ruffled hair, black against the orange sky. And the tree glows. Small orange dots. On and off. On and off. Dozens of them. Hundreds of them. The tree is covered in them. Filled with them. And the dots drift through the branches towards us. Through the air. And land on my arms and glow on my arms and in my hair and on my sweater. And she's pointing at me.

"Look." She says. "Look."

And I'm covered. And each dot is warm. Very warm. Almost hot. And now hot. And I'm completely covered and my skin is burning and my face is, too. I can't see anything except the light and I can't breathe because there are too many of them and when I try they fill my mouth and my lungs and my stomach. It huts and burns and I try to struggle and try to make a sound, but I can't. I can't move. There are too many of them. So many they're heavy. And so bright. So bright that when I close my eyes I still see the blinding white light. And it hurts. It's burning. And I can't move and I can't make a sound and I can't breathe. I can't breathe.

I open my eyes and it's dark and she's still asleep in my arms and I'm breathing heavily. I'm sweating and the sweat chills quickly when I push the heavy blanket off of my shoulders. I stare at the ceiling until it's too dark to see the individual planks and then I wake her up.

Her hair is dry, and her skin is soft under my fingers and she opens her eyes a little and looks at me and closes them and stretches and smiles. The one where her cheeks pull back and bulge and her forehead goes flat without wrinkles and she makes a small sound. A precious sound. I kiss her. It's already dark. We should go. I kiss her forehead and pull the blanket off of us. The cold is good on my hot skin and she hugs me tighter and shivers a little and I put the blanket back over her. She opens her eyes again and her eyelashes tickle my chest.

We stay in bed for a little longer, until she's more awake and she sits up and looks younger and happier and climbs out from under the sheets and into the cold. I can see her pale skin in the darkens. She looks so thin. She gets dressed and I get dressed and the clothes feel scratchy and dirty and she wrinkles her nose and says they smell and we drink water from the jug, but she doesn't want to eat anything, and we leave. Even just outside the door the wind is rough. And it gets very hard and cold when we get over the hill and follow the bends of the mountain to the edge of the trees. The black trees. It's hard to see them. We walk along the edge holding hands. Like we used to. We walk until we get to the gap where the street used to cut through and now it's just trash, and twigs and we follow that through. On the other side she lets go of my hand and looks through a bag and I follow behind her.

She finds something. She holds it up. A bike chain. It clinks against itself as I put it in the bag. She keeps looking. She looks happy when she finds something. And she finds a coffee mug with a lid that actually fits. But that's all she finds before we can see the old town across from the row of lampposts sticking up over the trash, and we stay far from it. Just close enough to keep it in sight. The wind is loud, and I huddle into my coat, but it's very cold and her hair flaps and lashes out, and she tries to tie it back again, but it comes loose again and again. We circle the town before it gets light. I look through a bag that feels hard, but everything inside is frozen and I can't pull it apart.

It starts to get bright and we head home. We found a little. Maybe enough. It might be enough. The hammer will be good. Splintered handle and all. That will be good. Maybe we have enough.

The sky is gray and pale, but it looks a little clearer today and I can see the hill of trash clearly before we get to it. And I can see the cliff, not far beyond that, but at least to the edge. And where the tree used to be. At the edge. It was so loud when it fell. Asleep, and then crack and we were sitting up and my ears were ringing and my chest was pounding and she was shaking so I held her and it was raining and she didn't say she wanted to go outside. That was the first time she didn't say it. She didn't say it ever again after that, either. And we heard it fall and slide down the cliff and we listened to the rain all night and it leaked through the wood and she was shaking all night even though it was very warm under the blankets. The rain made a sizzling sound when it leaked through the holes in the chimney and landed in the fireplace. And later it made the same sound wherever it landed. And we didn't have enough to fix the leaks in the roof. We lost a lot of food that way.

She starts to climb over the hill on all fours, but I walk to the edge and look out. It looks a little clearer today. It does. I think. I can see most of the way down the cliff from here. And I can see the brown dirt and lighter brown rocks and the black stems of twigs and bushes. The sky is gray, but the smog and clouds don't look so thick. They look thinner, I think. The wind is very hard and blows the dirt and ash on the cliff around and the twigs around and they swirl and slide down the side. It's very hard on my face, and cold and she's next to me and takes my hand and pulls me back. I sit down in the dirt against the door and she sit next to me and puts her head on my shoulder. I put my arm around her. It does look clearer. The sky. It's starting to turn brown, and it's pale and the light makes her skin look pale, too, but it's clearing a little. The sky is clearing a little.

"It's clear." I say.

She looks at me and then at the sky.

"It looks clear." I say.

"It looks the same." She says.

We sit for a long time in the cold and we listen to the wind and watch the sky. When we hear them we go in. She lights the candle. Her face is blank and she's staring into her hands. She shows me the empty box of matches.

"We'll get more."

"All right."

"We'll go tomorrow."

"Do we have enough?" She asks.

"I think so."

She stares at the candle. Her eyes are big and they look tired, and the wrinkles around them are deep.

We watch the little flame for a long time. Even when I can see the color of the wood, and the light from outside is brighter than the candle and it makes the flame look very small, even then we stare at it and watch it burn down slowly. The wax melts and rolls down the smooth side of the candle in small droplets. They catch the pale light from outside and glow.

"Let's go to sleep." I say.

"Not yet."

"Tomorrow is going to be a long day."

"Not yet, though. Not yet."

"Okay."

"I don't want to put it out yet."

"Okay, love."

"It looks so small, now. Doesn't it?"

"Yes, love."

"Small and dim."

Her face is blank and pale from the gray light and the orange light only shows on her flushed cheeks a little bit.

"I dreamt about the fireflies again last night." She says. "They're all I dream about, now."

"That must have been a good dream."

"And there were so many of them."

"I would like to see that."

"Did you dream?"

"I can't remember. I can never remember."

"It's good to dream. I see them all the time in my dreams. And I used to see her." She pauses. "I wish I could again. I wish that very much."

The flame is dim and I stare at it; dim and small in the pale light that's turning brown and turning the wood brown.

"And there isn't any trash in my dreams. And it's just us." She says. "But now I only dream about the fireflies."

I stand up and she watches me. I bring the peanut butter and spoons, but she doesn't want any. I leave them on the table and after a while we eat a spoonful each.

The candle is already almost halfway gone now and there's a lot of newly dried wax on the table around it. It still looks a little wet, but the globs are solid now and look pale. She holds her hands near the small flame, her thumb twisting the gold ring.

"Let's go to sleep."

"Not yet. A little longer."

They're out there. I hear them I the distance. Not clearly over the wind. But clear enough. The wind is strong and shakes the house, and the flame flickers and gets taller, but doesn't go out.

Her face is blank for a long time. She stares directly at the flame and she doesn't move. But after a while she shivers and stiffens, and the wrinkles show again in her face. She doesn't look at me.

"Good night, Hailey." She says and blows out the candle.

My throat knots. She hasn't said that in a long time, and it scares me. And my eyes burn a little and feel wet and the wetness chills quickly and in the dim light I can see her face. It's blank again. And the blankness scares me the most. The small purple and pink blankets and the small pudgy hands and cheeks and her crystal blue eyes. Two pairs, looking at each other, and when she smiled her cheeks were so pudgy and the little bit of hair on her head, and her toothless, awkward smile. And Alex was so happy, and she glowed. The purple and pink blankets in her arms. And it was so good, and the smell of trash didn't bother us. It wasn't too bad back then. There wasn't so much trash, yet. But it was enough. Dirty enough. And she was so vulnerable. And delicate. And little. And her pudgy hands. And Alex didn't cry after. She didn't talk either. Just sitting in the chair with her empty lap and empty arms and blank face. And it had been so good. It had all been so good. Too good. Perfect. And we were so happy. And the little bundle of blankets in her arms and both of their faces glowing in the orange light staring at the tree. And at the fireflies.

It's hard to swallow, and I blink quickly but my eyes are still wet. She's still turning the gold ring on her finger. She shivers, and I put my arm around her. She's shaking, but her face is blank, and she presses her head into my chest. I breathe deep and imagine I can smell her, but the air is very cold on my nose and I can't smell her.

I start to stand up, but she doesn't move, and she holds me tightly.

"Not yet." She says. "Not yet."

We sit for a long time. It's cold, but we don't move. We'll go to the City tomorrow and find more matches and more food. We have a little. It's enough, I think. It's enough. We're okay. We're okay. I run my finger through her dry hair.

She looks up at me as if she's about to say something. But she doesn't. Her eyes big and scared. She puts her head down. I know. I know, love.

In the brown morning light, I see the grooves and scratches and dried wax on the table. The plastic peanut butter jar. The two, licked-clean spoons. The broken looks sharp. The jug of water, the waterline a little darker against the opaque plastic. The empty can of beans. Past the table, the empty dresser. The kitchen. The stovetop collecting dust. The window with boards over it. The pictures tacked to the cabinets faded. Unrecognizable. I hold her tight in my arms and see her breath and all we have left. We're okay. We're not lost yet. She holds me back and closes her eyes. We're okay. I kiss the top of her head. We're okay.

Chapter Twenty-One

I feel hot. And I push hard through them. They grumble. Someone steps on my foot and I shout at him and he cowers back, his face wrinkling even more and he looks down and holds his hands over his head and other people turn to look and I push through. The piss-stained coats are gross, and I don't like touching them, but they all move so slowly, and waddle and their waddling makes me angry. And it's hard to breathe. The smoke is very thick, and we walk slow, and I cough often and hard, and the more I cough the harder it is to breathe, and I feel trapped. I feel trapped down here, and the ceilings are low, and the space is filled with smoke from the candles. I walk as quickly as I can through the crowd and push hard to get through until I'm out of the market and on the tracks that lead back down to my apartment, walking in the dark between the tracks. But the dark isn't comforting like it should be. I still can't breathe. And I feel hot. And itchy. And I scratch and pull large fistfuls of hair out and try to wipe it off my fingers, but it doesn't come off. I cough and groan in the darkness and I hear people on the tracks walking and they walk faster, afraid of what they've heard.

I trip in the darkness and fall into the trash on the side and cough and scratch at my chest because it itches badly now. I'm almost running, and I climb onto the platform and up the stairs and onto the surface and I can breathe. I don't mind the smell of the trash or the ocean. I can breathe. And I feel better and I breathe deep and calm down and I don't itch so much in the cold. I stand at the entrance for a while, and don't want to go back, but this isn't my stop, and I should get home. I'm still hungry and I don't have anything else to eat besides beans. Dry and sour and syrupy beans. I feel sick thinking about it. I need something else. But that's all I have now. Beans.

I stand for a while and watch the sky start to get darker, and more red. It's still brown. And the brown makes the world look surreal, and like an old movie. One of the old ones from before they could actually do color. And any second now a cowboy with boots and spurs and a six-shot on his hip and a hat will strut out from one of those bars and spit into the dust. But there's no dust. Only trash. And the trash is piled especially high against the wall of the building across the street. And the large glass window of that one is completely shattered except for a few jagged shards still in the sill and inside looks very black. I walk over to it and climb through.

The counter of the bar is wooden and covered in a layer of dust. The handles of the tap are all down and empty and the bottles behind the counter are all cracked, and the mirror behind the bottle is cracked. The booths are torn up, and the foam padding is coming out between the sliced rubber. The floors are dusty and there's trash everywhere, but not in bags, and it smells like something dead. The back room is dark, and the shelves are empty, and I can hardly see them except for where a thin stream of brown light comes in from the door I'm holding open. I go back down the steps and onto the tracks and start itching again immediately. And scratching. Hard. And it burns, but I still itch. I walk fast, and it doesn't take too long to get back to my apartment, and again the cold air is nice and stops the itching until I'm upstairs.

My stomach grumbles and I open the can of beans, but too quickly and the opener snaps and I shout and hit the can against the marble counter and scratch at my arms until they look red with long streaks from my fingernails. I take the sharp end of the snapped opener and jab it into the can and it goes through, but it cuts deep into my palm and the pain is white-hot and I shout again and hold my hand to my mouth to clean the cut. The sour of blood on my teeth and tongue. I calm down a little. It's warm and it's a deep cut so there's plenty of blood. I sit on the bed with my hand in my mouth and hold the blinds open with my other hand.

I watch the sky get a little more red. The wind blows hard enough to pull some shards of glass out of one of the windows across the way and I watch them fall. One shatters on a windowsill and a thousand specs glint in the reddening light, dusting the air. But my arm gets tired of holding the blinds open and I let them go. I lean back, but I start to itch again, and I get frustrated and want to see outside. I pull hard on the blinds and they come down and fall onto the floor in a crumpled clump with a loud thud and rustle and I stand. Looking at the highest places I can see. The red sky swallowing the tops of the buildings, but I can still see balcony's and ledges and I imagine falling from them. Fast and then nothing. Into the trash. Out this window. It's high, but not that high. Not high enough. I can feel the cold coming through the glass and it feels good on my hot face. And in the glass with the red light behind it I can see my reflection. I can see the tufts of hair on my head sticking up. And I can see the bald spots. And how pale I am. And ugly. And the scar on my cheek. It's deep, but thin. Thinner than the ones they make. Because the bullet was fast, and the knives they use are dull and they tear more than they cut. I look at the cut on my palm. It's still bleeding, but not as bad, and the blood is very bright in the red light at sunset. I put it back in my mouth. The warm liquid is comforting, and I don't feel so sick now. Some of it rolls down my chin and I wipe it away.

I lean my forehead into the glass and the cold feels good. But the itching comes back. Intensely now. And I scratch, but it doesn't help, and I scratch harder and claw across my chest where the itching is the worst, until my chest burns and the burning hurts and I wince when I scratch again, but I keep scratching because it still itches. I hit my head against the glass. The pain is sharp and calming, but only for a second. And I hit again and the glass bends. And again, and the glass cracks. I stop and look at the crack and feel warm liquid coming down my forehead. But only a drop. It rolls down my cheek next to the crease of my eye and tickles. The cracks in the glass look white against the red sky.

The sky moves slowly overhead, and the red smog and cloud get darker and I watch them for a while and the bleeding in my hand stops and I look at the cut and it looks dirty. I hope it doesn't infect. The street is getting darker and harder to see, but I still see the lamp posts sticking up, and I can still see the stump from where the tree used to be across the street.

The other stumps are buried under the trash. I hear a crash and a howl from around the corner. But I can't see them. They're running though. I can hear them running. And howling, and snarling, and bottles break and echo, and off in the distance I hear more of them. And I can hear the wind. It's louder because of the crack in the glass. I look out at the red, rotting cityscape, sinking into trash, the sour of blood still in my teeth.

BOOK TWO

Chapter Twenty-Two

It was bright. So bright. So bright I was blinded. By the sun reflecting off the hot white sand. Black smoke rising up from it to the crystal blue sky. Black smoke. Billowing. Shouting. Cracks of guns and bombs and more shouting. I heard the bullet whistle past before I felt it tearing at my cheek. White and hot like the sand. Tearing, searing, burning pain. I run my dirty fingers along the thick, puffy groove. It stings. And my eye stings. Don't touch it. It'll infect. I think I shouted, but I don't know now. We were all shouting. And the rifle was hot and sharp, and I dropped down into the hole and it pushed into my stomach and I coughed and spit and the sand was grainy and hot and blood-muddied. I didn't know I could be so afraid. The smoke from the guns smelled bitter and musty and chalky and thin and gray, not black like from the bombs and the grenades, and I could see it rising up into the air, away from us, slowly. The screams and shouts and gurgling sounds and thuds and cracks and the rich, sour, coppery smell of blood and the musty smell of gunpowder and of the bombs and the sand was white and hot and the hot white sand was cooled and muddied by blood. My eyes open. It's black. Completely black. Don't look. Don't look.

I remember heat and the sand, the white sand, so hot against my hands and the metal butt of the gun had been baking under the sun and it burned to touch my cheek to it. And being rained on by clods and flakes of sand that scattered over me. I felt the dry mounds crumble and smear across my face. Sergeant was shouting to us again, but I couldn't hear what he was saying. I wanted to shoot something. But we were so afraid. My hands shaking and the rifle shaking and over the louder noises and cracks and shouts I could hear the metal clip from my coat tapping against the metal butt of the gun. And the hill in front of us was steep and white and there were small flashes from the gunfire and thick gray smoke from the shelling. And it was hot and sweat rolled down my cheek from my hair into the cut and it stung, but it didn't hurt too bad then. I didn't feel too much. Except afraid.

My back starts to ache, and I pull my knees to my chest, keeping my eyes closed. Don't look. I lean my head back against the hot cinderblock wall, the rough cinderblock, it scrapes against my short hair and presses into my scalp. I didn't think it would be like this. This war. I thought - it doesn't matter now. I blink, realizing my eyes are open. It's black. And hot. I can't breathe it's so hot and I sweat more, and my shirt is damp and drenched and my hands are shaking, and my breath is shaky.

He never said it would be like this. His bulky, funny-looking mustache. He never said it would be so hot and smell like this. Sour. The posters in his office all looked so proud and they all had such serious looks on their faces - proud looks. But none of us looked like that. And his pen was thick, and his mustache was thick and the office was brown and looked dull under the white light and outside was cold and snowy and he made it sound good and something to be proud of. It's better than dull. This is better than dull. Maybe not better. But not dull. The fear. That wasn't dull. At least it's not dull. The fear wasn't dull. Of being killed. Of being wounded - worse than being killed. The quiet before you pulled the trigger. Like a hunter. Ironic. I try to smile but my cheek stings and my eye stings. At least it isn't dull.

Crawling to the edge of the mound of sand, and we were all shaking so terribly, and poking my head out and looking down across the white hill that looked so hot the air rippled and the smoke from the shelling rose quickly and in thick gray billows and I didn't see the blood stains at first because it was so bright. My rifle to my shoulder and it was hot on my cheek. I could see them down there like we were, dug in, they were a darker brown against the hot white sand. Their colors are darker than ours. Without my sight they just looked like dark spots on a horizon, running about, bright muzzle flashes, shouting, screaming, cracks of bombs and smaller cracks of rifles. Looking down the sight they were a little bigger, but it wasn't a very good sight.

I push my back against the rough wall. Hot. Dusty. Silent. Black. So black. So black I can't breathe. So black the blackness swallows blackness swallows blackness swallows blackness. It was so bright. And loud. So loud. So loud when I pulled the trigger that I couldn't keep my eyes open and I held it down until my ears rang too bad and my head was spinning. And did I yell then too? And I don't know if I hit one. I might have. I lick my dry lips. Bright red mist. The sudden shock and then nothing, or maybe it took a long time. Agonizing. Coughing up blood like Ricky. Maybe I didn't hit anything. I lick my dry lips, but my tongue is dry, and my mouth is dry and my lips are chapped and sting and I'm so thirsty.

I try to swallow but my mouth is so dry, and my throat is dry and I cough and stare hard into the darkness with my one, not-swollen eye and try not to smell the piss and the dirt and the sweat. It's so dark. Completely dark. I wave my hand in front of my face, but only black. Don't look. It's too dark. Don't look. I stand up and circle the small room, running my palm over the rough surface of the walls, and then the smoother surface of the metal door, and then rougher cinderblock. And I kick at the dust and cough on the dust and my cheek stings when I cough, and so does my swollen eye. I touch it again with my dirty fingers. The sand on my fingers rubs into the cut and stings more. It's very tender. It's gonna be a good scar. I might have been embarrassed by a scar before. That's funny. I might have been embarrassed by this. Scars are good. And there's no one to call me ugly now.

So lost. So stupid. I was stupid. Pathetic. I chew on the stretch of scar tissue in my bottom lip and stare at the darkness. Pathetic. And they thought I was happy. I thought I was happy. Stupid. And useless. And dull. Always dull. Staring out the window at it all. The bright blue sky, the green trees. Oh, and how I used to think they looked good and pretty and green and pretty, and stupid. So stupid. That was my life. The best years of my life, she called them. Staring out the windows at everything else, and nothing else. Happiness, the fiction of the pitiful idea that my life would ever mean something. Ha. It's so dark. So sudden and severely dark. I shift my weight. I hear grains of sand and dirt grinding against my pants. I hear my breath. I hear my heart beating. And it makes it darker. My shirt is soaked with sweat. It smells like it. Salty like it. And my piss too. So dark. Don't think about it. Don't look.

Chapter Twenty-Three

He looks quiet and calm, a thin orange swath of light coming
over him and across his leg sticking out of the blanket. I love
that leg. The wood floors are cold on my bare feet and the air is
chilly, but nice. And I lean against the wood post in the middle
of the room between the bed and the table and the wood is
rough. I can see my breath. The birds are chirping off and on
and the wind is whistling quietly. The small window in the
kitchen lets most of the late November morning light in, and it's
very bright behind me and makes the bed look even darker than
it is and I climb back next to him and he rolls over but doesn't
open his eyes. His hands are soft and trace my spine and he
smiles a little at the corners of his mouth and his dimples start
to show and I kiss him and he kisses me back and opens his eyes.

"Good morning." I say.

"How'd you sleep?"

"Well."

"Good."

He closes his eyes again and stretches and groans and pulls
the big blanket tighter around us. My toes are cold and his are
warm. I feel good and happy and I hold him tightly. It's good

out here. I like the birds and the space. I breathe deeply. It's so good out here. And noisy in the right sort of way. The quiet sort of way. Not like the honking and bustle and busy in the City. Oh, I'm just so glad we're here. And he's holding me. And I breathe his smell deeply. And all of a sudden, the birds chirp wildly, and back and forth. I look over the blankets and the white light from the kitchen makes the wood glow. The dream catcher hanging in the window with the thin blue feather and the edges are glowing bright and it rocks back and forth calmly in the wind. It was an upsetting dream. But I don't remember it now so well. So I'm not bothered by it. But it was upsetting.

I close my eyes again and run my teeth over the bone in his shoulder. His skin is warm and alive and his hands are calloused and strong and he holds me tightly and I feel happy. I look over his shoulder and imagine the crib by the wall across from the dresser. But it would be on my side of the bed. And it would be small, and pink, and she would be all bundled up, and I feel warm thinking about her. Her pudgy little hands and cheeks and when she smiles I would smile and she would have his eyes. His eyes are so pretty. I pull them open and look at the blue with the little bit of green around the edges that gets brighter when he gets angry. But they're very blue when he first wakes up.

We don't get out of bed for a while. Not until the chirping is constant and the wind is getting a little louder and the light in the kitchen doesn't come through the window so directly and then we get up and I make him breakfast and we eat the eggs. He doesn't like them unless they're scrambled very well. He washes the dishes and I hold him and rub my cheek against his beard, and it's scratchy. Scruff really. He never could grow a real beard.

"Let's go walking." I say.

"Now?"

"I want to find a river."

"Are there any out here?"

"Yes. Probably."

"I'm going in later."

"All right."

"Come with me."

"All right."

"You're very sweet, you know that?"

"You're crazy."

"And you're beautiful."

I kiss his cheek and he finishes the dishes and we take our coats and leave through the small wood door. The big oak tree on the edge of the cliff around the side is thick and the edges of the rough bark are glowing in the morning light, and down the cliff I can see far because it's very clear today and the sky is very blue and bright already and there are only a couple clouds and they're small, fluffy and white. Down the cliff I can see the forest and the trees are mostly bare except for the pines, and there are many of those, and then behind them a ways I can see the tops of the brick buildings sticking up.

"Where's this river?"

"This way." I pull his hand along down the dirt driveway to the road and we walk to the mountain and walk along the winding road until we get to the tunnel and we walk through it on the sidewalk and a car drives past us and the humming of the tires on the pavement echoes along the rock ceiling. It's cold out here, but his hands are warm, and I feel good. We walk for a long time in quiet. There's the path. I pull him across the road and into the brambles.

"It's beautiful isn't it?" I point out to where you can see the sky turn white in a streak against the trees at the horizon. He squeezes my hand. He smiles but his eyes look concerned. "We'll be back in time."

He smiles again. "You're very sweet to come with me, love."

"I don't like going. But I like being with you."

"It'll be quick today. Really."

"I wish you didn't have to go in so often."

"I know, love. Me too."

"Isn't it wonderful out here."

"It is. It's so wonderful. I just don't like leaving you by yourself. So far away." "You don't have to."

"I have to go."

"I mean I don't have to be by myself."

He's quiet. And the wind is loud on the side of the mountain. I shouldn't have said that. "I'm sorry, don't mind me, sweet. I'm happy to come with you. I'm sorry I said that."

"We will. Soon. We will."

"I know. I didn't mean to say it."

"Okay."

We hold hands all the way down the mountain and walk into the forest at the foot, and we walk between the thick trunks of the trees. The light comes through the branches and pine needles in thin shoots and makes the brown and dry twigs on the ground look bright in patches. We walk for a long time, but we don't find a river. He looks at me calmly, but a little impatient. We walk back. There's still plenty of time. I know it's out here.

Chapter Twenty-Four

I'm sweating. Sweat rolls into the cut and the cut stings and the hot sticky air doesn't cool it and make it better. It smells sour. It even smells dark. I miss the sun. Awful sun. Heavy sun. Sweating through my shirt so much it soaked the Kevlar. Heavy and awful and burning my neck and my cheeks. They felt red. But at least it wasn't dark. And I could see. And the white sand and the small dunes in the distance barely scraping the horizon and the blue sky and the pale brown trucks and the grease-shined black metal of the guns that glinted in the bright sun and looked very black against the white sand. And the air was hot and muggy and thick and smelled like diesel, but that was better than this. At least outside it was bright.

Smooth sand far out. Cracked and baking and flat, flat sand right under us and stretching forever in all directions. Blinding bright through the gaps in the flapping green tarp. And bright. Bumping heavily over the cracks. The wind whistled between the gaps where it was tied down. They all looked so afraid. White knuckles on black guns. The steel floor under our boots was covered in the white sand and small pebbles and spots of dried blood that I inched the heal of my boot away from. Nervous. And we didn't look at each other. Staring at the rifle in my hands. The metal was still cool in the shade of the truck. Later it was so hot that it hurt to touch. The bombs like thuds in the distance and the ground shook a little and they sounded closer than they were. The truck going very fast. A big bump. So afraid. The shouts, the cries the blood and his pale face, blood smeared and smooth, and his quickly-clouding eyes. The red mist suspended in the air, falling slowly after. It was so loud out there. Like a constant thunder storm. The rain, the hissing of bullets; the thunder, the thudding of the bombs that weren't so close; the lightning, the flashes from the muzzles and the brighter flashes from the grenades. Blinding. The shouting. The roar of jets through the sky.

I hate this darkness. I squeeze my eyes shut but the skin around my left eye is sore and tender and hurts to press shut too tightly. The dust and sand on the hot cement floor grind into my dry palm. I push myself to my feet. My legs ache. I didn't realize they were cramping. I stretch and groan and in the quiet my groan is loud. I press my ear to the warm metal door. Listening. Hard. For anything. But nothing. So quiet. So dark. Think about something else. You'll go crazy thinking about it too much.

Sergeant yelling. Think about that. The veins in his neck and forehead pushing through his skin. Reddening skin because he was yelling so hard. And it was so loud and bright and he spit when he yelled. The sour of the blood. The chalky smell of gunpowder. Someone cried out next to me, but he sounded like he was far away because my ears were ringing so bad. And there would be small pauses in the noise. But it was so loud. And now it's so quiet.

Someone kicked mud and sand into my face as he dropped down next to me. I'd seen him before, but he wasn't in my company and he was holding his machine gun over the edge of the hole with his head ducked into his shoulder and shouting and squeezing the trigger and the gun was so loud it hurt. He said something to me. I don't know what.

It's hot and my throat is dry. My legs are stiff, and my back is aching, and I stretch, but it doesn't help much. I walk around more, and I sit back down. The leg of my sweat pants brushes across the dust and chalk and sand covering the hot cement. I cough. And he said something else. Cowboy, he called me, I think. What the --- you looking at, cowboy? And he spit, and his spit was brown and gross and landed near me. And he was saying something else too and looked angry and his helmet was black on his forehead and he collapsed over his machine gun and red mist was all around him and I could smell it and it smelled sour and he leaked over the gun and onto the hot sand and it steamed and smelled sour and bitter and I didn't even hear the thud. And the red mist falling slowly.

His last words weren't very meaningful, were they? I wonder if that counts against him. To swear in your last words. It probably wouldn't make a difference, we're all damned anyways. All of us soldiers. But for normal people, according to religion, that probably counts against him. But we're damned regardless. There was blood on my lips and I liked it and it tasted sour and I lick my lips now, but my tongue is dry and I'm so thirsty. I need water.

I watch the darkness. And feel along the grooves in the cinderblocks and at the base where they meet the hot cement and in the nook between cement and cinderblock there's a thick line of dust and dirt and sand. I scrape it away and run my finger along the crack. The cinderblock is rough, and the cement is a little smoother, but the dirt scrapes the dry skin on my finger. It's very dark. Too dark. Don't look.

It wasn't dark back home. And the sky was big, but not as big as out here because the mountains. And up there looking down to the ocean and if it was windy the ocean had teeth and the bushes had voices. Dry yellow bushes. Brown grass. Hot wind. And the air would be dry and hot and filled with dirt and the smell of lavender and not like this. Not muggy and thick like this. It would be thin. And we'd be inside with the air-conditioning on high and mom would be in the kitchen like always.

But it's so hot and thick and dark and muggy and I can't see even the wall in front of me touching my nose. And I'm so thirsty. I need water. But they don't bring water. And I wait. I wait a long time staring at the wall touching my nose and running my finger along the grooves in the cinderblock. They haven't come for me in a long time. I don't know how long. It's been so long.

My fingers are sore from tracing the wall, but they're not cramping anymore. In the pit they were cramping and holding the rifle so tightly that I couldn't drop it even if I wanted to. Never let that gun go. Never let that gun go. And then a crack and the ground shook and we were covered in ash and dirt and tiny bits. I think it was a piece of bone, but there was still skin on it, bloody skin, on my hand and I shook it off and wanted to yell, but I don't think I did yell - it was too loud to yell anyway. And we were so afraid and too afraid to move, and I didn't know I could be so scared. And they didn't look pale because there was so much mud and dirt and ash and blood smeared across their faces and hands and uniforms, but I felt pale and sick and scared.

Quieter tucked into the hole. I wanted to curl up. But I couldn't move. Thud and crack and another dusting. It's too dark. I strain my eyes. I blink them a hundred times but there's no difference. It's hard to breathe. I pull at my shirt and scratch at my chest and throat. Thud and crack and dusting. And all the shouting and swearing at each other and everything else. And the white sand was very bright against the blood and the ashes and the black gunmetal and I kept thinking we should probably stop swearing because we're going to die and we don't want to die swearing. But we're already dammed. It didn't matter. And Sergeant was yelling and the veins in his red neck were bulging and his forehead was very red, and he kept shouting and when he stopped we shouted *Yes Sergeant*, but I don't know what he said.

It's quiet. In this darkness it's silent. This silent, black, thick darkness. I can't see anything. Maybe I'm dead. I died in that hole. This is what death is. Blackness. Nothingness. Nothing and waiting in a silent, dark, hot and sticky cinderblock room with a dusty cement floor and piss and sweat and waiting forever. Don't. I breathe. Don't look. The sun. It was so bright on the bleached dunes in the distance and the white sand was so white and hot and the small rocks were white too and I couldn't tell them apart from the sand unless I looked closely. And the larger rocks and the cliffs, dusty and tan and baking in the sun. So hot. So bright. It was never that bright in the City. It was bright though, not that bright, but it was bright and made the glass bright and the glass hurt to stare at too long. The tall buildings, glass and stone and metal, and the view from the rooftops at night and the lights of the buildings that twinkle inside the cloudy sky and make it glow orange. It was a good view. And it was good up there with her. And the wind was hard up there and cold and the cold was good, and I felt better up there because it was quieter and colder. But this is too quiet. I can't stand this quiet. It's so quiet. Up there it was just muffled. That's best. Muffled. And it was a good view. The only good part about the City.

The cut on my cheek stings. I touch it again but it's tender and it hurts to touch, and my hands are dirty. I hope it doesn't infect. It probably won't. But it might. My fingers are dirty and bloody and smell bad. They smell sour. My skin itches and more sweat breaks through. I try to breath, but the breaths I take are shallow and the air is thick and muggy. The cold was good. I like the cold better. And it got cold in the City. Especially when it was windy. The tall buildings made the winds even harder and colder and I would lean into them so much that if it weren't windy I would have fallen over.

It's black. And I wait. I wait a long time and feel thirsty and hungry and chew on my bottom lip and spit, but I don't have anything to spit. And it's black. And silent. My pant leg rustles against the dirt and dust on the ground. My sweat soaked shirt peels off my chest when I sit up straight and I hear it like sandpaper coming loose, but it sticks again. My breath is shaky. And shallow. It's so quiet.

Muffled. That's better than quiet. The honking and diesel engines rumbling and the hum of the generators and it all sounded far away. Leaning against the cold red cracking-brick parapet at elbow height, and it was all muffled and the wind was loud. And when it snowed it was even more muffled. That was nice. The snow was nice. And cold. And it looked clean and white and I watched it fall and become dirty. Looking down on the smaller buildings, and up the avenues and beads of light in thick trails up and down and the taller, glass buildings off in the distance disappeared into clouds, and they made the clouds glow.

Chapter Twenty-Five

It's a hard walk to the train station. Cold and windy. But it's pretty too. I walk as close as I can to the dirty guardrail so I can see down, down, down. Steep slope and thick bushes and then flat and far out the mountains look blue and hazy. Like father's painting. I didn't like it above the fireplace. But I like the painting. And listening to him paint. Orange nightlight on red sheets made wood walls glow mauve. I smile and feel warm. I love that room. And the alphabet along the ceiling with animal pictures over each letter. And the sound of father painting through the wall. Except when he was drunk. And he was drunk a lot coming home from the hospital. And he stopped entirely after mother passed. Oh. I sigh. And don't feel warm anymore. And Tommy said that's a hurt that'll never go away. And isn't that a sad thought? But at least he stopped eating so much after. Still chubby around the cheeks, little Tomtom. But he used to be so chubby.

We walk quietly and listen to the afternoon air and the cars are driving by more frequently and his hand is big and warm on mine. His feet are turned out a little when he walks and so cute. He notices me looking and tries to straighten them.

They're straight for a little bit, but I watch his thoughts drift to something else and his feet turn out again. I smile. He straights up. He really should pay more attention to his posture. Under his other arm is the small brown box he's delivering.

I can't even see the station yet. But I guess we're walking quickly. Quicker than last time at least. The mountain is very big to my left. I can't see the top. But the sky is nice and blue over it. I like it up there. And the hike getting there. And holding his hand while we walk together. Oh, and the view from the top. So far. And so peaceful. Better than from his old place for sure. But it was a nice place. But not like this. Nothing like from the top. The trees for miles and miles and the silver snaking river way out in the distance and the bright blue sky. And how it's brown over towards the direction of the city. So good we moved out here. I hope he's happy like I am. I think he is. I look at him. He smiles at me and the corners of his eyes wrinkle in that way that makes me feel like he's thinking something that's not very happy. Maybe he misses the City. But he doesn't say it. I wish he would say it if he does.

It was fun in some ways. We could move back if he wanted. The glass buildings were pretty. And it was fun. Oh, but it's just not nearly as nice as this. I hope he doesn't want to. I'm glad we were there. And all the memories from it. But it was cramped. Like the dresser being too big for where it was and the edge of it sticking out over the door to the bathroom so it couldn't close anymore. But being in it with him was fun. I'd be happy with him anywhere. It's just so much nicer having all this counter space in the kitchen. And now we have the birds and the trees and the space. Like New Mexico. On the compound with Tensu and all the long walks through the trees. So much nicer with trees and mountains and views like that. Where would we put a crib in that apartment? I feel my cheeks get hot a little. I surprised myself with that one. I smile. He'd be so good at it. He doesn't think so. But he will be. He's scared, but he'll be so good. I squeeze his hand.

"We'll be in and out." He says. "And then we'll come back."

"I don't mind."

"You're very sweet to come, love."

"I don't mind."

"In and out. I promise."

"All right."

We walk, and the wind gets harder when we get closer to the foot of the mountain and the road slopes more. I wish it was less cold. Or just that we wouldn't walk it when it's this cold. And he went in every day last week and already twice this week.

"I wish you didn't have to go in so often."

"I miss you too, my love. I miss you every second I'm not with you. And it won't last. It'll be over soon."

"And we'll have more time? Together? Won't we darling?"

"We will."

"Good. Because I miss you when you're away."

"It won't last."

"But how much longer?"

"Soon."

"It's always soon."

"Don't say that. It will be."

"You're right. I didn't mean to say that."

"It won't last."

"But it's good it lasts. We need it."

"We'll be okay."

"I just don't like it when you have to go so often."

"You're very sweet to come with me."

"I don't mind it all that much. And we need it. So I don't mind."

"Well, you're very sweet to come."

"I just hope it doesn't last much longer. It was every day last week, and it'll be every day this week. Oh, but I know we need it. I just don't like it is all."

"I know. And it won't last too much longer. I know it won't."

"And then we'll be together. And have all the time we want. And that will be good, won't it?"

"It'll be very good."

"I can't wait. And I'll have you all to myself." I almost said it again. I'm glad I didn't say it again. He doesn't like it when I bring it up. But I can't help thinking about her. Because she'll be so cute, with her pudgy cheeks and pudgy fingers and when she sneezes. Babies always have the cutest sneezes.

"I wish you'd let me help." I say. "I could go back to the restaurant. Or find a new job out here. That would be good, wouldn't it, sweet?"

"We really don't need it, love. We'll be okay."

I want to say more. But I know what it'll turn to. Because it doesn't make sense. I mean it does, because I know he's sacred of it. But it doesn't make sense because he won't say he's scared of it.

We walk along the main road behind the mountain that goes along the edge of the forest on this side. And on this side, it's almost all pine trees and it still looks green, but the green is a pale green and not the deep green of the birch and chestnut trees. We walk through the little town and past the small stores that are only one or two stories high and through the sloping streets with old black lampposts. On the far side of the town are the train tracks and we walk up the stone steps and across the overpass to the far tracks and buy our tickets from the automated machines and wait for the train to come. It doesn't come for a long time, and the wind is bad on the tracks and it blows a newspaper along the platform and it gets caught on the post of a trashcan. I can see far up and down the tracks. I think there's the light of the train, but I can't be sure.

He holds me and puts his chin on my head and my hair gets into his face. I can feel his scratchy beard through my hair. He holds my hands and I put them on my belly and run my fingers though his knuckles.

"Soon, love." He says.

"I know." But it's always soon.

"When we can."

"I wish you'd let me help."

"I don't want you to if we don't need it. And we'll be okay."

"But it would be sooner if I helped, wouldn't it? It's always soon but never happens."

"Don't say that."

"I'm sorry. I didn't mean that. I know you work hard for us, sweet. That wasn't fair. I'm sorry I said it."

"You don't need to be sorry, love. I know. I know how badly you want it."

"You want it too, right?"

"I do."

"It's not just me."

"I want it too."

"Because if it's just me, you'd tell me, right? You wouldn't keep it from me, would you, darling?"

"Of course, I want it."

"All right. I'm sorry I brought it up again. I know you don't like it when I bring it up."

"No, no. I'm sorry. I just get sad not to give you everything you want." He puts his chin back on my head and I hold his hands, but not to my belly because he doesn't like it when I bring it up, and I didn't mean to that time, but I guess it was my fault. I wish he'd let me help though.

The platform is concrete and very gray and the blue-green paint on the metal pillars is chipping away and the wood bench next to us looks dirty and sticky with something that spilled and dried across it. I see the steam pluming in the distance. I can't hear it yet, though. I run my fingers though his knuckles and toy with the small gold ring on my finger. It's small but looks good and shines in the bright light.

I can hear the train now, and feel it rumbling along. I hold his hands. But I don't feel good. I feel worried, but I don't know why. The air is cold, and I shiver. And his beard scratches the top of my head and I don't like it now and I move, and he can tell something's wrong. The train will be here soon, and it will be warm and maybe that will be better. It comes, and we get on and it's hot and muggy inside and I feel worse. I don't like the heat as much. I like the cold better. We find a seat in an empty car and I sit against the window and I can feel the cold coming through. The train hisses and rattles and rocks back and forth as it goes along.

Chapter Twenty-Six

I was running so fast. I didn't know I could run that fast, and I thought I would lose my footing on the steep slope and the sand was loose and so white and blinding. And I knew it was coming. I could hear them whistling past and thudding lightly into the sand, but I didn't know that then. I just knew I was running. And that I was afraid. And so afraid. So afraid I was yelling and sprinting even faster. And I tripped. I forgot that. Something soft. The ground came at me and I rolled through the hot sand and then I was up again and running. And yelling. And couldn't breathe. And couldn't see – it was too bright. The sun was hitting directly onto the white sand. We were all shouting. And screaming and running. And red mist and he stopped shouting and fell in front of me and I almost fell over him. Or maybe it was him I fell over. And the red mist tasted sour. And so many bodies. Some of them still crawling when I ran past them yelling. And the smell. It got bad.

I coughed on the rank smell. A lot. And then couldn't yell because my throat hurt from coughing and had to slow down. And then whistles and thuds and I was running again without even knowing it. And there was the bottom of the hill. And

I could see the muzzle flashes better now. But I couldn't hear the men anymore. Just the cracks and thuds and whistles and the rain sound of dust and bits. And the sand was so white and then so red. Glowing in the hot sun. The ground got softer. And blood splashed up against my pant legs and boots. And I was white hot with fear. And there was a hole. I was in the hole. Curled up. Like a little baby. Into a little ball. Pathetic. Closing my eyes so tight, hugging my rifle, tensing every muscle. And then I pulled the bodies and limbs over me. My shoulder still hurts from the gun falling on me. Maybe it's bruised. I press at the spot tenderly. Little baby. So many sounds. So much blood smell. And the bodies and soggy Kevlar were heavy and it was hard to breathe under there. It's hard to breathe in here.

I kick at the dust and hear it puff up and settle back on the hot cement. It's harder to breathe now. It's too hot. And there aren't any windows. And I'm using all the air. I breathe fast, but I shouldn't, but I can't help it. I feel sick. This is hell. I'm dead. I didn't kill him, he killed me. And this is hell. And I have to sit in this blackness that smells like piss and blood forever. Thirsty. Hungry. Forever. I can't breathe. I'm choking. There's not enough air in here. I've sucked it all up. I pound the back of my head against the cinderblocks until I calm down. And I feel a little better and wait. I wait for a long time. And it's just dark. And I stand up and walk around the small space and sit back down. And there's no sound except my shirt scraping down the cinderblock wall when I slide onto the floor and put my head into my hands. I'm shaking. And I'm so thirsty. And the smell is getting worse. Not as bad as the hole, but it's getting bad.

Blood. And bloody faces. And my face was pressed up against them and their skin was still warm. I could smell them.

The sour of their blood but also the rest of it. And I couldn't breathe and when I did I wanted to throw up. I think I did through up, and that only made it worse. And then one of the bodies moved and I yelled and pulled out my pistol and shot with my eyes closed until it only clicked lightly, and my ears rang so bad. And even then, I didn't open my eyes. It took a while until I saw his pale face, so white under the red streaks and he was coughing, and I didn't notice his uniform until I stopped staring at his eyes going cloudy, until after they were gray and the blood stopped squirting. And then I saw the patch on his sleeve was the same as mine, and the color was the same only darker because of the blood. His name tag was covered in blood, so I couldn't read it. And I threw up again. My jaw was sore. I think I clenched it too hard and then stretched it too hard when I was throwing up. It doesn't hurt now. My cheek still hurts though. And around my eye. He was crying. But he didn't say anything. He just died. Sputtering.

I feel sick. But don't throw up. It'll just make the smell worse. Don't throw up. Maybe this is my punishment. This darkness.

The sky was black with smoke and the sun would poke through and be very bright for a second and then it was covered again by the thick billowing smoke and I was lying on my back watching it. Then voices. Then hot muzzles prodding me out of the hole. Shouting things. I don't know what. And it was hot. And my uniform was heavy with blood that wasn't mine. And up the hill I saw us running away. Scurrying like little roaches though the white and blurry heat. Bombs were still falling and they shook the white sand and the sky was black and billowing.

Chapter Twenty-Seven

He reads a newspaper and flicks at the edges as the train rocks back and forth. He doesn't look pleased. He never looks pleased when he reads about the war. I wish he wouldn't. The car isn't empty now, and there's an old man asleep a couple rows ahead of us and a woman with a sleeping baby in her lap. Out the window I can see the bright fields and the rows of planted trees bending as we speed along the track. It doesn't look so cold from in here because it's very bright and the sun makes the fields glow. It looks warm, like a mid-summer afternoon, bright and glowing and the sky is blue and big overhead and there are only a few white, airy, high-floating clouds. He flicks at the edges of the newspaper and the small flicking is the only other sound in the car.

"Stop it." I whisper. My voice is loud because the car is quiet.

"Stop what?" He stops.

"Nothing."

I go back to leaning against the window, and he starts flicking at the edges again when he goes back to reading. I hold his hands still.

The baby starts to cry and it's crying is loud. He looks annoyed. I feel hot and I can tell my cheeks are flushed.

I feel angry, and I don't know why. And the cold glass doesn't help. The seats are dusty, and I can see the dust drifting in the light coming in through the windows. The car is silent again and the baby must be sleeping. We pass through more farm lands and then through another town with small buildings, but this one is larger, and the station is wide with big advertisements and the awning over the people waiting on the platform is wide and large and catches most of the light, so all the people are in shadow. The train rattles to a stop and people get on and more people sit down around us and the noise from outside comes in and it's not so quiet anymore. The doors close and now it's quiet again and we rattle off and pass through more low lands and follow the curve of a freeway for a while, but then we turn off of it and pass through a forest of all chestnut trees and none of them have any leaves left, except on the ground around their thick, dry trunks. On the other side of the wood is a big bridge over a freeway and we cross it and I can see down to the cars below and they look bright in the afternoon light.

He flicks at the edges of the newspaper again. I look at him and his hair is covering part of his face, so I can't see his eyes, but he looks annoyed still. And tired. His hair looks good, though. He used to always have it short. Like a military man or something. And he looked so intense. And he was intense. Always fighting something. I like it longer. He looks kinder. Softer.

"Where are you taking it?" I ask. The package is on the seat across from him and looks small all by itself.

"To the old post office."

"To the post office?"

"Next to it, actually."

"We should go by the old dorm, then."

"Okay."

"Do you ever miss the it?"

"Yes. I miss visiting you, and the courtyard and how your roommates would complain about us."

"You're very sweet. But I meant the City. Do you ever miss the City?"

"Yes."

"I don't. I'm glad we're not there."

"Me too. But it's a very handsome City."

"I don't think so."

"I think it's a very impressive City. But I'm glad we moved too."

"You'd tell me if you weren't, right?"

"Of course, love."

"All right."

"I'm very glad we left."

"I am too. And you're very sweet. I'm sorry I make you angry."

"You don't, love. Don't say that." He holds my hand. I like the feel of his skin on mine. His dry, calloused palm. He works so hard for them.

We pass several more stations, but not many people get on and he gets up to get food from the food car, but I don't go with him and he asks if I want anything and I say no, and he asks if I want anything to drink and I say no, and he goes out through the door with a hiss.

I watch the traffic on the side roads next to us. They're stopped so it looks like we're going very fast, and when they drive it looks like we're hardly moving, except when I look at how fast the buildings are rushing by. And we pass the town and we go back into a thick wood that looks like the compound and I imagine I see Tensu walking with his brown robe and his sandals and his bald head. Those were good walks and we wouldn't talk a word all the way through to the top, through the tall grass meadows and through the dense wood on the other side where the twigs and leaves on the ground were always wet with morning dew and would stick to my bare feet and we'd walk all the way to the top of the mountain and sit and I'd watch him. I miss the compound and the small wood kivas with their incense and the smoke was very thick and smelled very thick and they'd chant and meditate and I was the youngest one there by far. The train rocks hard against a bend and I watch the dust float through the air. It floats quietly. It was so noisy on the way there. People talking loudly and talking on phones and the man next to me in a suit was looking out the window the whole time and never once looked at me and the little boys in the front were screaming at each other and their mother couldn't quiet them, but she was trying. And I was scared and lonely and I didn't know if I'd ever see father again or Tommy. I was so angry.

Hunter comes back and sits next to me and hands me a bottle of water.

"Thank you. You're sweet."

He smiles and folds the newspaper he left on his seat and puts it in the pocket by the side and eats the apple and closes his eyes. He looks tired. I give him such a hard time. I shouldn't do that. He works so hard for us. But I wish he'd just tell me what he wants. He doesn't tell me what he wants, and it makes me so scared sometimes.

"We should call Tommy." He says.

"Oh, that would be lovely."

"It would be good to see him."

"You're very sweet to think of that."

He holds my hand.

"Did you know he used to want to be a painter." I say.

"Tommy?"

"A painter, just like father. But he was never any good."

"I thought your dad was a doctor."

"He was. But he painted, too."

"I didn't know that."

"And Tommy thought he'd be a great painter one day."

"Why did he stop?"

"I don't know. I wasn't there. But he was never any good. He used to love it, though."

"I'll call him when we get in."

"All right."

I miss Tommy. I hope we see him. Hunter's so good with him. Like his own brothers. I miss them too. I know Hunter does. He wishes they lived out here. Or we lived out there. Maybe that's it. Maybe it's not the City he misses. I wish they'd come visit, at least. But that's not fair. He's just so sweet around them. I smile and squeeze his hand. The train rocks. He looks peaceful. So timid when they're around. And slouches a lot more. Making fun of him and laughing and he laughs with them, but a small laugh, and when he does I think I know what he sounded like when he was a child. But how is it they never fight? Not in years, he said, I think. Tommy and I fight all the time. But not them. He's protective. Especially when they're drunk. I don't know what I'd do if Tommy was ever drunk. But he'll never drink. Not after father.

We pass another station and the car starts to fill up and more people are talking now and it's not as quiet. The noise makes me feel awake, and I'm excited to see Tommy. I haven't seen him in ages. And he changes so quickly these days. He used to be so chubby. Before I left. And then he wasn't. He never said he was losing weight in his letters. He left out a lot in those letters. But then I saw him in college, and there he was, coming down the stairs, carrying a big box, all strong and fit and manly-looking and not at all chubby. And we cried, and it was so good to see him, and he was all grown up and manly. He still has baby fat around the cheeks though.

My hand is in my pocket, but I don't have his letters anymore. It's still an odd feeling not having them. Even now. Thumbing through them in my pocket. Always. It was like a tick. Especially during fasts. Just knowing they were there made me feel better. He always had such bad writing.

Hunter stretches, and yawns and I lean my head on his shoulder. Across the aisle from us a man sits very straight typing away on his lap top. Through the window to the side of him I can see hills off in the distance. We must be getting close to the City now because the sky is looking brown and it makes the hills look hazy. I pick at the fabric on the seat and feel Hunter breathing. Him and Tommy got along splendidly. They're a lot alike. But he's not moody like Tommy. God, he's so moody sometimes. Laughing, him and his new skinniness. That chicken laugh. And then like a switch. And he didn't need my help with that question. Or didn't ask me for an opinion. Or just got all depressed for no reason. And then a minute later it was back to his jokes.

"I'm going to take you to a nice dinner tonight." Hunter says.

"You're very sweet."

"A real nice dinner. With candles and everything."

"You're sweet, but we can't."

"Sure, we can."

"We can't. We can't afford to, but you're sweet."

I can see his reflection in the window when I look back outside. He starts drumming on the side of the cardboard box and then stops. "We'll be okay."

"We can't. Not yet."

"What about the Saxon. You like that one, don't you?"

"It's very expensive, sweetie."

"For you, only the best."

"But we can't. You know we can't. And it'll only make it last longer. And it's already been lasting so long, and you know we can't."

"It won't last long, now. Only the rest of the winter. It won't be anything."

"Don't say that. Don't say that, darling. You know we can't. Let's not. I don't want a nice dinner anyways. I don't have the clothes for it."

"You look lovely as it is."

"You're sweet. But I look a mess. Some other time, sweetie. Some other time."

He goes back to drumming his fingers on the cardboard box.

"And besides, sweetie, you've never liked the expensive dinners. You wouldn't be happy there."

"But you do."

"That's not the point, sweet."

"Sure, it is."

"It's not. You have to want it too, otherwise there's no point. No point to any of it."

"Then I do. I like the dinners just fine."

"Don't say that, darling, if you don't mean it. Don't say it."

"I wouldn't say it if I didn't mean it."

"All right, darling. If you say so. But we can't as it is, so there's no point in arguing about it. But you're very sweet."

"We'll be okay if we go."

"We won't. There are more important things to save for. But I'm sorry. Look at me, I've just about brought it up again. I'm sorry, sweetie. Don't mind me."

"We'll be okay. It won't be anything."

"I don't want to. Please stop. I don't. And we can't. Just stop."

He looks tired, and then looks away, and I feel bad for getting frustrated, but he makes me so frustrated sometimes, but he's struggling too, I know he is, and I'm not helping any. I wish there was something to say, but there's nothing to say I guess. I hold his hand. He leans back and drums lightly on the box and takes a big breath and I can't tell if he's frustrated at me now or if he's just tired. I sit against the window and watch the dry trees, bright in the sun, and behind them I can see a road and beyond the road more trees. There's a hill just past the road and there's a row of bushes there that look gold in the yellow light. We come out of the wood and rattle along the raised track past apartment complexes with swing-sets and playgrounds out front. And dip down under bridges and roll along the pebbled track between large brown rock walls and then we're in the tunnel and it looks dim at first because there's still light coming through from behind us, and I can see the different tracks converging, and then we're deeper in and it's dark and the little orange lights in the car come on and make the green fabric of the seats look a dirty brown shade of green. It's quiet except the humming of the train. The baby starts crying again. I pick at the fabric of the seat. Hunter drums lightly on the box. His eyes closed. He looks tired.

Chapter Twenty-Eight

The roar of jet engines and the silence after. Like a vacuum came on and sucked up all the sound and then it all came crashing back. But for a second, we all stopped and looked and what if they were dropping it? Just like that. You just hear it more and more and the more of them that get involved the more you hear it, and they all have them and you just hear it so much it gets to you. And it got to Charlie. I don't think he meant to kill himself. Just to get wounded probably. But he missed or didn't miss. And they shipped him home quick after that.

It's dark and the cement is hard on my back and on my head and I can't tell if I was dreaming or was just remembering, and my hand moves up and down with my chest and my fingers are dry and I can feel the dirt under my fingernails. I try to swallow but my throat is too dry still and they haven't brought me any water, not since the first time and I don't know how long ago that ways. It could have been days ago. Maybe it was days ago. Or minutes ago. Or seconds ago. And I'm thirsty and my lips sting because they're so chapped that the skin is peeling, and I lick them, but my tongue is dry too. Maybe they forgot about me. Or they're dead. Or it dropped already and

I'm underground, so I didn't feel it. But I would have felt it. Or maybe it happened a long way off and I'm just waiting till the radiation gets to me or I starve first or die of thirst. Maybe I'm already dead. My eye hurts and my cheek hurts and I'm hungry and thirsty and it's too dark.

The skin around my eye isn't so swollen anymore, but it's still tender to push on. And his fist was really big, and his knuckles stuck out and his hand had scars on the back. I didn't see it coming the first time. The lights were in my eyes and the bag had been so dark and they pulled it off and then it was bright, and his fist hit really very hard and I coughed, and they held me up by the hair, but my hair isn't long enough to get a good hold and my head kept slipping out from his fingers. I saw it the second time. And I saw his scars in the bright light. And I deserved it. It was my punishment. My eye never hurt too bad, anyways. The rope was worse. And that cut deep, and my wrists feel good without it on now, but they still sting if I touch them. Thick rope. And dry. And the bristles were stiff and thick and cut deep and it was tied very tight. My knees on the concrete floor. The rope stinging my wrists. My eye was already swollen. The light swinging back and forth over head and the other lights in my eye. I cough and taste blood and dirt. My lips are bleeding a little and I taste the sour blood, but at least it makes them not so dry. And I can swallow it. But I feel sick after swallowing too much.

I forget to blink because it's so dark and my eyes burn. My breath is shaky and shallow and it's hard to breathe and I'm breathing very fast, but I can't calm down. My throat knots. I hate this. This darkness. I hate it. My eyes burn but they're still closed. I try not to cry but I'm shaking. We shouldn't have run down that hill. The white sand kicking up everywhere. I didn't have to be here. Somewhere else. It would have been easier to crumple over the bullets. That would have been easier. Like them. And the red mist. And a moment of pain. And then nothing. And it wouldn't be so hot and dirty and dark, and I wouldn't be so thirsty. I should never have come. I was just stupid and pathetic and thought I was being brave and finding meaning and it sounded better than being so numb all the time and the monotony and the pointlessness of it all. Better than dreaming about her. And she'd say she wanted to see me, and that she missed me. I meant a lot to her, she'd say. But she'd go home to him and kiss him. Come visit, she'd say. But she lived with him. And the sick feeling and the numb feeling and it was supposed to be so much better than the numb feeling. But it's not. It's so not. I hate it. I hate this. I wish I never came. I was so stupid. And mom must have been so disappointed. He was, I know he was. Stupid. He would have said that. And that I was wasting my potential. I wish I hadn't. She could have talked me out of it. If she picked up. But it was too late, wasn't it? I'd already signed. God, it was forever ago. Just that voicemail was forever ago. I wonder how he heard. She probably called him. I bet she did. He doesn't get to tell me what he thinks. I don't want to know. I don't care. But she was probably crying to him. I bet she's crying right now if she's heard. And so is Benji. But Leo wouldn't. I wonder if they've heard.

I hit my fists into the hard floor and the dust comes up and I cough on it and my hands hurt from hitting so hard and my wrists sting and my eye stings from coughing. I shouldn't have come. The darkness is heavy and thick, and I feel along the grooves between the cinderblocks. And count them. And count them again. And stretch my legs out and try and stretch as far as I can, but that only makes me light headed. And the air is so thick. And hot. And it was hot out there. And it smelled worse too. By the medical tent. So thick and hot that the smell gets stuck in the air and it was like swallowing their blood to breathe. And they said the paper masks would help, and they did a little, but not much, and we'd rub different oils and parts of twigs and chap stick and whatever we could find, we'd rub it under our noses to help, and that helped some, too, but not much. Nothing helped much.

And patrol was worse. The orange road and the orange dust and the orange rocks and it was so hard to see because everything blended together, and the Humvee kicked up so much dust and the village wasn't supposed to be hostile. And then we were taking fire from some kids playing soccer and Dylan was yelling and cursing and blood covering his hand and his shoulder and his cheek. He came back quick from that. He recovered in Miami he said and sent us post cards and pictures of the girls in bikinis with very brown skin and brightly-colored bikinis and the ocean, and the sand that didn't looks so white, but it was still pretty white, and the water was very blue.

I'm breathing slower and deeper and I stand up and walk around the small space and trace the wall and count the cinderblocks again.

The door is heavy and metal and thick and there's no light coming from the other side where I can feel the cracks. And the hinges aren't on the inside. It's smoother than the cinderblocks and I rub my palm against it. It's warm. And dusty. And the dust scratches my dry palm.

Bright orange dusty sand in my eyes, and I covered my mouth with my bandana because I couldn't breathe the sand and I squinted but the sand would still sting my eyes. But I could see the smoke from the other Humvee and the ashes and the twisted and smoldering metal and we drove quickly and that made the dust worse. We were so afraid. And always tense. And I could never sleep, and I was always tired. And I needed more sleep. But it was too much.

I lie down. I should sleep now. That will be good. I feel a little tired. I think I can sleep. But the ground is hard on my back and I roll over, and it's hard on my shoulder and I can't get comfortable, but I lie here for a long time. Staring. Until my eyes burn and I close them and see the orange sand and the Humvee driving quickly and the crack behind us and I pulled the trigger and then the red mist in the orange sand and we didn't see them until we came back around later and it was a little darker and the sand wasn't so thick because the wind had died down. She was holding her baby and there were large holes through both of them and her face wasn't fully together anymore. And she was young too. Probably not even twenty yet. But I was never any good at guessing someone's age. Leo was. He could guess anyone's age. But I was never any good at it.

I try and sleep on my back again. And I feel comfortable, a little. And maybe I'm sleeping. And after a long while I stand up again and bounce on the toes of my feet. But that only makes me tired and I sit back against the cinderblocks directly across from the door and imagine I can see it. And I'll see them when they come in. And the clacking of their steel-toed rubber boots on the cement. American. And their rifles pointed at me felt like being watched by a thousand eyes. And ice water. It felt good at first because of the heat. But I choked and then it didn't feel good and then it was bright and white and sterile and the whole room was white tiles and tearing off my uniform and hosing me down with more ice water and the water ran red and brown and swirled around my feet. I thought it would stain the white tiles. All so clean. Except that corner where they were scrubbing off dried blood. The butt of the rifle was hard and I was down before I knew what it was and my knees hurt bad against the hard cement. And these clothes are too big for me.

Why didn't they ask me anything? What could I have said? Maybe that's why, I guess. I wish they didn't retie that rope so tight. That stung worse than my knees.

Darkness wasn't bad at first. The shapes made the room feel small. A door. A wall. A shadow. Until the shapes moved when I moved. And that door wasn't there. And that wall wasn't there. And then it was bad. It was really bad. And I couldn't breathe. And I tried to yell and cry out and tears burned the cut and stung my eye and no matter how hard I opened my eyes – even to the point of burning – it was just all black. Pressing burning eyes into sucking blackness. It was like I would see what I imagined I saw, but I never did have a good imagination. Seeing the door that wasn't a door. Seeing the rifle that wasn't a rifle. Seeing the snake that wasn't a snake. And blackness. So much crushing blackness.

I'm sweating, again. And I'm shaking. And the sweat rolls down my forehead and tickles the bridge of my nose. And my hands are trembling. I try and breathe slower, but I can't and all I can see is blackness.

Chapter Twenty-Nine

The subway rattles and is very crowded, and I hold tightly to him and he holds the metal handrail and I can hear the music from the headphones of someone behind me. The train rocks back and forth and I step on someone's shoes and apologize, and I can smell something sour under the seat. Everyone sitting looks unhappy and sleepy, and they don't notice the smell. Same smell as when we got off at the train station. And I didn't realize how many people were in the train. All pushed together like fish in a can. And then swimming fish until that really long escalator and then back into the can little fish. People are cuter as fish.

I wonder if he liked the station as much as I did. The pretty stonework all around the walls and pillars and it all looks so old. And tan dots on the green ceiling in the shapes of constellations. He hardly looked up.

The train rocks again around a sharp turn and it's going very fast so we're all pulled hard against each other. It squeaks to a stop as it rolls into the next station and we push through people to get through the doors that are trying to close, and we walk slowly in the crowd through the turnstiles and up the stairs under the metal awning in the middle of the square. It's very windy because we've come out on the avenue side and down the avenue is always very windy. We walk along the brick square in the cold wind through the thick crowd and he squeezes my hand tightly so that we don't get separated, and the cold ring digs into my finger. It's loud up here with all the people and the taxis and busses and diesel trucks rumbling by. I like it better at night.

Steam comes from the top of one of the buildings across the street. A tall glass building that didn't used to be here reflects the bright gray light coming through the smoggy sky and hurts to look at for too long. We cross the street and pass a bank with large glass windows and long lines for the ATM machines. The movie theater is across the street. He was so cute about the movies and about the theaters he liked best. I never understood why this one. There were three closer to us. Or maybe even four. The crowd is thick, and I can't see over their heads and everyone moves so slowly. A halal cart on the corner smells like spiced meat and smoke and onions. The meat is on fire.

The crowd is thicker. And I feel anxious. I don't like this. It gets harder to breathe. I squeeze his hand hard. He pulls me with him through the crowd. There are too many people. But at least in the crowd the wind isn't so bad.

Hunter turns and shouts something to me, but I can't hear him. He pulls me off to the side, pushing through the crowd and we cross the street through the slow-moving traffic with bicyclists weaving between the gridlocked cars. We pass a gym and through the big tinted windows I can see the people sweating, riding the stationaries. The sky is gray and smoggy, and I can smell trash on the corner somewhere. Someone pushes past me and I almost lose Hunter's hand, but I don't. I'm breathing very fast and I my chest is beating hard and I don't like it. I try to breathe slower, but I can't. I try to breathe like Tensu. Deep and slow and holding it in my nose and then out for eight seconds. Like Tensu by the river with his eyes closed and his legs crossed and the river quiet and slow. Father would have laughed at me. But the river was quiet and slow. Someone else bumps into me and I stumble and squeeze Hunter's hand even tighter and the ring digs in even harder. But the river was quiet and slow. The honking and the diesel engines and the humming roar of talking. But the river was quiet and slow. And I breathe easier and we walk slowly with the crowd. We're not in a hurry and I feel better and breathe like Tensu. And his fat balled head and it would shine in the morning light where the sun came through the tall trees and never saying a word on those walks. Never. I miss those walks. And he never asked me about home. Not once. I would have told him.

Didn't this used to be a record store? A long line of people at the register. So crowded. Everywhere. How does Tommy live here? A siren wails in the distance. Someone on the corner hails a cab and gets in but doesn't go anywhere. The intersection by the back side of the church is filled with cars squeezing through. It's a big intersection and the sky is bigger above it.

The post office is close up ahead. I can't see it through the crowd. Always busy and noisy. Not like this. Not this many people. But so noisy. Except late at night or early in the morning, and then on my bench in the square under the big pagoda tree with my book. We come to the corner and I can see the big pillars of the post office and the round dome and it's large from close up, but small compared to the big glass buildings above it. We turn down Twelfth Street and there are fewer people. A large driveway with a mound of trash in front of it. Further down the windows of what used to be a bar are boarded up. The planks torn away on that one. The glass is black and cracked, silver webs spiraling outward. I follow Hunter across the street. We push through a small glass door that doesn't look like anything. It closes and the sounds muffle and small bells on the door handle are chiming.

It's a dark shop. The only light is the gray light coming through the glass door and carving out a patch in the floor in front of us. It's warm. And dusty, too. And the dust drifts through the air and when it comes into the light I can see how thick it is, and behind the dust are rows and rows of shelves cluttered with trinkets. I look at him and he calls out and someone from far off in the back calls to us and we start down one of the aisles. Porcelain dancing figurines in three different sizes, china dolls - all painted in pastel colors. A large glass monkey, dark red, with a sword and bearing its teeth and a hand written sign under it: *For Stop Evil.* Next to it the same one, but a smaller size. At the end of the aisle are bamboo plants in stone pots filled with little gray pebbles.

On the far wall are boxes, and in front of the boxes a cluttered, wooden counter. A small Asian man stands up behind the counter when he sees us. It's very dark back here, but there's gray light from somewhere and it streaks across his desk and I can see how white his long beard is. "Hello. Hello. How can I help you?" His voice is small and his accent is thick.

Hunter shows him the box and says he has a delivery and the small old man rubs his hands excitedly and takes the small box and his eyes shine and his beard comes down almost touching the box. He signs for it on the paper receipt that Hunter holds out to him and he says thank you several times and Hunter turns to leave, but he looks so happy and keeps saying thank you and I ask him what it is. Hunter pulls on my sleeve.

"A Gift. *Very* special gift. I've waited long time."

"Come on." Hunter whispers.

"What gift?"

He smiles a big toothy smile and puts the box on the papers on the table. "I show you. *Very* special. *Very* special." He tears at the tape on the box and pulls out a thin bronze statue of a ballerina. He brushes papers to the side and puts it on the counter in a patch of gray light. The bronze looks faded. It's a beautiful figure.

"It's very lovely. Isn't it lovely?"

"*Very* special. *Very* special." He looks happy. And claps his hands together. His smile is big and the wrinkles in his face are deep and his hands are gray and shriveled and have spots from the sun.

"Let's go." Hunter says to me.

"Wait. Wait. You give gift, I give gift." The small man says and bends down behind the desk and rummages. Some papers fall off the desk quietly. I pick them up.

"Here. Take." He says and holds out a small velvet pouch.

"No, we can't." Hunter says.

"Take. Take."

"We can't."

"Take. Very special. You give gift. I give gift. *Very* special." I take the pouch. It's soft. And heavier than I expected. "Thank you." I say. "Isn't that sweet?"

"Very special. Very special. You take. It good luck. Bring you luck."

"Thank you. You're very sweet. Isn't he sweet?" I say. Hunter pulls at my arm.

We leave through the same aisle we walked down. The shelves are so narrow and all the statues look so delicate and I'm afraid of bumping into them and breaking them. And then he would be so cross. And he would probably take back this little pouch. The muffled roar from the street gets louder. The gray light gets brighter.

"Let's not go out there yet." I say.

"Okay." He holds my hand. "What's in that?" He asks.

"Let's open it later. It'll be lovely to open it when we're alone, don't you think, darling?"

"Okay."

"Can we call Tommy? Are you all done now?"

I'm still toying with the small pouch and he waits with the phone to his ear watching me. I can hear it ringing. He talks to Tommy for only a second, but he looks pleased when he puts the phone back in his pocket and says Tommy says hi, and I ask if we're getting lunch and he says that he's close by and that we'll go to Café. I don't want to go outside just yet. I lean into him and he holds me and we listen to the traffic. I like the smell of this shop. It smells old. Like there's history to it that I want to know about. And then we go out and it's loud again and fast and bright and big. And we pass the movie theater on the corner. Across the street is the dorm and I look up at the large square windows and at the purple flag flapping in the strong wind and the smooth round pillars under the entrance. We cross the street and walk past the dorm to Café and enter on the avenue side.

It's all black and white, with a black awning and black walls, and black and white checkered tiles on the floor with black tables and black chairs and white cotton table cloths, and the waitresses all wear black pants with black aprons that have their names embroidered in white letters on them, and there are black and white pictures on the walls of old movie actors that I don't know any of. Hunter probably knows who they are. Or his brother would. Probably. His brother knew about all of the actors. It's very crowded. And loud from the talk. The waitress shows us to a table in back. I can still see the door. She brings another chair for Tommy. I watch Hunter from across the table. The white table cloth. The black pepper shaker, the white salt shaker, the small white flower in a vase with only a little water at the bottom. He's slouching. His eyes are so blue today.

Hunter orders tap water, but they don't serve tap water anymore, and so he pays for a bottle and I order a coffee and the waitress walks away.

"So what's in there, love?" He asks.

"Not yet. It will be lovely when we're alone."

"We're alone now."

"Not really. Not really alone. When we're really alone we'll open it together." I toy with the drawstring and the pouch feels soft and I feel two lumps inside it.

Hunter stares at the flower and scrapes his fork along the table cloth. The table cloth doesn't cover the sides of the black table. The waitress comes back with the coffee and a bottle of water.

"It's strange, isn't it?" I say.

"What is?"

"Being back here. It's very strange, isn't it? It hasn't changed at all."

He fills his glass with the water and drinks it quickly and refills it. I smell the coffee and hold the white ceramic glass in my hands. It's very hot and smells good and bitter.

"So much hasn't changed." I say. And I feel like I'm right back here. And we'll have class tomorrow.

"And I feel like I'm twenty again."

"I don't think I want to be twenty again." He says.

"Me neither."

A glass falls and the loud chatter gets quiet for a second and then starts up again.

"Love, remember when you spilled your pasta sauce all over that guy's pants?" He says.

"Yes. That wasn't very funny, though. I don't think it was funny."

Sorry, love. I was just trying to think of when our first time here was. It was that time though, wasn't it?"

"It might have been. I can't remember, sweet. But let's come up with another time that was our first time. Not that time."

"Okay, love. That time was our second time."

"Stop it." I try not to laugh, but he laughs and I really like it when he laughs. I pour the white milk from the sliver saucer into the hot, nearly-black coffee and it clouds over and the coffee turns brown and I sip, but it's very hot. Too hot to taste, but I put my nose to the cup and smell and it smells warm and bitter and good, and I offer some to Hunter. He shakes his head. I don't know why I keep offering. But I like offering it to him. And he might want some one day and if I don't offer what if he does and then there won't be any for him. He reads the menu. I pour a little of the water from his bottle into the vase with the flower.

"Tommy's meeting us here?"

"He said he'd meet us, but he said he might be a little late and to get started without him."

"Can we not talk about the time with the pasta sauce in front of him? Please, darling?"

"Of course, love."

I sip the coffee again.

He smiles and his dimples show and he reads the menu and drinks off another glass of water very quickly.

Chapter Thirty

It's so hot and dark and hard to breathe, and I'm breathing very quickly and shallowly, and I feel sick. This smell makes me sick. And all I can taste is blood from my cracked lips, but they've stopped bleeding now, dry and cracked and dusty. I need water. So thirsty. I roll onto my side and cough and coughing hurts. Praying didn't help anything, either. That was embarrassing. I don't think I did it quite right. I think it should have been both knees on the ground. Someone would have laughed at me. I feel a blush coming even through how hot my cheeks are. So stupid. But thank God it's dark. Ha. God. Does that count? At least it's dark. And they couldn't see me. No one will ever know. About any of it. I'm alone. In this dark, piss-smelling hole. And no one will ever know. I might as well pray. But the cement is hard, and my knees are sore. Maybe later. I breathe, but it's too hot and thick and it doesn't feel like air. It feels like water. Hot water. And I don't feel like I've breathed at all. But my lungs are already filled with this hot water and can't hold anymore. I'm suffocating. There's no more air in here. It's just heat now. And I breathe fast and groan and whimper and feel embarrassed that I whimpered. My hand on my chest moves up and down and I know I'm breathing and I calm down, but only a little. I sit, and that helps, but only a little, too. I push against the wall. Grinding my teeth. I push my back against the wall until my back aches and until the rough surface of the cinderblocks scratches through my sweat-soaked shirt.

I push air out. Hard. It hisses quietly and vibrates my chest and the small sound feels good and I can breathe a little easier. And I make the sound again louder and again, but even louder, and breathe deeper and I yell, and the yell is loud in the small space and vibrates my chest and feels good. My breathing slows. Slow. Deep. I feel better. And I sit like I did at the foot of her bed with my knees to my chest and my elbows on my knees and the book was heavy and it was sunny and dry outside in the mountains, but her blinds were drawn and the lampshade by her bed was purple and made everything in the room look purple and she was brushing her hair in the big round mirror by her bed. And I was reading and asking her about the words I didn't know and Leo came in. She stopped brushing her hair and he sat with me at the foot of the bed and we looked at the edges of the big shades that looked purple and the light was bright around them. And she was happier then, and she didn't cry all the time and she didn't always look so tired or talk so slow.

I sleep a little. And get up and walk around and count and recount the cinderblocks. How's that? They've changed. I count them again. The first time was right. I kick at the dust and cough. The darkness is so thick and heavy, and the heat is thick and heavy, too, and I walk back and forth until my legs are tired and my head hurts and I sleep a little more, but not for long because it's very uncomfortable on the hard, hot, piss-smelling, slab of dusty cement, but I'm getting used to it. I get up and count the cinderblocks again.

I sit back down and hit the back of my head lightly against the blocks, staring. At nothing. Blackness. So much time to do nothing. Too much time to do nothing. Back in the City I did nothing also, but I pretended it was something. In the windowless rooms and the dirty white tile floors under the florescent white lights and the rows of dusty books and I would study before and after class and then more and do well enough on the exams and then back to the rooms. And no one ever agreed with me that the library looked pretty from the outside, especially when the sun was going down in the winter and the light would be golden and it would hit the brown building at just the right time and it would look red, but no one else liked it. And across from it, the park, and the trees, when they had leaves on them, they'd look golden and deep green and the grass looked yellow and the fountain would still be going strong until the sun was just about set and then it would shut off and the water would look dark and smooth. And so much time doing nothing in the windowless rooms of the brown-that-looked-red building across from the park with the fountain. And it was quiet just like now, except when you turned the page or scribbled something and the scratching of pencil on dry paper and then erasing and blowing the eraser shavings off the page. Tapping your foot. Coughing on the dust. Groaning when you looked ahead at how much was left to read. The buzzing from the small light bulb overhead. And the smell. Old wood smell and old books and dust. That smell even now. I get that same feeling in my stomach that made me stop going. And then the hum of traffic and staring out the window for hours and hours when I was supposed to be reading. And watching the light change against the buildings across the street.

I piss in the corner. There's not much left in me. And it smells rotten. I go back to sitting and staring at the darkness. So much darkness. I can't breathe again. I sweat and my skin itches and my eyes throb and I can't breathe. And this smell is rotten.

Something else. Anything else. In the rain with Sergeant yelling in his green poncho with rain flowing over the plastic and off the brim of his large hat, yelling over the thunder and over the grunts of the men. The grass was wet and stuck to my hands and made my fingers itch and the mud was cold. It was gray, and his jacket was dark, and his hat was dark and heavy with rain and only his eyes were shining and the veins in his neck were bulging. Up and down and up and down and my arms were getting tired, but they were strong, and I wasn't tired and up and down and up and down. And he was never happy with us and always angry and up and down and up and down and more rain and more thunder and more yelling.

He has a big voice. And he must have yelled his head off for us to retreat, but I never heard it. I would have been back at camp. Safe. There would have been silence in the ride back, but once we got there we would have joked about it. At least until we saw the empty bunks. Of the ones that didn't get to hate the silence on the way back, or the tortured jokes. Then the guilt.

But my bunk is empty. And they've probably moved past the guilt now and are playing cards for cigarettes. I hate cards. And cigarettes. And I hate this pit. With this stench and this sweat and the heat. I roll onto my side and the cement is hard against my shoulder and my hair rubs against the dirt.

My beard is getting scratchy now. His face was smooth. Very smooth and the blood shimmered on his chin and his eyes were bright but turning gray quickly and he looked so afraid and I could tell he was pale. And he looked at me with his graying eyes and his pale, smooth skin and I stared at him until my eyes burned and I think I threw up when I noticed his uniform and his patches and his name tag. I should have taken his tags with me. I feel slick.

My stomach rumbles and I pull my knees up to my chest like at the foot of mom's bed. That feels a little better, but I'm still hungry. I'd even take the beans. Still cold from the can. And they tasted metallic, and the brown liquid spilled onto my boots and the dry, chewy, and stiff potatoes never cooked enough and everything was stale - especially the slices of bread we got. I'd take it. It sounds sweet now. And good. And I'd drink all the brown syrupy liquid left at the bottom of the metal tray and sop the bread in it. I think I miss breakfast most. Oh, eggs when they're cooked right with sausages and potato and the sausages still oily and chewy and salty and lightly brown. That's the best. And I could probably eat a whole stack of pancakes right now. With that good fake syrup that's real thick and with a good amount of butter and how it gets all greasy over the pancakes. And sausages with those too. Or even bacon. I half chuckle thinking what he'd say. He'd probably be so angry and disappointed. But I don't care. He doesn't get to say. And meat is so good and salty and chewy.

My stomach rumbles again and I try and sleep, but I can't sleep. I'm too hungry. And thirsty. And my lips are very dry and cracked and they sting. I open my eyes as wide as they'll go and try to see something. Anything. The grooves of cement between cinderblocks. The edge of the large metal door. My hand. I wave it and feel the wind against my nose, but I can't see it. I can't see anything. I hate this darkness. I hate it. And worse than this darkness I hate this waiting. I'd rather them torture me. I can handle pain. But not this waiting. I listen. Hard. For anything. Any sound or creek or crack.

Keys rattling. I heard it. The rattle. Silence. I don't breathe. I know I heard it. I crawl to the door and grope ahead in the darkens until I find it and press my ear to the warm metal and listen and listen hard and I hear it. Keys rattling. And boots. Clacking of rubber boots on the cement. They're coming. Finally. At least it won't be waiting. The rusty, dull knives. Tearing more than cutting. Or the batteries and wires and whatever else. But at least it won't be waiting. I can handle pain. I feel my chest beating hard, and it makes it hard to hear the keys rattling, but I hear them. Coming. And getting closer. And getting quieter and farther away and then nothing. Silence. I listen hard. Silence. Waiting.

Chapter Thirty-One

"What are you ordering, darling? I haven't a clue what I want."

"I'm thinking about the soup."

"What kind is it?"

"Squash. I think I'll have that." He closes his menu.

"That sounds lovely."

"We'll both get it."

"We can't get the same thing, sweetie. You know we can't get the same thing."

"Well, then you get the soup, and I'll have something else."

"No, no. You have the soup."

"I'll have the sandwich."

"But you want the soup, darling. You have the soup."

"I want the sandwich."

"No you don't. You're very sweet, but you want the soup. It's okay to say so."

"I've changed my mind. I like the sound of the mozzarella sandwich."

"You're sweet, darling. But don't say that if you don't mean it."

"I do mean it."

"But you don't. I know you don't. Just tell me what you want. I'll be okay with it, but I have to know, darling."

"The sandwich. I want the sandwich."

"All right, darling. You're very sweet."

I put my menu down and sip the coffee. It's very good coffee and strong. "Oh, but now I feel guilty, darling. I know you want the soup."

"I don't mind, love. I really don't mind. Please believe me."

"Not minding is different than having what you want. It's very different, darling."

"Don't be like this. I'm happy with the sandwich."

"All right, darling. All right. Don't mind me. I'm sorry to frustrate you. Don't mind me."

Oh, I wish he'd just tell me what he wants. I hate it when he does this. But I hate frustrating him. It's loud in here, and I like the fresh-bread smell and freshly-ground-coffee smell and I hear clinks of glasses and metal forks on ceramic plates and we're close to the kitchen back here and I can hear the sounds of oil sizzling. I hold the mug of coffee in my hands and it's warm on my palms.

"Tommy!" I see him coming through the crowd with his big shoulders and his thick eyebrows and he smiles and I jump up and hug him around the neck.

"Haven't you ordered already?" He asks.

"Not yet." I say.

"Good to see you, Tommy."

"Likewise."

They both sit down and I sit down and I'm so happy to see him. He looks so big and strong.

"How have you been?" I ask. "It's so very good to see you, Tomtom. I miss you so much, you know? It's so very good to see you." He looks older.

"It's good to see you, too." He says. "I've been excellent. Very busy. They keep me busy down here, but I'll come up and visit soon."

"Do. It would be so lovely to have you over."

"How long do we have you for today?" Hunter asks.

"Just for lunch." He says. "I have to get back."

"That's too bad, Tommy." I say. "But let's not talk about that now. Tell me how you've been. When are you going to find a girlfriend? I want a sister."

He laughs and blushes, but he hides it well. "Not me. No, not me." He says. "What's new with you, two?"

"Nothing is new, Tommy. But it's so awfully good to see you."

"What do they have you doing now?"

"Nothing any interesting. Just more communications things. Pretty much the same old. I'd rather hear about you two."

The waitress brings a third menu for Tommy, and he says he's ready if we are and we order. Tommy and I order the soup and Hunter gets the mozzarella sandwich.

"And things are good with you two?"

"Things are good." Hunter says. "As good as can be."

I sip the coffee, but it's still hot and burns at the tip of my tongue. "That's excellent. Excellent to hear. So, when's it going to be?"

"Don't ask that, Tommy." I say looking at Hunter.

"It's been long enough, don't you think? And I've been waiting."

UNTIL WE ARE LOST

"Don't ask that, Tommy. We will when we can."

"All right. All right. But just so you know my opinion, I think it should be soon."

"It'll be soon." Hunter says. "We will when we can."

I twist the ring on my finger. Hunter and Tommy talk about an old teacher of theirs, and it's so very good to see Hunter smiling without that something else behind it. It's like it's only with me that it's there. But that's not fair. Don't think that. I twist the ring. The waitress brings the food. I take a small spoonful because it's hot and steaming and oh, it's very nice. Very sweet. He'd like this. It's good with the coffee. Tommy eats sloppily and some of it rolls down his chin and I smile at him and he blushes. He wipes it away with the back of his hand and then wipes the back of his hand on the napkin. Nothing has changed, has it?

"But in all seriousness," he says, "you two really should. Not just for my sake. It'll make things easier for you two."

"We know, Tomtom. Thank you. We will."

"We definitely will. Very soon. As soon as we can." Hunter says and takes my hand. I stop twisting the ring. I hadn't even noticed I was still twisting it.

"I'm just saying it's been long enough, is all." He sops a large chunk of bread in the soup and bites it off. "Just get it over with." He says with his mouthful. He looks so much older. And his thick eyebrows are dark and he's still so thin. I can only remember him chubby. But he looks so thin.

"Let's not talk about this. We will when we can." I say.

"If you need money, I'll pay for the church. And we'll just have a small ceremony, and then it will be over."

"When we can." Hunter says.

"All right. All right."

"When are we going to find you a girlfriend and get you off our backs?" I ask.

"Not me." He says. "A bachelor for life. Not for me."

We eat and it's pleasant. And they talk for a long time together, about the war, he always brings it up around Tommy, and we talk about Tommy's work for the City and I talk so much I forget to eat.

"It's awfully strange." I say. "The three of us back in Café."

"Café!" They cheer and clink glasses and laugh.

"It feels like nothing's changed."

"Nothing has." Tommy says.

"Everything has. Don't say that, Tommy. So much is different. But it feels like it hasn't, and that's the strange part. And it's an awfully strange feeling. Darling, do you want some soup?"

"No, thank you. I'm fine."

"Have some soup, sweetie. It's very good."

"I'm okay."

"All right, darling. Oh, but now I feel guilty, sweetie. I'm sorry you didn't get your soup."

"I don't mind it, love. I don't mind at all."

"All right, darling. All right. But isn't it strange? It's like it's all the same, but it's all different too."

"We haven't changed all that much." Tommy says.

He smiles and his cheeks look chubby again for a second and I've really missed him. It's so very lovely to see him. I squeeze Hunter's hand.

Chapter Thirty-Two

My back is cramping, but I don't want to move. The corner is small, and my knees are hugged to my chest, and the rough walls are digging into my back and my short hair, that feels longer now. Sweat rolls down from it and I hear it dripping onto the dusty hot cement floor. A drop rolls down the side of my cheek and onto my dry lips. My dry and cracked and pealing lips. My tongue feels like sand. And tastes like sand. I cough. And more sweat rolls down my forehead. I need water. Water. Cold water. Fresh. And sunlight. Bright. Blinding. Light. White. And gold. Palm trees. The brims of the leaves shimmering white. Glowing. A lake. Crystal blue. And calm. Surrounded by sand and trees. And bright under the sun. White light. Golden sand. Shimmering. All of it shimmering. But it's so black. So much black. Don't look. But I can't help looking. I stare so hard into it that my eyes sting and burn and I blink, and it doesn't look any different. Just black. And blacker. My eye is still sore. But not swollen. And my chin scratches and I scratch it and the hairs are long. Longer than they've ever been, I think. Never really could grow one. But this is the longest it's ever been, I think.

My back cramps. I push myself forward and straighten out a little and my foot kicks something that scratches along the floor. I yank back. Bite. Snake. White hot. Like I was just slapped by lightning. Not a snake. I feel around in the darkness for the rope. It's almost as if I can smell the fear as it leaves. Dry, bristly, thick. I hate snakes. I kick the rope away. That was one of the best parts of the City. Not like home. I hate them so much. Rattle snakes. I shiver. God, that time Leo almost got bit. And we were running so fast after that as if it was chasing us. In the shade of the bush and it rattled but we didn't hear it and then we heard it and in the shade of the big tree he was laughing and laughing and I told him to quit it because it wasn't funny and he could have died. God, I hate snakes. And this darkness. And this quiet.

I lie on my side and the cement hurts my shoulder and my neck aches, but my back isn't so bad anymore. Sweat drips down and my shirt is sticking to parts of my chest and drooping with sweat where it's not sticking. And where it droops it brushes against the dirt and makes a small noise. I count the cinder-blocks in my head. And count them again. And kick my foot against the wall until it hurts, and I stop kicking. And push my finger into the grooves between the blocks until the skin starts to feel sore from the rough cement in between and I stop doing that, too. I cough. My throat is scratchy and dry. I hold my breath and it's very quiet. So quiet. And I hold it as long as I can. Until my chest stings and then throbs and then my heart beats loud and it's not quiet anymore, but I keep holding it until I feel dizzy and can't hold it anymore. And I breathe hard and the breathing is loud.

It's never quiet at camp. Always noisy. The rumbling of diesel trucks and Humvees and tanks, and the buzz of the electric lights, and the clatter from the mess tent, and the men running, and the shouting from the card games, and the complaining about the heat and the smell and the sand. And the boredom. It's never quiet at camp. Always noisy. The green sheets on the bunks. I tried to stuff my ears with cotton, and cover them with pillows, but it was still loud. No sleep. Only lying down with your eyes closed. And the City wasn't quiet. Always humming from the street and sirens and you could hear the sirens even when they weren't close and the honking and people yelling. Here it's quiet, at least.

The roof was nice. And the City was muffled and sounded very far away, even though it wasn't. And it was still nice after she left. For a while. But then it wasn't nice anymore. All I did was remember her. I can't stand her anymore. But for a while it was okay up there. And the people looked small and I could look down at the tops of the trees on the sidewalk. And especially when it snowed. It was nice when it snowed. I like the cold better than heat. But at least it's quiet here. Until they come for me. It could be now. They could be coming. With the knives. And the buckets of water. But they don't come. They never come. They've forgotten me, maybe. They've just left me here. And no one knows I'm here. Deserted hallways. I crawl toward the door. Nothing. No sounds. No keys or boot steps. They've forgotten me. In this blackness. And this quiet. It's better than the noise. It's better than the noise, at least. But I hate it. This darkness. I hate it. And they've forgotten me. And I'm going to be here forever. Until I rot. And it's so dark. Don't look. At least it's quiet, though. The quiet is okay, now. I don't mind it as much. The quiet. So quiet.

I lie on my back and look up. Where the stars would be. Like in the mountains back home. The lights from the town were dim enough and the town was small anyways and we were in the hills and so the orange glow didn't reach up to us, not like the City. The orange glow throughout the night against the smog and cloud and it was never really black unless you were under the lights and then behind the lights looked black. But from the roof you could always see orange hanging in the sky. The ever-thickening smog. And the stars weren't stars they were planes. Except a few. I look up. The big dipper. Benji liked the big dipper. Because he could always find it. Mostly always. It was the only one he could find for years. And it was the first one he showed me. The pine trees whistling in the breeze. It was cold, but we wouldn't move. Because we were looking at the big dipper. And the dirt and prickly twigs and brambles from the clearing sticking to our sweaters and poking my arms, but we wouldn't move. All three of us, we'd lie there as long as we could. I wouldn't move first. They had to. And there were so many stars. So many. Infinite. And bright, too. White little specs, and bright and thousands of them. Everywhere. And even where I thought there was a dark spot I could find stars if I stared at it long enough. And Benji would say mom wanted us back, but we wouldn't move. And then we saw the Orion's Belt because of that movie. I never saw a shooting star, though. I wanted to. And Benji said he did once. Leo saw a couple, but that was after I left for school and he would call me. And I never saw one. And I never said goodbye, either. To either of them. A message for mom. I didn't want to talk to her. I'm glad it went to her voicemail. She would have cried. And they would have been disappointed in me. And they would have tried to talk me out of it. And she wouldn't have said anything except cry. Pathetic. She used to be strong.

But then she never could be after he left. And she never could say what she wanted anymore. I was always so different from her, anyways. Leo was so much like here. I was like Benji, and we were like him. But I'm not like him anymore. Not anymore. But I could have said goodbye. That would have hurt too much. And there wasn't any point to it. I was going, and it didn't matter. It doesn't matter whether or not I said it. I left. And nothing changed for them after. I was already gone, practically. Nothing changed. Probably. Unless something happened. I would have heard if something happened. They've probably heard, now. And mom's probably crying. And they probably cried a little. Except Leo. He never cries. And Benji probably cried and he's probably still living off mom. And Leo. He's probably okay. Not hurt or anything. He's probably okay. Probably still playing guitar and watching all the movies. Still. He's probably really good now. He was good then. But he's probably really good now. Unless something happened. I would have heard. I would have.

I roll over onto my side and stare at where the wall is. I reach my hand out, so I know where to focus. It's black. So black. The floor is hard against my shoulder. The dust crunches against my damp hair. The hair on my chin itches and feels scratchy. My throat hurts and it's dry and my lips are dry. The cut on my cheek doesn't hurt anymore. But my eye is still throbbing. My shoulder pinches against the ground and aches. I close my eyes, but I'm not tired. The air is heavy and sticky and thick and it's hard to breathe because it's so thick.

I've never seem them so bright like out here. And big. Big bright white and sharp dots. Not from camp. From out of camp. And the sky is so big. And the small pale dunes, ghost-like from how white the stars are. And the moon too when it's up. But I still can't find the Dipper out here. Or Orion. Benji probably could.

Black tops of pines poking at the sky. And when the moon was up – and milky white – and there were fewer stars because of it, it made the grass and the trees and their faces pale like we were all dead. I miss it. With them. I wish we didn't stop going. But she was crying so much we had to stay with her. I guess it just lost its magic after that. After he was there but not there. I feel hot with anger suddenly. That really was the worst part, wasn't it? I wished he'd just moved his things out. To her house. That's the normal thing, isn't it? That would have been easier for mom. I'm glad they didn't last. I bet he knew they wouldn't and that's why he never really left. My fists are clenched and my nails are digging into my palms and I try to relax them. I would punch him if he were here right now. I would. I should have then. Or at least said something. I'm surprised Leo didn't. But any of us should have.

I stand and walk quickly around the edge of the room. Dragging my finger along the grooves between cinderblocks. My footsteps are loud in the sucking silence. I stop. My breathing is fast. There's just nothing. Waiting. Standing. Darkness. I can't tell which way is which. And that could be up or down, and I start to sway and feel dizzy and then almost fall. I close my eyes tight. And sit down. But sitting hurts. And I walk again. Walking keeps it straight. I jump a little but my legs are tired. I try push-ups, but my arms are so weak and tired and what's the point? They left me. I'm forgotten. Or even dead already. This is death. Just in the black and quiet and piss on the floor that smells very thick and hangs in the muggy air. This is death. And, I don't know, it's just so dark and I can't breathe, and the smell is so bad and I'm so hungry and thirsty and maybe I'm going crazy. And I hear so many thoughts. It's actually loud. It's all a blur and my head is spinning and I can't tell if I'm standing or lying down. And I fall and hit my head on the wall on the way down. That feels better. But now my head is throbbing. But it's not bleeding, I don't think. I can't tell. I put my fingers to the sore spot, but I can't tell if they're wet. I taste them, and they taste sour, and dirty, but not like blood. I feel better now. And it's quiet again.

I lie down again and look at the stars and Benji is on this side and Leo on this one and it's cool and the wind smells nice. Couldn't tell me apart, she said. Everyone says that. But I can't see it. Neither can they. I liked that she looked at the photo, though. I wonder if she's heard. And feels sorry for me. Or if any of them have. Or what they're doing. I bet Leo's playing guitar really well now. Unless, what if, something could have happened, and he, what if, it could be bad. And I wouldn't have heard. What if it was something bad? Oh man, mom would be crying so hard. Her favorite. And I never said goodbye. What if they're all gone? And I never said goodbye. And I'm the only one left and all alone and they're not there. I close my eyes tightly. Stop, stop. Not like this. Something else. Where are the stars? But there aren't stars up there. Just blackness. Emptiness. And I am alone. Completely alone. And I never said goodbye.

Chapter Thirty-Three

It's cold and the wind is crisp, but his arms around me keep me warm enough and I'm very comfortable leaning against him in our puffy jackets against the tree in the courtyard of the old church. The ground is dirt and the dirt is hard with cold and the red bricks around the trees look pale and worn down. The iron gate around the courtyard is old and rusting and small pieces of it have broken off, but it always looked this way. And the black paint is chipping away, and I can see the rusty iron. Cars rush past on the street. Now they're waiting, rumbling, and I can hear the humming and buzzing of blenders from the smoothie shop across the street. I hold his hand around me tightly and watch my breath and it glints in the spaces where the light comes between the bare branches. It's become a lovely day. The gray smog and cloud burned off and the late afternoon sun is showing through the branches now and feels good on my face.

His back must be getting stiff from leaning against the tree because he shifts positions and shifts again. I lean back against him and kiss his cheek.

"I love you." And he smiles and his dimples look dark.

I look back out at the street and the dirt of the court-yard and the honey yellow stones in the dirt and the big roots erupting and the smooth gray bark. The courtyard looks smaller, like seeing a playground for the first time as a grown-up and realizing it never was really that big.

"What's in the pouch?" He asks.

"Oh, darling, I had forgotten." I take it out and look at the small dark velvet. The two lumps clack against each other.

I pull the top open and empty two small, round, perfectly smooth, black stones into my palm. They're cold and heavier than they look, and wonderfully smooth.

"Rocks?" He says.

"I think they're lovely. Aren't they lovely, darling?"

"If you say so, love."

I put one into his hand and watch his thumb feel around the smooth surface.

"Aren't they smooth, sweet? Aren't they wonderfully smooth?"

"What are they for?"

"They'll bring us luck. Isn't that right? They'll bring us luck."

"Okay."

"But I want that one."

I can feel him chuckling. I lean back into him and close my eyes in the light coming through the trees. It's bright, but it's not so warm, and I feel rather cold. The wind is picking up again. But I feel better than I did this morning. I felt rotten on the train, and that was silly. But thinking about it makes me feel rotten again. I feel the smooth stone in my pocket and turn it over in my fingers. It's cold and magnificently smooth, without a single dimple or crack or crease of any kind. And very black. Just like his. Identical. I like that. Isn't that lovely? Identical.

We sit for a while longer. My nose is so cold it's starting to go numb. We get up and walk back to the square. We pass the statue of the man on the horse. I think it's a president. Roosevelt maybe? It's windy in the square. And the crowd is very thick and it's slow walking and loud and I feel overwhelmed again waiting to get down into the subway. Hunter holds my hands tight and I turn the rock over and over again. I'm cold until we get onto the platform and then it's not so cold and we pile onto the train and it's warm on the train and my hands stop shivering. But I'm tired and there's no room to sit, and hardly room to stand, and I lean against him, rocking with the subway. We wait at the station for our train home. I'm heavy with tiredness. His back must be bothering him today. He keeps fidgeting.

"We're happy aren't we, sweetie?" I ask. He's leaning back into the wooden bench in the food court and I'm leaning into him and I can feel him look down at me, but I don't look at him. "We have a good life, don't we?"

"As good as we can, love."

"That's what I think, too."

"You're happy, aren't you, love?"

"Yes. I'm very happy with you. You make me happy, darling."

"I love you so much." He says and kisses the top of my head.

"It's why I don't like that you have to come in so often now, sweetie. You're always coming in, and I can't stand to let you go alone." I look up at him. He looks tired.

"I can't stand to leave you alone. You're very sweet to come."

"But I don't have anything to do. I wish you'd let me help."

"I know, my love. I just can't stand the thought of you having to work. And it won't be long. It really won't be."

"But there's nothing for me, darling."

"It'll be better soon. Once we have enough. And then we can try."

Oh, I want that to be true. Can it be true? "But it won't be soon, will it darling? It won't be soon."

"This won't last. I promise it won't last."

"Don't promise that, darling. You can't promise that."

"But it won't. It won't, my love."

"All right, darling. If you say so. But I wish you'd let me help. Just until we're ready. Until then I have nothing, and it's so hard doing nothing without you. With you I don't care if we do nothing, or anything, or everything. With you, I'm happy, darling. With you, the rest of the world could disappear, and I'd be happy."

"It won't last, love. I promise it won't last."

"You're very sweet to promise that. You're very sweet." I kiss his palm and put it against my cheek and close my eyes.

The train is late. Finally, we can board and we find a nearly empty car. He reads the newspaper. I wish he wouldn't. He always looks concerned when he reads about the war. And he gets that look he used to get when we first met; that intense look like he's fighting something. But if he doesn't read about it he daydreams about it, and that's worse I think.

I watch the city roll by. He finishes and folds the paper and puts it away and leans back and closes his eyes. I watch the wrinkles in his forehead smooth. That's better. A white-brick warehouse rushes past. A thick wood with a dark road cutting sharply through it. The clouds look as big as mountains up there beyond the smog.

The smog clears and the light fades. The train hisses to a stop at our station. Fresh air hits us coldly and feels nice after the stuffy ride. The sun is almost down and the light is dim, making the trees dark and the sky pale. Moths flutter at the lights on the platform. The hill is steep and the wind is hard on my face and it's a long walk. Winding with the mountain road. There it is. No. It's a different bend and we walk further. Finally, the dirt road leading to the cliff and the little house at the end of it and the big oak tree with the thick trunk and the branches that first poke up at the sky and then curve back down towards the house, and beyond the house the sky is black and the stars are out. My face is numb and inside it starts to thaw and stings a little. We eat dinner in silence. It's a long way for him to go for so little. I wish he could find something else. But that's not fair I don't think. He likes it, and that's what matters, and it's usually not just for one package. We make a fire and lie in the bed and the fire is warm on my cheeks and makes the walls look orange and rich and I fall asleep with the flames on my face and his arms around me. I wake up and the fire is out and the night is thick and quiet, and the crickets are chattering, and I can tell Hunter is awake.

"Can't you sleep?"

"I'm okay, love. Just got a lot of nonsense on my mind."

"What nonsense, darling?" I'm very sleepy.

"Nothing important. Go back to sleep."

"What nonsense, darling? Tell me."

"It's not worth the trouble. We'll talk about it in the morning. Go back to sleep, love."

Sleep comes again easily. When I wake up I know I had that same dream. The man with the knife and the sharp blue eyes. And it's more upsetting the second time. But I don't want to think about it, it was just a dream and it's silly to get too upset by a dream. The light is coming in through the kitchen widow. It's bright and the wood is glowing and the ashes in the fireplace are gray but look bright in the bright white morning light. The November air is cold and crisp and good to breathe under the hot blankets with Hunter still asleep next to me and his warm body against mine. I wonder when he fell asleep. Was he up all night? I shouldn't wake him. I hope he doesn't have to go in again today. I want him here all day. I feel good when he's here, and he doesn't get to stay hardly ever now. But it won't last, he says. And then we'll be so happy. And then we'll go shopping for baby things. And the crib. And the little bundle of sheets. And in the mornings like this one I will hold her in bed and he'll wake up and not have to go in and we'll all three of us stay in bed together and be happy and feel lovely. That will be so lovely. And she'll have little pudgy fingers that will poke at my face and I'll stare at her for hours and she'll stare back, and how lovely that will be. And when he has to go in I won't, and I'll stay with her out here and when he comes back we'll be so happy to see him, and we'll have been thinking about him all day.

He rolls over and I kiss his forehead and he looks at me with his big blue eyes and the light comes in through the wood right onto them and they glow bright and deep in the light. And for a second, I feel the hair stand up on the back of my neck, but it passes quickly and I just love looking at his eyes.

"You're very cute when you're asleep." I say. "You're very cute always, but especially when you're asleep."

It's so nice and warm under the blankets with him, and his skin is so soft. I don't want to get up. Not ever. I watch the light slowly change. He strokes my hair.

"I have to go back in later. But not all the way. Just to Thornwood. So it won't take nearly as long as yesterday."

"Okay, darling." I feel my chest sink.

"I'm sorry, love."

"You have nothing to be sorry about. Nothing in the world. I just like you right here in bed with me." He smiles and rolls over and kisses me and holds me against him and I close my eyes and try to forget what he just said.

"We can go walking again this morning if you like? And try to find that river."

I smile and open my eyes and he's looking right down at me with those beautiful blue marbles of his. "Let's not get up just yet, okay?"

"Okay, love."

"But a walk sounds lovely."

"And maybe you want to come with me again today? I just hate leaving you."

"Of course, darling. I would love to."

"You're very sweet. The sweetest thing in the whole world."

I like his voice the best in the mornings. When there's still a heavy twang of sleep, like his throat isn't awake yet. And he's happiest in the mornings. So I'm happiest in the mornings. And the white light and warm blankets and the chilly air just above the warm blankets. He makes me breakfast and we eat the toast quietly, but the toast is crunchy, and the butter is good and the coffee is good with the toast.

"What kept you up last night?"

"Nonsense, love. Only nonsense."

"Tell me about it, darling. I want to know about all your nonsense."

"It was about the war. I told you it was nonsense."

"What about the war, darling?"

"It just makes me upset to think about. And then I can't stop, you know?"

"You're very sweet to be upset by it. I wish you wouldn't follow it so closely."

"I can't help it. I want to do something, but there's nothing to do. And it's only getting worse. All the papers say so."

"There's nothing for you to do, sweetie. It's not for us to worry about."

"I know, love. I know."

"You're not wanting to join it, are you, darling? Tell me you're not wanting to join."

"No. I'm not, love. I would never leave you."

"Good. Because I wouldn't be able to handle it if you joined. I wouldn't be able to, darling. That would be too much."

"I'm not wanting to. I told you it was nonsense."

"But if I weren't here, you would want to, wouldn't you? If you didn't have to leave me to do it, you'd want to. I know you'd want to."

"But you are here, love. And I could never be away from you. I'm only ever happy with you. I'm only ever anything when I'm with you."

"You're very sweet. Let's not talk about the war. It's not for us. Let's not talk about it, darling."

"Okay. I told you it was only nonsense."

"But if it bothers you we should talk about it. It's not nonsense if you're bothered by it, sweetie. Does it still bother you? I can see it does."

"It doesn't. Not today, love."

"All right. Then let's not talk about it."

I finish the coffee and wait for him to finish. We put the dishes in the sink and go walking bundled in our jackets in the hard, cold wind, my hand keeping warm in his pocket. It's a long way down the mountain. It smells like it might snow. Oh, wouldn't that be lovely. It's a long walk, but a nice walk, and I just love being anywhere with him.

The sun is starting to make me anxious. Seeming like it's already high up and we'll have to turn back. And we haven't found it yet. But the trees are nice to walk through. I like the sounds of the birds and the rustling of the dry bushes. We come through the trees and pass through the small town. On the far side are more trees and we'll probably have to turn back soon. I look at the sky. And then at Hunter. But he seems happy to keep walking.

The sky through the trees shines in spots of blue. The cool breeze and the smell of pine needles and sap and moss. Oh wait. Maybe a light trickling sound. Oh, could it be? I look at him and feel my heart racing a little and I think he hears it too and I drag his hand towards it and we climb over a low hill and there it is. It's beautiful. Just a tiny creak. A silvery snake coiling through the brown bank of the forest, the sun glinting as it does in the ripples. It's not very loud at all. That must be why we didn't find it before. Just a quiet trickle of the soft water on wet rock. I close my eyes and it's just like being back in New Mexico with Tensu. And I feel warm and happy.

We sit on the bank, the earth soft and wet, his arms around me, his chin on my head. And I know we'll have to go back soon, but I really don't want to. I just want to stay here with him forever. I'm so happy we found this. And we'll go back soon and to the station but at least we found this. I smell deeply the cool water and the wet rock smell. I knew there was one out here.

Chapter Thirty-Four

My chest rises and falls. I feel it with my hand. And my hand feels heavy against my chest. And the cotton shirt is soaked through with sweat. And my arms are wet. The dust and dirt on the ground gets stuck in the wet hairs of my arms. The ground is hard under my head. My hair rustles and scratches against the dirt as I roll over. The hair on my chin is scratchy and itches. But I can't move to scratch it. I'm too tired. And too hungry. And too thirsty. And too damn tired. I feel weak. And it's so dark. I can almost see the grooves between the cinderblocks. Almost. I think. Maybe not. Maybe it's nothing. It smells like piss. My stomach rumbles. I'm wasting away. Slowly. And waiting. I wait. Sweaty and hungry and thirsty and sick, I wait. Wasting. In darkness. This is all there is. Darkness. Thirst. And hunger. And more darkness. Can't get out. I can't get out. No way out. Just darkness. I breathe dust. And heat. I cough. My stomach rumbles. My throat is dry. I wait. In darkness. So black. Pure black. And I can't get out. No way out. And I'm so tired. I can't keep my eyes open. But I can't keep them closed, either. And I can't tell the difference between open and closed. I slept a little. I think. I think I slept. Did I sleep?

Standing. In the desert. Naked. Alone. Not alone. A line of us standing naked in the desert. Standing on clay. Gray and cracking clay. And we're looking forward, only forward, at a black cloud. A big black cloud. Monstrous cloud. Coming towards us. And the clay was hot. Crackling. And my feet are burning. And the cloud is the sky and the sky is black.

Not long enough. Never enough sleep. I'm tired. Globs of dirt and dust, matted into the sweat and the hair on my arms. Thirsty. Water. I need water. I cough. My throat scratches and I cough more. I wait. I don't stand. I can't stand. I'm too weak. The floor is hard. The air is thick and muggy and dusty, and I can't breathe. I wait. No sounds. Nothing but my breathing and the rising of my chest. Silent. At least it's quiet. So quiet. It's not so bad. And it's better than noise. At least it's quiet. And I'm so alone. There's no one out there. I'm alone. Alone to wait and rot and waste away. And once I've waited, once I've rotted and wasted away, only after all of that, and after my stomach eats itself and my throat is so dry that it crumbles into dust, only after all of that, then I'll die. And that will be nice. And it'll be over. And done. And then more black. Only black. But no exhaustion. And no hunger. And no thirst. Only black. And silence. Only death can be quieter and darker than this. Only death. That'll be nice.

But I waste away so slowly. I rot slowly. I wait slowly.

I'm nothing but a callous. That's all I am, now. A bit of dead skin. Hollow. And wasting away. That's all. A callous. I'll be dust soon.

Not soon. Soon would be too easy. Slowly. Speck by speck. I'll become dust. Speck by speck.

Then I'll be free. Free.

No. I'll be nothing. I'll be dust.

But I'll be free of this.

Then what? Nothing. Black. Silence. Nothing. Or is this death? Is this hell? And I'll never be free. Always wasting away. Always rotting in the stink. Always waiting. Did they kill me? Did they shoot me? With their guns prodding me, they shot, didn't they? The barrel against my cheek. It was cold. I remember it was cold because everything else was so hot. I'm dead. This is death. I didn't kill him. He killed me. So what am I waiting for? What's next? Nothing? Blackness. Silence. More rotting.

My stomach rumbles. I roll onto my side and tuck my knees into my chest. I'm not dead. Not yet. It rumbles again and aches. The stomach walls rubbing together, wasn't it? Someone said that. Professor Geer maybe? God, I don't miss it. This is at least better than that. Tired. But no, you have to study. Go and study. Have to study. Like holding your breath underwater. At least I feel something now. And the rest of them out there enjoying themselves and drinking and me studying and tired. Come out, she said, and she shouldn't have, and I shouldn't have, and I hate her for that too. It just added to the numbness. I hate numbness. I hate it. Let me die here slowly, painfully; let me feel it when dust becomes me, rather than exhibit in postures manicured of all discomfort.

I chew on my bottom lip and roll over in the dust and feel hot and sticky and cough on the piss smell and want to yell but I'm too tired to, and I just lie here coughing. The black. So dark. I press my foot into the cinderblocks but don't have the strength to push myself across the floor and can barely keep my foot up that high. I hate this. And I hate there. Both of them. All of them. And so alone. There and here. Alone. Me and this darkness. So dark. And hot. I'm sweating. Rolling in the dirt and it clumps together on my arms and forehead and hair, stuck in the sweat. I can't breathe. I need to get out of here. Out of this blackness. Of this heat. Where the air is thick but so little of it is air, and I feel like I'm never breathing. Never enough. It's just heat. The floor is hard on my head and my ribs. The skin on my heal scrapes against the rough cinderblock wall, and I press and it digs harder and I slide against the dust. I can't breathe. I need to get out of here. Out.

Where?

Out.

To what? More heat? More sand? The sun?

Back home. Home will be good. And better.

To the City. To the smog and the sidewalks. To the classrooms. To the exhaustion and the studying and the uselessness. The uselessness. To dreaming about her and waking up and feeling sick and broken and dull. To numbness.

Home. The mountains. And the stars. And it was nice and the breeze was cool and the tall grass looked gray in the milky-white light from the big moon.

The broken family. Always tense. Mom always about to cry and talking so slowly. Leo's gone. He's not there. Benji would be. Still living off her. Like a child. Expensive meals and luxury and she's probably washing his clothes for him.

But it's so hot and so dark in here, and so quiet. So miserable. So hungry and thirsty and exhausted. Only waiting and wasting and rotting.

There's nothing else. Nothing else for you. Not home, or the City or the desert with the men in our camouflage tents, and the cigarette smoke.

I hate cigarettes.

And the orange dust and the rocks and the tension. Always so tense. Nothing left. Except rotting. That's all. In darkness. Only a callous. Waiting to waste into dust. That's all. Wasting. In silence and darkness and heat. Wasting. That's all that's left.

I should have done this years ago. I was scared. Jumping would have been easier. Quicker. But I enlisted. And now I take the slow way.

It'll be nice. Quiet. Peaceful. Nothingness. Unless it's not. It'll be better than this. Than all of this. Whatever it is. It'll be better.

I open my eyes. Only black. I stare. Pushing myself to sitting and my arms almost give out, but they don't give out and I lean against the wall and rest my head against the cinderblock. It's easier to breath now that the cement floor isn't pressing against my back. It's quiet. No wind, no dust rustling, nothing at all. Only my breathing. I listen and stare. Darkness and silence. Nothing else. I wait. This is the slow way. Through hunger and thirst and exhaustion. I go the slow way. I should have jumped. There was no point to enlisting. There's never a point. I was just scared. Now I'm not. I'm not scared now, just impatient.

Chapter Thirty-Five

In the night we sit on the wood floor that's stiff from cold, bundled in the big blankets, with the fire crackling and big and bright and warm on our faces. It's so good to be back where it's quiet and calm and where the only sounds are the crickets and the wind and the fire. And his breathing. I hear his breathing, too. It's very lovely out here. And I feel good to be back and out of the City. I wish we could have seen Tommy again, though. Next time. Tomorrow. Ugh. Tomorrow. Today was so long. And I don't like waiting for him at the coffee shops. It's better when we're together. Better when it's only a couple days a week like it used to be, and not all day, and not eleven packages so his back starts hurting him, but he'd never tell me that. He works so hard for us.

The fire makes the wood glow orange, but the light doesn't reach the kitchen and the kitchen looks dark. The black blanket is soft and warm, and his body is warm and the scruff of a beard on his chin scratches along my cheek, and it's pleasant.

"I'm very glad to have found a river." I say.

"Me too."

"And it's not too far away. We can go all the time, can't we? It's just like in New Mexico. I'm very glad to have found it, darling."

"I'm very glad to have found you, love."

"You're a sweetie, aren't you?" He smiles and I hold him as tight as I can until I have to breathe. "I just wish we found each other sooner."

"Oh my love, we are so lucky. I'm so lucky. I'll take whatever we get."

"But I wish I could have known you when we were children. Do you think you would have liked me then? I wish I could have seen what you were like. You would have been so cute." He would have been the cutest little boy. With such a sweet little voice. Oh, I wish I could have seen him. "Or even just three years earlier, darling. We could have had three more years together. It's just like us to find each other right at the end."

"I would trade every year before I met you for just one minute with you, love."

"Oh, darling, I love you." A log rolls off the fire and crackles and sparks fly up. "And we're happy, aren't we, darling? So very happy."

"As happy as we can be."

"And it doesn't matter what happens, I'll be happy with you. As long as I have you, I'm happy."

"You'll always have me, love. We're not going to ever be apart."

"But even if everything goes wrong, we'll be happy, won't we? Even if it all goes horribly wrong - the war, I mean, darling - we'll still be happy won't we, darling?"

"Of course, we will, love."

"Because we'll be together."

"And we love each other."

"Oh, how much I love you, darling."

The log spars again and we watch the sparks drift up glowing and go out and they look like fireflies, like the ones in New Mexico, and Tensu used to look so happy when he watched fireflies. He was such a young little boy at heart, even though he was all wrinkled. Hunter holds me tight and I kiss him and feel very safe and good in his arms and I play with the hair on them. We sleep on the floor in the blankets and don't wake up until the early morning when the birds are chirping, and the fire has gone out and looks cold and the ashes are dark and gray and my toes are cold because they're sticking out from under the blanket.

Chapter Thirty-Six

My eyes open. It's hot in here. Dark. I breathe slowly. I slept. The ground isn't hard. It's soft. A bed. And a pillow. And it all smells clean and like new paint. And there's a little light coming through the edges of the blinds. The edges glow slightly. The blankets over me are warm and heavy and I push them off and roll onto my side. An apartment. My apartment. Right. I'm not there anymore. Not in the blackness. Not in the stench of my own piss. Not in the dust and the sweat and the heat. And black. It's cool. It's so good to breathe deep. And the pillow is so nice and soft and cool. And the light. It's beautiful. I can't remember it. Was it long ago? I just remember darkness. Oh, they came. That's right. And back to this. The chaos and noise and all these people and cameras and lights. Blinding. And handshakes. So many handshakes. And salutes. What was the medal? I roll over. I think it's on the counter. So many questions. So many lights. Click. Click-flash. Click. So many handshakes. If they only knew. But I'll never say. They'll never know. All those lights. And people. So many people. And this room. A large room. A reward. But it's not a reward. This crowded, bright, and hurried City. Always noisy. Never quiet.

The hum on the street, constant. And the rush of the wind and the honking and the shouting. It'll get quieter as the sunsets. But even at sunrise it's humming. The false, early morning quiet. Cluttered with anticipation of the sounds to come. I know true silence. And it just gets louder. And brighter. No more darkness. But I'm clean. Not dusty and soaked in sweat and smothered by the thick stench of my own piss and the dirt matted into my hair and on my skin and the hard cement and the cinderblocks. Twenty-six cinderblocks around.

The bed is soft and nice, and rustles when I roll over. And clean. It's all clean; my sheets are clean, my apparent is clean, my hair is clean and short again, and it all smells clean and new and like paint and like the fresh stain on the dark wood floor. And I'm not hungry anymore. Or thirsty. It's good not to be hungry or thirsty. And it's cold, and the cold is good too. So much better than the heat. But it's never dark or quiet anymore. And why all the trash? That rotten sour trash smell. I can't stand it. At least up here it smells clean.

I stand. The air is chilly on my skin and the little bit of sweat from being under the heavy blankets is gone quickly and the dampness chills. I wipe my eyes and stretch and groan and I press the switch by the lamp on the night stand and the blinds withdraw mechanically. Humming. Always noise. Always humming. Orange light comes through across the sleek, stained-wood floor. The smog is thick and the sky is brown. And turns almost red with the sunset. The street lamps glow like a procession of little orange beetles. At least the view is nice. The lights in the tall buildings wink sporadically. Up the avenue and down, cars roll in a slow progression like mourners. They should mourn. Look what they've done. Black mounds of trash on almost every sidewalk I can see. The street is a black gash of sludge. It's a narrow avenue. And the side streets are narrow. And the buildings tall. Not like before. Forever ago.

Light rings the streetlamps. The sun is lower. The sky is redder. The dusting of snow on roofs of the parked cars looks crimson. I stand close to the glass and I feel the cold air coming through and press my forehead to it to see further down. The cold is nice on my hot skin. Steam from sewers billowing in the wind. The bright sign in the ground-floor window across the street for the liquor store. It's a good view. And it's all so bright.

The wood is smooth, and it looks dark and red in the light, a little cold against my bare feet. The marble of the kitchen is colder. Black. The light from the fridge is bright and I squint. Cold air pours out from the open door and I shiver. Eggs on the shelf, butter in the tray, a loaf of bread. I don't like that they gave her a key. The vegetables in the drawer smell rotten. She's not even doing her job. I wish they'd just leave me alone. Ha. Never.

I close the fridge and take my whisky from the freezer. She'd never approve. Vets shouldn't drink, she said. It's a slippery slope. Ha. The whisky is good and coldly burns on the way down. I drink and get dressed and put the bottle on the counter by the bed. The large walk-in closet with its own light, and the large wood dresser that's filled with clothes they bought me, and the ties and suits on hangers. I liked it better when I only had a uniform. And it was all uniform. I dress and sit on the edge of the large, soft bed and tie my shoes and the leather looks sleek in the darkness. Two small wooden counters on both sides of the bed. My pistol in the drawer. The table in the middle of the large space with brown-cushioned chairs on all four sides. The stools at the marble-topped counter in the kitchen. The dark wooden drawers and cabinets. The large window, and from the bed I can see the roof of the hotel across the way with plotted pine trees and Christmas lights strung up on wires and wrapped around the pine trees. White Christmas lights. A thin thread hangs off my shirt sleeve. I pull on it. It gets longer and doesn't break, and I bite it off.

I drink. And stand. The thick heals of my shoes clack on the wood. All this. For what? What piss and dirt and darkness can make. A hero. Ha. If they only knew. I drink a large sip and it tastes sweeter and less cold and burns a little less on the way down and I feel alright.

I fold the sheets and blankets over the bed and smooth them out and smooth out the pillow. I take my jacket from the hook by the door and leave. And now I'm back to this. I lock the deadbolt behind me. All I do is walk - like I did before the war - and waste away - like always - but doing nothing - also like always. There's nothing to do. And they want me to shake more hands and talk to people and go on TV and it's all so dull and noisy and bright. The hallway is bright. And it's always lit because if it weren't it would be dark, and they don't like darkness. The carpet was cleaned recently and still smells like soap. It's chilly in the hallway and I like the cold air. The cold is better. The elevator is slow and old, and it's lined with rusted metal railings that make it look a little interesting. And a marble face where the buttons are. And the lobby is hot and dim with high ceilings and marble walls and stone pillars that are old and rustic looking, like in the elevator, and the only light in the lobby comes from the lamps in the corners with green lamp shades on them, and the light makes the stone and marble a little green. The doorman behind his booth. I can hear the TV on and he stares at it blank-faced. I leave through the revolving doors and walk down the stone steps. It's very cold, and the wind is strong through the tall buildings. I tuck the whisky into my jacket pocket and duck my head into the wind. I look up as high as I can see, but the stones disappear into the smog. I like the stonework up there when I can see it. I walk and pass a pile of black trash bags and try not to breathe, but I can't help it after a while and the smell makes me feel sick and I sip the whisky. That helps a little. The subway station is close, and I pass it and hear the train screeching to a stop. If I had anything to do or anywhere to go that might be convenient.

The streets are angled, and I can see the white headlights of a car brush along the glass and brick walls in front of me, and then they pass, and I hear the car going fast. Down the street and up a series of short stone steps I pass an open quad and can see a little more of the sky and it looks dark from under the bright lampposts. The clouds and smog are low, and I can't tell how tall the buildings are. In the middle of the open quad is a planted tree surrounded by benches and I pass it, my shoes clacking on the dry, cold stones. Across the quad there's more sludge and the sludge dirties my shoes. The trash is piled close to the wall on the sidewalk and I walk along narrow foot path and smell the sour garbage and drink whisky when it smells too bad. I pass a couple holding hands. She's not very pretty. And I get a strong whiff of her perfume and his cologne. There's so much of it. On everyone. It gives me a headache.

The cold feels good for a while, but it starts to get too cold. I don't want to stop. I drink more whisky and it warms me a little and I keep walking. Just walking. What else is there? This is all. Just like before. Nothing. Only I know it's nothing, and before I thought it was something. I kick at a glass bottle and it cracks against the lamppost. The sky is dark behind the lights. A woman passes. She's pretty. I hate her because she's pretty. Just like before. All exactly like before. But now I drink.

A car passes and sprays sludge against the cars that are parked. The sidewalks are mostly empty. I like that better. Better than the crowds and thunder of talking and shuffling and honking and humming and rumbling and shouting over the thunder of talking. So many people now. Wasn't it always this many? I guess it could have been.

The headlights are bright and stinging. Even the streetlamps are too bright. I half miss the dark and quiet and heat. No not the heat. But the darkness and the quiet. Not the thirst or hunger either. But the blackness. I'll never see such blackness again.

My hand fiddles with the glass bottle in my jacket pocket, but the glass is cold and so my hands are cold, and the wind is very strong along the avenue. I turn off it and feel a little less cold. A dead and rotting pigeon on its back, slunk over the corner of a trash bag. It smells. I walk under the low-ceilinged construction scaffolding. A string of white lights along the center of the metal-planked-roof makes the silver glow white. An old man snores and mutters, sleeping under cardboard under the scaffolding. His hair is long and matted and dirty and pokes up from the cardboard like snakes. I can see his breath in the light. He smells like piss. Thick like piss. I know that smell. I drink and cough a little because it burned bad that time. And I drink more. Around the corner a bar that smells like cigarettes. The music is loud. It looks empty.

It's just like it was before. I have nothing to do. And there's nothing for me. I feel angry. And a little drunk. And I hate that this is all there is. This is all I have. And I'm still alone. Still forgotten. By all of them. Except Leo. Maybe I should call him back. And say what? But it would be nice to hear him. I wonder why they didn't call. If they're okay. Maybe I should call. But no. They're fine. They would have told me if there was something wrong. They just don't care. I feel hot. I don't want to talk to any of them. The wind picks up as I cross the avenue and feels good on my flushed cheeks. There's no home, or anything else. Nowhere else. I'm stuck here. Trapped here.

A grate over a subway rumbles and warm, sour air pushes up through the cracks and rustles the plastic of the trash on top of it. The white lights from inside a twenty-four-hour market on the corner are bright and make the sludge stand out on the sidewalk in front of it. The door frame and window frames are red. The walls are white. I pass it and pass a liquor store and look at the bottle of whisky, but I have enough. The whisky looks gold in the orange light from the street lamps. I'm cold and my hands are getting numb and I cross the street and start back towards my apartment. But I don't want to be back there yet. I don't want to be in that empty space, with nothing to do but sit and drink and I don't have enough whisky for that anyways.

A tall, pointy-looking building in front of me reminds me of the churches around here. It's odd I haven't passed one yet. On the far side of the pointy building I can see where the wide avenue flows onto the bridge, the string of white lights arcing up into the low cloud lighting gray the cloud and the stone pillars. Across the avenue is the park, but the park is closed now, and I walk along the outside of the gate until the sidewalk ends and I walk back across the wide avenue.

Someone in the shadows with a hood across the street is spray-painting something elaborate on the side of a building. The hissing of the spray bottle is loud, and I can hear it over the wind. And I can smell the metallic paint smell from here. I hate it here. All of it. Except the view from my apartment. It's a good view. But I hate it here. The noise. And the lights. Especially the lights. And how they always want me to talk to someone or wave or shake someone's hand or say something. But I have nothing to say. They want hope. I don't have it. Pathetic. I would go back if they'd let me. Would I? It'd be better than this. Maybe not. I look up at the highest places I can see. The ledges and balconies of the nicer apartments, but I can't see very high up. It would kill me. That seems easier. Find something high and be done with it. No more of this. No more of the sour-smelling, constant hum of a City. I was so close to dead back there. It would have been easier if they just forgot me. Everyone else did. Except Leo. It would have been so much easier. I should just do it now. It sounds easy. Dangerously easy. I should have before. But I was just scared. And then the sand and the heat and the dust and the fear and then darkness. So much darkness. And the piss-filled, muggy air. And hunger. And thirst. Worse than anything was the thirst. I feel the scar on my cheek with my cold fingers. It would have been so much easier if the bullet was just a little more to the left. Just a little bit more. A tiny bit more. And then done. But it wasn't.

The sign for *Williams Street* dangles and rattles in the wind. The clank of bottles and cans from a bag as it slinks into the street with a lazy sag. Cardboard, soggy, stacked by the fire hydrant. A rat scurries out from a gutter and nibbles on vomit. His fur is damp and matted. He doesn't seem to mind me as I pass. A newspaper rustles in the breeze.

The wind is hard, and I feel cold and angry and more than a little drunk and the lights are starting to look blurry with long tails. I pass under a brightly lit awning of a strip club with a large black bouncer sitting on a stool in front, shivering in the cold. I hear the base drum from inside. Past the strip club I hear more music coming from a bar with green lights overhead that make the sidewalk look green and the trash out front look green and the people smoking cigarettes outside the window look green. And the smoke from the cigarettes looks green, too. A drunk man stumbles out, still with a flask in his hands, and he trips and falls into the pile of trash out front. He kicks, and squirms and shouts and they laugh and point, and I pass him and smell the bitter smell of beer and cigarettes and the sour of the trash. I drink and keep walking and don't look back, but I can hear him coughing and them laughing and shouting and the music even as I pass the church. Finally found one. The sidewalk in front has been cleared of trash and the large bricks have been bleached. The stained-glass windows are lit from inside and look colorful. It looks clean. All of it clean and shining from within. The high peaking spire is lit with bright white lights from below, and it looks ominous with it's high, sharp peeks jabbing at the low clouds. It's notably shorter than the buildings around it.

They give false meaning to it all. They clean the sidewalk and light themselves, filled with self-importance - their god gives them importance - and they give the ignorant a reason to feel important. But none of it is important. Nothing is. It's all useless, but they don't know that. None of them know that. They can't face it. That we're not. We're so not. So meaningless, so purposeless. I drink. A drop rolls down my chin. I lick it away and then wipe it away with the back of my hand. There's nothing for me here. Nothing for anyone.

What will happen when the sidewalks are full, and the trash bags overflow into the streets and the cars can't drive anymore? What will happen when it smells so bad that people can't go outside anymore? Will they stop their drinking and laughing, then? Finally? They still won't get it. Louder. Brighter. Smellier. Gross. So much trash. Whatever's in there, rotting, wasting, like me. I don't need to wait around. Find something high and be done with it. It sounds so easy. Maybe I will. I drink again, a big drink and it takes a while to swallow it, but it doesn't burn when I do. Maybe I will. Like I should have before. But I was too scared. Maybe I will.

I'm drunk. The glass bottle is almost half empty and I drink more. I feel hot and the wind is cool and refreshing. A large puddle in the street with small bits of food or something floating in it and a car rushes through it and I cover my face but the splash doesn't reach me. I walk more and around more corners and stare at the highest places I can see. A siren cries out in the distance. Most of the windows above me are dark except a few. But the sky is still glowing. And the trash on the corner is high and a lot of it isn't in the black bags.

I walk under a bright gold sign for a hotel that I've never seen before and I keep walking past the doorman standing under the awning with bright lights directly above him with his white hat and white collar and green vest and white gloves on his hands that he cups over his mouth and nose and I can see his breath coming through his gloved-fingers. The collar of his coat up and by his ears. The sidewalk clears a little up ahead and there's a diner on the corner with people seated against the large windows from floor to ceiling. A young-looking, skinny, black-haired woman in a short black dress that doesn't even reach the middle of her thighs, and her dress is thin and hardly covers anything of her shoulders or her breasts, and her slender neck, and an equally skinny man with wavy blond hair across from her. She's very pretty, and her shoulders are thin and bony and her arms are thin, and she's tall. I feel angry looking at her. Her ankles are thin and they lean against his under the table. And she smiles at him. I feel hot and I drink and keep walking.

Chapter Thirty-Seven

It's already a little warmer today, I think. The snow on ground looks white and clean, but it's already melting and brown grass is poking through in splotches. I wish it would stay. But it's too early for the snow still, isn't it? Larger drifts collected against the tree trunks look like miniature ski slopes for the squirrels. Hunter has a bag of packages at his feet. The train leaves the station slowly, picking up speed. The sky is bright and blue, and some clouds crossing over block the sun and the world gets a little darker, but the clouds pass and the snow sparkles again and the trees look bright and tan and the fields out beyond the wood look bright. We pass under a bridge and the shadow streaks across the car and the train dips down between the two large rock walls with spray painted numbers on some of the rocks, and the pebbled track way looks very brown and rusty and Hunter holds my hand.

"Are you feeling better, love?" He asks.

"Much better. I don't know what it was this morning, but it passed quickly, darling, and I'm better now."

"I'm glad you're better. You're very sweet to come with me even when you're sick."

"I'm not sick, darling. It was just a passing flu or something. I'm not sick, honestly."

The sky disappears and we're in the tunnel and the orange lights come on. The train moves slowly through the tunnel and takes a long while to reach the platform. We climb the stairs and make our way into the main station with the high green ceiling and the lovely stone work and I follow hunter outside into the cold. It's very windy because of the tall buildings. I can't see their tops because they disappear into the smog and cloud and we walk as quickly as we can through the crowd and around the corner onto a side street and pass a steakhouse with large autographed pictures of famous people. The roar from the crowd is loud even on the smaller streets and we walk past the small lumps of melting snow on the edge of the sidewalk by a pile of trash that doesn't smell, and the snow here isn't white or clear; it's black and gray and I try not to step in it. I follow him up past the train station and around to Fifth Avenue and I look in the expensive clothing stores that are all brightly lit with slender mannequins in the windows and I look in the widows of the jewelry stores, but I don't ever like this kind of jewelry. It's the kind that sparkles and has diamonds and is inconvenient. In the street the snow is already turned to slush, and cars drive over it and it sprays against the edge of the sidewalk and along the pants of the people walking closest to the edge. We go into one of the expensive looking clothing stores and he delivers the box to the man in a nice suit with a colorful tie and sleek leather shoes, and we go out and I follow him around the block filled with people and kiss him before he walks into a tall building, lugging that big bag of packages. His back must be so sore. I wait for him in the crowded coffee shop across the street.

It's a lovely shop, and the walls are brick, and the benches and stools and tables around the brick walls are all concrete and the gray concrete looks good against the brick. In the middle of the large space is the counter with several registers to order from, and I order my coffee. They make the coffee well. It's crowded and I lean against the brick wall and sip the hot coffee and the steam warms my face and I wait for a seat to free up. I've almost finished it by time a man in a big gray rain coat stands up and puts his computer in his bag and leaves, and I take his seat and try not to drink the coffee so that I don't finish it and have to leave before Hunter is done.

It's busy, but it's not too loud and I feel warm and pleasant sipping the bitter, creamy coffee. It's good coffee. A man in an apron comes around with a tray of water glasses. He puts one on the table in front of me.

"Thank you."

He nods.

The water is cold and it washes out the coffee flavor. I stare at the drips stuck to the side of the glass. I didn't think it would take this long. I finish the coffee and set it beside the water glass. I look around embarrassed that I'm still sitting. It's not as crowded, I don't think. It should be okay for at least a little longer. My feet are sore and I don't want to stand. I watch the light change against the brick wall. I wish I had a book with me. I should have known to bring a book. I lean back against the concrete bench. Hunter should be done soon.

I feel sick again. I try not to stare at one place for too long. But I might throw up. I should go to the bathroom. But I'll lose the seat. It gets a little better. Maybe it is the flu. I hope it's not. Oh, I hate being sick. But I don't feel like I have the flu. Just nauseated. I hate that word. It could be something else… oh, don't think that. Stop, stop. He won't be happy if it is. I shouldn't hope it, but I do. I so do. Wouldn't it just be wonderful? How can he not think he'll be amazing at it? He'll be so wonderful. Stop, stop. He's not ready yet. I wish he'd just tell me that. I hate when he keeps things like that from me. Oh, but now I'm getting angry and he hasn't done anything. It's probably just the flu. That's all. Just the flu. The concrete table is cold on my hands, and I wish I had more coffee. It's getting very dark outside, and the street lights are on now, and I watch the door every time it opens, but Hunter doesn't come. The people against the walls waiting for a seat aren't happy with me, but they can wait a little longer.

It's almost completely night now, the sky just barely a touch of dark, dark blue, the orange lights on in the windows across the street, the lampposts bright. The door opens with another jingle, oh, and it's him! I wave to him and can't help smiling so big and he waves and I love his tired eyes. He sits down and I hug him and stroke his hair and kiss his scratchy cheek and his lips and he kisses my forehead and my eyelids. The bag over his shoulder is empty now.

"How was it? That took ages."

"I know. I'm so sorry. It was fine. What have you been doing?"

"Oh, nothing. I forgot to bring a book, so I've just been sitting and not wanting to make eye contact when people look at me angry."

"Angry? At you? Impossible."

I smile and he smiles and we leave. We check the train times. We eat sandwiches from the diner across the street from the station. Orange incandescent light bulbs on the red-tiled walls and black and white checkered floor and the sandwiches aren't very nice. But they're cheap. And the bread is soft and I like it alright. We finish and hurry back across the street.

We wait on the steps looking at the constellations pained on the ceiling. I watch the big hands of the clock tick and watch the sign saying delayed flash. He looks so very tired it breaks my heart. I run my fingers over the back of his neck. We board the train. He sleeps. I watch the sky clear of smog and the stars sparkle in the midnight blue and the pale light makes the trim of snow shine on the black branches. We walk home in the cold and the strong wind. He doesn't say anything. I light the fire while he lies down. I undress him and hold him close and feel his heat on my chest and the heat from the fire on my back. Him rolling wakes me up. I put my hand on his shoulder. He hasn't been sleeping.

"Is everything okay, darling?"

"It's fine my love."

I don't know why he does that. It doesn't make sense to me. The nights can be so scary and lonely if you let them, and it's so very hard once the nonsense starts, but it doesn't have to be when we're together. I wish he would talk about it. And then maybe he could sleep better. And in the morning it's already so far away that it doesn't make much sense to talk about it. I never feel lonely in the night with him against me. But maybe it's not the same for him. I try sleep again. But I can't. He's awake. How can I sleep? I sit up.

"What is it, sweet?"

"Just nonsense. More nonsense. I'm sorry to trouble you with it."

"Talk to me. I want all the nonsense that bothers you to bother me, too. I don't want you to be bothered by anything in the whole world. But if you are I want it also."

"You're very sweet, love. I love you so much. But it's not worth it. Let's just sleep."

"It is. It is worth it, darling. If it's bothering you it is worth it."

"You're too sweet, love."

"Is it more about the war? It's about the war, isn't it? You want to go off and join it, don't you?"

"It's not about the war. Sometimes it is, but it's not. It's about it all. I just feel sick about it all; the war is part of it, I guess."

"You want to go off and join, don't you?"

"I don't. I hate war. I hate it. But I feel so helpless with it going on all the time. Doesn't it bother you at all?"

"I don't know, darling. I don't think it does. I never really think about it going on, but you're very sweet and brave to think about it."

"It's nonsense, I don't want you worrying about it, love. It's good it doesn't bother you. And I'm not going to go off and join the war. I hate war. I just want it to be over. I don't like what the papers say is happening."

"I know, darling. You shouldn't read them."

"I just feel useless. So useless."

"But there's no use in you going off to join the war. There's no use in that either. You have me."

"I know, my love. I'd never leave you."

"But sometimes you don't say what you mean. I know you want something but you say you don't. And that scares me a lot, darling."

"I don't do that, love. I'd tell you if I wanted to join. I really don't."

"It's not even just this. It's lots of little things. You never tell me what you really want. And then I don't know what you really want anymore."

"That's not fair. I don't keep things from you. That's not fair."

Oh, I didn't mean to start this. I just wanted to make him feel better, and now I'm making him feel worse. I can tell he's getting irritated. His breathing his shallower. "I'm sorry darling. I just want you to have everything you want. That's all."

"You're sweet. I'd tell you if there was something."

"Okay darling. I believe you. I just get scared that sometimes maybe you don't mean it. And that I'm forcing it on you. And we never have to if you don't want to."

"It's okay, my love. Let's go back to sleep. It's all nonsense, really."

"All right, sweet. But if it bothers you more in the night, wake me up. I don't want you to be bothered again without me."

I feel sleep coming on. My eyes are heavy. I wake up feeling a little sick. The frogs are belching loudly outside. The crickets creaking. I lie on my back and stare at the shadows on the ceiling. It's not quite night anymore, but it's not morning yet. It's that gray time when all, itself waking, looks alien, as if I'm seeing it for the first time before it takes form in the light. He didn't wake me up. Maybe it didn't bother him anymore. But I bet it did. He's very sweet not to wake me, but I wish he would. And I know he wants to go off and join up with the army, too, but he won't say so. I wish he would just tell me what he wants. I hate guessing. I would hate it if he did join, though. But I wish he would just tell me.

He's sleeping heavily. I'm glad he's sleeping. And he looks so peaceful. I want to touch his face, he looks so soft. But I shouldn't. That would wake him, and he should sleep. My stomach turns over and I feel very sick all of a sudden. It turns again and I hurry out of bed and to the bathroom and he hears me and comes over and covers me in a blanket. I get the chills and my stomach turns and up it comes and the sound of it hitting the water makes me feel gross. He runs his fingers through my hair and sits next to me on the cold tiles. I feel a cold sweat on the back of my neck. And my hairs stand on end. It passes and the feeling is gone and I feel better.

"Are you alright, love?"

"I'm fine, I think. I'm not sure what that was. But I feel better now, I think."

He sits with me awhile, running his fingers through my hair. It come back and my stomach turns again. He looks so worried.

"I'm sorry, darling."

"Don't be sorry, love. I'm sorry."

It's gone again and I feel better and we go back to bed. The light is stronger now and the gray is gone and his hands are soft through my hair.

"What's going on with you?"

"I'm not sure, darling. Sorry to wake you."

"Don't be sorry. I hope you're alight. Do you want to go see a doctor?"

"No, sweetie, I'm feeling much better now. Maybe some breakfast will be good for me. What time do you have to go?"

"I won't go if you're still feeling this way."

"I'm feeling much better already, honestly. I don't feel sick at all, now."

"I don't know, love. I think you're sick with something."

"I'm really okay, darling." Oh, but I think it is. It really could be. But I can't tell him. He won't be happy. Maybe he will. I'm so excited I could burst, but I can't tell him. Not yet. Maybe later. Maybe if we go for a walk and we're both in good moods, maybe then I'll tell him. But I'm sure it is, now. I'm sure of it. And everything looks so lovely, and the light is coming in beautifully through the kitchen window and glowing in the wood and the wood looks so pale and nice and strong. It's a very fine table, a lovely table. He still looks worried, but I can't tell him yet. Maybe later. I'll tell him later.

We eat a little breakfast, but I can't keep it down and I know that will scare him more.

"I'm going to call in sick today, love. I don't like the thought of leaving you here when you're sick." Oh, that would be so lovely. A whole day together. But he shouldn't. He can't do that.

"Don't, darling. Honestly, please don't."

He kisses the top of my head. "It's okay, love. It's the right thing." He calls and I hear him talking. He sits back down beside me beside the toilet. But I feel better now.

"Do you want to go for a walk? That could be nice."

"Love, you should stay in bed. I can make you soup or something. But let's not walk today. Just rest."

Oh, it's so wonderful that he's not going in. I just want to spend the whole day by the river with him. But he looks so concerned. I lie in bed and he lies with me, and I feel fine and so happy. I kiss him and he looks at me with loving eyes but concerned eyes.

The afternoon is chilly and the chill is nice and I feel great and am itching to go to the river. He's so sweet to stay today. He's the sweetest man in the whole world.

"I think a walk would be nice, darling. I haven't felt sick in hours. And I think it would feel really nice."

He doesn't like it. I can tell. But he doesn't say anything. So I kiss him and start getting dressed.

"Are you sure, love?"

"Absolutely sure, darling." He follows me down the hill towards the train station. At the bottom we walk along the edge of the wide road that cuts through the wood at the foot of the cliff and turn off when we see the small town and walk through the town. There are big parking lots in front of most of the stores and people are going about their business, and grocery shopping, and sitting in the windows of the small coffee shops looking out - and I almost wave to them. I'm so happy to see them. They look kind enough. It's a very lovely town and the light from the clear blue sky makes it look very fine, and on the other side we come to the wood and in the wood the ground is crunching under our feet from the cold and we walk through the wood a long ways until we hear it and go down and sit by the damp bank of the river. The water is lower today. The tops of the rocks sticking out over the silvery blue water are dry. We sit and lean back into the wet dirt and he puts his arm around me and I put my head on his chest. The small sound of the water against the rock and pebbles is so beautiful and gentle. The air is so clean. Oh, a deer. On the crest of the far bank. It stands in the light and we watch it, it's strong neck and smooth brown hairs and large black nose, and I can see its breath coming from its nose, and its small ears. It's very beautiful and sacred and the light makes the white spots on its back glow bright against its brown coat. It leaps away, and I lean against him and feel very good and very healthy and strong and excited. The sound of the river is wonderful, and the light shimmers in the ripples around the rocks. and it's really happening. I think. I hope. I put my hand on my belly. Oh, I bet it's a girl.

"I don't think I'm sick." I say.

"What do you think it is, love?"

"Oh, don't be mad, darling. I'm so very happy."

"Mad about what?"

"Just promise, darling. Promise you won't be mad."

"I promise, love. What's going on with you?"

"I think I'm pregnant, darling."

He's quiet, and I'm so worried he's frustrated, but he's smiling, and his eyes are bright, and he kisses me and holds me so tight and the lets go and looks concerned and I giggle.

"It's okay. You can hold me tight. It won't hurt her."

And he holds me tight again and he's not mad at all at all, or at least he's not telling me. He talks very quickly and his eyes are bright and shining and blue, so blue, and he says he's so happy and that makes me so happy, and that he should have known because of how I was glowing and that he never believed that a woman could glow, but that he had heard they do when they're pregnant, and that I was glowing and that he should have known, and he kisses me and smiles so big. Oh, I love that smile. It's gone of anything pained or stale, and just as free and innocent as when we first met. He says he's so happy and holds me tight again.

"Are you, darling? I know you wanted to wait. You did, didn't you?"

"I wouldn't ever want anything else. Not for the whole wide world, love. I'm happier than I've ever been."

"Really, darling? Don't say it if you don't mean it. Oh, don't say it if you don't mean it, darling, I must know. Really, I must know."

"I have never been happier, love. I don't think I could be happier than I am now. I am the luckiest man in the world."

He holds me tight and kisses me all over and I kiss him and we're very happy together. And the river is so nice and the sound fills me.

"You should go in today, darling. You really don't need to stay."

"Are you kidding? I couldn't possibly leave your side. Not today. Oh, my love, I'm so happy. And so happy to be here. And you'll have to stop coming in, won't you? That smog isn't good for it."

I can't even tell how big I'm smiling, but I know it's big because my cheeks are hurting, but I can't stop. And he's right, isn't he? Oh, I shouldn't have gone in at all. But I didn't know. Oh, I hope she's okay. She must be. She really must be. I won't go anymore. Just in case. But then he'll be all alone. Oh, that's sad too. But he looks so happy, and his eyes are wet, and his smile is so big and his dimples are especially deep and especially cute. And I already miss him thinking of him going in by himself.

And the missing him is terrible. The days are so long and the house is so empty while he's in the City. But when he gets home the world is bright again. And every day he says my belly looks bigger. But I miss him terribly when he's gone. At least she's here with me. Ouch. That was your hardest kick yet.

"Calm down, please."

I giggle remembering how squeamish he gets when he feels her kick.

I sit in the chair with the sun setting and making the pile of snow on the driveway look fiery. The wind pulls my hair and ruffles the bare branches of the oak. The colors in the sky are striking and rich and deep. I guess that's the only nice part to the smog spreading this far up. I still hate it. But I'm sure it'll go away once they start collecting trash again. There he is. My heart tickles. He walks with his feet out-turned and his shoulders slouching, and oh, I love him so much. I wonder if she'll walk like that. He smiles that tired smile, but it's different. It's all happy now. Nothing more hiding back there. And the golden light looks so nice on his face. He sits in the chair with me and strokes my hair.

"Aren't we happy, darling? Isn't it wonderful?"

"I've never been happier. I don't think I could handle being any happier, love. You've made me so happy. And I love you."

"I love you, too, darling. And nothing can spoil this, can it? Nothing. Not anything in the whole world, and I love you, and you love me, and we have our family, darling. We have our family."

"We do, my love."

We watch the orange sky and the streaking plum colored clouds and the pink wisps and the golden glow against the mountain. The few birds still hanging around in the early winter chill chirp goodnight. The crickets start to reply. I feel him breathing against me. It's so wonderful up here. Night settles in and the few starts come out. It gets cold, but I don't want to go in yet. The snow piles look blue and eerie. The shoveled driveway looks black.

It's too cold and windy and we go in. We make the fire together and lie in each other's arms with the big blanket over us and the warmth and the light flickering against our faces. So happy. So wonderfully happy. This is how I hope it always is. Nothing lurking behind his eyes anymore. No more soon. It's all now. And it's so wonderfully wonderful. How lucky we are. He puts his hand on my belly and I put my hand on the top of his, and he looks at me with that look he's just started. It's not piercing because it's not sharp, but it reaches far into me and holds in it the warmth of a loving father, as if he's looking right down onto her for the first time. I love him. Unconditionally. Truly. Oh, I love him. He kisses me. We fall asleep in each other's arms.

Chapter Thirty-Eight

The bottle of whisky is almost empty now. But there's a bit left. And it looks amber colored under the orange streetlights. The wind is cold, but I can't feel it very much. I'm walking fast, and hard, and my feet are kicking up sludge and my head is spinning a little and the lights look blurry. The buildings all look the same now. And I walk quickly down the avenue and turn back towards my apartment. It'll start getting light soon, I think. I've been out here for a while, I think. I pass another bar, but it's closed, and the pizza place next to it is closed and the metal grate is pulled down over the windows and the metal looks rusty.

Another church, but this one isn't lit. Maybe it's too late. And a park next to it. With a short iron gate and fence around it. The bushes are nothing more than twigs now, and there are leaves in the melting snow under the bare trees. The brick walkway looks dark and wet and the only light comes from the small lamppost at the entrance. Past it a car drives slow, it's headlights white and bright, sweeping across the small park and they light up the metal statue in the middle surrounded by wooden benches. Across the street the buildings have old looking fire escapes and on one of them there's a row of plotted plants.

Up ahead at a bus stop a tall woman stands in the wind, her red hair looks especially red in the orange light, and she holds her coat around her tightly. She's thin. And pretty. And I hate her already. And she turns a little and I can see the freckles on her nose and her bright round eyes and her lips. Full lips. And I almost stumble, but I don't, and I feel dizzier. I can see her breath in the air and the curves of her body though the coat and her thin legs showing under her tight jeans. She hasn't seen me yet and I lean against the brick wall by the alley behind her and drink and drink her in, and feel angry. And hot. The church back down the street is in shadows and is hard to distinguish against the dark, smoggy sky. The bust stop looks gray. The road and the slush black, the snow drifts brown. Her hair is the only thing bright. Bright red.

She stands next to the metal post with the bus schedule on it and looks down the street, but there's nothing coming. And the wind is loud and hard, and her hair is lashing out. It's curly, and red, and long. I drink again and put the bottle back in the pocket of my jacket. I can't taste it now. It just tastes like water, and I'm already drunk. I breathe deep and feel the cold on my lungs and chest and it feels good because I feel hot. And I don't taste the trash too badly. She walks back and forth next to the pole. Her hands in her pockets and her thin legs taking large steps and her head high. She's very pretty. And I hate her for that. Her neck is thin, and shadowy, and her hair falls down around it when the wind stops for a second, but then it starts again and picks up the red curls. I hate her for being pretty. And she'll always be pretty. And beautiful. And she'll have whatever she wants. And take whatever she can. Which is everything. And she'll never know. Never know how meaningless she is.

The wind blows her perfume to me and I smell it and breathe deep and it smells sweet and like peppermint and makes my chest pound very hard and my hands feel hot and moist. And the lights look blurry and have large trails and large rings around them, and I feel dizzy. And I'm walking towards her. She's beautiful. So beautiful. And her neck is thin and smooth, and I smell her peppermint perfume and my head is spinning. She needs to know. She needs to know. I'm close enough to touch her now, but the wind is loud, and she didn't hear me and she's still looking down the street. There's no bus. Or cars. Or people. It's empty. And the alley behind us is dark. Very dark. And her peppermint perfume. And her red, curly red hair. She needs to know. That she's not important. That she means nothing. I hate her. She needs to know that. She needs to know. My arms are around her and she screams into my hand and jumps a little, which scares me, and I pull her hard into me. And back. Back into the alley and the darkness and she's kicking and trying to scream, and her breath is hot on my hand and her lips are soft and I push her into the bricks. Hard. And she sputters and coughs. And I feel hot. And angry. And her eyes are bright even in the dark alley and her neck is soft. So soft. And I squeeze, and she coughs and tries to scream. And I breathe deep her perfume. She's even prettier than I thought. I hear her sputter. And strain. And the veins are showing in her forehead. I can see them in the shadows. She kicks, and I push harder and squeeze harder and she doesn't kick as hard and there's cardboard under my feet and I kick it back and away. Her neck is soft, and her breath is warm on my palm. I hear the rats squeak and scurry behind us.

Chapter Thirty-Nine

The sun is coming up. And the sky is looking a little grayer and the buildings are looking more pale and the streetlights are turning off and the streets are filling with people and cars and noise. It's cold. But I'm too awake to go inside. And I'm still drunk. And I don't feel angry anymore. I feel calm. I breathe, and the trash still makes the air sour but the cold feels good to breathe deep. Her breath was sour too. Her perfume like peppermint. Her eyes were bright even in the shadows. I feel good and calm and only a little drunk. Mostly just good. And the people aren't so bad. The slush in the streets looks pale and gray and there're still some dirty white peaks where the snow hasn't completely melted.

My fingers toy with the earring in my jacket pocket. It clicks lightly against the almost empty whisky bottle. It's a small earring. A silver hoop. I look at it. My fingers are cold and numb, and the hoop looks small between my thumb and finger. It shines in the morning light, but it's not polished and looks cloudy. A small fleck of dried blood near the clasp. I scratch it off and put it away. Cars honk. People shout over each other and talk loudly on their phones and push past me.

Most of them in suits. Their shoes clack on the cold ground and kick up slush. My face is cold and stiff, and the wind is strong, but it's not as strong as it was earlier. The glass in the building ahead looks black in the gray light. Except on the lower floors where the lights are on already. Thick billows of white steam push up through the orange and white construction cone. A subway rattles under the ground. People shout.

I walk back towards my apartment, but I'm a long way away still. And I pass a particularly sour smelling pile of trash with the black plastic stretched so thin it looks gray. And some of them are torn open in places and brown pulpy looking grime is pouring out. I walk in the thickening crowd.

Exchange Place leads back to my apartment, past a deli with flowers out front. Most of them look withered and droop. The roses especially, they look pathetic. The edges are browning. The white ones - whatever they're called - they still look a little fresh. A small man with a thick winter cap stands behind the plastic screen cutting the stems off a bouquet. The sidewalk in front smells sweet and like the cheap coffee inside. The breaks of a large diesel truck squeak, and the truck rumbles at the red light and all I smell now is the diesel. I stop and go in to buy more whisky. I pay and leave and finish off what's left of the bottle in my pocket. I throw it away in one of the smaller looking mounds of trash on the sidewalk. The stone steps up to my apartment building under the yellow sign with the address have been washed since I went out and they're still damp and look dark and smell like wet stone and bleach. The revolving doors have been cleaned, too, and the glass looks clear. The same doorman's behind the counter, still watching TV. I can hear the sound from the small TV well in the large, high-ceilinged, marble room.

"Good morning, sir." He says. His eyes droop, and his white shirt and black vest and black tie all look too big for him. My shoes squeak on the marble floor. It's always hot in the lobby. I open the new whisky in the elevator and start it off. She's waiting by my door. I forget her name. Something with a 'K' sound. Cunningham? She has another brown bag of groceries in her arms. Plump hands. Small hands. And a small almost round face. I put the bottle back in my pocket. It clicks against the earring.

"Good morning, dear. You're out early again." She says and steps towards me. She's short. And plump. And her eyebrows are picked thin. "It's good to see you getting outside."

She lets us into the apartment. I wish they didn't give her a key. I lock it behind us. Her hair is cut short to her ears. She sets the bag on the marble counter and her leather purse, too. "How are you?" She says.

"Good." She starts unloading the vegetables into the fridge. And removing the ones I never ate. They look rotten and brown and droop.

"What did you do this morning so early?"

"I walked."

"Good for you. It's good to get out. Help me with this, dear." She says. I take the bundle of old and sagging carrots from her and drop them into the garbage. I wash my hands. The water is cold. She smiles and her dirty-blond hair sways across her forehead. It bulges out over her ears. Like from the fifties or something. She has silver hoop earrings, too. Hers are larger and look clean and shine. I can't even fit my little finger through the one in my pocket. The light coming through the window makes the silver refrigerator door shine, and light streaks across it as she closes it. She holds herself upright and rigid. She's short and her hips are wide, and her legs are plump, and she looks disproportionate.

"So, what now?" She asks. She walks out of the kitchen and sits on the stool on the other side of the marble-topped counter, folding the brown paper bag.

"What are you going to do with yourself?"

"Nothing."

"Well, you can't do nothing." She says and looks at me with her small eyes.

I open the door to the freezer and look in and the cold comes out. It's empty. I close it.

"What was there before the army?" She asks. "What did you used to like doing?" I poke my finger into the tip of the earring in my pocket until it stings.

"Nothing."

"Well that's no help."

"I'm fine."

"Of course, you are, dear. What do your parents do?"

"Nothing."

"They're retired?"

"I don't know."

"What did they do?"

"Nothing important."

"Alright. How about your brothers? Your file says two?"

"They don't do anything either."

"You have to have wanted something else. And you can't just do nothing. What about when you were a kid."

"I don't know."

"Did you ever want to be an astronaut? Or a fireman, or a doctor, or something? My kids want to be astronauts. The both of them. Running around with their spaceships held high and making sounds. Of course, the one follows the other. First it was submarines."

"A doctor."

"That's great. Good for you. You wanted to help people. Of course, you did. You're such a good boy."

"I wanted to be a surgeon."

"Well that's a fine thing to be, dear."

"I don't think so."

"There's plenty you can do. We can get you volunteering in a hospital. That will be very fine. They'll love to see that. And it won't be nothing of your time."

"I'm fine."

"Of course. Of course, you are, dear." She takes a notebook out of her brown leather purse and jots a couple notes down and then closes it and looks up at me, fiddling with the pen still. "You know something funny? My little ones can't stand hospitals. Can't stand the smell of them. And you know what else, dear? I can't either. I wonder if that's genetic. They should do a test for that. But we'll get you all set up. A very fine thing for you to do, dear. Very fine, indeed. What a good boy you are. Such a good boy. Of course, you come back from that horrible place and want to help people. You're such a good boy."

She stands up and puts her things back into her purse and looks through it and drapes it over her shoulder.

"Are you doing alright, dear?" She asks.

"I'm fine."

"Of course. Of course, you are. You're such a good boy. But I'm here if you ever want to talk with anyone about anything. You're such a good boy."

We shake hands. Her little plump hands. Her straight and ridged posture. Her small eyes. They glow hazel in the gray morning light. Her eyes are bright. Not cloudy like hers got. Surprisingly cloudy and gray. My hand still smells sweet. And like peppermint. She leaves the folded brown paper bag at the foot of the counter.

"It's always nice to see you, dear. It's so very nice to see you. You're such a good boy. Of course, you come back and want to help people. Such a good boy, dear."

I lock the door behind her and take another big sip of the whisky and sit on the bed and look at the earring. It's small. It was easier than I thought it would be. To pull it out. Her red hair. Her thin lips. And thin legs. Strong legs. And peppermint. I smell my hand. I breathe deep and feel good. I shouldn't feel good. But I do. I feel really good, and calm and I lie back. The pillow is soft, and the bed is soft, and it'll take a while before I get used to it, but it feels good on my head. I touch my fingers to the side of my cheek where the scar is. It doesn't hurt. Not at all. I trace it with the little hoop earring. My heart beats quickly and hard. I feel good. And calm. And I breathe deep and put the earring on the bed-side table and close my eyes. I smell my hand. The stretch of skin between my thumb and first finger, that's where it smells most like her. Like peppermint. I wonder what this part's called. This stretch of skin. I breathe deep and feel good.

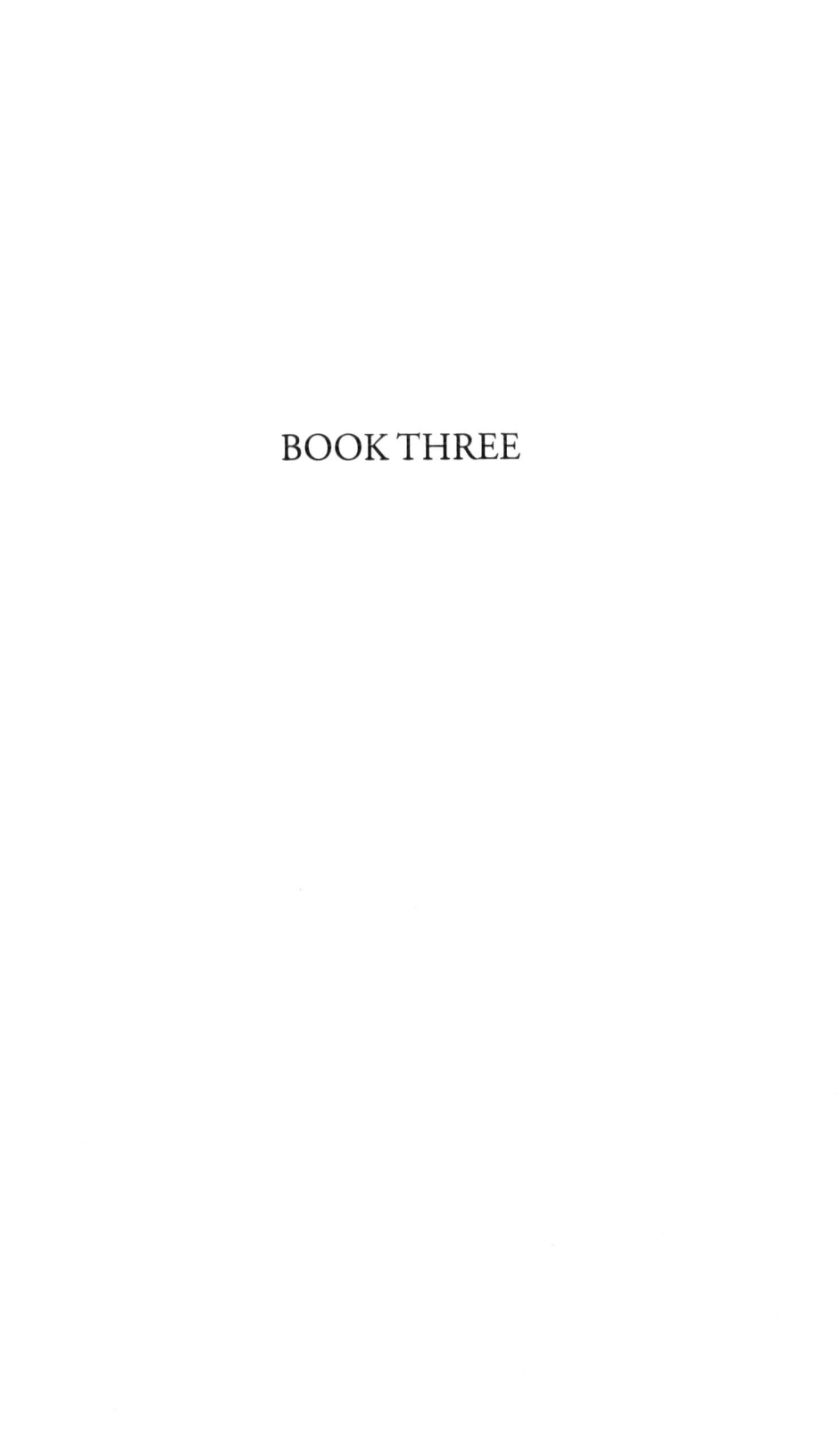

BOOK THREE

Chapter Forty

It's hot in here. My skin itches and my eyes feel heavy and the blankets are heavy, and the air is thick. I kick off the heavy blanket, but I miss its weight, and my damp skin chills. The white walls look pale and blue in the morning light coming through the blinds. I close my eyes. Sleep. Back to the dream. The same stupid dream. Every night. Where was I? Mom in the kitchen. And Steve's there, too. By the screen door. And it's bright, but I think it's night outside, and the wood floor is bright and scratched and I'm leaving. Going. Somewhere. Where was it? Upstairs, I think. But there are two staircases. Leading up and away from each other. Two stairs. It's hot in here. And my skin itches and I roll over. Streaks of light from the cars on the street cross the ceiling. The air is hot and muggy. I don't usually wake up before my alarm. It must be the heater.

I stand. Everything looks blurry. The wood floor of my apartment is cold on my feet. The air is nice on my hot skin. I like mornings. They're quiet. And calm. I like the quiet. I can hear the hum from the cars down there. Humming and fading away and then coming closer and fading away again. Light pokes through the sides of the blinds and the streak crosses my arm and the hairs on my arms glint where the light comes across them. I dress.

The small apartment with the white walls, bare walls, and the single painting over the desk behind the couch with the leather chair that's drooping in the middle because it's losing its screws. The couch, the brown couch in the middle of the room looking at the small TV on the dusty glass coffee table. The bed with dark blue sheets. A muted version of it all. Dull. So dull. And gray. And pale blue. And this checkered shirt is hard to button. My fingers feel numb. But it's a nice shirt. I look good in it. Maybe someone will like it, and she'll smile, and I'll smile back. I don't want to go to class. I want to sleep. My eyes feel heavy. I brush my teeth. The water is cold. Even my reflection looks tired. And shadowy. And blurry. Like there's two of me. I'm tired.

I slouch into the cushions of the sofa and turn on the TV. The sound is off, and the screen is bright and the white light stings my eyes and makes the dust on glass table look gray and grainy. The light makes the walls look ghostly and the ceiling look pale and ghostly. I tie my shoes and stare. The small bonsai tree on the glass table looks ghostly, too, and prickly, and the leaves are brown. I haven't watered it in days. I should do that. Later. The little porcelain fisherman standing in the soil with a small wood fish on an invisible string that swings lightly over a ceramic bowl. The bowl is empty. And the soil looks dry. The light from the TV makes it all look pale, and flat. I feel tired. I need more sleep. Steve always said to get more sleep. At least eight hours, he said. But these classes are so early, and they give so much work, and then there's always a test, and I have to stay up so late studying, and then wake up so early again. And I should go to class. But I'm not in a hurry. My alarm hasn't gone off yet, even. I'm tired. Always tired.

I'm complaining. I shouldn't complain. Don't do that. It'll get better. Better than dull. Dull and unimportant. And he'd say he told me so if he knew I thought like this. But no. He's wrong. It'll get better. And at least it's different from what he wanted. I'm glad he was so upset by it and so red in the face and I could see the veins in his neck and the pink birthmark over his eye looked especially pink. And I said being a doctor is something important and that he doesn't know anything important and that I'm going to be important and he said I was going to start therapy and that I'd understand when I grow up and hopefully it won't be too late by then. I feel hot. The screen is bright. It'll get better.

The edges of the blinds start to look a little golden with the rising sun. I sink deeper into the cushiony couch and breathe, and the air feels muggy. The advertisement for the marines is just ending. A tall man on a red rock mountain. Sweating. He looks proud. His sweat pants and tank-top fade into full military attire with a sword and everything, and medals, and the hat and white gloves. And he looks proud. And his face fades into the mountain. *The Marines. The Few. The Proud.* I stand and groan and my alarm goes off and I silence it and turn off the TV and turn off the heater and pick up my backpack and jacket and leave. I don't want to go to class. The hallway is bright with the white lights overhead and quiet. Outside is cold. And noisy. And I zip up my jacket and duck my head into the wind. My backpack is heavy and makes my back ache.

The pool hall across the street is open, but there's no one inside and all the pool tables look brightly lit and green and I walk past it and past the spray-painted brick wall. Maybe it's not worth it. The studying. The hours and weeks and months of working and studying and not sleeping enough. And it's only the beginning. But I'm just tired. And it'll be good once it's done and I'm a doctor and he'll choke on his words. Good and important. Doctor Roth.

The wind hits hard on the avenue and cold, and I cross the street before the light changes and pass the coffee shop that smells like burnt coffee and the halal cart that smells like meat cooking and the smoke from the meat is thick and comes out under the metal awning. The man cooking the meat looks sleepy too. It's freezing. I wish it would snow already. The cold is good, and the snow is better, and Steve doesn't like the cold or the snow. I like it. It's good that it's cold.

But not now. I wish I was back in bed and it was warm and I would be staring at the white walls, pale, and bare, and I should put things on them. She wanted me to. She always complained about it. So empty, she said. And white and pale and gray. She'd decorate them.

I wait for the taxis to pass. The yellow paint shines in the young light. The sun comes through between the buildings in the crisp air and cuts sharply a patch of pale cobblestones out of the blue shadows. I wish there were more streets like this. And that it was longer than two blocks. It's like I imagine it was a long time ago, when the world was more than the picture of excitement. It's fitting, in a way. Just two blocks of cobblestones, a picture in a picture of when something meant anything. I cross and walk under the construction scaffolding with men overhead hammering and calling to each other, and I smell the smoke from their cigarettes. I walk over the grate above a subway and hear it rattling below and warm air that smells sour comes up.

I stand in line to get into the large lecture hall. We're all too early, and it's cold, but we have to wait. I should have waited in bed. No one talks. The sounds of morning traffic and the wind and the pigeons. Inside, the security guard doesn't look at us. Sitting at his podium and looking at his watch. My nose starts to sting from cold. Starts to numb. I shift impatiently. Finally, he stands and walks slowly to us and unlocks the door. I show him my ID as we pass. Down the large staircase, into the brightly lit, high-ceilinged, rosewood room and the hundreds of bright, red-cushioned chairs. I find my regular seat and wait, staring at my notes blankly. The professor comes in and takes off his jacket and takes out his dry-erase markers and starts to lecture.

Chapter Forty-One

The subway rattles. Rocking back and forth. I'm tired. One strap of my backpack hangs across my knee. I hold my head up with my fist and lean heavily on my elbow. I yawn, and my eyes water and I blink away the water. Almost home. I want to sleep. Or watch TV. The books are heavy in the bag. The blue plastic seats are smooth, but they don't look very clean. The silver poles shine in the bright white subway lighting. The advertisements overhead. The family across from me. My backpack is heavy and pulls on my leg as the train rocks.

The family sitting across from me is quiet. The boy, sandwiched between the two parents. The only one with his eyes open. Wide open. He looks from mom to dad. Up at them. His legs don't touch the floor and he swings them. Something spilled on the floor and dried under his seat. He twists the corner of his yellow shirt and creases the embossed picture of a skateboarder. The fat man eating sunflower seeds next to me spits the shells back into the bag. One misses and lands near my shoe. Gross.

In the far corner of the subway, an old lady in layers of dirty sweaters and coats and scarves and gloves with trash bags full of more clothes. She's very wrinkly. Her cheeks are creased, and the creases are deep and around her eyes and across her forehead. Her pale thin hands tremble holding the trash bags. She's also holding a doll. It used to have hair. It's dirty too. She's mumbling to herself. Most of her front teeth are missing. Her lips are thin, and one eye is squinting. The subway rocks back and forth. Water on the floor rolls quietly towards my shoe. I wiggle my feet away. The shell of the sunflower seed floats and drifts about in the water. The wrinkly old lady coughs and mutters.

I close my eyes. Maybe I'll take a nap when I get back. I shouldn't. I have to work. And review my notes from today. He covered a lot today. The room smelled like dry erase markers by the end of lecture. And bright red seats and bright yellow lights and my hand hurts from writing so much. I'll review the notes. And then read the chapter. And then nap. And eat. I forgot to eat. I need to eat first. I'm hungry. The fat man spits more shells into the bag. He grunts and sits up straight. And slouches back again. His bald head is shiny.

The train screeches as it stops. And pulls me into the fat man.

"Sorry." I say and stand, hanging my bag over my shoulder. It's heavy.

The boy is still swinging his legs and chewing on the collar of his shirt. And the dad is showing him pictures on the camera that's on a string around his neck.

I watch my feet. The white tiles of the platform are dirty. So are the rails of the of the turnstile. I push through, and they click as they spin and walking up the stairs I feel the cold wind pushing me back. I pull my jacket tighter around me. A dump-truck beeps backing up and I smell the trash. It smells bad and sour and I try not to breathe too much. A jackhammer thumps and gruff men in bright vests holding clipboards and all of them with beards, they shout over the noise to the other men with the jackhammers and the shovels and point. The middle of the street is fenced off around them. Them, and the large chunks of pavement and dirt and orange and yellow safety barricades. Always under construction. Unfinished. Always. And messy. It's ugly. And noisy. And they're building something sleek, probably. Something modern. I like the old brick buildings that are only a couple of stories high. The ones with the red bricks and the old fire-escapes. Everything is all glass and metal now. And tall. Really tall. At least in the City. I should move. Just outside. It's quieter out there too. And I can breathe. And the sky is large and wide. That would be nice. I should move. When the semester ends maybe. And I don't have to wake up so early anymore. And I won't have to commute. That would be nice. This is a nice area, too, Steve said. And expensive. And where he used to live. And that I would like it. And he doesn't complain about the rent. And it's close to school. And then I said I wanted to be a doctor. And he said I was ignorant. Or I'd become ignorant. Close-minded; that's what he said. And I said he was close-minded. And he called me ungrateful. And that if I wanted to be independent I could pay my own rent, but he didn't mean it. I'm not ungrateful.

The sky is bright. And blue. And clear. It makes the glass shine, and it looks like it should be summer. But it's cold. And the trees don't have leaves on them. And everyone's wearing a jacket. But the sun makes the sidewalk look bright. And then I hear a bird. Or maybe it's just the squeak of a car. The jackhammering is loud, and I cover my ears as I walk by it. I cross the street. The awning of my apartment is big and has gold numbers on it. *284.* The railings inside are gold, too, and the light makes them sparkle. The tiled floor is brown and looks gold. And it's warm. I unzip my jacket. My nose tingles, thawing, and looks red in the large mirror.

I stare at my phone in the elevator. It's bright. My hallway is ugly. And the sea green rug is polka dot and the brown polka dots make it look dirty, and the walls are brown and make the rug look especially dirty. And the lights are bright and white and always on, so the hallway always looks the same. The same color. The same dirty green and brown. My back hurts. I hang my backpack on my other shoulder. My phone beeps. I open the door to my apartment. The key sticks in the lock and I jiggle it and it comes loose and I close the door and slide the metal chain latch across it. I breathe. It's dim and pale and makes me feel more tired. I should open the blinds. I put my bag by the door and sit down at the desk in the slouching leather chair. It's dark. I don't want to work. I want to sleep.

I stare at my phone. Charlotte. I wish she'd call. Or even text. But an email? Her black hair makes her green eyes shine. And she's thin and curvy and taller than Abbey, and really pretty. And kisses me on the cheek and hugs me for too long and calls us friends. Her email is long. Probably wants help with something. At the bottom she says: Lunch? Don't do it. She's not interested. She'll cancel. I erase it.

I open the note book. It's too dark to see the pencil marks. The paper looks blue and pale. And the phone was bright so everything else looks especially dark. I should open the blinds. And I should respond to her. She might actually want to get lunch. That would be nice. Finally. She probably doesn't. Maybe she does. A siren passes on the street and fades. I call her. It rings. She doesn't pick up and I hang up. Pointless. It's never going to happen. But she always plays along. And smiles at me too long. And stares at me. And it seems like it's possible. Like holding sand. Like trying to hold sand. I like that. I write it down in the margins of the pale blue-looking paper. Like trying to hold sand. I scribble it out. Stupid.

The desk is smooth. The lamp on the right is crooked and I fix it so that it's at a right angle to the corner of the desk. The light from outside glows at the edges of the blinds. But it's a paler light. Bluer. Not golden white like this morning. It's getting late. And I should do work before it gets too late and I have to stay up all night and wake up early tomorrow. I'm already tired. I need sleep. And food. I stand and walk to the kitchen. It's still dark and the light from the fridge is dim. Butter on the shelf. Milk in the door. Probably sour. Empty, white racks and drawers. And yogurt. I take the yogurt. I should go grocery shopping. The front of the fridge is bare and white like the walls, but it's yellower. The red tiles on the floor are cracking and dusty and the walls and cabinets are all painted white. I sit on the couch and eat the yogurt. It's tart and bitter and I don't like it very much. It's very plain. The bonsai tree still looks like it's dying. But the couch is comfortable. I put the spoon in the sink and throw the container away.

The jackhammering starts again. I go to the window and open the blinds. The sun isn't as bright as it was, and the sky is darker too, but it's not sunset yet. Everything just looks faded. And dim. And the street looks messy with fences and traffic and chunks of pavement and jackhammers and shovels. Messy. Mom doesn't like it either. What a mess down there, she pointed and Steve ignored her. She would have swept the sidewalk if she'd had a broom, I bet. Always clean. Ordered. And in their hotel room the clothes folded and put into the drawers and hung up in the closet. Moved in. It's more comfortable that way, she said. I don't think anyone else does that. All her pills lined up on the bathroom counter in little boxes. Shorter than Steve by a lot, but she holds herself well. Strongly. Proudly. Well, she used to. I didn't like it. Made me feel strained looking at her. But I miss it now. She looked almost as tall as him.

I should work. I sit again. I can see what I wrote, now. Scribbles. I'm tired. God, it used to be better than this. Exciting at least, if not interesting. But how quickly interest fades when born of novelty. Like starting a fire with twigs but forgetting to put a dry log on top. Poetry was better. But he said it had to be Politics. Politics and law. And then I said medicine. And he still said politics. I miss poetry.

The epoxide opens. 1) acids, 2) bases. Differente! Acid first protonates. Postive charge unequal. Arrow. *Positive charge unequal.* Star. I can't remember this. But I should. I need to. This one's important. I trace over the star. He said something about it. Something…Muffled and his beard was wet today, and his hair was wet and curly and gray. Dry-erase markers sticking out of each knuckle. Different colors. He always looks at his feet when he talks to us. *Positive charge unequal.* What did he say? Unequal. I'm tired. I should nap. And eat. And eat and watch TV. And then work. That sounds nice. After this, though. My eyes follow the notes again. But I'm looking more at how the light shines along the gray pencil marks than what the marks mean. I read again. *Therefore, longer bond = weaker.* Arrow. Exclamation mark. I don't know what he said. I wasn't listening. The pretty girl a couple rows in front wasn't there today.

The jackhammer is distracting. The brick building across the street looks pink and the sky looks pink and the glass shimmers because the sun hits it directly. My floor looks a little pink too. And the white walls look a little pink. And further out other buildings look bright and brown and the white parts look a little pink too. The paper in front of me, too, and the pencil marks are dull and silvery and pink. I retrace the arrows with my pencil. My eyes feel heavy and tired. And *The epoxide opens.* What are epoxides, again?

It didn't used to be hard. Not this hard. I lean back and slouch and my back hurts and I breathe. Doctor Roth. I want that. To be a doctor. I'll be a good doctor. And it sounds important. And I won't feel so useless and small and tired. It just takes time. That doesn't feel comforting. So much time. And what if it's a waste? I close my eyes. What if it's a waste and I just waste time and then I don't have any more time and then I'm stuck. And not important. My eyes burn, and I can't focus and I stare out the window not looking at anything. I'm tired.

I close the book. The wood of the desk looks shiny and pink. It's bright in here. But it'll be dark soon. I stand up. My back feels better. Don't watch TV. Something else. Anything else. What? Anything else. My phone rings. The screen says *Mom.*

"Hey, mom."

""Hi, sweetie." She talks slowly. So slowly it hurts me. It's his fault. He left and now she talks slowly. "How are you?" It's so slow I can't sit still. I walk in circles around the couch.

"I'm good, mom. Just trying to do some homework."

"Oh, I don't need to keep you. I was just wondering if you'd gotten a package recently."

I look across the room to the kitchen for no reason. I think the last bag is still in the fridge. Or maybe I threw them out. "I haven't. But I've been busy. Maybe it got left with my super. I'll check."

"Oh good. I didn't have time to bake them for you, but I hope you like them. They're from this new bakery that opened up on State Street, right off of Cota." The names sound familiar.

"Thanks. I'll ask my super."

"Do. And please tell him I say hello. How is he?"

"I will. He's fine."

"I know you have to go. Thanks for taking my call."

"Anytime, mom."

"Do you like what you're doing?"

"Sure."

"That's good."

"I do." I lean against my door.

"And you still like where you are? And your apartment? It's a good apparent, isn't it? I used to love it there."

"Yeah. I do."

"That's good."

She's quiet.

"How are you?" I ask.

"I'm good. It's just so quiet over here."

"I know."

"But I'm so happy you're happy, sweetie." She coughs. "And I can't wait to see you for Christmas. Leo is going to be back, too."

"Is Steve coming back?"

"He said he doesn't know yet."

"Okay."

"But it'll be so great to have you home, sweetie. But I know you're busy. And I don't need to keep you. But let's talk soon, okay? I miss you, sweetie."

"Of course, mom."

"Bye, sweetie."

"By, mom."

I hang up. She always sounds sad now. I don't blame her. And I do miss her, too. And Steve. How close we were. In high school. I was just like him. I am just like him. Mom says so. She says I look just like him. I hope I'm not like him.

I sit on the sofa and slouch and my back hurts, but I don't want to move and it doesn't hurt that badly. The bonsai tree looks brown. And the small fisherman with the fish on the string. He has a painted white mustache and beard. And the soil looks dry. And brown. And a little pink. The light's fading quickly and I can see the corners of my ceiling getting darker and darker. And the shadows stretch down along the bare white walls. The jackhammering stops. Finally. It's quiet. And the sounds from the street are muffled. The hum of the refrigerator. It smells musty and it's stuffy and it's warm. And quiet.

The TV is bright. And it makes the outside look darker than it is. I rub my eyes and slouch more.

Chapter Forty-Two

I turn off the TV. Bored. More tired than bored, and more tired than when I started, and my eyes burn. Outside is almost completely dark. The sky is still a little blue. From here I can only see a corner of it above the roof of the building across the street. I stretch. And groan. And stand. The room spins. And looks blurry. I almost fall back into the couch, but I don't. Everything is dim. Just like this morning. Dim and dull. I should do work. Just do it. Sit and read and get it done. It'll feel good to be productive. I fill the glass on the counter in the kitchen with water and drink quickly and fill it again. It's cold and feels good because the air is hot and stuffy. The bright white light in the kitchen makes the red cracking tiles look pale. And the white counters look especially white. I stare at the building across the street. Its windows are dark now. And the brown bricks are dim and orange because of the street lamps. I close the blinds. Don't get distracted. Just work. And be done with it. I go to the desk and reach for my phone. My pocket's empty. Did I lose it? When did I have it last? I see it on the couch. Must have fallen out of my pocket. I put it back in my pocket and sit at the desk. The kitchen light is still on but it's not enough to read by. The desk lamp is yellow and makes the desk look yellow. And the pencil scribbles look yellow and gray.

I stare at the wall behind the desk. A shadow of the desk stretching across it. I feel tired. I should nap. But it's getting late. And I haven't done anything. And I'm always tired. Just read. Is this all there is? The City is supposed to be exciting. Is this all? *The best years of our lives,* she said. Class and sit and read and sleep and study and study. There should be more than this. But there's nothing. Nothing I want. It's busy out there. And messy. And overwhelming. Concrete and crowds and people and fences and chunks of concrete and jackhammers. I guess this is it. Dull. And tired. Maybe if I had a girlfriend.

I tap my foot on the cords under the desk. It's quiet. And still. Except for the hum of the refrigerator, it's silent. The walls are bare. The floor looks yellow. The blinds are down. And they look yellow, too. No one can see me. I'm completely alone and no one knows what I'm doing. I can do anything. These four walls. Alone. I look at my phone. No one calls. No one will. Except mom or Steve. No one will. I should drink. They'd call if I drank. But how do they have time? There's so much to do. Too much to do. And it's gross. Abbey likes vodka. Vodka cranberry, or vodka soda. Or just vodka. And I liked watching her drink and be drunk and she was softer when she was drunk. But I don't like bars either. They smell like beer.

I stretch and the corners of the chair dig into my shoulder blades. Scapulas. I read and scratch my fingernail along the underside of the desk. It's not smooth like the top. It's coarse. And makes me shiver. I stop. I read more. The light is gone from the sky now. Focus.

The cation mor stable on most substituted. No cation in base. Exclamation mark. *Sterics.* I get that. It makes more sense this time. He drew a graph that I copied. I don't get it. Not important. He won't test us on it. Maybe. More arrows. And positive charges and negative charges and more arrows and exclamation marks. Done. But not done. There's a chapter. Two chapters? But done.

I grab the jacket off the hook and the door locks automatically behind me. The lights in the stairwell buzz and I zip my jacket up. I run up the stairs. The door to the roof is open with a big sign saying not to go out. The wind rushes around me. It's cold. And the sky is dark blue but the air glows orange from all the lights and it's hard to see the blue. I feel better. Muffled sounds from the street, and the wind, and the hum from the generators. I lean on the red brick railing and look straight down and out across the avenue. A line of bright red break lights and traffic lights. Glowing. And in the distance, flickering. Winking. And on the other side bright white headlights. The lights in the windows of the buildings far away twinkle. And the tops of some buildings are lit up in colors. Small spots of light drift across the sky and it's hard to tell the airplanes apart from the few stars. Light everywhere. Dots of it everywhere.

I follow the railing around the roof, hands in my pockets. My shoulders are hunched, and I straighten them, but it's tiring. I slouch again. More buildings. Smaller ones. And fewer lights. The church isn't lit up yet, and it's pointed roof sticks out above the flat-toped buildings surrounding it. The bare branches of the trees in the courtyard of the church jab at the air. Further down more lights. And taller buildings. Very tall. And shiny. And the lights are brighter. I like it up here.

I stand where Abbey stood. I miss being near her. There. Right here. Her head on my shoulder. My heart jumped and beat so fast. She probably shouldn't have done that. My arm going around her. Surprised even me. She probably shouldn't have let me do that. But I was so glad she did. Standing there with her. Right here with her. For so long. Despite the cold. And she smelled so nice. I breathe deep but it just smells like cold air now. I feel like I'm holding the air now hard. So hard. As if to keep her from going down. Packing her books. She said she didn't want to go. And good luck on the exam and kissed me on the cheek. She shouldn't have done that. I was so happy when she did. And she smelled so nice. And her hair tickled my nose when she did. And I should have stopped her. I knew when I put my arm around her that I loved her. And I knew it when she kissed my cheek, too.

Stop. Stop, stop. I close my eyes and shake my head. As if to shake away the feeling. But 'feeling' is the wrong word. It's too small of a word. Appendage is a better. Trying to shake it away is like trying to shake off my arm. Stupid.

The wind picks up and the clouds come in. They glow. And it's hard to see the buildings farther away, now. The prettier ones. I follow the brick railing back to the water tower. I climb the ladder and sit under it, protected from the wind. My fingers are freezing. The railings are greasy, and I try not to touch them. It's cold even without the wind. I wish I had tea. Or hot cider. I sit against the greasy railing and watch the clouds roll over the lights and the lights disappear and make the gray clouds glow. A siren wails. I see the red and white flashing lights against the buildings. A fire engine honks. The sound and the flashing lights fade. On the roof across the way a few people drink beers. A string of Christmas lights hung from the antenna above them. They laugh. I can't hear it, but I can see them laughing. The wall below them is spray-painted with silver and black letters that I can't read. A black-and-white cat crawls along in the shadows of the roof below the spray-painted wall and curls up on a lawn chair that faces the street.

I sit and watch the sky for a while. It's getting colder. I should do more work. I have a lot left. Read the chapter he lectured on. And the next one. And do the problem sets for Linear Algebra. And something else. I can't remember. The ground under me is dirty and damp and the water tower over my head is dark and I can hear water dripping from it. I'm cold. I climb down. The stairwell is warm and bright. I unlock the door. It's quiet and warm and the lights are still on in my apartment. The leather chair looks uncomfortable, and sags in the middle and the leather looks scraped and faded. My notes and computer and lamp. That's all. More to read. I'll read. I slouch and look at my phone. No one calls. I read. Slowly. My eyes are tired and it's hard to focus. My phone beeps. Another email from Charlotte.

Saw you called. Sorry I missed it. Lunch this week? Char.

Maybe she does want to get lunch this time. Why does she email? I put it down. Ignore her. I read. The pictures and diagrams are colorful. And the structures are cool. I like the structures. But I don't get the arrows. Or the thing about stability. I re-read. I feel tired. I run my fingers along the edge of the book and flick at edges of the pages and the small flicking sound distracts me so I stop. I'm tired. And the words look blurry and very small. I need to focus. I re-read.

Chapter Forty-Three

My back hurts. And the wind is loud, and people are loud and shout to each other, happy to be getting out of class. I walk behind the library. Tourists with cameras stand in the middle of the sidewalk. The late afternoon sky is bright and clear and blue, and the sun makes the library look more red than brown. I cut through the faculty apartment complex, past the playground and the parking garage. It smells like cooking by one of the ground-floor windows. I'm hungry. I hear kids laughing inside. On the other side of the apartment complex the wind picks back up. I duck my head and walk quicker. The trees are bare and pointy and rock back and forth in the strong wind.

My backpack is heavy and pulls down on my back. I walk quicker. I toy with my phone in my pocket. I should call her again. Maybe she does want to get lunch. I'll call her. When I get back. She would have called back if she wanted to. Or emailed. Maybe she was busy today. It was probably better we didn't get lunch today, anyways. I had to study. Maybe tomorrow. I'll call her. I still have a lot to study, but at least I did something. I walk home past the pool hall and the coffee shop and the taco shop and the liquor store and pull my keys out of my pocket, but I don't want to go inside. It's cold, but I don't want to study. I studied a lot today. And I can take a break. There's still more. But I can take a break. I'll go for a walk. I walk down the sidewalk. Good. This is nice. I can breathe easier. It's not as windy here. The buildings aren't as tall. And it smells like baking bread and meat from the Moroccan café on the corner. The short girl behind the counter waves to me. I smile and wave. She's pretty. But only from a distance. Her teeth are weird. Kitty. Katie? Something with a "K." Across from the café is the brown church without any windows and with a large cross on the peak of the pointed roof. It's a nice color, but it looks plain. Boring. The courtyard in front of it is nice though.

I look through the window of the cupcake shop across the street from the café. It looks cozy, with big windows and a Christmas tree with lights on it. I hear muffled Christmas songs from inside. But I don't want a cupcake. It smells like sugar baking and the smell is nice. And even down the street it smells nice. I pass a lot of clothing shops. Probably fancy clothing shops. Mom loves this neighborhood. Loved. When she lived with Steve here before they were married. And then un-married. And whatever they are now.

The sun is behind the buildings, but it makes the red bricks on the tops of them glow orange and the shadows and the cracks in the stones look dark. I step out of the way of a man talking loudly on his phone, almost bumping into him. An older woman in a dark green puffy jacket pushes a stroller with a giggling baby. She's making faces at it. Her faces are ugly. I'm tired. I try not to breathe in the smoke from the man standing on the corner with a cigarette.

I walk away from him and around a fenced yard of antique statues. Probably really expensive. The stone statues on the gray-green grass, a small stone birdbath without water and with stone birds around the rim, the stone walkway between patches of grass; all of it bright under the bright clear sky. The fence around the yard is rusting and brown. Planks of wood leaning against the side of the adjacent building. My face is cold, but the sun is coming down through the bare branches of the trees and feels warm and good. My heavy backpack makes my back ache. I should go home. And study. Maybe not yet. I'll eat. And take a break. And watch TV. That'll be nice. And relaxing. I worked hard today. I can take a break. I kick my shoe through a small pile of dried brown and orange leaves. They crunch as I step on them. I like that sound. The trees are thin along the street. Thin and bare and the sun makes them shine and look brown, with small lights strung around the branches in green wire, but the lights aren't lit yet. It's not dark enough.

"No way." Someone says from behind me. I turn around. "Can it be true?" John says. "Good day, mate."

"John. It's good to see you."

We shake hands awkwardly. His thin blond hair longer than it was before, falling into his eyes.

"How've you been?" I ask. "What are you doing down here?"

"I've been great. Really great. What about you? Where have you been, mate? I haven't seen you since forever."

"I've been busy. A lot of work these days."

"You still pre-med?"

"Yeah."

"Good for you, mate."

"You're in Organic, too, right? Have you read the chapter yet?"

"No."

"Me neither."

"I mean I'm not pre-med anymore."

"Oh."

"No more pre-med --- for me."

We keep walking the way I was going.

"Yeah, I'm happy about it." He says.

"What are you doing instead?"

"Drugs."

He laughs.

"I'm not too sure, mate. Still trying to figure it all out." We circle the block and pass the Cuban restaurant that smells like beans and walk towards my place. "You're still living down here?" He asks.

"Yeah."

"Good. Let's go there. It's cold as hell out here."

"Okay." It's good to see him again.

"Yeah. So happy to not be pre-med. It was so stressful." He says. He waves his hands in front of his face when he talks.

My hands are numb and stiff and the key digs into my finger when I twist it in the lock and open the door. It's warm. He stares at the legs of the woman in the elevator with us the entire way up. He talks loudly in the hallway and his voice echoes. "It's good to see you, mate. It's been too long."

I unlock the door and draw the latch behind us and put my bag down. My back feels better without the bag pulling on it. He puts his bag next to mine and I hang my jacket up. The apartment is dim, and I open the blinds. The light from outside makes the black rim of the TV shine.

My face feels cold. He falls into the couch and spreads his arms out. "When was the last time?" He asks. "It feels like forever ago."

"I don't know."

"Has to have been before the summer, right?"

"I think so. I've been busy."

"What'd you do for the summer. You were talking about going home, right?"

"I did. For the most part."

"I was planning on going on vacation with my family. And it was gonna be our first vacation in years, and we were going to go to Costa Rica, and I was going surfing."

"That sounds great."

"Yeah. Yeah it did."

"What happened?" I sit on the couch next to him and look at the TV.

"My idiot brother." He crosses his shoe on top of his knee. His shoe is close to the cushion. His feet are probably dirty. "My dad had everything planned." He says. "He had taken time off from his practice, and so had my mom, but my brother was like, 'I want to spend time with my girlfriend.' And my dad got pissed.

"My brother was like, 'I never get to see her, and this is going to be my only summer vacation.' And my dad cancelled the whole thing."

"Sorry."

"And I haven't been out of the country since forever."

"Sorry."

"It's alright." He brushes his hair out of his eyes. "What have you been doing?"

"Nothing."

"Really, mate. I want to hear."

"Really, nothing. And studying."

"Any girls?"

"No." I should call Charlotte.

"You work too hard, mate."

"I know."

"I'm so much less stressed, now."

"Yeah?"

"It's so nice."

"How are things with Anna?" Is that her name?

"Hanna? Oh, mate, that ended badly."

"Sorry."

"It's alright." He says and waves his hands and puts his foot back on the ground, leaning forward. His hair falls into his eyes again. He looks like he's from California or something. But he's not.

"Mind if I grab some water?"

"Sure."

He stands up and walks into the kitchen.

"Yeah, that ended badly. Apparently she was cheating on me, or was cheating on her boyfriend with me. I don't know, mate. Where are your cups?"

I point to the cabinet in front of him. "Sorry." I say. He fills it and drinks. It's good to see him. It's been a long time. He shakes his hair out of his eyes again. It's getting longer. It was buzzed before. Like mine. In the bars. With Abbey. And they would drink and I would drink my soda. It's good to see him, though. It's been a long time.

"Girls are crazy, mate. They're crazy." He laughs and sits back down, putting the glass with water on the glass coffee table. "Did you ever work things out with Abbey?" He asks. "I haven't seen her since forever, either."

"No."

"We're a lot alike, you know?"

The sun is hitting directly on the windows across the street and they look bright and the brown bricks look gold and I stare at the bright spots until my eyes hurt.

"We're searchers." He says. "We're looking for something real."

I don't say anything. I missed and didn't miss when he said these things. But it's really nice to see him.

"Most people are waiters."

I lean back into the couch. I'm tired. And hungry. And I should study. I pick at the thread poking out of the cushion.

"They wait for something to happen, and don't try and make anything happen for themselves. It's sad, you know?" He rubs his hands together. His shirt is tight on him and I can see the thread of his neckless sticking out from under his tight shirt. "It's sad."

I nod.

"Let's go do something." He says.

"What?"

"Anything. Let's go."

"I don't know. I should do work soon."

"Let's go to a bar."

"I don't think so."

"Come on. It'll be fun. Like old times."

"I'm okay. I have to study."

"Not tonight. Just take a night off. I haven't seen you since forever."

"I have a lot to do. Not tonight."

"You always have a lot to do. Let's go. You won't have to drink. Just like old times." He's standing up and moving towards the door. I should study. I look at the leather chair. Drooping. I feel tired. And my back hurts. I studied today. A little. But there's more to do. I should study. And I don't like beer. Or bars. Because they smell like beer.

"Not now. Soon, though."

"I won't take no for an answer, mate." He throws my jacket onto my lap.

"I have to work."

"Let's go meet girls. At a bar. Like in the movies." He's waving his hands around again. "Just come for a second. And then you'll come back and study all you want. But let's go. Just like old times."

"I'll walk you to a bar."

"Maybe you'll stay for one drink." He smiles.

"I'll walk you to the bar." The door locks behind us. I should study. I'll study when I get back. This feels good, though. It's good to be getting out.

Chapter Forty-Four

I'm drunk. I can hardly taste the liquor anymore. It's brown and dark and syrupy and the candle makes it glow amber. And the counter of the bar is dark brown wood. And smooth. But sticky in some places. Glasses clink and people talk loudly and there's music on but all I can hear is the rhythm. Steve wouldn't be happy. *You're killing your brain*, he'd say. *It's poison*, he'd say. But I feel good. And warm. And the dim lights are pretty. And the bottles of liquor are brightly lit from behind, and they look pretty. And the funny looking bartender in a white apron and a black shirt and black pants. He looks blurry.

"Cheers." John says.

We clink glasses. And drink. It tastes like water until I've swallowed it. And then it tastes sweet and burns a little at the back of my throat.

I spilt a drop on the back of my hand. I lick it. My hand feels numb. He smiles. I put the glass down. My head spins.

"Good to see you, mate."

"You, too." We're shouting to hear each other.

"I just have to say, it's great. How hard you work. It's great."

"Thanks."

"Really. It's great." He swallows. "Great. But it's been forever, mate. And it's good to see you."

"Good to see you, too."

"It's good to take a break sometimes, too, you know?"

"It is."

"Damn straight. Damn straight, mate." He smiles. His hair is in his eyes again. He straightens up. "And don't think *I'm* not working hard."

"I don't."

"I am."

"I know."

"Good." I drink. "I am." He says. "Very hard." He drinks. And puckers and swallows and waves over the bartender pointing to his drink and the bartender nods and hands us another round. I finish what's left in mine. It was a big sip. I feel dizzy. And my eyelids droop and feel heavy. But I feel good, too. And warm. And it's nice to breathe. Someone shouts something, and a bunch of people clap. John claps, too. Glasses clink. John leans forward and looks like he's thinking hard about something. He sips his glass. The small ice cubes in it float around. The ones in mine look shiny because of the candle.

"Talk to me, mate." He says. "Tell me something important."

I drink. And lean back, but there's no back to this chair. It's a stool. He laughs and slaps his knee and I smile and blush and steady myself. And breathe. Breathing feels good. I feel good.

"Tell me."

"I don't know. I don't know anything important, I don't think."

"Something important. Anything important. What's important to you, mate?"

"I don't know."

"Just say something. Anything."

"Epoxides open differently in acids and bases." I smile.

He doesn't look happy with that. And drinks. And I drink. I'm drunk. I'm not studying tonight. Good. That's good.

"What are epoxides?"

"That's the question! That's the question. I wish I knew."

He cracks his knuckles one at a time and shakes out his hands. He looks very serious. I thought that would make him laugh. He leans on the counter again and looks at me. "There's more, you know?"

"More what?"

"To life." He says. He's holding his head up with his fist.

"I know."

"More than studying."

"I know."

I'm worried about you mate."

"It's just this semester. Or this year. I have to get through this. Then it will be better."

"But it's too much. You're working too much. It's not worth all this."

"I'm fine."

"It's not fine. You're becoming a waiter."

"I'm becoming a doctor."

"You're becoming boring."

"I'm fine."

"You're sleeping." He drinks and coughs and puts his glass down but keeps his hand on it. "And waiting. You're just waiting."

"I'm not just waiting."

"And you know I only say this because I respect you. I do."

I drink. It smells like cigarettes from outside.

"Remember how you were? You were excited, you know?" I pick at the wood of the counter with my nails. "You, Abbey, me, that was fun. We had fun. And you were excited."

I lean on the counter. Someone bumps into me and apologizes and his breath smells like beer. It was fun. For a while. And then it wasn't.

"And you guys were cute together."

"We weren't together."

"That's not the point."

"What's the point?"

"You're different, mate. You've changed."

"It's just this year. Just organic. And all the other ones." I feel hot. And defensive.

He fiddles with the empty glass. There's still a little left at the bottom and it rolls around and catches light and glints. He stares at the candle through the glass. It makes his face glow. His blond hair glints, too. And hangs over his forehead.

"I think it's great that you work so hard, you know." He keeps looking at the candle through the glass. "But you're different now. And I used to want to be a doctor. Since forever. Being a doctor is great. And working hard is important for everything. But it can be too much, you know? That's why I stopped. It can be too much, mate."

"Yeah."

"I just don't want you to become this person that only studies and doesn't see his friends. And you've changed, is all. That's all."

"So have you."

He orders another round and pushes his glass away from him. I still haven't finished mine.

"Forget it." He says. "Cheers." He says. "I'm glad you came out tonight."

"Yeah."

"Don't be mad."

"I not."

"I'm just saying, you know? I'm worried about you."

"I'm not mad."

"Alright."

We click glasses and drink. I drink slowly. It tastes like water. But sweeter and thicker. And smoother. And it burns, but only a little, and my nose feels funny and tingly. And the mirror behind the bottles that are lit up looks shiny. And bright. And I can't see myself in it because the bottles are in the way. But the bottles glow and the liquor in them shines and looks pretty.

"Just don't change, mate. That's all I'm saying."

"Okay."

"It's not worth it. It's not *that* important, you know?"

"Okay."

"I'm serious"

My head pulses. I don't feel as good now. The glass is cold on my fingers.

"But it's great what you're doing." He says. "Great."

"How come you stopped?"

"It wasn't for me."

"What wasn't?"

"All of it, you know? All the work."

"Why not?"

"I don't know. It just wasn't. It wasn't worth it."

"Okay."

"How much I was giving, you know? It just wasn't worth it."

"Okay."

"It wasn't for me. I want to help people. But there are other ways to do that."

"That's what my dad says."

"There are other ways that are more worth it."

"So, what are you going to do now?"

"That's what *my* dad says." He laughs. His hair rocks back and forth on his forehead and shimmers in the dim candle light. The bartender walks past us, but we're not done with our drinks and he keep walking. He has a funny looking mustache that curls at the ends. He's bald and his bland head shines. Some girls at the other end of the bar giggle. They're cute. But they're not looking at us. Their lipstick is bright. And they have glitter on their cheeks. John looks at them.

The music changes and between songs there's a gap where it's not as loud. But it starts again. Even louder. My ears are ringing.

"Girls. They're crazy, mate." He's still looking at them.

"Yeah."

"Crazy."

"I know."

"What actually happened?" He pauses. "With you and Abbey, I mean."

"Nothing happened."

"Seriously, mate. What was it? You both just disappeared on me."

"Really. Nothing happened. That's what happened."

"Alright. If you say so, mate."

I swallow. My throat feels scratchy. I hope I don't get sick. I better not. I'll sleep it off. But I have class tomorrow. "What time is it?" I ask and reach for my phone, but it's not there.

"What?"

"I think I lost my phone." I say, standing up and looking under the stool. I feel wobbly when I stand, and it's hard to see anything clearly. And especially under the stool where it's dark.

He stands up and shines his phone on the ground, so I can see. I still can't see. It's all blurry. And I don't want to touch the ground. It's gross. And sticky. I kick around with my shoe. I can't find it. "It's not here." I say.

"Maybe it's back at your place."

"Maybe." My pocket feels weird without my phone. Empty. "What time is it?" I ask. And standing feels weird. I'm dizzy. I sit back on the stool. Maybe it's at my place.

"It's not that late." He says, looking at his phone.

"What time."

"A little after midnight."

That's late. That's too late. I have to sleep. I have class tomorrow. I have to sleep. And find my phone. I hope I don't get sick. I'm gonna get sick. I know it. And then I'll fall behind. I have to sleep. "I should go."

"Not yet. I made you mad. Let me buy you one more drink."

"I need to go."

"Come on, mate. Don't be like that."

"It's not that. And I'm not mad. Really. I just have to get some sleep. I have class early tomorrow."

"One more." He waves at the bartender and points to his glass again and the bartender nods. "Last one." He says.

"Last one."

"Cheers." We finish what's left in our glasses."

The bar is loud and people laugh and drink and shout. And it smells like beer and the ground is sticky. I don't like bars. Or beer. Or liquor. But at least I can't taste it. I'm tired. And drunk. And he's drunk. It's good to see him, though. And being drunk feels good. It's a rarity, and it doesn't usually, but it feels good now. The funny-looking bartender brings the next round.

Chapter Forty-Five

It's dark. And late. And I'm tired and my throat feels scratchy. And it's cold. The wind is blowing hard. And I don't have my phone. I walk quickly. And heavily. And John was annoying. And stubborn. His subway stop was in the opposite direction as my apartment. But he's so stubborn. And now it's even later. And I have to sleep. And I'm drunk. But the cold makes me feel sober, and the alcohol makes me feel the cold less. I walk past a paint supplies store. It's closed, but the lights are on and in the window there's a canvas with a picture printed on it to look like a painting. Next to it is the post office. The round dome is lit up from below and the large stone pillars are lit, and the windows are gray and faded and big. It's small compared to the buildings around it. But it looks large up close. Abbey liked it. She said the pillars reminded her of Greece or something. Ancient Greece. She wanted to go. To Greece. Walking back to her dorm after class, she'd look up at the pillars and smile and bump into me because she couldn't walk straight looking up. She might still live in the area. She liked it here. I do, too. It's nice. And not so busy.

The wind stops but the leaves on the ground blow across the street and rustle and they look yellow in the yellow light against the black pavement. And the trees look black. It's a nice night. The construction site is quiet, and the scaffolding is strung with bright white lights. The street splits and I walk on the edge of the sidewalk past a subway station and past a coffee shop with the chairs on the tables and the lights on inside. There's a square in the middle of the intersection and the sky looks large above it. The clouds are low, but thin, and I can see a couple stars. A girl walks out from around the other side of the coffee shop. She's pretty. And short. And sort of looks like Abbey. Her hair is tied back like Abbey used to have it. And she has the same brown book bag over her shoulder. She crosses the street towards me. It is Abbey. My heart is beating really fast suddenly. Really fast and hard. And my hands feel weird. Shaky. She sees me and smiles. And I smile. And wave. And feel shaky.

"Hey." She says. She has that same smile.

"Hey." She hugs me. Her perfume. That same perfume. She fits perfectly in my arms.

"What are you doing out here this late?"

"Nothing. Drinking." I say.

"*You?*"

"Yeah. With John."

She holds the strap of her bag with one hand. The hand with the little black mole on it. Her small hands. "Good for you." She says. "How have you been? It's been ages."

"Good. How are you?"

"I'm good. I'm really good. It's been ages. It's so good to see you."

"I've been busy."

"Me too. But it's so good to see you."

"It's good to see you too."

It's late. She probably wants to go home. I should go home. I need to sleep.

"Why don't we ever see each other anymore?" She asks.

"I don't know. We should catch up, though. I've just been busy. But it would be great to catch up."

"Busy with what?"

"Classes. Pre-med."

"You're still doing it?"

"Yeah."

"Good for you."

"John's not."

"Me neither."

"Why not?"

"I couldn't do it."

"Sure, you could."

"No." She smiles. That same smile. "I really couldn't. You saw my grades." She laughs. Always laughing. And a short strand of her burnt-brown hair would come loose from her hair-tie and fall across her cheek when she laughed too much, falling almost to her mouth. "You were too distracting." She says and laughs more. I smile. Her wide front teeth. They look especially white.

"That's Joe's world anyways."

"Right."

"He loves it."

"When does he start?"

"Next year. He's a little nervous."

"Tell him I say good luck."

"I will. I'm nervous, too."

"For him?"

"Because I'll never get to see him once he starts." She sticks out her bottom lip. She's cute. I walk with her back up the avenue. I can smell her perfume. It makes me sad. I remember it. From class. From her hand writing on my notes. Drawing faces. She smiled without looking at me. And her perfume smelled nice. It was all I could smell. Or think about.

The street is quiet and there aren't any cars. She looks up at the big pillars and the rounded top of the Post Office as we pass it. Her neck is thin. And creased with thin shadows. And she almost bumps into me. But she doesn't.

"So what's new with you? I've really missed you." She talks without looking down.

"I've missed you too." My throat knots and I feel my stomach sink even as my heart beats hard and fast. "I've just been studying, really. Nothing interesting."

"Good for you. That's great."

"What are you doing instead of pre-med?" I ask.

"Environmental science. I think."

"That's great."

"I like it."

"You're gonna save the world."

She smiles.

"And now you drink?" She asks. And smiles. And I smile.

"Not really. It's a onetime thing."

"If you say so. I'm not one to judge."

My steps are heavy. All the lights are pulsing when I look at them. And very bright. We walk and turn down Thirteenth Street and walk past the movie theater and her face looks pretty in the red lights from the advertisements. Her dorm is the other way.

"Are you still living in the dorm?"

"No. But still in the same area. I like it up here."

"I didn't know there was another dorm up here."

"No. An apartment."

"Oh, that's cool."

"Yeah. It's small. But it's ours."

"Whose?"

"Me and Joe."

"Great."

"You should come visit some time. And see it."

"Sure."

It's cold. My nose feels cold. And my cheeks are stiff. And my hands, even though they're in my pockets, they feel cold, too.

"You don't have to walk me, you know. It's late."

"I want to."

"Good. Because it's good to see you. And it's been ages."

She keeps looking up at the buildings. But she doesn't walk into me anymore. Her hair is longer.

"It's good to see you, too, Abbey."

"It's been ages."

"I've been busy."

"I can't wait for you to see the new place. We don't have enough chairs yet. But we're getting more soon. And the kitchen is in the living room. And the bed room fits only the bed. We've got a queen size. It's wonderful."

We wait on the curb for the light to change. We cross when it does. Her hands are in her pockets. Her brown book-bag hangs over her shoulder and bounces against her back. We walk past brown stone buildings with stone stairways and large doors and intricate hand rails and fences. The buildings are short, but the streets are narrow, and I can't see much of the sky.

The leaves on the sidewalk rustle under our feet and she kicks at a larger pile. And giggles. And I smile. She's cute.

"Are you still in the same place?" She asks.

"Yeah."

"It's a nice place." She says.

"I like it."

"Have you put anything on your walls yet?"

"No. One thing. A painting."

"That's a start."

"Yeah."

Laying across the couch and her feet wouldn't touch the other side. And the pillows would smell like her after that. Complaining that my walls are too boring, and she'd be studying, and I'd distract her and then she'd complain about that and stick out her bottom lip and pretend to be upset. But then we wouldn't do so well on the exams. And she got actually upset. And Joe knew, of course. But he didn't say anything at first.

"I'm still decorating our walls." She says. "Joe doesn't want anything to do with it. You two are so much alike."

"What's he doing with his year off?"

"He's working. Trying to get experience before he starts."

"Has he chosen a school?"

"He's working on his application. He won't hear back until the spring."

"Oh. Well good luck to him."

"I'll tell him. I'm really proud of him. He's worked so hard. I'm sure he'll get in somewhere amazing."

"He'll be a good doctor."

"I'll tell him you said so."

"Do."

"So will you. You know?"

"Right."

She's quiet.

"Why don't we see each other anymore?" She asks.

"You know why."

"But hasn't it been long enough?"

"Sure."

The wind blows the leaves in front of us.

"I miss you." She says. "We used to have so much fun to-gether."

"We did."

"It's really good to see you."

"You too."

"I really do want you to come see the new place. And see Joe."

"Sure."

"He's not bitter at all."

"Okay."

"It would be so fun to have you over."

"I'll come."

"Good. Soon?"

"Sure."

"Great. It's right here." She points to an old brick building with a rusty fire-escape. And small windows. Most of which are dark. She points to one on the top floor. The window with the light on inside. "That's ours. That one up there." She says.

"It looks like a nice building." I say.

"It's old. And small. But it's ours."

We've walked far. And my legs are tired. And I don't feel so drunk anymore. I just want to sleep. I should sleep. I have class early tomorrow.

"It's so great to see you. You look really good."

"It's good to see you, too, Abbey."

"I'll see you soon."

"Yeah. We'll get coffee or something."

"You drink coffee now, too?" She laughs. "Boy, you've changed."

"So I've heard."

"Coffee sounds great. And you have to come see the new place. I'd invite you up now, but it's late and I need to get to sleep. And Joe's been waiting for me."

"Some other time."

"Please. It's great to see you. It's been ages. And tell John I say hi. I haven't seen him in ages either."

She hugs me. And kisses me on the cheek. She feels warm. Her perfume is sweet. She walks inside, and I can't move. I feel low. The street lamp makes the old, dirty stone steps look orange and the cracks look black. I feel heavy. I'd cut off this arm if I could. I just want to sleep. I look up at her window. Yellow light. The street is quiet except for a taxi that drives past. And the leaves that rustle behind it. I walk away slowly. Feeling heavy. And cold. And tired. And I think I'm getting sick. I need to sleep. But I have to wake up so early. I could skip class. I don't want to go anyways. But I can't. I have to go. Or else I'll fall behind.

I walk back down the street and towards my apartment. The wind is cold on the avenue. And loud. I still smell her perfume on me from when she hugged me. Her smile. And her teeth. And when she stuck out her bottom lip. She's the same. The same as I remember.

Chapter Forty-Six

I need to sleep. I need eight hours every night. At least. That's what Steve said. *Eight hours.* Not tonight, though. Unless I skip class. I can't. I'll fall behind. I can't fall behind. But I'm tired. And drunk. And I'm getting sick. I hate getting sick. Houston street is wide and windy, and I cross it. Past the fences and the crumbling chunks of pavement that look dark and black and past the orange and yellow and white guardrails. It's quiet. All quiet. And the street lights are orange and make the freshly laid pavement look dark and black. And the headlights from the car waiting at the light are bright and blinding and make my shadow stretch across the sidewalk and the building in front of me. Planks over the windows. Spray-paint on the planks. The ladders have been removed from the fire escapes. The red bricks are cracked in places. There's some nice stone work along the roof though. Abbey'd like that. She'd look up. And those thin grooves of shadow along her neck. And bump into me. And I'd smell her perfume again. My hand doesn't smell like her anymore. It wore off.

I should call her. Not now. But tomorrow. I should call her. And we'll see each other again. That will be nice. But not nice. She'll go back home. To Joe. And I'll go home to my couch. And TV. And dull room. And dull classes. And dull everything.

An old woman is asleep on some cardboard under layers of blankets, and I step around her. I can see her cheek. Wrinkly. And old. And pale. The blankets are dirty and brown, and she has several sweaters on I can see because the blanket is too small for her. Like a child's blanket. The white light from the car passes over her and sweeps along the building and the bars ahead. It smells like cigarettes and beer. And I hear people laughing and talking and clinking glasses inside. I don't know why John didn't want to come to this bar. It's right across the street from me. But he's stubborn. And he wanted a different one. So we went to that one. The red lights over the window make the glass look red and cloudy so I can't see inside, and the cracking sidewalk looks red and the tree without leaves looks red. I don't like the smell of beer, and it smells a lot like beer. And I don't know the difference between cheap beer and expensive beer, but I imagine this is what cheap beer smells like.

Three dunk men stumble out. They look pale and red also. One starts puking next to the tree. The other two laugh. And one of them punches the air with his fat fists. His bald head looking shiny and red. He keeps punching at things.

"I'd do it." He says. "I'd do it." He's fat. And doesn't have very good balance. And his grey-green rain jacket rustles. I step past them and one of them taps my shoulder.

"Hey, buddy." I turn around. His fist is big and hits my face hard and it it's rough and stale and my eyes close my head rocks back and I almost fall. But I don't fall. And I open my eyes. My lip buzzes but doesn't hurt. He's walking away, his gray-green rain-jacket billowing behind him, and he throws his hands up.

"See, for no reason. I told you I'd do it. For no reason."

He pulls a black cap over his head. I should chase him. I should hit him. He doesn't look back.

"I'm really sorry, man." His friend says. "It didn't have anything to do with you. I'm really sorry."

"For no reason." The fat man shouts. "See."

I should hit him. Before he gets too far away. My head buzzes. I should hit him. Steve wouldn't approve. Do nothing, he'd say. Just nothing. I have to do something. I feel hot. And my lip is hurting now. And I taste blood. I touch it. It stings. And my fingers come away bloody. And the blood glistens in the red light. Blood tastes sour. I didn't know that. I should hit him back.

"Sorry, man. You need a tissue."

The fat man is around the corner and I can't see him anymore. But I should chase him. And hit him. And beat him. For no reason? I have a reason. I should hit him. I don't move. But I should.

Sounds of coughing and gaging. Sounds of laughter in the bar. And glasses clinking and people shouting and the base of the music. The stink of vomit and beer and cigarettes. The tang of blood. I feel dizzy. And tired. And my lip hurts. My head buzzes. My neck hurts too.

I look down the sidewalk again. Chase him. Hit him. Beat him. Blood tastes sour. He's gone. I should have hit him. He's gone now. I should go too. I didn't realize my fists were clenched. My nails digging into my palm. I should go. To sleep. I walk. And stumble. And catch myself on the tree, and almost step in the vomit.

"You okay, man?" The guy asks from behind me. "I'm really sorry."

I walk. My lip stings. I don't like the taste of blood. I feel it roll down my chin and I wipe it away with the back of my hand. My jaw feels sore. So, does my neck. And the skin around the right side of my mouth does too. But the cold makes it all hurt less. My head pulses. I feel tired. Blood seeps in between my teeth. I spit. But that hurts. And it's red and frothy and I still taste it. My hands are shaking. I should have hit him. I should have. Steve would be proud I didn't. I can't fit the key into the lock with my hands shaking. I manage. And pull the door open. My fingers are cold, and the metal handle is cold, too. But inside is warm, and my fingers thaw. And my lip stings more.

I can't spit. But my mouth is full of blood. And I don't want to swallow it. The elevator ride is long. I wipe more blood off my chin. It smears on the back of my hand. I don't latch the door behind me, I just spit in the kitchen sink. I feel the cut again. It stings. And my fingers come away bloody. They're probably dirty. And his fist was dirty. And crusty. And cracked. Dirt in the cracks of his fat knuckles in the red light. And stale. Dry. I feel hot. And angry. His fist was big. And hit hard. And it was dirty. I hope this doesn't infect. I wash my hands and my mouth and the cut. I saw it so clearly in the red light. I wash it more. And spit. And my mouth still tastes like blood, but it's watered down and not as sour or tangy. I slide the latch over the door. I run my tongue along the groove of the cut. I can't help playing with the flap of skin. It doesn't hurt so bad. And it wiggles.

I hold a piece of toilet paper to my lip to soak up the blood and sit in the middle of the couch. I feel dizzy. And drunk. And heavy. I'm tired, but I can't sleep. My head is buzzing. I should have hit him back. He deserves it. I should have hit him. Steve would be proud I didn't. I could have dodged him. Made him miss. And then hit him. Or not. Steve wouldn't be proud if I did. But he deserved it. And I've never hit anyone. I could have ducked it instead. I feel hot. And I'm breathing fast. And my heart is beating fast again. Like when I saw Abbey. And she saw me. And she smiled her smile with her narrow eyes and her thin lips and her perfume and her hair tied back. My lip hurts. My eyes droop. And my head buzzes. I could have hit him. Should have. Hurt him. I should have.

I pull the toilet paper away from my lip. It sticks. But it comes off. A large red spot of blood. I stand and throw it in the trash under the sink and get undressed and fold my clothes and put them at the foot of the bed. It will be good to sleep. I'll be tired when I wake up, but it will be good to sleep. I turn off the light and find my way to the bed and fold the sheet and blanket over me. It's warm. And I feel tired. And my lip doesn't hurt that badly. But I still taste blood. And I swallow, and feel sick. The bed is soft and the room is dark. And my head pulses a little and my eyes are heavy and I breathe slowly. *For no reason,* he said. No reason. I should have hit him. I close my eyes. No reason.

Chapter Forty-Seven

It's hot in here. My eyes open. My throat is dry and my head aches. I'm sick. The air is muggy. I had that stupid dream again. Dark redwood steps. Two different staircases. One going up left. One going up right. I roll over and shut off the radiator. I'm only covered in a sheet, paper thin, but I feel hot. Almost sweating. I close my eyes. It's easier to leave them open. The room is bright even though the blinds are drawn. Very bright. At the edge of the blinds where the light is the brightest, perfect white. It stings my eyes to look at. It must be sunny outside. It's quiet though. What time is it? My phone isn't on my desk. My lip stings. My head pulses. My throat is dry and scratchy. I close my eyes. I'll go back to sleep. All day. I'll feel better. But I can't sleep. It's too bright. And I have class.

Class. I sit up. But too fast and my head pulses and spins and I feel dizzy and sick and my lip stings. What time is it? I can't find my phone. The alarm didn't go off. Did it? Where is it? I need to get to class. Everything looks blurry. I rub my eyes and dress in the clothes at the foot of the bed and my throat feels dry and scratchy. And my lip stings. I should never have gone out last night. I shouldn't have let John talk me into it.

Now I'm behind. I feel sick. I never go to bars. Or drink. And now I'm behind. And can't find my phone. I feel dizzy. A thin stretch of light cuts across the couch. It looks white. And the rest of the couch looks dark and brown and soft. And the walls look pale. And pale blue. Dust in the air above the couch, the tiny specs glint and wink when they catch light and drift quietly. I feel dizzy. I shouldn't have gone out. The bar. So many drinks. The sticky floor. It all smelled like beer and cigarettes and perfume. And Abbey's perfume. And her teeth. And when she stuck out her lip and when she kissed my cheek. I sit down on the couch. I feel my phone under my leg. Its battery is dead. I breathe, and the air feels muggy and warm. The couch is soft and comfortable, and I lean my head back and stare at the ceiling. Slow moving streaks of light. White and yellow. Pretty.

I plug my phone into the charger and open the blinds. It's bright outside and my eyes sting. I missed class. Maybe I can make the afternoon lecture. The white walls across the street are especially bright and white in the afternoon light. And the windows shine and glint and the silver spray-painted writing shines. And the shines hurt my eyes and my head starts to throb bad. The cat isn't there today. I can feel the cold coming through the window. I shiver. Traffic is busy on the street. It must be late in the afternoon. I'm behind. I'll do work. All of it. All of the assignments. I'll do them all today. And I'll go to the afternoon lecture. My backpack is in the corner. So is John's. He forgot he left it here. I'll do work. All of the assignments. I'll sit, and read, and I'll do all of it and catch up. Maybe I'll even get ahead. And I'll go to the afternoon lecture.

A knock at the door. Loud. It startles me. John? Wanting his bag back? The knock comes again before I have a chance to open it. A short man. With a mustache. And a package that he hands me.

"Sign here." He says. I sign. He walks away. I close the door and re-latch it.

A small, cardboard box. I cut the tape with my keys and put the box down on the kitchen counter and my keys next to it.

I hope you like them. Love, mom.

It's a small note on light purple paper in darker purple ink. A ziplock bag of cookies under the note. I'll call her and thank her. When my phone is charged. What if she called? Or Abbey. Abbey might have called. I throw the note away and feel guilty I did. I'll call her when my phone is charged. I should do work.

The room is bright now. And the scratched wood is pale, and tan and the white walls are bright and my head aches and I squint to see without the light stinging, but the bare walls are bright and still sting. I feel dizzy. I need more on my walls. And the bonsai tree looks brown. It needs more water. The tips of the small leaves look pointy and sharp and stiff and brown. I fill a glass with water and drink half. It's cold and feels good against the back of my dry, hot throat. But the glass stings when it touches my lip and when the water runs over the cut. I give the rest to the bonsai tree. It pools around the feet of the fisherman. The top of the water ripples and the tops of the ripples catch the light and shimmer. My jaw feels sore.

I should study. I should sit and study. The drooping leather chair. Tan and pale leather, scratched and sagging. Tan wood frame. I should sit and study. My head is buzzing. And I feel sick. I can't. Not right now. I feel hot. I'll to it later. Later. I grab my jacket and leave. The hallway is chilly. Someone left the window open. The stairwell is cold too, and the roof is windy and loud. They're jack hammering again. Thudding. And thundering. So loud it makes me blink. The cold air is good. And refreshing. I get antsy when it gets hot. Hot and muggy. I feel better now. A little. The sun is bright and makes the empty branches down there look bright and the church look bright and brown. Its pointy roof sticking above the flat roofs around it. Without leaves on the branches I can see the cemetery in the courtyard next to the church and the small and large head stones. The grass is brown and yellow leaves are piled next to the brick wall.

I lean against the railing and look up at the water tower. The metallic roofing and the pipes around the base reflect the sun. I squint. The wind whips at my jacket. In the pauses of the jack hammering I can hear the hum of the generator and the rattling of the radiators.

My hands are cold, and the metal ladder up to the water tower is cold and greasy and the grease shines under the bright sky and I climb it quickly. I sit on the ground and lean against the brick wall under the grease-sheened pipes and wipe my hands on my pants. My clothes are dirty anyways. I'll change before lecture. I don't like wearing dirty clothes. But the cold is good. And I feel calm up here. And not so sick. And the buildings across the wide street are bright under the sun. Bright and brown and clean. Looking up the avenue I can see the taller buildings of the skyline. They look so different in the daytime. They shine and glint, and the metal and glass start to confuse with each other and the skyline blurs together a little in the smoggy haze. The bright blue sky over them; white, slow-moving clouds high in the sky. The jackhammer is loud, and I can hear traffic below. But I feel calm up here. I can breathe easier. I'll go down soon. And then go to lecture. So, I'm not behind in both classes. I'll catch up this weekend. That will be good.

Under the water tower the wind is blocked, and it's not so cold. Only a small breeze comes from over the sides and rustles the collar of my jacket. The sky looks bright and blue directly above the shining buildings, and only a little muggy with brown smog off in the distance.

I bring my legs to my chest. My pocket feels empty without my phone. My leg feels lighter. I push my hands in my pockets to keep them warm and feel along the edge of my wallet. But not my keys. They're not there. I forgot my keys. I never forget my keys. I'm locked out. Stupid. I'm so stupid. My super has a spare. I should get them. I breathe the cold air and sit for a bit longer. The air feels fresh. But I should go. I have to get my keys. I never forget my keys. I'm so stupid. I climb down the latter and wipe the grease off my hands on my pants again. I look over edge to the street one last time. Straight down. Cars slowly push past each other. People zigzag between the cars. Bikers zigzag between the people and the cars. On the balcony across the street I see pale wisps of smoke hovering over the heads of a couple sitting and smoking cigarettes. The smoke hangs and drifts back and forth. Rising, until it's caught by the wind and disappears. I don't like cigarettes, but the smoke looks pretty.

I walk quickly down the first flight of stairs and take the elevator from there to the ground floor. I knock on his door, but no one answers. It's quiet and the knocking echoes in the hallway and the lobby. I wait and knock again. I feel hot. And

I can't stand still. And I'm breathing quickly. I lean against the gold railing on the entrance stairs. The gold hasn't been polished recently and looks cloudy. The large Christmas tree is up in the lobby with lights on it and ornaments and everything. They must have done that last night. Or this morning. I walk back and forth and knock on the door again. Of course, no one answers. I can't believe I forgot my keys. And I missed class. Probably both classes now. Stupid. I'm behind. So far behind. What if I can't catch up? What then? I knock again because there's nothing else to do. And louder. And it echoes more. I feel hot. I want to hit something. Anything. For no reason. Like the fat man last night. I should have hit him. If I see him again I will. Him and his fat crusty fist. And fat head. I feel hot. I leave. Outside is cold, and that's better than hot. And the jackhammer is loud. The sun is bright.

I walk past the bar. Dried puke on the sidewalk. It still smells like beer and cigarettes. But mostly cigarettes. I hate cigarettes. I cover my ears as I pass the jackhammer and the dusty fence and the gruff men in bright reflective vests. I walk quickly and down a side street away from them. And the noise. I still hear it all the way down the block.

I sit inside the window of a cafe and try not to think about class. It's hot in the cafe but cold by the window. I order a sandwich and water. I drink the water quickly and the waiter refills it. The sandwich isn't very good. The bread is dry. I drink more water but that doesn't help. Not many people walk by the window and I stare at the books in the front of the book store across the street.

I missed both classes. I'm behind in both classes. I'll catch up. I'll do all the assignments today. I have nothing else to do.

Just read. Sit and read. And do the problem sets and read more and sit more. I can't believe I missed both classes. Drinking? I never drink. I hate drinking. And bars. I finish another glass of water and pay and leave.

I keep walking. I'll go back soon. But the cold is good. And I feel calm. And I can see my breath. I walk down Mulberry into Little Italy. With the tourists. And rows of identical restaurants all the way down the block and on both sides of the street. With the same bread in the same baskets in the middle of the tables with olive oil in the same little round-bottom vials. A fat man sits just inside under a heater with his napkin in the collar of his shirt and his face smeared with red sauce and he chews sloppily and noisily.

I circle the block, past the souvenir stores with the small license plates with common names on them and with small replica statues. The Statute of Liberty. The Eiffel Tower. Different sizes. All of them filled with tourists. And little tourist-children. And all of the tourist-parents have cameras, either around their necks or in their hands.

The wind is blowing hard and the restaurants are pulling in their signs, so they don't get blown away. And the sky is clouding over. Dark clouds in the distance. I should get back. And work. I have to work. So much to do. John's lucky. Not to have this. The pressure. He's lucky. He's probably sitting on his couch right now. Drinking Pepsi - always Pepsi. Watching TV. He's lucky. Not to feel this.

I walk up Mott street to my apartment. The clouds are dark and lower in the sky further south, but it's still bright overhead. The cupcake shop with the big windows looks bright and warm and smells like sugar baking. The cafe on the corner smells like fresh bread. It's busy inside. A flock of pigeons rises in front of me fluttering. Scared away from a loaf of moldy bread by a passing car. They perch on the top of the red brick building above the cafe. Their feathers glisten in the sun.

I pull on the door. It doesn't open. I wait outside for someone to leave. A couple I've seen before. They nod to me and I hold the door for them.

"What happened to your lip?" He asks. He's tall and wearing sunglasses.

"Long story." I say.

He chuckles and takes his wife's hand, walking down the way I came.

It's warm in the lobby. And I catch sight of my lip in one of the large mirrors. It's swollen and purple. I knock on the door to my super's apartment again. I hear his kids crying inside and a TV on. Someone is shouting. Probably him. The smell of onions cooking in oil. No one comes. I knock again. It swings open quickly.

"What you want?" He says. The bags under his eyes are deep and purple. The thin hair around his ears. The shiny bald top of his head.

"I'm locked out of my apartment." His kids are still crying and yelling and it's loud in the hallway.

"Which apartment you are?"

"8G."

"8G, 8G." He mutters. He pulls a key ring out from behind the door and unlatches a key from it. "How's father and mother?"

"Good."

"Good. They always good. Okay, here you go." He hands me a key and closes the door.

Always wearing that stained white tank-top. Even in winter. I wait for the elevator and turn the key over in my finger. It's good I have it. I can work. I don't want to. But I should. I have a lot to do. I hear my phone ringing before I get to my door. Abbey? I latch the door behind me. *Dad Cell*.

"Hey, Steve."

"Hi."

"What's up?"

"I just wanted to say hi."

"Hi."

"How're you doing?"

"I'm good."

"Studying hard?"

"Yeah."

"Good for you." He's quiet. Just waiting. I can hear him breathing. I hate when he does this.

"How's mom?" I ask.

"She's great. She misses you."

"Tell her I said thanks for the cookies."

"You should call her."

"Okay."

He's quiet again. I'm tired. My throat hurts. My lip stings.

"How are you?" I ask.

"I'm great. Really, really great." I'm bending down so that the phone can stay plugged into the charger, but my back is hurting. I unplug it and sit down.

"How's school going?" He asks.

"I missed class today."

"It's good to take a day off every now and then."

"Yeah."

"Did you know Maria went to medical school for a year and decided she didn't like it and left to become a teacher?"

"Oh."

"I just thought that was really interesting. Thought you might like to hear it."

"Right."

"She says she doesn't think you'll like it very much."

"Okay."

He's quiet again.

"You should call your mom."

"Okay."

"She misses you."

"Okay."

I flick at the pages of my books on my desk and hear him breathing on the other end, but I don't have anything to say.

"Are you home, yet?" I ask.

"Not yet. We're staying a couple more days here."

"Oh."

"Maria knows the island. She's showing me around."

"Great."

I stare at the bright spots in the windows across the street until my eyes hurt.

"Are you going back for Christmas?" I ask.

"I'm not sure yet."

I hear her in the background. "Tell him I say hi." She says.

"Maria says hi." He says.

"Right. Steve, I have to go. I have to study."

"Okay. Thanks for taking my call."

"Bye."

I plug the phone back into the charger and stare at the wall. I feel tired. Tired and dull. And low. I stand and walk to the window. The sky is almost completely gray now. Except for one bright spot over by the North dorms. I stare at the gray clouds. They look close. And the street looks busy. All the cars and the people, all busy and honking and walking fast and talking on their phones. And no one notices the white flakes that fall quietly from the dark gray clouds. They're thick. And there aren't many of them. They get caught in the breeze and swirl around.

That's nice. I like the snow. I sink into the couch and turn on the TV. The screen is bright and I squint. That same commercial is on. The one for the army. His face fades into the red rocks with other faces. *The Few. The Proud. The Marines.* Not the army. The marines. I'm tired. My throat hurts. My lip stings. I'll study later. Everything seems dull. Dull. But I'm comfortable staring at the bright screen. The commercial ends and the movie comes back. I don't know this movie. I know that actor though. What's his name? Leo would know. He knows all the actors. Michael something? Martin? I lean back, slouching more. I'm tired. I'll do work later.

Chapter Forty-Eight

My phone rings from behind me on the desk. The couch is comfortable. I don't stand up to get it. It could be Abbey. Probably not. But it could be. I push myself up and stretch and groan and feel tired and the room spins. I don't turn off the TV. John's calling again. His voice sounds weird over the phone and he wants to know if he can come pick his bag up. I tell him he can, and he says he has big news and he'll tell me when he gets here.

I sit in the drooping leather chair and close my eyes and lean back. It's good he's coming. I'm glad. But I have to work. I should work. Just read. Something. I'll do it later. I don't want to read. Or study. Or do the problem sets. None of it. It's all so dull and unimportant. But I have to. To be a doctor one day. Doctor Roth. I wish that still sounded important.

Breaks squeak on the street. A truck rumbles. The wind outside hisses though the window. The air is still in here, though. The sky is gray and it's still snowing. Thick flakes. More of them, too. Coming down at an angle through the tall buildings. The room looks gray and pale and dull. I walk to the window and lean against it. It's cold on my forehead.

The bones of the trees down there are catching some of the snow. And in the divider in the middle of the street, some of it is sticking. White against the brown grass and twigs. A man sitting on the bench outside the building across the street. Smoking a cigarette. Even in the snow. A woman passes him, and he follows her with his eyes. The wind makes the snow swirl, and it sweeps back and forth. It's pretty.

The sky is still bright in the distance above the North dorms. Still blue, but all around it is dark and gray. And the tops of the buildings over there are bright and shine especially because everything around them is so dark. And in here is dark. And gray. I should turn on a light. I should probably do work, too. I yawn, and my eyes hurt and my lip stings.

I turn on the light in the brown-tiled bathroom and look in the mirror at my lip. It looks worse than it feels. Swollen. And purple. And it still tastes bloody but it's not bleeding. John's gonna like this story. It's a good story. For no reason? The row of lights over the mirror are bright and make my face look orange. And blurry. I feel dizzy. And my face looks blurry. Hazy. Like there are two of me. I turn off the light and stare at the man on the bench again. I feel tired. The gray hangs low over all of us. Cars and people rush and rush and the gray hangs low over all of us. All of us lost. Searching for something without knowing we're even searching. And so we'll never know what it is we're really searching for. And we'll always be lost.

A knock at my door.

"Room service." He calls. I'm glad he's here.

His shaggy hair has snow in it. And on the shoulders of his jacket. I close the door and latch it behind him.

"Good day, mate. How're you feeling?" He says.

"Good."

"Me too. What happened to your face?"

"I got punched."

"When?"

"Last night. I got punched."

"Did we fight?"

"No."

"Good." He sits on the couch and puts is foot on his knee. I sit next to him and lean back. The snow in his hair is melting and dripping onto the couch.

"The craziest thing happened this morning." He says. "You'll never believe it. I was watching TV and guess who called."

"Who?"

"Abbey. Abbey called."

"She called you?"

"Yeah. Said it had been ages and that we should all catch up."

"Oh."

"So we're all going to get drinks this weekend! Great, right? You're welcome."

"I can't."

"Why not?"

"I have to study."

"Mate, don't do this. Please don't do this." He waves his hands in front of his face again.

"I missed class today."

"Good for you. You work too hard, anyways."

"I have to study this weekend."

"You always do this."

"Do what? I'm not doing anything."

"You're running away again." He's not looking at me.

"I have to study."

"Sure, you do."

My phone rings and I get it from my desk, but don't answer because it's Steve calling again.

"This is just like last time, mate. When you disappeared." He says.

"I can't fall behind right now. I just can't. I really have to study. But maybe next weekend?"

"Whatever you say, mate."

"And last time was different."

"Whatever you say."

"I have to study."

He's still looking at his phone. His jacket is on his lap and his hair is in his eyes. My phone buzzes. *One New Voicemail.*

"Funny story." He says, not looking up. "I can't tell you the shock of walking into class and realizing I forgot my bag. And then I remembered I didn't have class. So the bag didn't matter."

"Was it cancelled?"

"I just don't have class on Friday's. It's so nice."

"You're lucky."

"And I don't have anything to study over the weekend."

"Good for you."

He puts his foot back on the floor and looks at me. I stare at the blank TV.

"Abbey and I are still getting drinks this weekend."

"Okay."

"You should come if you can." He says.

"Okay."

He leans back and shakes his hair out of his eyes. Drops of water splatter onto the couch. "Does your lip hurt?" He asks.

"No."

"It looks pretty bad."

"It's not."

"Who hit you?"

"I don't know."

"Were you that drunk?"

"No. I just never met him."

"Picking fights with strangers is dangerous."

"It wasn't a fight. I just got punched."

"What'd you do? Hit on his girlfriend?"

"I didn't do anything. He just hit me?"

"For no reason?"

"Yeah. Exactly."

"Well, it looks bad."

"Okay."

"Don't be mad."

"I'm not."

"You look mad."

"I'm not."

"Is this about Abbey?"

"I'm not mad."

"Alright. If you say so, mate."

"Okay."

The wind hisses and we look out the window. The snow is falling harder, and the flakes are thick. It all looks gray, but it's bright enough out there.

He stands up. "I have to get an email out to my professor." He says. "Do you want to come back with me to my dorm?"

"I really should get to work."

"Of course."

"You're an ass."

"Don't be mad."

"I have to study."

"Just don't disappear again."

"Some of us still have exams to study for."

"And some of us don't run away from things we want."

"I'm not."

"If you say so, mate."

"There's nothing there."

"If you say so."

"And I have work to do."

"Don't disappear again. That's all I'm saying."

He puts his jacket back on.

"*Stay gold, Ponyboy.*" He says and laughs. And I watch the snow. It swirls in the wind, falling in thick sheets.

He takes his bag and leaves. I latch the door behind him. It's dark. And gray. I feel tired. And low. And I don't want to study. But I have to. I have to catch up. Doctor Roth. I wish that still sounded important.

Chapter Forty-Nine

The wind hisses and we look out the window. The snow is falling harder, and the flakes are thick. It all looks gray, but it's bright enough out there.

He stands up. "I have to get an email out to my professor." He says. "Do you want to come back with me to my dorm?"

"I really should get to work."

"Of course."

"You're an ass."

"Don't be mad."

"I have to study."

"Just don't disappear again."

"Some of us still have exams to study for."

"And some of us don't run away from things we want."

"I'm not."

"If you say so, mate."

"There's nothing there."

"If you say so."

"And I have work to do."

"Don't disappear again. That's all I'm saying."

He puts his jacket back on.

" *'Stay gold, Pony Boy.'* " He says and laughs. It's not funny.

"I'm not running away from her." I say. "I'm moving on."

"Alright, mate." He says. "I'm just worried about you, is all."

"I'm fine."

"Alright."

"Maybe you don't remember how much work there is."

"That's not fair, mate. You know I work just as hard."

I don't say anything.

"But you're disappearing, mate. You're disappearing." He waves his hands in front of his face.

"I'm fine."

"Come with me to my dorm. It'll only be a minute, and then we'll grab another drink and keep talking."

"I can't."

"It'll be good for you."

"Why?"

"No reason. I don't know. Just come. It's something to do. So you don't disappear again, mate."

"I have to work."

"You have all weekend."

He throws me my jacket.

"Why not?" He asks.

"I'll walk you up." I say. It'll be good to get outside.

"Great."

We leave. I zip up my jacket and duck my head into the snow and wind until we turn the corner and the wind stops. It's quieter out here with the snow. The cars sound muffled. And it falls silently. The snow is starting to stick to the sidewalk and it crunches a little under my feet.

He's walking fast, his hands in his pockets and his shoulders up by his ears. I keep up. My shoes feel wet already from the snow. And cold. I can't see the tops of the taller buildings because the clouds are low and gray, and the snow is thick. I like the snow. And the cold air is nice.

"She's cute, mate." He says.

"Who?"

"Abbey. She's cute."

We walk over the grate above the subway and I hear it rattling down there in the darkness and the sound fades away quickly.

"And you two were cute together. And annoying." He says.

"We weren't together."

"I didn't learn a thing because of you two."

"Me neither."

"You obviously learned enough."

The sky above the open square is big. And I can see the lights in the buildings turning on. At least on the lower floors. And they shine and look gold and we walk quickly keeping our heads low. The wind is loud in the square, and traffic is slow, and the cars are noisy. I smell smoke from somewhere. But it passes, and we cross the avenue. His dorm is close. And up ahead I can see the sun hitting the tops of the cars and the sides of the buildings. The snow thins and stops, and we slow down.

It feels good not to be in that room. Gray and dull. And stuffy. Outside is nice. And I feel good. John kicks at snow on the sidewalk. It fluffs around his shoe and sparkles in the bright sunlight. The wind whips the purple school flags. They snap back and forth, yanking on their tethers. Inside is warm.

John talks to the security guard at the desk and we give him our IDs and he swipes them and John signs something and I sign something, and we go in. John holds open the glass door for four girls. They giggle, passing us. They're cute. They look young. The courtyard is empty, and there's snow on the purple benches and tables and the sun makes the snow look bright.

We walk up the stairs. The walls of the stairwell are white and cinderblock, and the stairs are gray, and the handrail is gray and the paint on the handrail is chipping. John's voice echoes in the stairwell.

"This will only take a second." He says.

"Okay."

The hallway is brightly lit and his room is across from the stairwell. It's unlocked, and he pushes through.

"You leave your door unlocked?" I ask.

"Tommy's here." He says. "Have you met Tommy?"

"No."

He calls out, but no one answers. And he knocks on the white wooden door to the right of the entrance. "I guess he's not here. This is the living room. My room is just back here."

He throws his jacket on the couch facing us. It's a small living area. The couch looks dirty in the flickering yellow light from the lamp. And the light makes the white walls look yellow. A mostly empty bookshelf next to the couch. On one shelf are framed photos of John and his family. The rest of them in white coats. He looks the shortest. His dad is bald, but they look the same. The same pointy chin. And his brother has it too and the same color hair. John's hair is buzzed like it used to be. And they all have the same blue eyes. All four of them.

"Make yourself comfortable." He calls from his room.

I look closer at the picture. I feel strange looking at it. Like somehow I know a storm is coming and am looking at people who don't. And they look so happy. But it's happened now. He won't have a white coat like the rest of them, now. I bet that was tough for him. It's quiet except for his typing and the buzzing from the light in the kitchen. And it's hot. I unzip my jacket. The kitchen is filled with dirty dishes. The TV across from the couch is small, but larger than mine. John comes out.

"Tommy's a good guy." He says. "You'll meet him. His sister's an RA here, too."

"Sure." I feel relief. It's all still there. All the books. All my notes. And I'm behind. My heart beats hard again. But I don't have to right now. I don't have to. I can do it this weekend."

"Not bad, right?" He looks around.

"It's nice."

"Perks of being an RA, mate."

"Do you mind the freshmen?"

"No. They're alright. Annoying, but alright."

He grabs his jacket from the couch.

"A drink?" He asks.

"I can't."

"Right. Coffee, then."

"Okay."

"There's a good Café across the street."

We leave. He doesn't lock the door.

"Where are you and Abbey going this weekend?" I ask. My voice sounds louder than I meant it to in the stairwell.

"Not sure yet. But you should come, mate."

He jumps down the last flight of stairs. His hair ruffles and falls into his eyes again. He holds the door open for me and the wind rushes in.

"Mind if we have a cigarette in the courtyard first?" He asks. "Café won't let me smoke in there."

"I don't smoke."

"I do."

"Sure."

We find a seat on one of the purple benches dusted with snow. He sits on the table and takes a pack of cigarettes out of his jacket.

Chapter Fifty

Doctor Roth. Right. I can't remember now why that was important. It was, though. It was. Doctor Roth. I flick at the
edges of the book. The paper ruffles and creases. It's thin paper,
but it shines in the light from my desk lamp. Always colorful
pictures on every page. Supposed to make it interesting. Epoxides aren't interesting. Color doesn't help. I stare out the
window. The snow is thinning, and the wind is dying down. It
looks quiet out there. It's quiet in here, too, but it doesn't feel
quiet. It feels loud. Loud. And heavy. I look back at the book.
So much more to do. And I've done so little.

I push the chair back, but I don't stand up. I lean my
elbows on my knees and my head on the desk. I feel tired. Always tired. I feel tired and low and sick and my lip hurts. The
ground by my feet is dusty and the wires under my desk are
tangled. My head aches. I feel hot. I should have gone with
John. Outside. In the snow. It's cold. But it would have been
nice. It would have been different. New. This is all I do. Study.
And pretend to study. And then study more. My head aches.
I run my finger around the edge of the desk. The polished
wood is smooth. Like the table in the living room - but it was

a darker wood. And I'd run my palm over it and stare at mom in the kitchen. Mom was always in the kitchen. Leo on the counter watching her cook. Or bake. She loved backing then. And her hair was long then. And Steve came in from outside. It was bright outside. And dry. And I couldn't see him well because it was so bright. There were windows everywhere, and the light made the wood glow. Everything was wood. And all the wood in the house would glow. The wood table in the living room was big. And it looked even bigger because I could barely see over the top. I swung and kicked my feet over the edge of the big chair. Wooden chair. Steve and mom kissed a lot back then. Squealing and hiding because it was gross. And they laughed. And I laughed because they laughed. And Benji came out from the family room because we were laughing. And then we all watched a movie. Because it was Sunday and there was nothing else to do on a Sunday morning besides watch a movie. And Leo would sit on mom's lap. And Steve between Benji and me. And the TV would be bright, and big, and I would laugh when they would laugh.

Sunday's aren't like that now. Nothing is like that now. My head aches. I look at the book. The thick book on the desk. The shiny paper. The colorful pictures. The small print. I can't. Not right now. I can't. I stand up and feel dizzy and I look out the window. The snow's stopped, but the sky is still dark with heavy clouds. And it's not so blue over the North dorms anymore. I take my jacket from the hook and my keys from the counter by the box of cookies and leave. It locks behind me. I feel low. And the chilly hallway doesn't help. I drag my feet along the sea-green carpet. The floor of the lobby isn't carpeted and my shoes squeak on the shiny tiles. Outside is cold.

I walk. And duck my cheeks into the collar of my jacket. It's quiet out here. Especially around the corner from the avenue where there's no wind. I like it.

I don't have time for this. There's too much to do. But I can't. There's *too* much, and I can't focus, and everyone else is out enjoying themselves. Down the smaller streets, where less people walk, the snow is thicker on the sidewalks. And untouched. A thin, untouched, perfect white that contrasts the dark red bricks and the black pavement, wet with melted snow. I cross the street and walk down the avenue. Most of the bars are already open but they look empty. And the music isn't loud inside. I think this is the one Abbey used to tell me about. With the sawdust on the floor and the old Irish men. Or maybe that was further up. She wouldn't let me work this weekend if she knew. She never let me study. *The best years of our lives*, she said, and then put her head on my shoulder. The best years of our lives. It was so pretty on the roof. With her. And she smelled so nice.

The best years of our lives. Those are the years I'm wasting. Alone, studying in the pale room with the small light, and the rest of everyone out there enjoying themselves. She wouldn't let me. But she can't say anything now. She doesn't get to. I know what she'd say. And she doesn't get to.

The alley is narrow, and the buildings block most of the gray sky. The side door of the library opens out into the alley right across from me, and next to the door a window with children's books on display. The covers are colorful. But that's not a very good drawing of a lion for the cover of a book.

I like this alley. It's brick, and narrow, and old looking. Another picture of how it used to be. At the corner, a wide avenue and lots of wind and lots of cars rushing past, kicking up slush from the street, and the picture is ruined. I cross. The wind is cold. It's snowing again.

The snowflakes are smaller now and fall quickly and in thick sheets. They muffle the sounds of traffic. I walk fast. My shoes are wet and cold, and I don't have another pair. I turn down a smaller street. The buildings are shorter and made of stone with wooden windowsills. They look old too. But metal and glass buildings tower over them. Of course. And the glass looks black and bleak. Snow lands on my cheeks. It's cold. I look down at my feet again and tighten my hold on my jacket. Everything is empty on this street. No people. No cars. It's nice. Even the small pizza shop with the long red awning stretching over the sidewalk almost to the street - even the pizza shop is empty. It's bright inside, and smells like cheese and bread. A large man comes from a room in back with a grease-stained white apron rubbing his knobby hands on a towel that he throws over his shoulder. Maybe I should eat something. But I don't want pizza.

A pile of black trash bags covers a fire-hydrant. A thin layer of snow dusted on top of them. A bar with a wooden horses head over the door. It's closed. A few doors down, a recruitment office; inside a man in uniform and with a thick, bushy mustache behind a dark wooden desk, his mustache bouncing as he talks to a couple sitting in front of him; large posters of strong men in uniform with large guns hang in the large glass windows. *The Few. The Proud. The Marines.* They look proud. I used to be. Doctor Roth. That used to sound important. And I felt proud. I don't feel proud now. I feel low. And tired. And my lip hurts. And my head aches. And it's cold. I could stop. I don't have to keep going. I could just stop.

It sounds so easy. Dangerously easy. Steve would be happy. Good for you, he'd say. Now you can actually make a difference. On a significant scale, he'd say. But what then? Drinking with John and Abbey. Abbey with her smile, and her laugh, and her shiny eyes. And she'll laugh and put her hand on my leg like she always does. The one with the little black mole on it. And she'll want to dance. And she'd hold herself close to me when we danced. Her hair on my chin. One of her hands on the back of my neck. And her perfume. And after that? Just watching TV. My best years. That's how I'd spend them. On a couch. And drinking. And I don't even like drinking. Or I'd study. I could drop out. Leave. Go somewhere. Steve wouldn't let me.

I'm walking faster. My hands are shaking in my pockets. The street ends and opens up onto a small square with a black wrought iron fence and a fountain in the middle. I run my finger along the spine of a branch poking through the fence and brush off the white powder collecting on it. The branch is thin and pointy and stiff with cold. I circle the fence until I find the entrance. The gate is open. There's no water in the fountain. It's too cold. But there are benches and I brush the snow off and sit on one. It's a nice fountain. With three levels. A ridge of snow lines the rim of each tier. The rattling of a chain in the breeze. The distant hum of the city. But mostly the quiet of falling snow. I hunch over myself and huddle into my jacket.

I kick away the snow on the ground with my shoe. The dark stone under it, damp. My nose burns with cold. My skin feels stiff. I'm cold, but at least I'm not in my apartment. Something different. Not dull. I lean back. I can see my breath. A small brown bird flies to the second rim of the fountain.

White powder sprinkles into the air. It cocks its head looking for water. Or just looking. And flies off. Through the layers of falling snow, the branches of the trees lining the fence are barely distinguishable. Pale brown. White, gray and pale brown. That's all. A blur of very pale colors. Mostly white, though. And I can't see the detail of the stonework around the rims of the fountain through the thickly falling snow, but on top there's a fish, and an angel riding on its back, it's wings spread out and it's head up to the sky. Snow is collecting around the grooves of its eyes.

The snow doesn't melt when it lands on my jeans. I'll be covered soon. Buried. If I sit here long enough. There's not much wind, and the fat flakes fall straight. Quietly. It collects in the creases of my jacket. Burying me. I can't keep my foot from taping and scraping away more snow from the dark stone. I'm tired. And my lip stings again. His fist was so dry, and cracking, and dirty. And hard. And for no reason.

I should go. I have to study. But I can't. It's so dull. And meaningless. And no reason. For any of it. But I should go. I should. I stand. And shiver and shake the snow off of me. The vapor of my breath is thick. The snow has made my shoes damp and my feet cold, and I hunch my shoulders and leave the small square shivering. Back to my apartment. Small, dimly lit, dull apartment. And the empty walls. And the drooping chair. Leather. Steve doesn't like that I have a leather chair. And the desk. And the books. So much to do. I'll do it. I have to. I'll catch up. I feel tired. So tired. I can't remember why I do this. But I do it. No reason, I guess. No reason. For any of it. I wish it still felt important. Meaningful. I brush more snow off a branch before I cross the street. The street is filling up with snow now, too. The sidewalk is almost completely white. And the snow crunches under my feet.

I walk back the way I came. Along the street with small old buildings, and the large, new, glass buildings above them. Past the recruitment office with the large posters. I'll join the army. That will be different. I smile, and my lip stings, and I duck my head lower as I walk along the edge of the snowy sidewalk. Steve would hate that most of all. I walk quickly, past the black trash bags almost completely white, now. Back to my apartment.

Chapter Fifty-One

The sun is bright on the fresh snow, sparkling, and on the purple benches. A thin trail of smoke stretches up from the end of John's cigarette. He takes a long drag, looking past me, and the thin trail of smoke disappears. He's thinking about it this time.

I squint looking up at him sitting on the table, me on the bench. He smiles at something behind me, and then looks back at me, letting out the smoke. The smoke makes my head ache.

"I don't know, mate." He says. And looks back over my shoulder. He smiles and waves to someone. "I just couldn't keep doing it." He says.

"Okay. No pressure to talk about it."

"It wasn't what I wanted, I don't think." He takes another drag and the thin trail disappears again. "And it's just so much work. You know?"

"That I do."

"You miss out on so much by studying all the time." The breeze carries the smoke into my face. My head throbs. I feel sick.

"Like this weekend, with Abbey. It's a chance to fix things."

"I don't think so."

"See, this is what I'm saying. You're becoming a waiter. Just waiting for something to happen."

"Okay."

"You used to be different. A searcher." He waves his hands in front of his face and ash falls off the tip of the cigarette onto the fresh snow.

"Right."

"Don't get moody. I'm only trying to help, mate."

"I'm not."

He breathes more smoke that the wind carries into my face. I grimace.

"Sorry, mate. Want to switch?"

"I'm okay."

"Alright. But you should come out this weekend."

"I can't."

"Abbey's going to ask where you are."

"Okay."

"And you won't be there to dance with her. You know she'll want to."

I stare at the bright snow and it sparkles and I stare until my eyes hurt, and that only makes my head ache worse and I look back at him.

"And if she asks me, I won't say no."

"Okay."

He taps the ash onto the table.

"My dad would be proud of your discipline." He says. "But it's not good for you." He takes another drag. "It's not good for you to do nothing except work all the time."

The smoke makes me sick, and I cough. My throat feels dry and my head aches.

"Sorry, mate. Switch with me." He hops off the table.

I take his seat. It's even brighter facing this direction. He sits on the bench where I was. The cold air is nice and tastes clean.

"That's why." He says. "That's why I stopped. Because it never ends. You'll always have this much work. Probably more. And then there's no room for life."

"There's room." I say. The sun is in my eyes from this angle and I squint to be able to see him.

"You can't even spare a single night. Not even for Abbey."

"Especially not for Abbey."

"That's cold."

A thin cloud passes overhead, and the shadow streaks across the sparkling snow. On the other side of the courtyard someone is reading with her back leaning against one of the large round pillars surrounding the square. A strand of her bright blond hair covering her cheek, her legs mostly extended and crossed at the ankles. She's pretty.

"Was it really that bad?" He asks.

"It's over is all."

"You could have at least given me a warning."

"Sorry."

"One day you two are annoying as usual, then you're gone."

The cloud passes and it's bright again. So bright that it's hard to see her across the yard because the snow around her is blindingly-white.

"She was upset, you know." He says. And smokes and taps the ash. "She was pretty wrecked."

"Did you guys spend a lot of time together after that?"

"For a short while. And then she left, too."

The sun makes the snow around her glitter and wink. From across the courtyard we see each other and smile. She's pretty.

Her cheeks are flushed, and her skin is pale and her hair is gold. I look back at John and she looks back at her book. John's almost finished his cigarette. He's drawn a line in the snow on the bench with his finger and he traces it back and forth.

"You can't wait forever, you know."

"I'm not waiting. I have work to do. A lot of it."

"Of course, you do. We all do."

"I'm not waiting."

"It's just not good to wait is all."

"The alternative isn't always a good option either. Sometimes you're just screwed."

"Don't get moody, mate."

Her skin was always tan, and her cheeks and face especially, but they went pale and red when I told her. And her lips stopped smiling and her eyes were very serious. I didn't expect that. I didn't expect her to get so serious when I told her. But she got so serious. And I couldn't look at her. She had been with Joe for two years, she said. And we were friends. Good friends, she said. But that was it. She had gotten so serious so quickly, and she had stopped laughing so suddenly. I could barely hear her, my chest was pounding so hard.

"You're going to realize one day." He says. "And I hope it's not too late then. Not too late for you to start living."

She brushes the strand of hair back across her ear and looks up at me again. I smile and look back at John quickly. And then back at her. She's still looking at me, she looks down at her book and blushes. I think.

"You don't see me letting my work get in the way of my life, do you?" He says.

"That's different."

"How? How is it any different?"

"I don't know."

"I work just as hard."

"Okay."

"And I still have time to see old friends."

"Okay."

Her hair shines in the sunlight. She sits mostly straight but bending her neck to read closer to the book. The book is small, but so are her hands, and her legs are thin and long, and I shouldn't keep staring. John takes another drag. There's nothing left, but he doesn't put it out. And even though the smoke isn't blowing at me anymore, I can still smell it. I don't like cigarettes. John swings his legs over the bench and leans back against the table. He puts one foot on top of one knee, head tilted back and up towards the sky, eyes closed and smiling in the sunlight.

"This is nice." He says, breathing the smoke out. "This is how life should be."

She's looking at me again. I smile. And she smiles. A big smile. But looks away quickly.

"Go talk to her." John says.

"Who?"

He laughs and blows smoke at me. "Go."

"I'm fine."

"Stop waiting."

"I'm not."

"Sure."

"I don't even know her."

"That's Tommy's sister."

He coughs and puts out his cigarette. "Go say hi. I'll introduce you."

He starts to stand up.

"It's okay. Really."

"Alright. But this is exactly what I'm talking about, you know?"

I'm more surprised by that than anything and don't know what to say.

"You've changed."

"People change."

"But you're not living anymore. You're just studying. And waiting. And running away."

"I'm not running away."

"Alright."

"Things are over between Abbey and me."

"Prove it."

"What?"

"Go talk to her."

"No."

He brushes some snow off the table and it sparkles as it falls. She might have heard us. John doesn't exactly talk quietly. What if she heard us? She's still looking down at her book. But I think she's smiling.

He closes his eyes again, face still up towards the sky. The sun makes his skin look tan. I should go talk to her. I should. My hands are shaking a little. I stand up.

"Good for you, mate."

It's a long walk over to her. And I can tell John's watching. But she doesn't look up. She's even prettier up close. And the snow sparkling around her makes her face light up. She looks up just as I get close enough to smell her perfume. It smells like that flower. The one along the driveway back home. The white one. She smiles. And I smile. Her eyes are bright and blue. Sharp and blue. And her lips are big and full and her teeth are very white. That strand of hair she tucked behind her ear gets loose again and in the breeze it bends across her face.

"Hi." I say.

"Hi." I like the sound of her voice.

I smile. And she smiles. And I can't think of what to say. She's so pretty.

"What's your name?" She asks.

"Hunter."

"I'm Alex." I take her hand. Her soft hand. It's small in mine. "It's nice to meet you, Hunter."

"Nice to meet you, too, Alex."

Her voice is soft, and so nice. I like listening to it. The sun warms the back of my neck, but it's still cold enough to see her breath when she talks. I feel like I'm outside myself watching. Watching us talk. And we talk easily and for a while. It's like her voice is all that matters, and she could say anything in the world and I would be happy. She says she likes the snow. And I say I do too. And she says it's very lovely the way it sparkles and that it reminds her of her grandmother who used to say that the sparkling snow looks like the stars. She's very pretty. Beautiful. I tell her I'm sorry when she says her grandmother passed away. I can only hear her voice. The only sound in the world is her voice. The warmth of the sun is gone and the snow has stopped sparkling. It's colder now. I didn't notice John leave. Did he go back up? Have we been talking that long?

"Want to go for a walk?" She says. And smiles. And something in my chest feels warm for the first time in a very long time.

The sky is gray with thick clouds that are tinged in pink around the edges. The streetlamps are on already and the orange light makes it seem darker than it is. And makes the snow lining the bare branches of the trees glow faintly. Yellow, stiff leaves brush along the fresh snow at our feet. She laughs as I tell her why my lip is swollen and purple. And she says she likes that I didn't fight him. And that warm feeling gets warmer.

She tells me about her home. And about leaving to live in New Mexico. She likes books more than movies, and red wine more than white wine, but she likes all wine really. She loves Hemingway. I tell her I think I've read something by him, but I'm not sure. And she makes a surprised face and says I simply must read more. Her eyes are bright and sharp and seem to catch light from nowhere.

We pass the movie theater and a pool hall and the post office with the round dome. It's getting dark but I don't want it to end. And I don't think she does either. It's really very nice to talk with her. We wait at the light as the cars push along. Strands of her hair blow across her face in the wind and she smiles back at me through them. I want to kiss her. My chest beats hard. But that's crazy. That's just crazy. The light changes and we're cross the street. We're walking back towards her dorm and I feel my chest sink a little.

Outside her dorm she stops. She brushes those strands of hair back behind her ear again. We're both looking at the snow around our shoes. She says she really likes talking with me. And I tell her I really like talking with her and that I would love it if I could see her again and she says she would love it too. And my heart is beating faster than I thought it could. Tomorrow, she says. And I say that sounds great. She hugs me goodbye for a long moment. Feeling her against me for the first time and enveloped in the smell of her, I feel a heavy calmness settle over me. The way a traveler feels after a thousand sleepless nights lost on the road, when he finally crosses the threshold of his home. Like all that I have been wrestling with until now suddenly means a little less than it did before. Like I have found whatever it was I was looking for. Something truly significant. Maybe. I walk back to my apartment feeling good and excited.

About the Author

Lao-Tzu Allan-Blitz graduated from the New York University with an inter-disciplinary degree in Happiness and earned his medical degree from the David Geffen School of Medicine, at UCLA. He is currently a resident physician in Internal Medicine and Pediatrics at Brigham and Women's Hospital and Boston Children's Hospital. A writer his entire life, he has written over twenty short stories and three novels. *Until We Are Lost* (Adelaide Books, 2019) is his first published novel.